WANDERING
SOULS
IN PARADISE
LOST

Fragments of the World II

WANDERING SOULS IN PARADISE LOST

HÉLÈNE RIOUX

A NOVEL TRANSLATED
BY JONATHAN KAPLANSKY

Cormorant Books

ALWAYS A GIFT
LITTLE FREE LIBRARY
NEVER FOR SALE

88 Waverly St. N.

Canada Council
for the Arts
 Conseil des Arts
du Canada
ONTARIO ARTS COUNCIL
CONSEIL DES ARTS DE L'ONTARIO

The publisher gratefully acknowledges the support of the Canada Council for the Arts
and the Ontario Arts Council for its publishing program. We acknowledge the
financial support of the Government of Canada through the Canada Book Fund for
our publishing activities.

 Canadian Patrimoine
Heritage canadien

We acknowledge the financial collaboration with the Department of Canadian
Heritage through the National Translation Program for Book Publishing.

LIBRARY AND ARCHIVES CANADA CATALOGUING IN PUBLICATION
Rioux, Hélène, 1949–
[Âmes en peine au paradis perdu. English]
Wandering souls in paradise lost / Hélène Rioux ; translated by Jonathan Kaplansky.

Translation of: Âmes en peine au paradis perdu.
ISBN 978-1-897151-89-1

1. Kaplansky, Jonathan, 1960–
II. Title: Âmes en peine au paradis perdu. English. III. Title.

PS8585.I46A7413 2010   C843.54   C2010-904412-6

Cover art and design: Angel Guerra/Archetype
Interior text design: Tannice Goddard/Soul Oasis Networking
Printer: Imprimerie Gauvin

Printed and bound in Canada

CORMORANT BOOKS INC.
215 SPADINA AVENUE, STUDIO 230, TORONTO, ONTARIO, CANADA M5T 2C7
www.cormorantbooks.com

CONTENTS

SPRING EQUINOX

I

WANDERING SOULS
AT THE END OF THE WORLD

... there's a restaurant of a similar name in the area.
A greasy spoon, to tell the truth.
Frequented mainly by taxi drivers.

FOR SOME IT IS AN earthly garden, an Eden filled with trees and flowers from where, long ago, Adam and Eve were banished after biting into the cursed apple. People speak of the Fall — with a capital. We remember old pen drawings in which our two guilty parties, naked, heads lowered, their private parts camouflaged modestly — for from now on they are modest — behind a vine leaf, exit the gates of the playground from which they are forever banned. Guilty or not, their descendants, sweat on their brows, will be subject to the same exile until the end of time. It is written. It is the curse of the human race. Non-believers shrug their shoulders: a legend, they dismiss, smiling contemptuously.

In the beginning there was the Big Bang; then things evolved for a few millennia, as everyone knows. Our ancestors were gorillas, more or less, and there weren't any apple trees on earth. At one time — not so long ago if we consider the age of the human race — they burned at the stake those who dared challenge dogmas. "We've gone beyond such black deeds, I hope," non-believers add smugly. Besides, how to believe that for a simple trifle, a harmless (and if you think about it, healthy) bit of greed, one recommended by doctors, nutritionists, and other inquisitors of our scientific era — for a healthy bit of greed, this God whom we qualify as just, would inflict such a punishment. It's incommensurable. And why should an apple be a forbidden fruit? "An allegory, or a symbol," suggest the less adamant, aware that science alone can't explain everything. Since the dawn of time, humanity has invented myths for the inexplicable: a plumed serpent, Cronus eating his children, a garden of delights. Why not? Deep down, it's poetic. And we'd still rather have Adam and Eve as our ancestors than a band of orangutans.

Researchers, however, claim to have discovered the site of an ancient garden in Persia, in Mesopotamia — they even speak of Cuba or other islands close to the Equator, and of Atlantis sunk to the bottom of the ocean, as other possible sites of Eden.

People — that is, Novalis — thought that after the Fall, the

Earthly Paradise imploded, its fragments scattered throughout the surface of the globe. We will never be able to find or reconstruct it.

But others believe the opposite. The place exists, sacred books describe it, milk and honey flow in its rivers; it's called the Promised Land. Or Arcadia.

PARADISE. FOR SOME, THE WORD calls to mind an unusual flower without petals or scent; for others a bird with shining plumage. Film buffs remember a movie or two. If they've made inquiries, they know seats are less expensive in the highest gallery of a theatre, what the French call "Paradis." They see images in black and white — sad Pierrot and Garance, and in *Les Enfants du Paradis* — or they think of the film *Cinema Paridiso*, set in Italy, in which a wide-eyed child listens to a projectionist philosophize. The literary ones quote Dante, Baudelaire, or Milton. Some like to recall Proust, remembering that his last servant — but she was so much more — was called Céleste and played the role of a guardian angel to the sickly genius. Others, a learned circle of hand-picked eighteenth-century scholars, think of Paradis de Moncrif, an accomplished courtier, formidable duellist, actor, and librettist from the Age of Enlightenment, to whom we owe the *Histoire des chats* and the libretto of a heroic ballet. The work was entitled *L'Empire de l'amour* — *The Empire of Love* — but who remembers? Booed by audiences, today it is no longer staged. Such is life. The man himself slipped into oblivion, but well, they can't all be Diderot or Voltaire.

Flipping absent-mindedly through the dictionary, we see paradise is also a place for the departed souls of the righteous awaiting resurrection. Because there is, of course, underlying this idea of waiting, the desire to regain ... what exactly? Innocence, perhaps. More original than sin, lost innocence, a faint light that glimmers at the end of a long tunnel in the memory of the world.

It is a distinctive, special corner of the Earth; for adventure lovers, the savannah with its elephants and big cats, an oasis in the desert, a lake in the heart of a wild forest; for history lovers, a village in the bush, a medieval city in Tuscany or Andalusia, surrounded by walls, filled with relics, the river meandering through it spanned by stone bridges. A castle, an uninhabited Moorish palace, still dominates the landscape. Each season has its scent: jasmine, orange blossom, lavender, or rosemary. And all those islands in shimmering seas, tropical — some would say fiscal — paradises. They form archipelagos in the Mediterranean, the Atlantic or Indian Ocean, and the Caribbean: the past hideouts of pirates, cruel wreckers, and adventurers — Corsica, Nassau, Paradise Island. Five-star resorts now extend their tentacles along the coast. On some of these islands, the Seychelles or Marquesas, painters and poets have followed a fickle muse. Some actually found the muse frolicking on the shore, flowers in her hair. Others, well ... others contracted tropical dysentery and died there, without further glory.

For the more modest, a chaise longue on the beach, a glass of rum under a palm tree suffice — their earthly paradise one week a year.

Others believe the bare, virgin expanses of the North are the last infinite spaces of paradise. Perhaps they've heard tell of the strange legend of the ancient Greeks. Arktikos was bear country, a continent with a mild climate filled with kindness, where unicorns, naiads, and other creatures of mythology lived together. A bear? The North Star. To the ear of these austere dreamers, Siberia sounds better than Tahiti. The whiteness appeals to them, the immobility, the solitude. They ponder for a long while, turning the glossy pages of albums, looking at maps of northern Canada. The water and the air there, so pure, they think, the silence so absolute. In the North, very far north, beyond the Arctic Circle, Nunavut, Baffin Island, Alaska, far beyond Kuujjuaq, Iqaluit, and farther still beyond, Radisson, Goose Bay, Cartwright City, and Labrador City. Their spirit hovers above unexplored islands; they whisper magic names: Cornwallis, Somerset, Ellesmere, Devon; they are as if in a trance, their entire being reaching toward the far reaches of the world. They think of a highway called the Freedom Road, in extreme eastern Quebec, of a valley called Happy Valley; they think of the polynyas, the areas of open water that remain mysteriously unfrozen despite the intense cold — in 1616, William Baffin discovered them on his ship called, in fact, *Discovery* — they think of the polar night that spreads over this forgotten world from September to February. They think of the white nights, the midnight sun, the slow drifting of icebergs that melt in the ocean in a ghostly procession.

Others, however, continue their reading. They are amazed to learn that forty-five million years ago, Ellesmere Island was a subtropical paradise. There stumps of dawn redwoods are found, skeletons of tapirs, turtles, and snakes. Another legend? The same? It doesn't matter. Images appear and fill them with wonder. Paradise existed. These spaces still intact, these undiscovered lands and seas are mermaids. Their calls are a trap. Perhaps they read stories of explorers — Hearne, Hubbard, Wallace, George Cartwright — and imagined accompanying them on their voyages. Rash in their thoughts, they start out armed with shotguns and worthless compasses. For what good is a compass in a gust of wind, or a shotgun when not a soul lives in the vicinity and even the large white bears have holed up in some cave to hibernate? They become those adventurers — that is, the unlucky ones — alone in the white, empty expanses; they go round in circles as if in a maze, bent over by the brutal wind, blinded by the blizzard. What were they thinking? Their paradise — their quest for the absolute — is truly lost. And yet it was so beautiful when they dreamed. They cling to their dream. They're hungry. If they still have matches, and gas in their portable stove, they melt snow in their mess kit, boil their moccasins and mittens and, trembling, swallow the thin soup. Then they stop being hungry. Sleep and night win out. They've reached the end. A final image fades beneath their frozen eyelids. Fade to white. Perhaps they've achieved what they were seeking.

But others — whether or not they've already gone — claim that in the North there is absolutely nothing.

YES, PARADISE: IT IS OFTEN dreamt of, and everyone has their own dream. It is the imagined country, the faraway land people long for without knowing it. It is always somewhere else. It is the life beyond this one.

What we never had, we miss. For the poor, it's opulence, and for the unknown, glory. People whose hearts have been wounded will say it's a loving mother, a faithful friend; people whose memories have been wounded will say it's childhood.

It is love. And here are little girls immersed in storybooks, girls in front of the mirror, smiling at their reflections. Musicians are tuning their instruments: the ball may begin. "Where are you?" they whisper. Crystal-clear laughter, trembling sighs. We see them thirty, forty years later. They have married a real estate agent, an electrical appliance salesman; their children will soon leave home, live their lives. What remains of their dreams lies in a heap on the grass, among the dead leaves, ready to be burned. Everything is ruined; everything has come too late. They forget that life is there, still there, or else it's life itself they want to forget. Old tunes of tangos in their wake, pillows wet with tears, a hoarse voice conjugating a verb in all tenses. What verb? To love too much. A rider gallops in the distance, wind sweeps into his cloak. A hairy guerrilla, covered in scars, bedecked with ammunition, shouts out — *¡Libertad o muerte!* Or it's a pale revolutionary, with round, steel-rimmed glasses, carrying the aura of his altruistic mission, a martyr or a messiah — both have the undeniable potential to charm — the big-hearted outlaw or his pitiless double. Prince Charming must be a myth invented by men. Any woman will tell you: she'd prefer a hundred times to have been Mata Hari, La Pasionaria, or Carmen the gypsy, red skirt lifting to reveal her tanned legs, peony in her hair, than the princess sleeping on a pink bed for a hundred years.

And then there are powerful men with a dubious past, all alike, in love with inaccessible blondes: Adam Worth, for instance, madly in love with the Duchess of Devonshire. Always the same model. Starting out with nothing, they climb, ready to defy all laws, break all taboos, climb the rungs toward an ideal that slips away — the blonde with the temperamental pout, the pinup in a negligee posing in their calendar — and when they reach it, if perchance they succeed, they never really possess it. The dream slips between their hands, sand or snow.

Paradise is something fleeting. It is a mirage; it is like the horizon receding. We don't reach it.

The Holy Grail.

There where death does not exist.

FOR OTHERS, IT IS CELESTIAL. It's called heaven, or nirvana; it's where the righteous go after they die. Somewhere beyond all known constellations. It's therefore useless to exhaust oneself seeking it here: it can only be earned. A place of meditation and disembodied ecstasy where all desires are excluded; sometimes it is represented as somewhat dreary, neither hot nor cold, where asexual cherubs play the lyre upon a cloud. How does one avoid yawning with boredom, faced with such a prospect? *Eternity*, they sigh, *must be very long up there*. But the visions of hell seem a hundred times more forbidding. When you think about it for too long, you regret being born, because then you have to die and end up in one of those places.

Music lovers say they catch a glimpse of it when they hear a chaconne by Johann Sebastian Bach. Alone in his music room, they insist, that remarkable man, that angel, was already there: he generously supplied us with the essence.

OR ELSE WE THINK OF its opposite, hell. "Abandon all hope, ye who enter here," is written at the entrance of the abyss where they hurl the condemned. For paradise is of course hope. As for hell — at the bottom of a funnel going down right to the centre of the earth — Dante described the torture in detail. The lustful, greedy, violent, treacherous, and heretical forever prey to tormentors. Too late, chimes the clock. Too bad for them. Even suicides, already miserable in their earthly existence, are not spared: the poet transforms them into trees: they cry and bleed for eternity. And if we think this punishment unjust, it is, quite simply that there is no justice in the other world either. Or if there is justice, its mystery remains unfathomable.

BUT YOU DON'T HAVE TO go that far: down here we find enough ravaged places, abscesses festering on the Earth's heaving body, disfiguring its face. Cesspools, pits, ossuaries, mass graves: there is no dearth of words. The Devil's Island — well-named — of grim memory: sadistic jailers, and convicts in chains, innocent or guilty. Names appear at regular intervals; we hear them, they come and go on the map of the world. We try to imagine places before catastrophe struck: they are called Rwanda, Darfur, Bosnia Herzegovina, Iraq, Burma, Lebanon. Others have come before them; others, on the waiting list, will soon offer their splendour for slaughter. And the cities, the magnificent cities with castles, domes, cathedrals, and stone bridges, will be reduced to ashes; the rivers will be the colour of blood.

WHAT REMAINS OF US AFTER the betrayal. When the earth suddenly breaks apart, when an abyss opens beneath our feet.

AND FOR SOME CYNICS, HELL and paradise do not exist, either down here, or in any kind of beyond. They do not believe in the beyond.

～

JULIE, A PINK, V-NECKED T-SHIRT emphasizing her arrogant chest — the boss insisted she wear sexy clothes — wipes the

Formica counter with a cloth. She's not sure she wants to stay there, but well, she hasn't worked in three months. Her savings — almost five thousand dollars — have melted like snow in the sun. The sun is, of course, a metaphor, because in Montreal in March there is more hope for sun than the reality of it. Hope or nostalgia, given the never-ending winter. In other words, Julie has no choice. Even if she doubts she'll be able to get back on her feet financially in a greasy spoon like this, with a grand total of two customers, one nursing a Coke, the other gaping at a cold cup of tea. Really, what possessed her to work in such a dive? She finishes at midnight, and the evening is likely to be long. But she couldn't conceive of returning to the Geisha Bar to dance nude. Anything but that. She's done with being a floozy. Besides, she still feels too fragile; she's not yet confident enough to try her luck at the "in" places — the bars and restaurants downtown or in the Plateau, where they say girls can easily make two hundred dollars an evening in tips alone. She earned at least double that when she danced. Whereas here … Twenty-five? Thirty at most, and she'd be lucky to get that. She's not even sure she can pay her rent next month.

When she arrived, Marjolaine, the cook, explained her responsibilities in detail: fresh coffee every hour — boiled coffee is spoiled coffee, everyone knows. The packets are ready; all she has to do is place them in the basket of the machine, add water, and press the button. Easy. Don't fill the breadbasket too full — otherwise there will be waste and with the price of bread ... For Marjolaine waste is worse than a sin. She says that throwing out bread is a crime against humanity. In the beginning, she made pudding with the leftovers, but her modest dessert wasn't very successful — the men prefer *pouding chômeur* — poor man's pudding, which is sweeter. The result: in addition to the bread, they also wasted the eggs and milk. Unacceptable — especially in a recession. She also has to clean the tables and counter, Marjolaine added, fill the sugar dispensers, salt and pepper shakers, and help out with the dishes. "The dishes? I'm not paid to wash dishes," Julie protested, insulted. Marjolaine sighed — she sighs a lot. "Only when business is slow. A youngster like you. You're young, you don't plan to stand around twiddling your thumbs, leaving me with all the hard work?" No answer to that. "And above all, smile and be polite with the customers. Most of them are regulars, taxi drivers. They come here to unwind, so the last thing they need is a waitress who sulks ... Their job is already stressful enough as it is ... As you see, nothing too complicated." Julie was already fed up. "Oh! I forgot. Do you smoke?" Julie nodded her head. She really wanted to quit. Her supplier from Kahnawake has disappeared, in jail or in Florida, how to know? Now she has to buy her smokes at the convenience store and even though she chooses the cheapest ones, they eat up a large part of her budget. But she can't manage without, no point even trying; she's already nervous enough. "So you'll smoke outside," Marjolaine continued. "Everyone does it; we have no choice. When there are no customers, of course. Any questions?" Julie indicated no. You don't need a university degree to understand instructions like that. She plans to remain a few months to get experience, then quickly find somewhere else.

AT THE END OF THE World nothing has really changed. That is, the decor: the same colourless fluorescent lights illuminating the same beige walls; the same scratched rectangular tables. The same menu, or almost, is written in the same black felt-tip pen on the same white board: soup of the day, chef salad, meatball stew, macaroni with meat sauce, regular or Italian-style poutine gratinée, or *galvaude*. Certain people find something here, a taste of their childhood, they say. That's probably true — if their mother made Italian-style poutine for them. They call it comfort food. Good for them. Everyone needs comfort in these times. The dishes are just a bit more expensive than last December — the increase in the price of grain made the cost of living soar everywhere on the planet.

If he or she pays attention, the observer will nevertheless notice some new items. The chocolate mousse, for example. And the calendar. This year, it features three caramel-coloured cats sleeping on a cushion in a basket. Last year, it was a horse in a meadow. At the end of the counter, beside the marble cake that has been cut into beneath its cover, a chocolate rabbit in its mauve and yellow cardboard wrapping has replaced the miniature artificial Christmas tree that occupied the place of honour three months ago. The idea, Marjolaine's, was to have the raffle on Sunday — Easter falls earlier than usual this year. For the raffle tickets — a dollar each — she cut out about a hundred squares of paper, and wrote a number in the middle. They're in a saucer beside the cash. No fuss, as she says. We're among friends, so let's keep it simple. With the profits she plans on buying potted flowers to decorate Doris's grave in the Cimetière de l'Est. The deceased's family has not shown much enthusiasm for flowers. Marjolaine will go with Raoul or Boris to buy them at the Jean-Talon Market. Impatiens, geraniums, daisies, bleeding hearts, perhaps — although that name, frankly … it's depressing, especially in a cemetery. She can already picture how nice it will all look in May with the snow melted. She'll bring a spray of tulips. Spring would be too sad without them. Doris was especially fond of tulips. There had always been some on the patch of land in front of her place — a lower duplex in Rosemont. She had conscientiously planted her bulbs in autumn. Marjolaine remembers that once the poor thing had brought her there on her birthday, April 20. Truth is, she is not over it.

Sitting on a stool, a middle-aged woman with dull mahogany hair sips a Coke, a magazine open in front of her.

At a table close to the window, a man with a dark complexion is scribbling in a lined notebook. Two deep wrinkles — more furrows than wrinkles — starting from his hook nose pull the rest of his face down. Marjolaine keeps an eye on him: recently, there was a guy like him who took off without paying his bill. To add insult to injury — or vice-versa — he left taking his cup with him. But this one seems okay. He's been showing up one day out of two for a couple of months now. Arrives in the late afternoon, stays until the middle of the evening, sometimes later, doesn't smile, drinks only tea — "no milk, a slice of lemon, please" — never orders anything to eat. Not surprising he is so emaciated. Writes in his notebook as if the commotion from the radio and hockey games, the conversations, and the noise of dishes clinking doesn't bother him. And when he's not writing, he sits, staring into space, mulling things over. More immobile than the statue of that writer — Dante, a poet of ancient times that the Italians revere — put up in the middle of a little park on the street of the same name, nearby. A plump girl, not very pretty, face marked with acne scars, sometimes joins him and they (she especially) speak in low voices: the topics don't seem very cheerful.

Twenty-five minutes to eight. All day long freezing rain has fallen, accompanied by gusts of wind. It's still windy, but the rain has changed to wet snow that's even more distressing, and the sidewalks now shimmer like skating rinks in the pale glimmer of the streetlamps.

After the "events" — that is how Marjolaine soberly refers to Doris's sudden death in the restaurant's washroom three months ago — she had to stand in for Ali at a moment's notice in the kitchen. He disappeared without warning after being

Héléne Rioux

questioned by police that night. The police questioned all
witnesses — who didn't have much to say; they were playing
cards when the incident occurred. Sometimes death comes
like that, quickly, on the sly, and there's nothing spectacular
about its appearance. Unnoticed, it does its job quickly and
then leaves. No, it isn't like in war movies or on the TV news,
where it hits hard in a racket of bombs and sub-machine
guns, with everyone shouting, crying, and begging, and
afterwards the scene is a mess of rubble and blood.

Since the "events," a few waitresses have come and gone
at the End of the World. In their eyes, the ambiance, not to
mention the tips, must have left something to be desired.
Even if, to entice customers, the boss placed a sign in the
window that said "New sexy waitresses." This is Julie's first
evening.

On the muted TV, two men seem to be roaring with
laughter without our knowing why. Comedians, probably.
Prime time revolves around them. The radio is on. It is playing a program — *Bonsoir Nostalgie*. Each evening between seven
and nine o'clock, they play songs that listeners requested the
day before. A singer long dead and buried is now wondering: *si tu n'existais pas*, if you did not exist, he repeats in a
melancholy voice — to someone who, obviously, exists. As
if a person's existence or non-existence could change the
course of things. If he thinks that, the poor man is deluding
himself. We are scarcely atoms in the universe. So, one more
or less ... No, the course of things does not change. And in

the end perhaps it's just as well. The change could be for the worse. How would one know? Might as well stay on familiar ground.

Marjolaine emerges from her lair. "That song always makes me think of Doris," she announces to Denise in a quavering voice. "Remember, he was her favourite singer." She wipes away a tear. "I can't help myself. I still see her, all huddled up, her lipstick on the floor, and her wig ..." Her voice breaks off. Disconcerted, Julie stops cleaning the counter for an instant. Denise grabs her purse. "Come with me," she says to Marjolaine. "We'll go out for a smoke. It'll cheer you up. You've gone all pale."

Julie glances at the abandoned magazine. Gels, creams, patches, pomades, exfoliants: an entire array to improve the complexion, slim the figure, brighten the hair, stop the craving for nicotine. Products at all prices, for all ages, for all defects. She turns the page. Oh, a young actress is on the verge of making her Broadway debut in the role of a duchess. Marjorie Dubois, Canadian, a rising star, specifies the journalist, comparing her to another Marjorie — Martinez — an idol from the time of black and white movies, whom Julie doesn't know. A full-page photo shows her running in the sand in sky-blue jeans, barefoot, her chestnut hair dancing in the wind. In another, a big smile reveals brilliant teeth. How do they manage to have such perfect teeth? In real life, no one has teeth like that. Dentures? No, that kind of girl doesn't have false teeth. She must have had her teeth done. Or else the photo was touched up; they have all kinds of software, for that, concludes Julie, who has a mouth full of fillings and can no longer even afford a dentist. In another photo, Marjorie Dubois is wearing a long white dress, sleeveless, in open-work cotton — organdie, according to the caption — she's sitting on a terrace; the sun is still glowing brightly. For her, apparently, it never stops glowing except to set, making the starlet even more beautiful in the orangey light. In the photo, an oblique ray makes her opalescent nails and the cat's-eye adorning her delicate middle finger sparkle. Her cheek rests in one palm, a half-full glass of golden liquid within reach of the other hand. The article talks about a movie she's going to act in next summer in Vancouver, and of her love affair with a well-known musician on the west coast. She also played the role of a young junkie in an episode of *The Jaguar*, a prestigious, tremendously popular American series. Her real first name is Marjolaine. "Like the cook," Julie says to herself, vaguely surprised that a star, even a rising star, shares something, and especially her first name, with that ... she seeks a plausible comparison. That patch of grey? That rainy day? That dull cliché? The date of birth is mentioned. "The same age as me." The observation jars her. Suddenly she feels worthless in the restaurant while the wet snow spits and lashes against the window pane — perhaps the sky crying; this evening the sky, the city, and the restaurant are crying, and their tears are flowing down the cold windowpane — worthless inside the beige walls, beneath the neon lights, yes, worthless and rotten, cloth in her hand. The tacky song makes her sad as well. Too many *whys* are buzzing around in her head. *Why is it always other people, never me? Why is there no justice on this earth? Why aren't I the one running on the beach with Stéphane? Why is my corner of the world like this?* She wonders why she exists.

Too many questions, and not a single answer.

STANDING UNDER THE AWNING, THE two women light their cigarettes, shivering. "I have an appointment at the hairdresser tomorrow morning," Denise announces, just to distract Marjolaine from her brooding. "My colour is long overdue. I also think I'm going to have it cut an inch or two."

"Good idea. At the end of winter, hair always needs a pick-me-up."

"Not only hair ... And today is supposed to be spring," grumbles Denise. "If I listened to myself, I'd go south right away. To the Dominican Republic, or Cuba."

"Any time. I'll go with you."

"You always say that. Then when the time comes, you have no money."

"Why don't you just say I'm for the birds? I don't know how to treat myself. Not used to it, I suppose ..."

"Maybe it's time you started. There's no point in waiting. Then one day it's too late. Think of Doris."

"I suppose," repeats Marjolaine distractedly — she doesn't feel like talking about it. "Or else I'm afraid of hurricanes ...

The problem is I can't help but feel responsible," she continues, with a sigh. "Poor Doris. I see her, I have nightmares, wake up bathed in sweat, heart beating as if it were going to leap out of my chest, then I can't get back to sleep. Marcel says it's hot flashes, part of menopause, but it isn't. If this keeps on, I'm sure to end up depressed."

"Stop tormenting yourself. You're worrying for no reason. You're no more responsible than I am. Doris was in the terminal stage; it could have happened at any time. It's just that we didn't know it."

"But I should have known it. She was in a worse state than usual that night. I can't forgive myself for not hearing her when she fell. A fall like that must have made some noise. I feel sick imagining the time she spent there, moaning."

"No one heard her, Marjo. Stop tormenting yourself."

They throw their butts into the slush at the same time. A muffled splattering sound — a car moves slowly down the street in front of them. In an instant, its headlights create halos in the grey; it's as if a ghost is passing by, eyes wide open to the night.

"We don't even know how long she lay there worrying, alone, with no one to help her," continues Marjolaine plaintively. "Or to hold her hand. We don't know if she suffered."

"An aneurism, that's what they said after the autopsy. It's like when the heart gives out. You can't predict it. I don't think you suffer long. And if you want my opinion, she was better off not ending up on a bed of pain. She didn't see herself go, and with cancer, that's the best thing that could have happened. My late husband — may he rot in hell, the way he treated me — had quite an ordeal for months in the hospital. In the end he was no better than a vegetable, as skinny as a rake, just skin and bones, frightening to behold and green around the gills. Pale green, actually, bordering on yellowish, with rust-coloured spots, like a head of celery past due going limp in the drawer at the bottom of the refrigerator. A bit like that guy, the one who spends his time scribbling things in a notebook. It's funny, I thought that now, with computers, no one wrote by hand anymore."

"True, that guy doesn't seem very modern."

"Anyway, he had it coming, I'll grant you that," continues Denise about her late husband, "but I wouldn't want my worst enemy to suffer the way he did."

"People can say what they like, but even so, passing away in the washroom ..."

"Lacks dignity."

Marjolaine nods her head, sighing deeply.

"How long do you think the new girl will tough it out?" asks Denise after a moment, to change the subject.

"I don't give her a week." She shrugs her shoulders, irritated. The boss's sign gets her goat. "Sexy! Give me a break! What am I then? A zombie? A broomstick?"

"No, no Marjo. I think you're well preserved for your age," Denise reassures her awkwardly.

"I don't claim to compete with the youth, but ..."

"Stop. You are the age you are. About the same as me. Your boss is an imbecile. It can't be his wife who comes up with those ideas."

Marjolaine shrugs her shoulders. "I don't know."

An awkward silence dampens the moment; Marjolaine sighs again, though not as deeply.

"It's not that I mind doing the cooking. No, in fact I even prefer it in a way. I don't get tips, of course ..."

"Don't tell me that the old cheapskate didn't give you a raise?"

"Yes, yes, I got a raise, that's not the problem. But I find that poster ..."

"Humiliating, I agree with you entirely," Denise concludes adamantly.

"And indecent. This has always been a respectable place. At this rate, he's going to ask them to dance at the tables."

Boris Savine then arrives in his taxi, exits, and slams the door. "It's slippery like you wouldn't believe," he comments, sliding on the icy sidewalk. Denise has a fleeting vision of his sturdy body — *quite a hunk, that Boris*, she thinks with a mixture of desire and spite — sprawled in a puddle. She suppresses a desire to laugh — why is it so funny to see people fall? But Boris doesn't fall. Once sheltered beneath the canopy, he lights a cigarette, and holds out his open pack to the two women. Marjolaine shakes her head. "I just put one out," she says. Denise takes one. "You're right; it looks pretty slippery to me. A good way to break a leg. I should have stayed home. Now I wonder how I'll manage to get back."

They smoke in silence. Marjolaine looks at her watch. "Well, there's more, but I have dishes waiting for me, and I'm not counting too much on that little thing to help me."

"She doesn't seem too strong," adds Denise.

"What little thing?" Boris asks.

"The new sexy waitress," replies Denise, in an acid tone of voice. "You'll judge for yourself. She started this evening."

"Is my brother there?"

Marjolaine shakes her head. "Haven't seen him all day."

He turns to Denise. "I could give you a lift home. I've finished for today. Decent people don't go to work in weather like this."

"I suppose we won't play this evening, either," says Denise. She seems disappointed.

Since the "events," they haven't played one single card game. Out of respect for the deceased, for years their partner at five hundred, an extension of euchre; it's as if they no longer feel like having fun.

"Perhaps we'd better start again," suggests Denise. "In books, they call that *coming to terms*. Laure was talking to me about it just the other day. She really would like to. So would I. And I think that, where she is, Doris would be happy."

Boris nods his head. "We'll discuss it ..."

"Even Raoul is just waiting for that, I'm sure of it," insists Denise. "We haven't seen him in ages. I miss our evenings."

"Maybe after the playoffs. These things need time. Meanwhile, I'm famished. There's some macaroni left, I hope?"

"You're lucky," replies Marjolaine. "I've just made another pot. It's in the oven, browning. You'll be the first to taste it."

ON THE TV, THE CAMERA pans in on about fifteen young people sitting, a bit primly, on cloud-shaped cushions. A black woman, a few Asians and Latinos among the blond and chestnut-coloured heads. Julie thinks she recognizes Daphné — a Chinese girl with platinum hair who danced in the same clubs as she not very long ago — but the camera moved too quickly. Now the hostess, a blonde in a lamé mini-dress, is giving her sales talk, smiling ear-to-ear. "It is our great pleasure this evening to ..." and so on. The audience applauds frenetically. It's the new reality TV show.

"You're not going to leave that on!" protests Boris. "I came for the hockey. If you don't change the channel, I might as well leave."

Denise shrugs her shoulders. The scribbler raises his head then returns to his writing. Marjolaine takes the remote control. "It's okay, Boris, it's not worth getting worked up."

"Besides, my brother is going to be here any minute," continues Boris, as if to justify himself. "We're supposed to watch the game together. There's hope: they were smart to put Mike Wallace back in front of the net. It's a crucial game. If they lose tonight, we've practically no chance of being in the playoffs. And turn off the music."

"Excuse me?"

"The radio, Marjolaine ... Please."

The end of the national anthem on TV replaces the beginning of an Elvis Presley song on the radio. *Love Me Tender*. "Really," mutters Denise. "Shutting off the King, that takes nerve."

"The customer is always king," declares Marjolaine wryly.

"I'm a customer too. I'm even the one who requested that song."

Boris sniggers. "In memory of your crazy youth?"

"I don't see why you're laughing. I danced quite a bit when I was young. I was very much in demand, you know. I have memories aside from those of a married woman."

Julie advances with a placemat, a glass of water, and a paper napkin. Boris eyes her appreciatively. Sexy indeed. She's wearing tight, low-waisted jeans, a T-shirt that goes below her ribs, her stomach is just flat enough — not too much, though: anorexics don't turn him on — a pearl set in a silver ring adorns her navel. "Doesn't it hurt getting pierced there?" She inclines her head in a way that can mean yes or no. Not very talkative. "So it'll be Marjolaine's famous macaroni au gratin, with a beer," he continues. "Never mind the bread; I've gone on a diet." To judge by his pot belly, he is in dire need of one. "If someone wanted to pierce my navel they would have trouble finding it in the folds," he says, bursting out laughing. Julie conscientiously notes the order — though one might wonder why; he's the only customer eating.

A QUARTER AFTER NINE. THE sullen man glances at his watch. Bizarre. The date was for nine o'clock, and she's never late. Looking annoyed, he motions to Julie to bring him another tea. The door opens. He looks up, makes what resembles the beginning of a slight smile. But it's Diderot Toussaint making his entrance, looking shattered. "I've had news of Ali," he announces to no one in particular. "His papers — his visitor's visa or work permit, I'm not too sure — weren't in order. He's leaving tomorrow. Deported. Returning to his country."

"Ali?" exclaims Denise. "They didn't take him for a terrorist, did they?"

Diderot shrugs his shoulders. "How to know what they think in those offices … You only have to have an Arab name, or one that's slightly foreign, to become suspicious in their eyes. Real paranoia since September 11. Fortunately I have my citizenship." He sits down across from Boris.

"Some folks have their citizenship," Boris grumbles. "But they're still in prison in Guantánamo."

Julie approaches with her order pad. "I'd like a good cup of coffee," says Diderot. "None of that reheated stuff, huh?"

She realizes she forgot the instructions — fresh coffee every hour. "Don't worry. I'll make fresh."

"Bring me some too," says Boris. "Is there any sugar pie left?"

"One slice."

"So I'll take it. Warm, with a scoop of ice cream."

He who was talking about a diet has already downed two portions of *pouding chômeur* — with whipped cream —

following his macaroni. Not about to lose his rolls of flesh.

Two hours have passed. A group of overexcited teenagers — perhaps enticed by the poster in the window — came in for poutine; Julie heard them chuckling nervously as she walked by. A few taxi drivers came in to drink coffee and then left. Diderot stayed to see the end of the match. Boris's brother didn't come. At one point they heard the echo of a siren — an ambulance or fire engine — in a nearby street and Marjolaine brought a hand to her throat, as if afraid of choking.

Julie looks gloomily at her new environment. She can't wait until midnight, can't bear it anymore. She only wants one thing: to go to bed. Even though for three months now she basically has not slept. But alone in her bed she's able to imagine Stéphane. She closes her eyes and the face of her beloved appears. She clasps her pillow. Her mind glides as if travelling along a river. One hand travels down her belly; her mind glides and drifts along the current. One hand between her thighs, she imagines him. Her mind, a swan, a duck, a seagull — her mind has wings, her mind glides, settles on the water, floats, follows the current, sliding along happy images. Such lightness. The past offers its promises. The future is closed, but the past remains open. She in a medieval dress — she had chosen it in a catalogue for her wedding. The two of them in summer, travelling to cities you see in movies; they're in Paris or in Italy, in Venice — their gondola moving slowly along the canals, the full moon flickering upon the water. Or they're on a tropical island. Running on the sand, jumping in the waves. Hand in hand, heads back, dazzling teeth, arms raised in a victory sign. In the background, waves carry the echo of their giggling. The hand speeds up. Pleasure is within reach; Julie calls to it, moaning. Come, come. It comes like an earthquake. Time stops in the space of an infinite second. The night will go by; the night goes by.

IN THE KITCHEN, MARJOLAINE FINISHES preparing dishes for the famished night owls — with the weather tonight, they won't be beating down the door. She leaves between midnight and one o'clock. The owner's son takes over till breakfast, then his wife will replace him, assisted by another sexy young thing — but less so than Julie. Marjolaine will return in the afternoon. Tomorrow morning, in her kitchen, over a second cup of coffee, she'll look at the stack of cooking magazines the boss lent her; he'd like to add one or two more sophisticated dishes to the menu. The competition — all the new trendy cafés and bistros opening — is becoming increasingly fierce in the neighbourhood. "Just because our customers are taxi drivers doesn't mean they don't appreciate fine cooking," he decreed. Actually, perhaps he isn't wrong. For the time being he has bought a powdered product to make what he calls "chocolate mousse." Marjolaine had shrugged her shoulders. *If that's his idea of fine cooking …* She made it a few times and found the taste too chemical. Doesn't even measure up to Jell-O instant pudding.

The Canadiens had a close win, one-nothing, the only goal

miraculously scored nineteen seconds before the end of the game. Now, a player — the star of the game — struggles to express himself in front of a microphone. "A hard game. Quite a few shots on the goal. We all fought like hell." Boris sighs, relieved. "You didn't miss anything," he says to his brother, Fédor, who has just arrived. "Aside from Leduc's goal at the end, it stank."

"Couldn't get here before. I had a fare to the airport, then went over to Saint-Bruno and on to Montreal North. But it's all right; I heard it on the radio."

MARJOLAINE PUTS THE TELEVISION ON mute and turns the radio back on. "With winds of one hundred and fifty-five kilometres an hour, Hurricane Jenny, now category two, is expected to reach Haiti by the end of the week ..." Diderot Toussaint puts his head in his hands — he still has family in the Gonaives region and in Cabarete. "A suicide bombing in Kandahar killed three Canadian soldiers, bringing the total to seventeen since January." This depressing report ends the news. Gilbert Bécaud's voice replaces it with an old song about Easter vacation in Le Tréport. The program *Romantic Cities* continues its odyssey around the world like it does every evening of the week.

Julie stands before Fédor with her pen and pad. "What's the soup of the day?" he asks. Then, without giving her time to answer, "Jenny," he exclaims, stupefied. "Fancy meeting you here ... What are you doing here?"

"The soup is chicken and rice. And my name is Julie."

"Come on. You're Jenny. I'm paid to know that. I went to pick you up often enough in the middle of the night, you and your friend, when you both finished dancing. Her name was Daphné. I brought you back home: Centre Street in Pointe-Saint-Charles."

"I don't understand a word you're saying. I never lived in Pointe-Saint-Charles. I don't know that area." Her voice wavers. "I've never seen you before."

"Leave her alone," Boris intervenes. "She should know who she is, after all. You've got the wrong girl. Jenny is the hurricane."

But Fédor insists. "You're not going to pretend you don't recognize me? The Geisha Bar. Doesn't that ring a bell? At the American border. Or the other one, in Terrebonne, the Olé Olé."

"I'm not a dancer." Now she's shouting. "My name is Julie. Julie Masson. I never danced. I work to pay for my education. I go to university."

She walks away — her heels clatter on the floor. Images of her shattered life, shattered to bits, come tumbling down. The snow storm one night in December, the twenty-first. Stéphane on Taschereau Boulevard, his dismembered body imprisoned in the car while she danced in a lousy bar near the border. The money saved, dance by dance, on the tables or in the booths. Table dances and lap dances. You do what you have to. A goal in sight. Images like shards of glass that make her memory bleed. But in the end, a kind of paradise surely awaited her; she'd had a glimpse of it when they went driving around the countryside in the afternoons — the house on a river, with a studio for Stéphane, with big windows that would have let in light, and for her, a garden in summer, and above it all, the sky with the moon and the stars. She would have learned to recognize the constellations, the Big Dipper and the Little Dipper, Cygnus, Sirius, and the others. You have to make your way, nothing is ever free; everything must be earned. Her entire childhood her father and mother had drummed that refrain into her head. They worked themselves to the bone fifteen hours a day in their convenience store, never taking a vacation. So she beavered away, valiant, cautious, patient. She worked every night, thinking that way doors would open more quickly. They opened all right, and sooner than she'd expected. Onto hell. No, it was more like a trap opening beneath her feet and she fell in. Everything must be earned? People who say that are full of it. Because she's still wondering what she did to earn that.

A few days after the — she doesn't say "events," she says "accident," she says "end of the world" — a letter arrived for Stéphane. A letter from his friend François, the so-called poet, the one living the good life in Spain at taxpayers' expense — he received a grant from the government whereas Stéphane ... Life is unfair, we well know. She read it. What does it matter now if she read his letters? Who could criticize her for it? She'd have been better off sending it back, writing on it "Deceased." It began with "My dear Tépha." He always called him that. Tépha. They were like brothers, with all kinds of memories and codes she didn't understand. Like brothers, and she, of course, was not their sister. "My dear Tépha." In his letter, he spoke of a dancer, an artist, he said, a genuine one. He loved her and she had a lot of friends almost as beautiful and as artistic as herself. Manuela and he were going to have a baby come summer. He'd written: "What are you waiting for to leave Julie? She won't be able to bring you out of it." He said that he'd seen her dance nude. She remembered perfectly the night he'd turned up at Geisha with another guy. They'd wanted her to dance at their table. Their words had entered her heart like a knife. "I'd more likely pity her, you see." That burned. "It was pretty low-level." She'd wanted to reply, but could not find the words.

"I HAVEN'T GOT THE WRONG girl. It's Jenny. This reminds me of another girl, last winter, in Cabarete, who claimed she was a tour guide. Afterwards, she named me her price. For what she had to sell, it was not cheap."

Diderot bursts out laughing despite his concern. "Did you buy?" Fédor shrugs his shoulders.

Julie turns back. "You're crazy. Off your rocker. Stark, raving mad." She is no longer shouting: she is spitting out her words, screaming, screeching. "You make me sick. You're just a lowlife like the others." She throws her order pad across the room, holds her pen like a weapon in her closed fist.

Marjolaine rushes over, tries to intervene, but Julie pushes her away. "Don't touch me. You're an old witch, a mean old witch." Now she's crying, shouting and crying at the same time. "I don't want anyone to touch me."

Everyone is wide-eyed, even the silent man, who has stopped his writing and observes the scene, dumbfounded. On the radio, Henri Salvador croons that he would like to see Syracuse. Tears roll down Julie's cheeks, streaming like rain. Standing in the middle of the room, her every limb shakes. She gasps pathetically, like a heroine in an old melodrama. "My name is Julie. I don't want anyone to touch me anymore."

"A hysterical crisis," decrees Denise. "We have to call 911."

But Marjolaine replies that no one is calling anyone. "Come, Julie," she says, "come with me. I'll make you some hot milk. Everything will be okay. Some nice hot milk with honey. You'll see, everything will be okay."

The door flies open, the wind rushes in and a woman in a raincoat enters. A few damp locks escape from her jet-black bun. She shakes her umbrella. An apparition, truly. The first time they've seen her here. Come from another world, suddenly appearing out of the night. And like a ray of sunshine, Diderot Toussaint thinks, never at a loss for comparisons, even trite ones. She glances around the room: everyone is suddenly frozen. "*Messieurs dames,*" she says with an accent. *Messieurs dames?* Except for Julie, who's still crying, they exchange dumbfounded looks.

"I've come for the poutine," she announces, after hanging her raincoat on a hook.

Marjolaine regains her composure. "Yes," she stammers. "Poutine, of course. Please have a seat. I'll bring you the menu."

She takes Julie by the shoulder, leads her toward the kitchen. "We know your name is Julie. Fedor's not bad guy, Fédor; he's a joker. He just wanted to tease you. Some nice warm milk with honey. You'll see, everything will be okay, everything will be okay. Don't cry." She repeats it in her gentle voice, like a litany, in her worn-out, lilting voice, like a lullaby. Even if she has lived enough to know that no, everything will not be okay. Not when the heart is affected. She knows that some wounds never heal.

2

ON THE ICY SIDEWALK,
EXITING THE SUBWAY

A good way to break a leg.

A QUARTER TO NINE. BÉATRICE Berger emerges from the subway at Jean-Talon station. She is greeted by flurries of melting snow, and pushed along by gusts of wind. Montreal spring in all its fury. Spring because today is the day, or rather the night — which, all things considered, doesn't change things much, it is hardly any less grey, just colder — of the equinox. It's funny: each year, we believe in it. As if the seasons conformed to a well-established calendar and, like soldiers in some perfect army, the heavens above stop and start at precise dates. People who think that are under an illusion: today proves it ... Or else they have short memories. Equinox only means that day is equal to night.

No promise of warmth or sunshine. *Does the phenomenon occur simultaneously throughout the planet?* Béatrice wonders. She tries to imagine the earth's inclination in its course around the sun, then gives up. The sky is a mystery. Despite her efforts, she has never managed to locate the constellations. Try as she may to crane her neck to observe the firmament, the stars always seem to be an anarchy, like dandelions in a field, and she can discern no order in the way they're arranged. As for the rotation of the planets, Béatrice knows only one thing: they revolve … Yet equinoxes, like solstices, have provided an occasion to rejoice since the dawn of time, in several countries around the world. Well, when we say rejoice … It's like for everything else: everything depends on the point of view. She thinks of human sacrifices that in an era not so long ago — the human race is relatively young — people offered to deities equally cruel and insatiable, in the Aztec Empire, for example. Sowing, harvesting: humanity must feed itself. In the end, everything revolves around that: the world's hunger and satisfying it. Everything revolves. You can get dizzy thinking about it too long. She opens her umbrella; hopes to have enough time to reach where she's going before the wind turns it inside out.

Beaubien station would have been closer, no question, but she wanted to walk a bit. She likes to walk, no matter what the weather. Especially when she has a date like this one. Strolling gives her the time to think without becoming dizzy, getting herself into a state, as she says. These weekly meetings make her nervous; she always has so many things to tell. In her head there is screeching, an uproar, like a pack of unruly kids in a schoolyard rundown area. Walking allows her to put her ideas in order. The umbrella is pink, strewn with white and blue polka dots; for Béatrice this lends the bad weather a frivolous, even joyful aspect. Thus equipped, she feels as if she's thumbing her nose at the elements. The border is adorned with fabric daisies she sewed on herself — tiny, impeccable stitches — one by one, in her spare time. Her rubber rain boots are pink as well. She walks down Chateaubriand, heading south. The End of the World isn't far, seven or eight minutes and she'll be there. She may even be early. It wouldn't be the first time.

THE WHOLE BUSINESS BEGAN A little over three months ago. A classified ad that appeared in Saturday's *Le Devoir* — she always reads them. Not in the Personals column, between "Camille, forties, wants to live intensely" or "Chubby blonde looking for exoticism seeks cultured black man" and "Prince consort, part-time, for household goddess" — although she reads them too. When she buys the newspaper, she intends to read it completely, from front page to last: sports, financial section, and classified ads included. Even if she's not looking for a prince and has nothing of a household goddess about her. But these concise descriptions amuse her. Certain requests are discreet: "F possessed with inner beauty wants to meet M with affinities." Everyone is seeking. "Retired but passionate literature professor seeks F for love and more." People have strange ways of expressing themselves. Why the unnatural "but"? Does passion go up in smoke when you retire? Along with the paycheque and employee benefits? Are people active in the job market more passionate or exciting than others? In other words: is passion the exclusive hunting ground of youth? Are golden-agers deprived of it? Casanova, however — she's read his memoirs — tells another tale. Even when he was completely shrivelled, he kept on loving. But people tell about whatever they like in their memoirs ... And then "love and more" ... *More what?* Béatrice asked herself, imagining God knows what acrobatic contortions taken from the *Kama Sutra*: the Crab, the Mare, and the others. Not very aesthetic, between two retired people. In the end she's not exempt from prejudice either, she'd concluded with a kind of melancholy. Perhaps, more simply — is it really simple? — the academic was looking for a soulmate with whom he would attain spiritual ecstasy. The inner beauty with which the other one said she was possessed. Perhaps they corresponded, who knows? Wandering souls in search of paradise lost, seekers of the mythical Grail. Strange, when you think of it: bottles containing the same message, floating side by side on the same ocean. Two trains leaving the station simultaneously in opposite directions; two calls, not hearing one another, two pathetic cries uttered by two deaf people in the desert. She'd almost been tempted to send the professor a letter — it would have been a precedent. Answering with a question, in fact: "When you have love, dear retired professor, what more can you want? Please explain. If I had it, know that I'd feel fulfilled; I wouldn't seek anything else." Truth be told, she'd cut out that ad and placed it in her night table drawer. Something for a rainy day. You never know.

But no, it was in the "Books and CDs" column, her favourite, and it was phrased as tersely as the others. "Seeking to collaborate with voracious reader." No indication about the gender of the person seeking.

A phone number followed.

Béatrice's heart had suddenly beaten more quickly. A call of destiny, surely, a message or a sign. Because she's voracious, has always, or almost always been. "The flesh is sad, alas! — and I've read all the books," as a poet said. She hasn't yet read all the books — there are so many — but it's a dream she cherishes, the inaccessible star to which everyone aspires in his or her own way. Books fill her life, true. Even though, in her case, "fill" seems a euphemism. Better to say they enchant and illuminate. They define it. To top it all off, she works in a used bookstore, Outre-mots, "beyond words" — a play on words, as the business is located in Outremont, on rue de l'Épée, between Fairmount and Laurier. A very friendly bookstore where regulars go, on the ground floor of a renovated house almost a hundred years old, with sagging but comfortable armchairs to sit in while leafing through books. There's a rocking chair with a faded pink cushion, and an area to sit down calmly with fruit juice, mineral water, chamomile tea — or linden tea, *tilleul*, for hard-line Proustians. A basket of apples, some muffins baked every morning by Madame Brunet, the owner — the couple lives upstairs with their two teenagers and an obese grey cat named Caramel, go figure why — croissants, palmier cookies, *pain au chocolat* from the home-style bakery, not to mention the madeleines in a flowered plate beneath a dome. Everything is designed either to satisfy ravenous book lovers — as is often the case with her, her curves bear witness — or to satisfy an attack of hypoglycaemia, which has already happened. Though a few walls have been knocked down, the overall look of the place still maintains its old-fashioned character with the creaking cherry wood floors, the mantelpiece of the con-demned chimney on which books are placed with calculated negligence, the raw lace curtains in the bay windows. A concept, really: customers must feel they're being welcomed into a friendly home. More a meeting place than a business. They are just asked — naturally enough — to take off their boots in winter, or cover them with those little socks or slightly grotesque slippers — which, bizarrely, resemble shower caps — in sky-blue embossed paper. There's a cash register at the entrance. Music, always, but not too loud, just background. Sure bets — Dylan, Reggiani, Nougaro — baroque music, a few unusual recordings, the Netchaev Group, Daphné — famous for her death-metal interpretation of an old hit, *Broken Wings*. This time, it's her latest, a slam album on the texts of Christine de Pisan (*Seulette suis et seulette veux être — All alone I am, and all alone I want to be*). Occasionally, book launches or poetry readings are organized. Five or six bottles of wine, a large plate of *crudités* on the coffee table, a bowl of whole-grain crackers without trans fat. At the end of the readings, books are sold and signed by a proud or disappointed author. When the good weather returns, they set up a table and a few garden chairs in the yard for those who like to read in the sun, an old wrought-iron park bench, and an ashtray on a stand for unrepentant smokers.

TODAY, TUESDAY, BÉATRICE IS OFF. She works six days a week, from noon to eight p.m., and doesn't complain. She likes her job. On busy days, she holds court at the counter in the back of the store — in the little room behind the kitchen that used to be a child's room or a maid's room — like a queen granting an audience. Saturdays and Sundays are particularly packed. Full of hope, the sycophants spread out their offerings before her. Her responsibilities then involve separating the wheat from the chaff. She examines the merchandise carefully, makes sure the volumes aren't annotated or scribbled in, and no pages are missing. Then she buys ones likely to find a buyer, publicly casting aside the ones that haven't the shadow of a chance. She'd take them all gladly, but the bookstore owners have another concept of business. Yet no, it's not true, she wouldn't take them all. Recently, for example, an older woman showed up with two grocery bags filled with novels from the *True Emotions* collection. There were about fifty of them, in very good condition, most in paperback, three or four hardcovers, all by the same author, an English-woman named — but perhaps it was a pseudonym — Hope Spencer. To have written so many books, for there are many others, the author must be a hundred years old, or else turn out three of them a year. Unless an army of ghost writers turns them out for her. On the covers, practically identical, couples are embracing in the moonlight, under an arbour. Or there in an exotic decor of palm trees swaying and sailboats, white sails billowing. Or there's thunder, leaden clouds running across the purple sky and, in the background, the tops of trees bending beneath the wind. No matter where, the couples — passionate, obviously not retirees — are always embracing just as closely. People don't read these anymore, especially not in Outremont. Or, if they do, they don't flaunt it. Béatrice knows customers' tastes well: women over forty have their favourite writers — the ones often seen on television, who take part in all debates and give their opinion on all topics — they are partial to artist biographies, recent bestsellers recommended in their magazines. Younger women read novels designed especially for them in which the heroines, audacious man-hunters who work in adver-tising or movies, have weekly meetings in trendy restaurants where they exchange confidences, calling a spade a spade — even though they are just as naively sentimental as any Harlequin romance; the bloody thrillers please all readers or almost; the classics, when they are not too damaged, as a rule are destined for penniless students. Her choice made, she offers a price, not too high but fair, which in any case is always accepted. At Outre-mots, the sycophants do not like to see their offerings scorned. The rest of the time, she classifies the titles selected in alphabetical order in their respective sections: novels, poetry, detective novels, history, philosophy, esotericism, biography, cooking. There is also a section for comic books and illustrated children's books, the one for vinyl LPs — now back in style — and CDs. The owners are considering adding a DVD section.

Béatrice considers the right to examine a privilege and, magnanimous, also sometimes gives one that's unsalable a chance. Sometimes, though admittedly only occasionally, she is offered a rare book. One day someone brought her a dedicated copy of Grignon's *Un homme et son péché* — a first edition, 1933 — that she, of course, kept for herself, thanks to the dedication. "To Marc — or was it Marie — an illegible surname — with very best wishes." Nothing compromising, but the author had left his mark and, for her, obsessive at times, that's what counts. However, she has no intention of rereading it. Once — for a course on Quebec literature at college — had been more than enough for her. And this week, a young man who had inherited the library of an uncle, a former university professor, sold a *Divine Comedy*, in English, a rather old edition, from 1948, translated by one Lawrence Grant White, with illustrations by Gustave Doré. When she comes across a gem like that, she says nothing to the owners, sets the price, buys it, and keeps it for herself. Is it honest? She doesn't know and refuses to ask herself the question. If it's not entirely honest, it's not dishonest either. She's taking advantage of an opportunity.

Once every three months, the unpopular books end up jumbled together at the door, in a bin topped by a sign saying "2 for 1 dollar. Clearance." It always breaks Béatrice's heart. At that price, frankly, she'd rather they give them away. "But if we start giving them away, no one will want to buy anymore," the owners justify, not unreasonably. They have more business sense than she. Fortunately, for that matter. They make it a question of principle. "Emotion has no place in business. People who show pity inevitably end up bankrupt." Yet, even at that price, some books interest no one. Then they are sent in boxes to institutions — processing centres and other prisons.

BÉATRICE ALWAYS HAS SEVERAL NOVELS on the go, can jump from a thriller to a poem, from Saint Augustine's *Confessions* to a gastronomic dictionary. She reads at work when no one is there; she comes home with a book and reads in the bus and in the subway; she reads in the kitchen while eating dinner, in the living room while listening to music, with a glass of fine Napoleon brandy, maybe two, or three; she even reads when the television is on — one dictionary or another, she has an entire collection. Ten pages an evening, three of proper names and seven general dictionaries: a person never stops learning. She takes her bath with a collection of poems, and a classical work keeps her company in her bed until sleep overtakes her — swoops down on her, she prefers to say, imagining sleep like a sly animal, a bird of prey lurking in a corner and watching her intently — often right in the middle of a sentence. She always falls asleep with the light on.

Her choices are random, never discriminating. Imagine a typical week of reading: at work, *The Missionary Instinct in Women*, a rather scathing essay by Florence Jordan — very instructive; in the subway, *The Flight and Fall of the Angels*, a Russian detective novel by Marina Ivanovna — macabre descriptions, goose flesh and cold sweat guaranteed. For when it comes to inflicting cruelty, whether by making a person who knows too much talk, or by shutting him up for good, the post-Soviet mafia has no cause to be jealous of the inquisitors of the Middle Ages or of Chinese tormentors in terms of imagination. "Angel" is the surname given to traffickers of heroine imported from Afghanistan, and as for their fall, well, it's brutal and not much is left of their wings. In the kitchen, *Recipes from the Ends of the Earth* by Victor Karr — "sauté, brown, braise, caramelize, cook until transparent ..." the translator, Han Rajon (a woman probably, but perhaps a man, hard to know with that first name), has more than one synonym up her sleeve — and in the living room, a few pages from the life of Cosima Wagner or of Robert Elkis, the legendary filmmaker, or the biography of Arthur Miller. While the miseries of the world, the tally of the day's victims, flash by on screen during the TV news, Béatrice will be flipping through the historical dictionary of the French language. Baudelaire's poems — she never tires of them — or Juan Garcia's — she's just discovered him — then accompany her in the bath and Byron's *Don Juan* — in the original — will share her bed, if not *La Cité des Dames* by Christine de Pisan. Daphné and her interpretation — even in slam — put a flea in her ear. The book is still resting on her night table, with the complete works of Pushkin, the next book she plans to read.

She's voracious that way. Or would like to be.

But since the telephone call she's had other reading. Since then she's been caught up in a mission, and now she only reads very black novels — or very red ones, if you think of the gallons of hemoglobin spattering their pages — the history of the contemporary wars — the First, the Second, Indochina, Algeria, Vietnam, the Gulf, Rwanda, Afghanistan — genocides and crimes against humanity of the twentieth century, biographies of crafty politicians or famous murderers, accounts of trials that made headlines — or didn't. Of her early reading, the dictionary is the only book she still reads. To educate herself. Or take her mind off things. However, even there, she sometimes comes across words and names she would rather never have discovered.

But back to the ad. Of course she phoned. How could she not? The call of destiny was irresistible.

A man with a deep, slightly husky voice, picked up. The

usual questions, then silence when she told him her name, Béatrice. "Impossible," he murmured. "Unexpected, I mean. I'll explain." He made a date with her at the Café Dante for eight o'clock that same evening. "I'll be wearing a red toque," she murmured before hanging up. She wanted to make sure he'd recognize her. As for what he looked like, he said nothing. In any case, she was the first to arrive, and didn't remove her toque. Italian music played softly; there were four or five quiet customers, men who looked Italian, drinking coffee in small cups. At regular intervals the espresso machine spluttered and a divine aroma filled the room. Béatrice ordered a cappuccino. When he entered, she recognized him without ever having seen him. While not handsome — that is, according to arbitrarily set standards — his face was ... how to say it ... intense. Serious. He seemed like he had a bit of a cold. He resembled his voice. Thin — slender, she thought — shoulders slightly bent. He hung up his coat, nodded to the waiter behind the counter, and sat across from her.

She was still thinking of that enigmatic "I'll explain." It must have been because of the "béa," as in "beatitude." Béatrice, *la lectrice*, the happy reader. It wasn't that at all.

Straight off he asked her if she had she read *The Divine Comedy*. "A long, long time ago," she stammered, caught up short, ashamed to have to admit to this gap in knowledge. Because no, she had not. The same as with Cervantes, Proust, and Homer: we know them by name, quote in conversation the lines about madeleines or windmills, the wooden horse, the city of Troy, and give our listeners the impression we know all that. They must do the same. Impressing people. Nothing shines beneath the veneer.

He remained unshakeable, didn't believe her. The conversation was off to a bad start. She retracted what she'd claimed. "Actually, no," she admitted. And he: "The opposite would have surprised me." She wanted to sink ten feet into the ground. She who claimed to be a big reader had not even read the first word of that classic. He said: "Don't worry about it."

They talked about her work in the bookstore. He wanted to know what people read. Her self-confidence returned.

"They read novels," she answered animatedly. "Detective novels are popular. Agatha Christie is still a safe bet, of course, although less and less. The favourite authors now come from all over the world, just about: Venice, Moscow, Barcelona, Peking, and a little city in Scania, Sweden — a name that ends in 'o.' Or is it in 'ad'? I'm not sure anymore. Serial killers and sexual predators, international scams, organ trafficking, pedophilia, schemes of corrupt politicians, heroine trafficking …"

"And arms dealing."

"Yes. Money laundering. Illegal immigration. Prostitution rings."

"They used to call it white slavery."

"And terrorism."

"Of course."

They were there, in a peaceful café in Little Italy, recording all the planet's defects. Surrealist, she thinks now.

"Topics that fascinate readers."

"Hell."

His tone when he said that. She'd been taken aback. Who was this guy? A crank? A mystic? Some kind of guru seeking to lure her into his sect? You can never be too careful. "For some, it's a way of understanding the world. At least that's what they tell me. They want to find out about how the legal system works, or about culinary oddities in other countries. And I believe them." He'd nodded his head.

If he was a mystic, he had nothing of a crank about him. No, he had — he has — his wits about him, and a solid head on his shoulders. Béatrice remembers in detail the conversation they had that evening, and the memory elates her; she is still moved by his attention as he listened to her. "Extreme" is the word. She said that a future historian wishing to study the customs of our era would no doubt recourse to detective novels. He answered: "Alberto Manguel, in his *A Reading Diary*, I believe." They'd read the same books; she had tears in her eyes. They'd known each other for scarcely ten minutes and already she felt so close to him. Both on the same wavelength; soulmates. *I am your reader*, she wanted to exclaim. *Don't look for anyone else. I'll read all you want.* But she contained her excitement, afraid he would take her for a hysteric. She got back on topic — they were discussing detective novels. "It's the fight between Good and Evil," she declared calmly, clearly seeing the capital letters in her mind. The knight versus the dragon. And the investigating knights, on the side of Good, are generally quite endearing. Vulnerable, disillusioned, lovers of fine food, often well-read. Grappling with what are usually pretty twisted love stories. They've changed since Maigret. Mind you he too, in his way ..."

"Heavy."

"A disillusioned *commissaire*, yes, but not at all vulnerable. And not very well-read. As for his loves ... A totally conventional married life. Deadly boring. The missus in the kitchen lovingly preparing the *blanquette*. You know what? I'd have hated being his wife ... And that of his author even more."

He smiles fleetingly. Emboldened, she forged ahead. She remembers everything, exactly, the words, the pauses, the smiles: she goes over the lines in her head, like those of a play rehearsed a hundred times.

"There's one in Barcelona, an ironic private eye that gives all his favourite recipes — I tested his paella: excellent. He burns the books that have disappointed him. Another one, in Venice, relaxes by rereading the classics in Latin. In his case, it's his wife who cooks. In between two bloody investigations, the Swedish policeman listens to opera. But eats very poorly. Hamburgers, frozen pizzas, anything ... even criminals have something ..."

"Appealing?"

"In a way."

"Dissenters have always fascinated the masses, you know as well as I. Think of Cartouche, Pugachev, Rasputin, Lacenaire, Mandrin. Popular heroes."

Except for Lacenaire — thanks to an old cult film — and Rasputin — *but was he a dissenter?* — she didn't know them. She nodded slightly, all the same. "I mean to say appealing in books ... Manguel reads detective novels, too. He particularly admires Sherlock Holmes. Not I. His Watson is ridiculous. And even Moriarty. Too evil to be plausible."

"No. Don't believe that. People invent nothing. Even, or especially, when it comes to evil. Everything has been invented." Had he read all the books? Was that why he seemed so sad? "The monotony with which the human race repeats itself is in fact depressing," he concluded.

She could find nothing to add.

They are in agreement on one point: despite all that's been said of his famous story — *The Murders in the Rue Morgue* — Poe did not invent the detective novel. It has existed ever since there have been stories. You only have to open a Bible; the plot is already in place — murderer, murder victim. And that brilliantly illustrated what he'd declared concerning monotony. People always rewrite the same story. A man kills his brother out of jealousy, another swindles his with a bowl of lentils, and a woman exchanges favours for the head of an innocent man. Lust and lechery have ruled, do rule, and will rule the world. No, we invent nothing; everything exists.

"And then there are the new heroes, the war photographers.

Always there when things are heating up. Adrenaline rushes and all that. The eye of the world."

"Virgil," he said. "He guides Dante in hell."

"But never mind," she added, "people also have other books. Fortunately, I'd say. They read pop psychology, you know, the genre that explains how to feel good about yourself, cure cancer by positive thought, survive the loss of a loved one. They buy biographies of famous people, novels — Marguerite Duras still has her fan club."

"Autofiction."

"A genre that has its enthusiasts. And then, history, especially when grand and violent passions are at stake — for that, England has a highly romantic aura. Henry VIII and his string of women. The unfortunate Anne Boleyn, her daughter Elizabeth, the ill-fated Mary Stuart."

"Foolhardy, above all."

"Tragic female destiny, Sissi and Marie-Antoinette. And cookbooks. A real frenzy, cooking. Everyone seems to go in for it."

"And what do they watch on television? Aside from game shows and variety shows, I mean?"

"Reality TV. People who broadcast their reality. Anyway, "reality" is a misnomer. To my mind, nothing is more fake. What's more, they're very bad actors … Then there are always the thrillers. Nowadays investigators are profilers, scientific investigators, medical examiners, experts in all kinds of esoteric techniques.

"Profilers?"

"Yes, they outline the killer's profile. So-and-so must be a white man in his thirties; he must have peed the bed in his childhood, is still traumatized by it, stuff like that. New investigators work in highly specialized laboratories with very precise instruments. Crime scenes are now the most chic places on the planet."

He looks cynical. "What do you think of that?"

She didn't know. She wasn't thinking anything.

"I don't know. Cutting up corpses has become the "in" job ... Hercule Poirot's day has passed, I mean. With his little grey cells, he is completely passé. The endearing Columbo as well, who is helpless before a fax or an answering machine."

He cracked what appeared to be the shadow of a smile.

"Crime represents a ... mathematical problem, so to speak," she continued. "Fingerprints are out of date. With time, criminals have learned and now wear gloves. But they always forget something, a detail. Investigators can smoke out a guilty person from the least little fibre found at the crime scene, from the slightest DNA particle — there is always a hair fallen somewhere, a microscopic drop of saliva projected onto a windshield."

"The how, rather than the why."

"Watching these series, you'd think the world was full of murderers."

"It is."

"They quote Shakespeare and Nietzsche."

"Dante?"

"Dante is the first name of an investigator, the hero in one of those in series. He concludes each of his inquiries with a quotation drawn from the *Inferno*. Dante Sullivan. The one they nickname the Jaguar, you know."

But of course he couldn't have known. He looked shattered, as if an idol had just been desecrated. "Immortality is sometimes a curse."

"Those series are short-lived," she hastened to resume. "Nietzsche is the one quoted most. 'God is dead.'"

"*Gott ist tot*. But he isn't."

"A song that's a big hit right now. From the Netchaev group. But it seems Nietzsche has been misunderstood."

"That's strange; in your list you've not mentioned love."

"Of course there's always love. Thwarted love, I mean. But death is more popular. A shame. Perhaps because people don't know how to talk about love in books. Writers are afraid of seeming saccharine. Only poets dare. And even then ..."

She replays their conversation. It's always like that when she's walking. In her mind, she asks questions that were or weren't asked, gives answers that were or weren't given. A customer of the bookstore — a mixed-up artist, a bit weird — told her he saw the paintings he was going to paint when he was driving in his car — a jalopy, in fact, all rusted and dilapidated. He parked it in front of the bookstore and the owners thought it clashed a bit with the rest of the street. Stéphane something, Gingras or Gélinas. She hadn't seen him in ages. Months. He used to come once or twice a week. Sitting in a battered armchair, feet on the coffee table when the owners weren't there, he would read biographies of painters, and sometimes would buy a book. He didn't have much money, she would always give him a discount. Didn't like Gainsborough, whom he found over-done, adored Gauguin and Picasso … But then people come and go, not feeling they have to provide explanations to their bookseller, or their grocer or baker. He would resurface one day, tanned, and tell her that he, like Ulysses, was returning from a fine voyage. Or he'd be pale and say he has been quite sick.

QUESTIONS AND ANSWERS, THAT EVENING, at Café Dante.

He said without ado: "I'd like to ask you a few … frivolous questions, if you will."

"Ah …"

He seemed anything except frivolous.

"A kind of abridged Proust questionnaire. For some background information, as it were. Of course you're not obliged to answer."

"I have nothing to hide. Well, almost nothing."

She stifled a little laugh. She didn't want to seem totally without mystery. To begin, he asked her what her favourite sound was. She hesitated. The choice was vast: water — sea or river — the soft sound of rain, a particularly tacky tango tune, the ticking of an antique clock in an empty house, the chirping of sparrows at sunrise, the song of the other bird whose name she doesn't know — six sad notes that arise at dusk in the country, the wind blowing, snow crunching beneath our steps. But this evening, really, wind and snow are not a soft sound. This evening, she would say silence.

"It's the purring of a cat."

"You have a cat?"

"Céleste. A grey cat. She's three years old."

"The sound that you hate?"

She replied: "Pneumatic drills in summer. They make a terrible racket." Not very original, really. You should never ask questions off-the-cuff. You get uninteresting answers and in the end it is just as ill-advised for the person asking as it is humiliating for the person questioned. Now she'd say something else. She'd say: a sound I imagine, like a bomb exploding in a marketplace, the cries of people being tortured, the obscene laughter of their torturers. Or else, she'd say silence again. She'd say: "Because true silence, the one they call the silence of death must be terrifying. The silence, perhaps, that you hear when you're dead." In fact it is assumed — rightly or wrongly — that once you are dead you hear nothing else. Other than the lutes of cherubs. But no one believes in that anymore. Besides, do cherubs still play the lute nowadays? Perhaps they are up-to-date and now play their music on a computer.

He also asked her her colour. She had no preference. Today, in this rain, she'd have a yen to say pink, like her boots and her umbrella, the flowers that wait to be sown.

Her season. She answered unhesitatingly: "Fall. I hate spring."

"People who like the fall are pessimists. Optimists prefer spring."

"I'm talking about spring in Montreal, of course. But in Montreal, is it a season?"

He nodded his head. She said she basically had always been a pessimist pretending to be the opposite. He asked her what character, real or fictional, she would like to have been, and she replied spontaneously: "Carmen."

"Why?"

"We always want to be the character who's most unlike us, I imagine. Can you see me in Carmen, in Seville, dancing the *seguidilla*?"

"I don't know."

He hadn't even smiled and she'd felt even worse. Even though, for the occasion, not knowing too much what to expect, she'd taken the trouble to put on makeup — discreetly — and worn her contacts.

Today, she'd answer differently. She'd say Byron or Bach, Johann Sebastian, when he composed a chaconne. Perhaps even Socrates.

She'd wanted to ask him: "And you? Just for some background information." Strangely, she didn't dare. They ordered more coffee. For her, a grappa.

CROSSING RUE BÉLANGER, HER FOOT slips on a sheet of ice; she manages to recover her balance just in time. "All I need is to break a leg." She should have cancelled her appointment when she heard the weather this morning. Crazy to go out in weather like this. And what she feared happened: the wind swept in beneath her umbrella, turned it inside out like a glove. Two ribs broke. It was not a good umbrella, but all the same ... This evening she was using it for the first time. She shakes it, closes it, and opens it again. One side hangs down miserably, like the wing of a maimed bird. She shakes her head. No, in Montreal, spring is not a season. You don't have to be a pessimist to observe that. Her hair is wet. "And now I must look like hell." She is almost crying over it. "Not that it's important, for him, appearance. He couldn't care less, he's not looking at me; I could just as well have turned up in old pyjamas with feet for as all he cares. In curlers. I'm a voice that talks, that's all." Once, he said she had a moving voice. And yet, when she speaks, he never seems moved.

THAT EVENING AT CAFÉ DANTE, he wanted to know how she had come to love reading. She could have answered that she hadn't come to it: she'd always loved reading. She saw herself again, a little girl in the schoolyard, head in a book while the others played all kinds of physical games. The not-very-pretty little girl, hopeless at sports, who was pudgy, who wore glasses. She could have said: "They used to call us bookworms. Today it is nerds or dweebs. The type of children never popular in school ... As a teenager, I had acne. You can see."

"You didn't like life?" he would have asked.

She'd have answered that she liked life in books, that at reality she wasn't very gifted. That books had consoled her.

She feels like that now because her hair is wet. An icy rain is lashing against her face, and her gay pink umbrella with flowers is ruined. After all those hours of patience, sewing on daisies — she, who is neither patient nor talented at needle-work and detests sewing. At Café Dante, she nevertheless answered — uninterestingly, once again — that it was because books make people laugh and cry, think, dream. Because they provoke emotions; because they enchant. Because they open up the conscience.

He said: "There you go." And he explained his project to her.

"People rewrite the same story," he repeated. He is rewriting *The Divine Comedy*. He has read and reread it, in Italian, in about twenty French translations and some English ones as well. He can recite it by heart, or almost, in the three languages. Dante used history. He placed ancient characters, saints or traitors, and people that he knew, his contemporaries, in heaven or in hell. A way to settle scores. He was an intransigent man. So he wants to do what Dante did, write a divine contemporary comedy. Dante had taken Virgil as a guide in the beyond. As for him, he's taking Dante. He is walking in his footsteps. He felt it was urgent, he added.

A mission. Pursue, persevere, prolong. Bring him out of oblivion. Enlighten, if that is still possible. Open people's consciences, if, that is, human beings still have them. But he wants to trust humanity. "Dante started writing his master-piece in the middle of his life. He was forty-two. I'm the same age as he. He worked at it for fourteen years. I'm giving myself the same time. Afterwards, we'll see."

He had been a voracious reader for about thirty years. That time had passed. He had no more time to devote to reading. Someone had to do it for him. He was to be fed, to be given details he could sink his teeth into. All kinds of details. Shocking, cruel ones for starters. He would tackle hell, would start up where Dante had left off: in the four-teenth century. He had assembled all the elements he needed for the six centuries that followed. Now someone had to take over, be in charge of the contemporary period, the twentieth century and beyond, that formed the heart of the work. This person would read newspapers, novels, essays for him; everything she came across. Occasionally, she could also watch television, note what images appeared, surf the net, explore covert sites — dungeons, torture chambers, brothels, and cesspools of our time. "You know what I'm talking about." She thought so.

"You have a computer, I presume?"

She has one. A dinosaur — it's five years old — but defin-itely connected to the Internet. Low speed. She even has an email address.

That evening, she, who is not very skilled at surfing, wasn't sure how to reach the sites he was describing.

"You'll learn. Even if nothing has been invented, I need to know. I'm not forcing you to do anything, of course."

She shuddered inwardly at this idea of herself bogged down in a cesspool. Could the police trace her, then come arrest her for obscenity, throw her into the depths of a dungeon?

He was nevertheless partial to the written word. "Images are fleeting. They're deceptive and ever-moving. But the written word is irrevocable. Writing remains. You know that, right?"

She nodded. "Novels?" she asked. She was amazed. He replied yes, novels, because people only imagine what is true. "Imagination is often our sole truth," he concluded. *A man who likes aphorisms*, she thought.

He said: "You understand, I won't be able to pay you. I've had to give up everything myself." Indeed, he did not look prosperous.

No need to pay her, she assured him. For her needs, relatively modest, her salary at the bookstore suffices. She is neither extravagant nor greedy. She felt all fired up. Before she had only read for her own selfish pleasure. Now he was suggesting that she collaborate — no, not *collaborate*, the word had too much bad press, had a very bitter aura about it, even for people like her who had not known the horrors of the war. *Resistance* was a lot nobler, but in this case did not apply. *Work in tandem* then. Better yet, *have an understanding* with him.

On the way out he lit a cigarette. So he did have weak-nesses; that was better, actually. She has her own: fine Napoleon brandy, Poire William, arak, grappa. A wide array of spirits awaits her at home — another way of knowing the world. He walked her back to the subway. Soft snow was falling slowly, glistening beneath the street lights. It looked like a scene from a postcard: "Winter's night in Montreal." The window of an Italian pastry shop was decorated with tricolour flags; among the cupcakes, *cornetti*, and cream puffs, was a large oval cake upon which tiny figurines were placed, like players on a rink. In red jelly the words *Go Habs Go* had been written. They stopped for a moment to look at it. He said. "You understand why for me Béatrice is an unexpected first name ... You will be my muse." Yes, Dante and Beatrice. An understanding.

On her way home, she realized she had forgotten to ask him his name.

RUBBER BOOTS WERE A BAD idea this evening. She keeps slipping — and is far less agile than a hockey player. She's too warm despite the snow seeping into her coat collar. Fortunately, rue Saint-Zotique is only a few steps away. They are meeting at the End of the World, a restaurant frequented by taxi drivers that's rather quiet in the evening.

She still doesn't know his name. In fact, aside from his age, she basically knows nothing about him. He certainly is not married. No, he lives alone; she'd swear to it. She imagines him in a house with walls covered in books, furnished with battered armchairs in dark colours, brown or navy. A bit like at the bookstore. His work table must be strewn with papers, occasional cigarette ashes and coffee stains. Or the opposite, immaculate. Just one notebook, just one pen — he writes by hand, she knows — perhaps a glass of water. If he puts on music, it must be baroque — Monteverdi, Johann Sebastian Bach, Henry Purcell's *The Cold Song*, probably in Klaus Nomi's unforgettable version. Perhaps he has a collection of scratchy records he plays on an ancient turntable. Or else he writes in silence. He has no TV. And definitely not a computer. Does he have work aside from writing? A mystery. He always makes dates with her in the evenings. Perhaps he lives off the interest of a small inheritance. Or perhaps, like Dante, he has a sponsor who pays his bills and gives him a cheque at the beginning of each month. Do people still find benefactors? Perhaps, more banally, he receives a welfare cheque on the first of the month. There is something one-sided in their relationship: she opened up while he remained — and continues to remain — a mystery.

On the telephone, he simply says: "It's me," which, after all, is a bit presumptuous. He suggests a time and a place. Always very courteously and she always agrees. And always in Little Italy or somewhere near. He must live around there. They've been meeting regularly for a little more than three months, and a certain formality still exists between them. When she thinks of him, she calls him "Dante", or "Mr. D."

She finds it funny to use the English form of address — he is so un-English. Though, if you think about it … The Brits are known for their composure, and Mr. D. certainly doesn't lack that. She spoke about it one evening to her friend Cora — more a customer than a close friend, a voracious reader as well, whom she rarely sees outside the bookstore, but they'll sometimes have a beer or a sandwich together when they leave at the same time. Cora said: "What's even funnier is that it makes me think of an eccentric character on TV. Mr. Bean." Eccentric. Impossible to imagine an adjective more removed from him. Béatrice experienced a kind of shame. They were in a café on Bernard that time, and Béatrice was on her third cognac, which perhaps explains her sudden impulse to pour out her feelings. "Well, there's got to be something enjoyable in all this for me." Cora did not look very convinced. She also declared that she didn't see the point in rewriting a book. Especially *The Divine Comedy*. She herself had already tried to read it and stopped after twenty-five pages. That was several years ago, but she had not forgotten the tedium. A veritable chore, this reading she had set for herself, the way you set out to read … *The Princesse de Clèves*, for instance. Or to sit through all of *Battleship Potemkin*. "Do you feel up to re-watching those old films that are considered masterpieces?" "Perhaps the translation was bad," Béatrice suggested and Cora admitted that was perhaps the case, but she had no intention of repeating the experience. There were too many good books to read. "Does he write in verse?" Béatrice had to admit she hadn't the slightest idea. He'd never shown her. "In any case, Dante and Beatrice's love was platonic," Cora concluded, leaving the restaurant. And now, even though he had never asked her to keep the secret, Béatrice felt as if she had betrayed his confidence, and was living, in the eyes of others, a slightly pathetic, if not zany, affair. Strange relationship. It's not love, or friendship — not yet. She doesn't know how to define it. She is touched, unsettled. In a way, enthralled. She feels a strange sensation, a kind of tickling inside, butterflies beating their wings in her chest — and further below — when she comes across a passage that he will, she thinks, enjoy. She would like to impress him.

Now that she has read all she could discover on Dante and has examined all the portraits — notably the one painted by Raphael, and another by Giotto — she finds he does look like him. The two deep wrinkles, especially, starting at the hook nose. He never smiles. He is almost invariably dressed in a turtleneck, navy or olive green, in fine quality wool — mohair or cashmere, and shapeless corduroy pants. A Scottish scarf. Ink stains on his skinny fingers. Boccaccio said Dante had a long face, an aquiline nose, eyes rather large than small, a long chin, and that his expression was melancholy ... "He praised delicate viands but for the most part ate plain food ..." If Mr. D ate at the End of the World ... Béatrice thinks of the menu written in black felt-tip pen on the white board. Pigs' feet or meatball stew, poutine, *pouding chômeur*, Jell-O ...

But he never eats in her presence, which means she doesn't dare to either. In Italian cafés he orders espresso; at the End of the World he drinks tea "with a slice of lemon, please." She does the same and comes home famished. But anyway, eating while describing what she's found … would be indecent, to say the least. She cannot imagine stuffing herself with what they call, for instance, their chocolate mousse — probably something out of a package — while describing crimes, massacres, slaughters, macabre enactments she has read about over the course of the week.

He listens gloomily — melancholy, Boccaccio would say. He then divides up the culprits, each according to the extent of his crime, in the circles established by Dante in the 1300s.

She goes by theme rather than chronologically: one week, she studies the civil wars — Spain has its quota of horrors; another, military putsches, when sadistic colonels and generals seized power — in that group, Idi Amin Dada wins the prize hands down. Then there was the week of the suicides, depressed stars, dried-up or disillusioned writers, teenagers with no future, betrayed lovers and other desperate types. She thinks of Picasso's grandson who swallowed a bottle of bleach and whose terrible agony lasted three months. Pitilessly, Dante placed suicides in the seventh circle. She doesn't know what her own Dante will do with them. Another week, she devoted herself to various forms of capital punishment, applied according to country and time period. More inventions to make your hair stand on end. He's right when he says we invent nothing. Try as she may to keep her distance, reading such as this drains her morale. And when her morale is too low, she thinks she would have done better to answer the retired professor, the one seeking love and more. She thinks the contortions, even geriatric ones she had imagined, giggling, would have been far more pleasant than what she's doing now. That even taken from the *Kama Sutra*, these contortions were nothing compared to her mission. Mission? Could she be one of the missionaries that Florence Jordan talks about in her essay? But whom does she want to rescue? Sometimes she thinks she's become involved in a futile venture. But she doesn't want to think that.

ONCE IN HIS LIFE, DANTE also took up arms, a rather muddled story of war — aren't they all in the end? — in Florence between the Guelphs and the Ghibellines. For Béatrice, the issue of the conflict is not very clear. Another war of religion, she understood. She wonders if Dante ever killed. She and Mr. D have never talked about that. This evening, she intends to broach the subject with him.

This week, she looked into criminal organizations, the mafia, their godfathers and their henchmen — Sicilian, Russian, Chinese. She has a funny story to tell him, and hopes it will extract a smile from him. What a victory should she succeed! Sometimes she'd really like to experience moments that were less ... spartan? ... monastic? ... austere? ... Moments that were less platonic with him. To feel that their connection — their understanding — truly exists. That they can link up somewhere beyond horror. *I can't wait for paradise*, she thinks. Mother Teresa and others like her. Yes, even reading about Mother Teresa's exemplary life would give her pleasure.

She had come across the story by chance — a book that for months had been gathering dust in the biography section and was going to end its career in the clearance bin. She rescued it out of compassion. The story takes place at the end of the nineteenth century, a time period not part of her research. She would, however, be amazed if Mr. D knew it. A famous crook had stolen a Gainsborough painting from a London gallery. But he couldn't bring himself to sell it, because he fell in love with ...

At the word *fell*, her right heel slips on the ice, and after inelegantly whirling her arms about a few times, she falls flat on her face. She tries to get up. A sharp pain paralyzes her. Her knee screams out — a broken kneecap or torn ligament. The cry — she cannot conceive of this pain any other way — throbs and radiates down her entire leg, spreads to her back, her belly, reaches her heart, grips her like a vice. Is so much suffering possible? In a flash, the torture described in all the works, a good hundred of them, that she has been devouring — without being hungry — for three months passes before her. She sees the images, unbearable in their brutality, conjured up by the words. Eyes poked out. Thrown into the sea. The river. The swamp. A stone around the neck. Feet in a block of cement. Scalded. Castrated. Thrown to the piranhas. Electrocuted. Burned alive. Thrown to the dogs. To the bears. To the bees. To the sharks. Into the snake-pit. Into the cage of starving tigers. Flayed. Put on the wheel. Burned alive. Immured. Buried. Alive. Thrown to the croco-diles. To the rats. The names of the weapons used, the blunt objects, baseball bats, cigarette butts, iron rods, blowtorches, riding crops, chainsaws, billy clubs, bludgeons. Fangs, fetid dribble, barking, growling. The names of the parts of the body burned, sawed off, torn off, mutilated, nails, fingers, eyes, hair, tongue, nipples. The head in. A *cesspool* — a word she always had found horrible. Oozing images, revolting odours. Each time a long shiver had run through her; her heart had stopped beating for an instant. Often, she'd had to close the book, break off her reading. We really want there to be a beyond and for it to put things right. Are things fairer in the beyond?

Afterwards, two, three days later, she told him that over a cup of tea — the stories of wounded prisoners dumped along a river in Somalia, left to bake in the sun while waiting for evening to fall and the crocodiles to come, and others hanged by their feet from a tree, incised skin waiting for flies to come nibble at them. And he remained stony-faced. No, not stony-faced. He merely nodded his head. Nothing has been invented. Dante already described everything, put every-thing in one circle or another of his hell. She insisted. She said: "I wonder if even the ninth circle of his hell can be worse than this."

"Is the work too difficult?" he had asked her last week.

"You have to stop if it is."

Is so much suffering possible?

Her umbrella is in the street — daisies lying in oily puddles, petals indelibly soiled. In jails, cellars, interrogation rooms and other places of tortures, some people surely wanted to call for help, but had no more voice. In any case, there was no one to hear them. Here she is in the labyrinth, all alone. Her guide has left her. Did he get lost? Her purse, cellphone inside, lies a few steps away. She has to call 911. She stretches out her hand, cannot reach it, tries to crawl. Her leg cries out.

The grey snow falls upon her.

3

CHEZ MARCEL,
AFTER THE THEATRE

Powerful men with a dubious past, all alike, in love
with inaccessible blondes: Adam Worth, for instance,
madly in love with the Duchess of Devonshire.

A famous crook had stolen a
Gainsborough painting in a London gallery.

AN OMINOUS MIST HOVERS OVER Broadway and what remains
of the greyish snow beneath the glow of the street lights. It's
drizzling. On the sidewalk, coming out of the theatre, Andy
N. Bloch — *N* for Newman, even though when he's asked
the question, he replies without flinching that it's for *Never*
Mind — holds in his left hand his black umbrella — jet
black, he likes to describe it — above his mother, Myriam;

with the right, he hails a taxi that pulls up into a puddle. Andy N. mutters a rather obscene curse, which Myriam pretends not to hear. Oily drops have splattered the bottom of his dove-coloured pants — picked up that same morning from the shop of the old Chinaman — the only person whom he trusts to dry clean his suits.

He'd like to smoke a cigarette and walk a bit, stretch his legs, but the weather is too bad. He's not going to risk seeing Myriam ruin her exquisitely supple kid leather boots in the slush. Myriam of course doesn't smoke — tobacco ruins the complexion, not to mention the teeth. So he thinks it better to refrain, which does not improve his humour. They're leaving the theatre: this evening was the premiere of *Moriarty and the Duchess of Devonshire*, a creation with the ineffable John Wallace in the role of Sherlock Holmes — appallingly miscast. *What was the director thinking?* Andy N. grumbles to himself. John Wallace's face is far too chubby to portray the austere detective. And the role of his sworn enemy, Professor Moriarty, was entrusted to the insufferable Fuller. Ineffable and insufferable. Everyone knows that a play's success is largely a matter of casting. When acted with a minimum amount of talent, if not brilliantly, even a mediocre script gets across to the audience. But a poorly acted masterpiece doesn't have a chance. In this case, the casting failed; that's the least that can be said. And Andy N. fully intends to say it. He's not accustomed to mincing his words.

The criminal and the detective … In real life, apparently,

the two actors can't stand one another, which is still no excuse. Behind the scenes people spoke of — Andy adores gossip — a liaison or a flirtation between Wallace, a nevertheless legitimately married and father of half a dozen kids, adopted or not, and the thrice-divorced playwright. This perhaps would explain ... The powerful woman, rumour had it, exerted pressure. Ensuring that her wishes carried weight — and her weight is considerable. Her name is Juliette Evanelli, but there is nothing evanescent about her. And Juliette, really! A forty-year-old woman, well-padded beneath her corset, like Anna Magnani — but bulk doubled and chin tripled — in the Italian post-war films, endowed with misplaced exuberance, very Latin. "More Latin than her and you die," murmured her entourage, admiring or disenchanted. Bloch had met her a few months ago at a launch — a book he was vaguely interested in — which he had gone to one evening with nothing better to do; he mostly remembers the contralto voice murmuring nonsense about he doesn't remember what, but his ears are still ringing. Calamity Juliette. Nevertheless, she had been awarded a couple of more-or-less prestigious prizes — less rather than more, actually — for her historical novels set during the Civil War, Prohibition, and other periods rich in tribulations of all sorts. A novelist people read a lot, too much, in his opinion, translated into a dozen languages, including Mandarin — or was it Cantonese? Go figure. But well, for the Middle Kingdom these sagas probably represent the quintessence of exoticism, or capitalist decadence. Even though, since the death of the Chairman Mao, the Chinese don't spit on capital either ... And now the diva of melodrama has taken it into her head to tackle the theatre. Ineptly, very ineptly, if people want Andy N. Bloch's opinion. And have it they will.

He often attends premieres with Myriam. He carefully chooses the plays she will most likely enjoy. For other plays, he's got a list of friends who are only too pleased. With Myriam he has a special relationship he compares to the intense one connecting Marcel Proust and his mother. Andy truly loves Proust and has since he was a teenager. A large black and white portrait showing the writer seated in a high-backed armchair, head slightly tilted to one side — an old-fashioned elegance that delights Andy, a fine impenetrable gaze, melancholy from having observed so much of the world, its defects and vicissitudes — hangs from a wall in his room, across from his bed. Thus the one he so admires watches over his sleep, and Andy sees him the moment he opens his eyes. That's enough to make him want to start a new day. He then gets up without too much reluctance.

He knows the author's life down to the slightest detail, has devoured all the biographies. It's to read *À la recherche du temps perdu* in the original, that he's been learning French — a terribly difficult language, with terribly perverse grammar — for the last two years. And what to say about the pronunciation? *Je me "souis" longtemps couché de bonne "hiure."* When he masters it sufficiently, he'll tackle Russian, even more

difficult, and read Dostoevsky, his other idol, in the original
— Cyrillic alphabet and all. Or Italian. Why not? It would
be less demanding than Russian. He has learned to say a
sentence of Dante's — the inscription written at the entrance
to hell in *The Divine Comedy*, and declaims it whenever the
occasion arises, without, however, being sure of his accent.
Lasciate ogne speranza, voi ch'intrate. That is, he must pronounce
it abominably, of which he is well aware.

Deep down, he identifies with his favourite author; he's
almost angry at him for existing before him, for living the
life he himself would have liked to live. For imagining it
before him. Social gatherings in the Guermantes' living
room, outings to upscale bordellos. And Swann. Swann. The
name itself is a stroke of inspiration, just one syllable that
glides voluptuously in the mouth. You picture a swan on a
lake. "I am not of my century," he repeats, sighing as he tells
himself Proust must have sighed. "I was made for the France
of the Third Republic." Top hat, gaiters, cane with a gold
knob, gloves the colour of fresh butter. A flower in the
buttonhole — Proust would have worn a cattleya. Rides in a
victoria in the Bois de Boulogne, young girls — and boys —
in flower, making eyes at people out for a stroll. Other times,
with deceptive seriousness, he claims he is Proust's reincarnation, as if he believed in such nonsense. It should be said
that, like Proust, Andy almost did not survive at birth; he
was asthmatic — still is, his puffer never leaves him — and
that, while he appreciates women's company and conversation,

his tastes lead him unquestionably to boys. Moreover, his father is a doctor — a cardiologist — like Proust's father — who was a general practitioner. And Proust was Jewish through his mother, an Israelite, as they said back then. He, Andy, is Jewish through both his parents. One last thing, and to this he attaches the importance it deserves, they both have the same astrological sign: Cancer. They are thus, in a way, cosmic twins. All the same, he prefers to forget Albert Bloch, one of the least sympathetic characters in *A la recherche du temps perdu*. Incongruous among so many similarities that delight him, Albert Bloch is like a thorn in his side. He consoles himself by saying that Proust perhaps — though it would be surprising — chose the name by chance. And that he, in the end, did not choose it. He chose *Never Mind* — Proust, a man of wit if ever there was, would certainly have appreciated the irony.

AFTER THE PERFORMANCE, MOTHER AND son invariably dine out together. One good turn deserves another: she is his guest at the theatre — as a critic for the magazine *The Big Apple Scene*, he gets comps, always the best rows; she pays for their meal at the restaurant — with her husband's money. Then they're even and pleased with their outing. Some people criticize him for perhaps taking advantage of her, imply he has passed the age of being supported by his mother. He replies to them readily with the proverb: "'The mother prefers the baby before he's grown, the sick child before he's healed, and the one who travels before he returns.' Old

Tuareg wisdom," he clarifies. Deadpan, he adds: "I fill mine with joy in every aspect. Ask her."

He gives the driver the address of Chez Marcel, their favourite restaurant — French. Victor Karr praises it highly in his *Gourmet & Gourmand*, a bible. One of the three finest in New York, the eminent gourmet decrees. It is as if Michelin had given it three stars. For, coming from his pen — often dipped in acid — it is praise worth its weight in gold.

During the ride, they don't speak much. Myriam's per fume, gardenia, lily of the valley, floats in the interior, a bit powdery. And the old-fashioned fragrance, comforting, an enchanting garden in May, a memory of protected childhood. A nursery, toys, tin soldiers, rocking horses and stories read in beautiful illustrated picture books, mother and child in symbiosis, curled up in a cushioned armchair. Of course, there was no nursery at home; he hadn't lived in an English novel of the century before last. Yet, in a way, it was almost the same. An imaginary memory — tip of the hat to Proust — brought on by the floral perfume. Most of the time imaginary reminiscences are more authentic than real memories. That's what he tells people — often the same ones, including his father — who criticize him for taking too many liberties with the truth. The truth? Imagination is our only truth, he retorts. That shuts them up. Our only truth. He enjoys flinging out a few aphorisms from time to time. And if some, sceptics, shrug their shoulders, others — artists, most of the time — share his opinion.

The taxi drops them at the door of the restaurant. Andy gets out first and while Myriam pays the fare, he opens his umbrella. Drizzle — damned New York drizzle. Unpredictable, insidious, changeable. All they need is for the *Siberian Express* to start blowing and the snow to resume. It happens in spring and everyone gets depressed, sighing: "So this is what they call global warming!" A cynical smile on their lips, their faces grim. "We've never frozen so much as since global warming began." They're right. Andy sometimes tells himself if he didn't like the Big Apple so much — probably because his family settled here three generations ago and he himself was born in a chic Manhattan apartment — he would go live on an island in the tropics. But on the islands there are hurricanes that carry away everything in their path. We give them innocuous names — the current one is called Jenny, her predecessor Igor still rages, but less vehemently, on the coast of the Yucatan. The next will probably be Kevin or Ken — they alternate between male and female, in alphabetical order. No, it's Karl; he heard it on the ratio this morning, a tropical storm gathering strength. Karl Marx? He giggles softly. Karl Marx, a hurricane? That's the least that can be said. Apparently we are four degrees of separation from the great reformer. Someone always knows someone who knows someone who knows. That's what they claim. He tried several times to imagine what handshakes could have separated him from Marcel Proust, but didn't get anywhere ... And then there is *El Niño*, the child, the warm water current responsible for all our woes. How ironic! Yes, despite the historical or charming names they give them, hurricanes are monsters, ogres as impossible to satisfy as the ancient Aztec gods. Then, when they've gone, you see disgusting creepy crawlies, scorpions, snakes, beetles, or trap door spiders with hairy legs, swarming in the ruins. The mere mention of it makes him shudder. A phobia. During his vacation in Mexico last January, a *cucaracha* as big as his thumb spotted in *flagrante delicto* in the bathroom gave him nightmares the rest of the week. Yet the hotel had a five-star rating and the room was priced accordingly. *No son peligrosas* the receptionist had repeated to him to calm him down when he complained. Truth be told, he had thrown a fit, demanding to change rooms. But, at that time, the hotel was *lleno, completo.* They had sent up an employee who turned out to be rather cute. He sprayed insecticide in every corner: in the end, the chemical odour had been even more unpleasant. As for theatre, in the islands — tiny theatres, amateur troupes playing light comedy or, worse yet, mangling Shakespeare's tragedies. He'd just as soon not think about it. In fact, he'd be bored in the tropics. Perhaps it would be more bearable on an island in the Mediterranean, the Aegean. Directly out of *The Odyssey*, containing millennia of history with mermaids, Cyclops, courageous warriors, wrathful gods. In the sixties and seventies everyone went to Mykonos, to Hydra. A must, that exodus. They settled into rustic, whitewashed homes. Leonard Cohen and all his gang: poets, musicians and painters, hippies with wooden jewellery, necklaces of shells on their embroidered shirts, garlands of flowers in their hair. They uncovered the true meaning of life, or at least looked for it; they had the means. "Returning to roots" — the expression must have been invented around then. At the first light of dawn, they climbed into small boats belonging to local fishermen with gnarled limbs, and lined faces, and they would set their nets offshore. When evening came, they took out their guitars, lit a fire to grill the sea bream, shared bottles of retsina or homemade raki — real panther piss — with the same fishermen, then danced manly folk dances on the beach, like in *Zorba the Greek* ... When he doesn't miss the France of the Guermantes, Andy fantasizes about the peace and love era. *Bonsoir nostalgie.*

They rush into the restaurant. The reservation was duly made that afternoon by Andy. They leave their raincoats and umbrellas at the coat check, and the maître d' leads them to their table in the centre of the room — they have a view of the entire establishment. Red tablecloth, two tulips in a vase, a beeswax candle that the maître d' immediately lights, mood music: Serge Reggiani, Henri Salvador, Gilbert Bécaud, that type, retro. They all sing softly of romantic cities and their charms. Reggiani evokes Paris and its wolves; the other two croon about Syracuse or Le Tréport.

The waiter, Bruno, agile and dark-complexioned, the way Andy likes them — and how he likes to imagine the young muscular fisherman of the island of Mykonos — soon appears, and gives a gracious, vaguely knowing smile, as he places a basket of bread on the table and fills the two water glasses. Their menus are presented.

Andy scans it attentively. *Poularde demi-deuil* — a classic on the menu; it's a young castrated fowl, a capon, in fact — *poêlée de Saint-Jacques au Pernod, thon mi-cuit et sa salsa mangue-citronnelle*. Traditional French cooking alongside nouvelle cuisine, with its cosmopolitan boldness. Everything is written in French in lovely ornate script, with the English translation — which Andy won't allow himself to read — in smaller Roman characters, just below, in parentheses. *Escalope d'autruche transibérienne* — gives rise to a somewhat sur-realistic vision of one of those flightless birds, chilled to the bone, shivering with all its feathers, on the snow-covered plains — or perhaps it made the trip on the Trans-Siberian, that most-romantic train. It's served with a *sauce onctueuse a l'infusion d'airelles, parfum de vodka impériale*. Interesting. Original, although in the end not very French. *Imperial vodka*, you wonder: *is it from the personal reserve of the unfortunate Nicolas II* — perhaps even of Rasputin, the damned drunk, if we go by the rumour — whom they went to exhume secretly from the cellar of the Winter Palace? No matter, his choice is made. The duchess's hat, a huge thing in felt-like fuchsia, mischievously cocked to one side, adorned with the feather of the large running bird, an imitation no doubt — Andy no longer knows if the ostrich is a disappearing species — that looked as if it were on the point of flying away each time the actress inclined even slightly, inspires him. "Those airelles ..."

"They're cranberries."

"*Airelles* are unquestionably more appealing. The sound I mean. I approve. And the vegetables?"

"Purée of celery-root, beet soufflé, caramelized salsifis," replies Bruno as if declaiming a monologue written by the great Shakespeare himself. He must be an actor.

"Better and better."

Mimi — the first syllable from her name, Myriam, and the second from Mommy — Andy practically never calls her by any other name, besides, she adores it; *La Bohème* is her favourite opera — eats lightly in the evening. She always eats lightly. She nibbles, as it were, pecks, a bird, and certainly not an ostrich. A hummingbird. Thanks to these deprivations and the daily torture sessions — some machines stand toe to toe with the most ingenious medieval tortures — at the exclusive gym where she goes, her figure, at fifty-five and a shade, remains irreproachable. Today the figure is moulded, no not moulded, that would be vulgar, rather it is draped in a black crêpe-de-Chine dress, with long sleeves, a high neck, the hem barely one centimetre above the knee, which is sheathed in smoky grey gossamer nylon. An emerald silk scarf, a large ring made of Mexican silver — a cat's head with jade eyes, Andy brought it back to her from his recent vacation in Puerto Escondido — on the middle finger of her right hand, a coat of clear polish on her nails. Classic.

Elegance personified. Her hair — which has always been black and will always be — Andy can't imagine his mother with white, or, horror of horrors, salt-and-pepper hair — parted on the side, falls straight, just below her ears. Her eyes — neither blue nor green but rather blue-green, slightly almond shaped — are emphasized by a very fine line; her lashes carry just the amount of mascara necessary to seem authentic, and her lipstick is called "Dawn." If her nose is a little too long, the oval shape of her face is almost perfect. Dr. Markovitch, renowned cosmetic surgeon, old family friend, had a role to play in that. And then, she only uses the best products on her skin, the most expensive; she has a wide array in the bathroom — champagne and ash this year, a creation the decorator dubbed "Normandy." Andy had tears in his eyes. Normandy. How refined. Proust went on holiday there with his mother.

She nibbles or pecks. Andy suspects that, deep down, she's very fond of food and is always depriving herself in the name of beauty. No pain, no gain. This evening she chooses to nibble on blinis accompanied by smoked sturgeon. "No sour cream, please. Or cucumbers." She's right; they're hard to digest, especially at night. To drink, they both agree on a bottle of Pomerol — a full-bodied wine that Bruno recommends with the ostrich. Mimi will only drink a glass of it.

"As a first course …" Andy hesitates.

"May I suggest the velouté of butternut squash and mirabelles? And when I say velouté …" — in his mouth, the word takes on an irresistibly sensual connotation — "sin." He smiles knowingly. Andy is already licking his lips, like a cat anticipating a treat. "Or there are warm gizzards over mesclun, which tonight consists of escarole, lamb's lettuce and oak leaves, and flavoured with raspberry vinegar. Or duck liver terrine and red onion confit flavoured Calvados and wild thyme," he recites in the same breath. "Delicious."

"Duck?" Myriam exclaims. "I only hope it isn't one of those poor mistreated animals they've talked about so much recently."

"The chef only buys his stock only from the most reliable suppliers," Bruno states, "where the ducks are treated ... humanely."

Myriam makes a face. "I don't know if 'humanely' is a well-chosen term, Bruno. Because when all is said and done, human treatment does not inspire me with much confidence."

Bruno remains silent. The topic is highly sensitive. The Holocaust, he knows is never too far away in the memory of the Jews.

"In that case, I'll have a half-dozen oysters," Andy decides, closing the menu.

They aren't kosher, of course, and, to think about it, neither is the ostrich. Even the sturgeon raises certain questions. But well, you have to move with the times; Myriam herself agrees. "The dietary laws come from times and ideas that are completely foreign to our current mental and spiritual condition," as was recently and rightly decreed at some conference of Reform Judaism.

"You're sure they're from the coast? Not from China, I hope?"

Bruno looks offended. "We serve Blue Points raised in New England, nothing else."

"I just wanted to be sure. These days it's hard to know where what goes on our plates come from. Besides, when it isn't genetically modified, it's filled with hormones or worse."

Bruno nods his head emphatically. "Such altered products have no place here."

"So the oysters to start, then the sin ..." — Andy laughs — "I mean the *velouté* ... followed by ..."

"Andy!" Myriam interrupts him in a reproachful tone.

"Okay ... Forget the sin, Bruno. *Meine liebe Rabenmutter* is trying to starve me. I'll make do with my molluscs ... And for you, Mimi?"

Evidently, the term "Mommy Dearest" has not sat well. Her lips are pinched. In any case, she does not want a first course. "You can bring me the blinis at the same time as his oysters. I eat slowly," she informs him. "He — I'm referring to my victim — will have time to devour two courses before I finish my first." Now they're even. She smiles indulgently. Andy nevertheless orders a martini to whet his appetite. As if he needed it. "Vodka, two olives ... Commander Bloch," jokes Bruno, accustomed to the whims of his regulars. Mimi shakes her head. Mineral water will be all for her.

"Come now, you're not going to drink just water while I down my aperitif all alone?" Andy protests. "I'll look like a pathetic alcoholic."

Which isn't very far from the truth, thinks Bruno. "A kir, perhaps?" he suggests. "A glass of white port?"

She gives in with a shrug of the shoulders. "Okay, something light then. A glass of champagne, say. But certainly not Veuve Clicquot. The word *widow* sends chills up my spine."

"Oh! Could you please bring a half bottle of Riesling," says Andy. "From Alsace, of course. With the oysters. They don't go well with Pomerol."

WON'T IT BE A BIT difficult to digest that red meat?" remarks Mimi after Bruno has moved away. "It's almost ten thirty, after all."

"You know very well I'll be up all night laying my paper."

She smiles. He says "laying my paper" because, in French, critics "pondent" their articles or papers. The way hens do eggs. The metaphor always amused him.

"And, when it comes to laying," he continues, "the ostrich seems to me entirely appropriate. After all, it lays impressive eggs. With just one, you can easily cook an omelette for the entire family. I just hope that this time what I'll derive pleasure from turns out to be a female." With great difficulty he represses a chuckle. "The French have a special relationship with the poultry yard," he continues dreamily. "Don't you find? They seem to spend their lives there. Their writers 'pondent' or 'lay' their works, their newspapers are 'canards' — ducks, their innocent girls are called 'oies blanches' — white feathers. Our gallery in the theatre they call the poulailler — literally, the henhouse."

"Or paradise. Remember the movie."

"By Marcel Carné."

"Bizarre. I don't understand what can be so paradisiacal about it. From up there, you only see the crowns of the protagonists' heads."

"Angels see us like that, I imagine. But there's a view of the orchestra and the people sitting there. Perhaps the connection is esoteric, but it is there. And then, as you said, it's up there … What the French call the poulailler — the gallery, but literally the henhouse, is their paradise. Their business leaders and statesmen have always had a fine time with what they call 'poules de luxe,' literally de luxe hens, but that can also mean high-class prostitutes, and 'cocottes' — which means 'hen' as well as 'promiscuous woman' …"

"And they have the rooster as their emblem," finishes Mimi.

"Apparently Dr. Proust very much liked the company of promiscuous young actresses to whom he gave little gifts. They accompanied him on his trips. I wonder if Izzy" — that's his father — "has the same odd habits or weaknesses. Or indulgences."

"Personally I stopped asking myself those questions a long time ago."

"He had a huge selection. Proust's father, I mean. He was the official doctor of the Opéra Comique! One of his soulmates, Laure Hayman, perhaps served as a model for the character of Odette. All with the blessing of sensible Maman Proust who healthily went to take in the sea air in Trouville or Cabourg with her Marcel. Oh, that makes me think, mother hen."

"Indeed."

"And we mustn't forget the divine Marquis who called the scarcely nubile young servant girls he enticed 'chicks.'"

Mimi looks at him disapprovingly as he spreads a thick — too thick — layer of butter on his roll. To her dismay, he has a tendency to gain weight. Already his chin is sagging, and he's only thirty-two. He eats — and especially drinks — to excess. She's worried about his liver. She's noticed some subtle changes lately. The whites of his eyes are a little less white; there's a hint of rosacea. She doesn't even want to think of his cholesterol count.

"Your verdict?" she asks. She knows he wants to talk about the play — an exercise that allows him to organize his ideas. At intermission, he was already fulminating.

"Over the top!" he exclaims, almost theatrically. "Syrupy melodrama. I hated it. And that implausible 'I loved her, I only loved her' at the end, with a quaver in Fuller's voice. Completely phoney! Can you imagine the despicable

Moriarty making that confession to Holmes?"

She smiles. "Come to think of it, why not?"

"Never!"

"Even the most hardened hearts can find grace."

This time, he's scandalized. The line seems to be out of a bad romance, one of those pathetic plots where poor but proud girls, innocent young things, end up winning the eminent lord of the manor. "You're joking, I hope."

"Barely. I quite like the idea of Professor Moriarty love-struck. Even if the object of his desire is only a painting."

"Mimi, your passion for opera is blinding you."

"Not at all. It seems to me I can hear Sir Arthur Conan Doyle stamping his feet in his grave and I don't mind. You'll admit the guy was rather stuffy. And his novels, my God, his novels ..."

BRUNO SETS DOWN COASTERS IN front of the guests, the martini, the glass of champagne, and a square white plate featuring appetizers — tapenade and liver mousse garnished with truffles — on the house. "I checked," he says. "Our mousse is made from grain-fed chicken, free range, treated ... animally." Myriam smiles. Andy seizes a canapé.

"I've changed my mind," he says suddenly. "About the Riesling. Bring a bottle. Am I the type to be content with half measures?"

"GOOD," HE CONTINUES, A BIT calmer. "Not that I want to be the champion of Conan Doyle and his heroes, far from it.

You're right when you say 'stuffy.' I've often yawned my head off reading his endless opuses. High-sounding and moralizing words, that silly Watson and even Holmes, at times ..."

Mimi agrees. "Movies and TV have made him more interesting than he is in the books. Conan Doyle didn't write with a pen, but with ..."

"A large brush, and that's being generous. If he could, he'd have written with a shovel. He didn't overburden himself with subtleties. But you seem to have liked the play more than I did."

"The story, my dear."

"I'll concede the play has a subject, even a good subject. After all, Mrs. Evanelli is a historian of sorts, if I'm not wrong; she knows, at least we hope, what she's talking about. She should stick to history precisely. Have you read any of her novels?"

"Of course I've read some of them. They make excellent vacation reading. Last year I brought *Oh Georgia!* to Italy. Another Civil War novel. Five hundred and forty-three pages, not one less. It was rather heavy to carry around, I swear; but when your father was napping, Georgia kept me company on café terraces in the afternoon."

Her gaze wanders for a moment, as if touched by the memory of trattorias under the sunshine of Pisa, Florence, and Venice. Andy pricks up his ears. "What are you remembering?" he asks. "Is there some dashing gondolier whose prowess you've forgotten to describe? Did a mandolin player with long, velvet lashes strike the right chord?"

She looks enigmatic, swallows some champagne.

"Come on, Mimi," he insists. "You've whetted my appetite. Don't leave me hanging. Confess everything."

"I already told you about the trip, my son. There's nothing to add … At least, nothing worthwhile."

"Let me be the judge."

"Another time. In any case, I'm glad your appetite's been whetted for the copious meal ahead … So you were saying that you hated *Moriarty and the Duchess*."

"I understand. I won't make you reveal your intimate moments tonight," Andy resigns himself. "As you like. I give in." He falls silent.

"Are you sulking?"

He sighs. "No."

"So, talk. Talk, dear. I love it when you tell me things."

He licks his fingers, dabs his mouth with a napkin.

"Evanelli based her book on a true story," he continues, finally — Andy likes creating suspense — "the story of one Adam Worth, a crook in the late eighteen hundreds who had begun his 'career,' so to speak, right here in New York, after the same Civil War — an apparently inexhaustible source of inspiration for our national Juliette … Little tricks, a few prison terms, some second offences, etc. Rather ordinary beginnings, all things considered, for someone of his kind. But he rapidly built a reputation for himself. Detective Pinkerton Jr. was his sworn enemy almost from the outset. When things started to heat up a bit, Worth decided to emigrate."

"Crooks have always been big on emigration," Mimi interrupts. "At the slightest gust of wind, you see them rushing for their sailboats, lifting anchor and setting sail. Crooks are inveterate travellers."

"He decided to pursue his activities in Europe and once there, after all kinds of adventures — I'll spare you the story ..."

"No, no. I don't want you to spare me. I'm dying to know them. The true story seems more thrilling to me than the play."

"It is, believe you me. Reality always surpasses fiction. Well, almost. But if I tell you about all of that nut's escapades we'll be here till noon tomorrow. Since the subject interests you, I can lend you a few books. You'll really enjoy them ... Where was I?"

"After all kinds of adventures ..."

"Yes. Well, he stole a Gainsborough painting, *The Duchess of Devonshire*, which the art dealer John Bentley had just unearthed in a remote village in the English countryside. You know me: I read all I could find on it before seeing the play. I like to know the territory ... Conan Doyle admitted he was inspired by the character in creating Moriarty. I can accept that. But to spin this ridiculous tale! Moriarty is everything but that. This time, Evanelli went too far. Or rather, let's say she surpassed herself ... By the way, you'll tell me it's not related, but did you know that the duchess was a great-great-

great-great aunt — I don't remember exactly how many generations separated them — of the melodramatic Lady Di?"

"The wheel keeps turning," Mimi replies. It's a sentence she says often.

Andy raises his glass. "Let's drink to that wheel." He takes a swallow of his martini; she wets her lips in the champagne glass.

"Worth landed in London with an accomplice, one Bullard, 'Piano' Charlie Bullard, a virtuoso on the keyboard and with the crowbar or God knows what burglar's tool. Apparently his fingers were so sensitive he needed nothing else to crack the combination of a safe ... Piano Bullard. I'm crazy about those stories. And I love the nicknames of the crooks. I found a Malloy Flesh, a Jack Wolf-them-down, a Doolcy the Baboon, and a Maggie the Tigress who sharpened her teeth with a nail file and had razor-sharp brass false fingernails. All these details are true. In a book, there were photos. You should have seen their mugs! When they say 'gallows birds,' these are exactly the faces you picture ... And I forgot Marm Mandelbaum, a kind of obese mama, queen of the underworld, who invited the pride of the city to her home for dinner. There, high-level criminals, police officers, and politicians, in no particular order feasted at the same table."

"Corrupt, needless to say."

"Their lairs had incredibly evocative names. Listen to this: The Door of Hell, The Morgue, The Suicide Room, and my personal favourite, the Blood Bath. Can you see yourself going to have a pint in the Blood Bath with Ludwig the Vampire? Because there was also a Ludwig the Vampire, who apparently was incredibly hairy, although I don't know how that trait makes a vampire out of him. Count Dracula was hairless, I recall."

"You recall. You speak as if you'd spent time with him."

"But I did spend time with him, Mimi!" He booms with laughter. "I even knew him very well. I'll tell you about our affair another time. After you tell me about yours in Venice."

"I told you: in Italy I was on my best behaviour."

"You told me but I didn't believe you ... That Ludwig, evidently, must have had other qualities."

He takes a second canapé — mousse garnished with truffles — and chews it slowly, an ecstatic expression on his face. Then a third, with tapenade. She'll let him finish the entire plate, he knows — she's one to avoid excess, so he takes the last one, empties his martini glass, and eats both olives. "Delicious," he comments. "But with all that, I've still lost the thread a bit. Where was I, dear Ariane?"

"Piano Bullard, the ace safe-breaker ... dear Thésée."

"I see myself more as a Minotaur. I'm awaiting my prey, the beautiful blond young men that city officials offer me every nine years to feast upon. Too long to wait, even for a half-bull."

"You're straying off-topic."

"I like to stray, in many respects."

She rolls her eyes, sighs as a matter of form. Always with the allusions. He can't help himself. Bizarrely, he has never introduced his conquests to her. Bizarrely, because they confide everything to each other, or almost. She sometimes wonders if his sex life isn't limited to that, an allusion.

"Worth and Bullard, the two associates ..." He bursts out laughing. "Excuse me, but I'm imagining them during the crossing, stealing passengers' wallets. One hoodwinks the dowager, Worth, I'd say, while the other filches her diamonds and rubies. It's amazing they didn't throw them overboard, a stone around each of their necks."

"Because they were also pickpockets? It's a bit lacklustre, you will admit."

"They were all that you want, except honest ... Once in London, almost upon arrival, our rogues both fell under the charm of the same courtesan, an Irishwoman with golden blond hair named Kitty, a beauty, going by the photos I've seen. They took her along with them to Paris where they opened the Bar Américain at 2, rue du Scribe, close to the Opéra," he recites from memory — his is almost infallible. "Upstairs, a gaming room where any sucker passing through the City of Light naturally would go and get ripped off."

"What else could a sucker expect?" she remarks — rather cleverly.

"As you say. Today, the rooms are part of the Grand Hôtel Intercontinental. On my next trip to Paris, I promise you I'll stay in a suite there and go wild. The Olde England store is located on the main floor. Entirely appropriate. Between two copulation sessions, I'll go buy myself ties. Or an umbrella."

—

He bursts out laughing, almost chokes, begins coughing. Myriam shakes her head. "Andy," she says, pretending to be offended. The she too laughs. He catches his breath. "Oh! Here's Bruno, finally. About time too. I'm dying of hunger."

Bruno sets both first courses down on the table. The Riesling is nimbly uncorked, tasted and approved by Andy, the glasses half-filled. Bruno wishes them "bon appétit" then slips away. Andy squeezes lemon juice over his oysters, stabs one with the small fork. Myriam starts on a blini, takes a swallow of water. Her plate is a bit spartan, but the chef has decorated it prettily with halved red and yellow cherry tomatoes, black olives, lemon wedges, and bouquets of parsley and dill. They fall silent for a moment and enjoy.

"It happened in 1871," he continues, finally. "France at the end of the reign of Napoleon III, a France that was perhaps a bit too frivolous, a bit too wild, but you know how I like those decadent time periods; France had just been crushed by the evil Prussians. The previous Christmas, Nietzsche had given Cosima Wagner the manuscript of the *The Birth of Tragedy*. That has no connection, you'll say. It's just an illustration of the famous wheel that keeps turning. To situate the facts, place them in context. Ten years earlier, *Tannhäuser* had been booed by the Parisian public. So, when Paris surrendered to Germania, Cosima was jubilant. She wrote in her diary that Wagner had finally been avenged."

He is teasing her. She has attended performances in the best opera houses in the world — la Scala is her favourite theatre, hands down; she is partial to Italy — but has never set foot in Bayreuth, ever. Obviously. She, enjoy Wagner? Forgive him? Never. Nor would she ever forgive Nietzsche his writing. Even if some claim he's been interpreted wrongly.

But Andy has recordings of all Wagner's operas — *Twilight of the Gods* draws tears from him, *Parsifal* introduced him to new orgasms — and has all Nietzsche's works in his library. They neither make him cry nor bring him to orgasm, but it is his rebellious side expressing itself — it has to come out, after all. As for the rest, mother and son are in perfect harmony.

"Wagner, that anti-Semite!" she scoffs.

"Come now, his conductor was Jewish," he pretends to protest.

"A traitor, don't talk about him to me."

"Besides, Nietzsche ended up renouncing Wagner. So I find it contradictory to hold it against both of them at the same time."

Silence; then, "I don't give a damn," she says. She says it in her approximation of Yiddish, "Ech care nisht." That's final. A flat refusal. Time to change the subject.

Andy even eats ham occasionally. He delights in the prosciutto from Trattoria Da Luigi. Served with fresh figs, and drizzled with three drops of very fruity Tuscan olive oil. Or the very fine, almost translucent slices he buys in a delicatessen in Little Italy and then enjoys at home, accompanied by a bottle of Brunello. Pig? Why not? "I have nothing against pigs," he says, when people are surprised. "I even find fat pink pigs rather endearing. All animals are brothers. And we are brothers of the animals. No discrimination, that's my motto." He is even crazy about — without Mimi's knowledge, she'd be furious if she knew — Beef Stroganoff, with sour cream and everything. While she doesn't go to synagogue any more often than him, she respects certain precepts — as it were, the ones that suit her — in accordance with her diet. She'd say: "Don't cook the lamb or calf or kid in its mother's milk." Jeanne Proust had surely renounced the dictates of the Torah and must have served her meat with butter or cream sauces like any self-respecting bourgeois French-woman. "But it's the father I'm eating," he would protest. "Or else it's the mother, the mother in her milk!" Which, in the end, is not more ethical — but who wants ethics?

"Once again, I'm getting off topic. What I mean is that Proust, his mother Jeanne, his madeleines and his duchesses on one hand, and on the other Adam Worth, Kitty, and Piano Bullard in their Bar Américain all co-existed. Or, almost. A few decades apart, but what are a few decades in the history of humanity? Wagner composed his operas, Nietzsche philosophized. It's exciting to imagine that time period. Everything happened simultaneously, so to speak, often in the same city — Paris."

"Nietzsche and Wagner in Paris? You're talking nonsense."

"Metaphorically. I simply mean they were contemporaries

... Because Proust was born in 1871 and Wagner died in 1882 ... or was it 1883? In any case, Proust was almost the same age as Siegfried, son of Wagner and Cosima, born in 1869 if I'm correct. As for Nietzsche ..."

She motions impatiently. "Enough with the dates. You're making me dizzy."

"It's the overall portrait that matters, I mean. People are fascinated by it. How can it be otherwise?"

"I don't see what's so exciting. The exact same thing is going on here now. In New York. We went to the premiere of a play, we're eating sophisticated food Chez Marcel ..."

"Very sophisticated."

"And all the while the international mafia are plotting their dirty tricks ..."

"I know, and terrorists are ordering their supplies on eBay; FedEx delivers them the next morning, then they meet in the evening in basements, quote Nechayev or recite suras as they make their home-made bombs to blow up our monuments and airplanes."

"*Voilà*," concludes Mimi in French.

"Okay, the criminals are there, as well as the mediocre leaders. It's just that they co-exist with Juliette Evanelli rather than with Marcel Proust. So, as you say, *voilà*. That's why I'm fascinated."

Myriam gives a start — he's almost shouting. "Lower your voice," she whispers.

"I'm getting carried away, excuse me."

He eats his last oyster, drains his glass, fills it. Mimi covers hers with her hand.

"To return to Kitty, Kitty Flynn was her maiden name. After a bit of shilly-shallying, she ended up marrying Piano Bullard. You wonder why — the safe-breaker was also an inveterate drunk. What's more, he was already married in America. She didn't know, of course. Women are sometimes unpredictable."

"The missionary instinct."

"As you say, although missionary — in her case, I have my doubts. She wasn't that type of woman. In a bed perhaps, if that. I have the feeling she was bolder than that ... Bold or not, she must have really lacked common sense. But she wasn't stingy, or prudish; and generously, or democratically, if you prefer, she divided her favours between two guys, lucky her. A *ménage à trois*. Oh, that makes me think, the Duchess, the real one I mean, Georgiana, Gainsborough's model, also had a *ménage à trois* with her husband the Duke and his mistress, one Lady Elizabeth Foster. What's more ..."

"What's more?"

"Apparently the two aristocrats — the women — had very tender feelings toward one another. They had a ball. Rather scandalous, at the time. But you'll say that the wheel keeps turning."

"It keeps turning."

"It keeps turning and it's a small world."

"It's a small world," hums Mimi, *mezza voce*.

"You used to sing that to me to put me to sleep, remember? And when we went to Disney World, I could never get enough of that ride ... So, to finish, Kitty, that rascal, got fed up and dumped her two thieves. She took off, settled in New York where she ensnared a naïve millionaire, a Cuban, whose family had made a fortune growing sugar cane. They ended up being wed. The marriage with Bullard hadn't been valid as he was already married. As for the unfortunate Adam, he consoled himself by stealing *The Duchess of Devonshire* one night at an art dealer's. A woman of great beauty who perhaps reminded him of his bird who had flown. At least this one would remain faithful. Some authors claim that he ended up really being in love with her."

"You see. As I told you, even hardened hearts ..."

"With her or the painting."

"People are much more often taken smitten with image than with its model."

"I've noticed, alas ... But anyway, that little-known episode inspired Juliette Evanelli. I give her points for her research. But Worth never said *I loved her, I only loved her*, at least not in those words. No. And he wasn't sinister like Moriarty. Rather nice, even, if you go by his biographer. A kind of Landru, but tender-hearted. Physically speaking, more or less the character that inspired Chaplin for his Monsieur Verdoux. Never armed. Quiet and good-natured. Vest, bowtie, pocket handkerchief, fob watch. Moustache and sideburns. Blue eyes. A real dandy. If you saw his photo, you'd never suspect.

Really, the parallel with Professor Moriarty is inconceivable. I find Worth closer to Arsène Lupin, the perfect gentleman. But apparently he had a real genius for criminal activity, which perhaps explains it. Conan Doyle met him on a ship, during a crossing. By the way, he was Jewish. I'm speaking of Worth."

"What does that prove?"

"It proves nothing. I was mentioning it in passing. He kept his duchess with him for twenty-five years, rolled up and concealed in the false bottom of his trunk when he travelled. Touching, isn't it? Alone in his hotel room, he'd take her out of her prison, unroll her to admire her. Even if she had wanted to, the poor woman couldn't have fled. Her legs were cut off."

Myriam raises an eyebrow.

"The old maid," explains Andy, "the retired schoolteacher, you know the type, who had the painting in her house some-where in the depths of the English countryside — without the slightest idea of its worth. The proof is she sold it for thirty-six pounds, the dealer's best transaction ever — wanted to hang it over her fireplace."

"Incredible, all the paintings by masters that have been found, and still are, in the most unlikely places, that people buy sometimes if they are lucky for next to nothing in bazaars and flea markets. It happened again recently in Florida, I think."

"But it happens less and less often … As the Gainsborough was too large, she altered it. She cut off the legs of the unfortunate Georgiana. By the way, some claimed it was a fake. In any case, it was authenticated."

"For what it's worth. Going by what they say, museums are full of fake paintings."

"I like to believe that one was genuine. And as for the genuine duchess, with her passion for gambling, she had ended up penniless a little over a century before. Ruined, fleeced. Her feathers plucked like a turtledove's, or a partridge's. An innocent young thing no more. Aside from her feathers she lost her property and money, an eye, and some of her teeth. The beauty was a bit bashed up, as you can imagine. But no doubt Worth knew none of that. He loved her immortalized at the height of her glory. You know what they said about her? That a man could light his pipe by the fire in her eyes. That sets you dreaming ... All in all, it's quite a romantic story, if you want my opinion. I'm not talking about amputated legs, of course, but of the gangster's infatuation with his aristocrat. Worthy of, I don't know, Jane Austen, or better yet, the Brontë sisters, Thomas Hardy or even Thackeray."

"Henry James?"

"Henry James, yes, probably, from one point of view. That's why the play disappointed me so much."

"For me it's always more or less the same story."

"Of course. What other story is there to tell?"

He falls silent for a moment, then continues in a more or less pompous tone — as if he knew his speech by heart: "Men start out with nothing and begin to climb, climb the ladder toward a nirvana that slips away — the beautiful blonde — and when they reach her, if ever they succeed, they don't really possess her. They possess only her image. The blonde is the ultimate goal, the inaccessible ideal. The carrot constantly dangled in front of the donkey's nose. I have a soft spot for these stories, distressing though they may be. Movies constantly provide examples. Gatsby and Daisy, Scarface in Brian de Palma's movie, with the depressive Michelle Pfeiffer. I forget the name of her character ... The gamekeeper, I forget his name too — if he even has one — and Lady Chatterley."

"With Lady Chatterley," interrupts Mimi, "it was she who wanted to go down as opposed to him wanting to go up."

"The other side of the coin. The indisputable charm of depravation. It's more the desire of a woman who's over the hill, I think."

She looks mortified. Adopting this type of expression is part of their game. She's not a prude, as he knows. Together, they speak freely of everything, or almost. Aside from Nietzsche and Wagner, Myriam's age is the only taboo subject. This time she is really mortified. Perhaps he went too far and his saying "over the hill" offended her."

"Don't frown like that ..." — will he add "it ages you"? No, he does not — "I was kidding, of course. Although ..."

He takes two swallows of wine, wipes his lips with his napkin.

'Slumming it' is the apt term. And I admit it doesn't apply

only to middle-aged women. Young people also want to. And men, of course. Go to a sex shop and you'll see."

"I don't go to sex shops. And I'll have you know that the female character in *Scarface* is called Elvira."

"Yes, Elvira, you're right ... What I meant is, why are people surprised that women want to slum it? Perhaps they're fed up with the pedestal they've been perched on for centuries. Virgin and martyr, Mother Courage, a wife who is frigid but — and even because of it — respected. Frustrated libido. It's so boring. Their fate isn't enviable and far be it from me to criticize those who choose to jump the fence. There's a pretty song in French: *Il faut bien que la chair exoulte* — You have to indulge the flesh."

"By whom?" now she's smiling.

"Jacques Brel, I think."

"And of course the ones who were neither virgins nor mothers were relegated to the rank of whore."

"Of course. Madonna — either the Virgin or the pop icon. It never ends. We can't get past it. The Christians tackled the embarrassing problem by making Jesus' mother a virgin. For whom they experience fanatical veneration. Admit that is really weird. Would you have agreed to that? I mean enduring pregnancy without experiencing the pleasure of conception?"

She nods her head. Perhaps for her conception was not such a delightful memory.

"Weird," she admits despite everything. "To return to the topic of blondness, was Chatterley a blonde?"

"Good question. Impossible for me to remember. What is certain, though, is that the gamekeeper had black hair. I'd swear on it. And he was hairy."

"It stands to reason."

"More recently, Ms. Atwood also found a worthy opportunity in her *Blind Assassin*. A blonde in the Canadian upper-middle class during the thirties, having a 'sexually explicit' liaison with an ironic revolutionary."

"Such affairs always end badly."

"And when you think of it, the women are always married."

"Against their wills."

"Married all the same. Which unquestionably spices up their sexual romps, their romantic frolicking, if you will. Very unorthodox … Such torrid passions in our neighbours to the north," he continues, a tad meditative. "Who would have thought?"

"In this case, the neighbour was a woman."

"Which explains it. For French-speakers, we can still understand: their origins are Latin. But in Toronto the Good? A bit like imagining libertines dancing the French cancan in Salt Lake City's Mormon communities … It must be the British blood in their veins. Because while they may be as cool as cucumbers, you only have to think of Anne Boleyn and Mary Stuart. Be wary of still waters. If someone asks me what historic character I'd like to have been, aside from Proust, of course, I'd choose one of those Englishwomen. Anne Boleyn, let's say."

He reaches for the wineglass: almost empty. So he empties it. Then fills it — nature abhors a vacuum. He looks rather vague. Mimi nibbles a mouthful of smoked sturgeon.

"You forgot Barry Lyndon and his Countess," she says, to get him back on track.

"I didn't forget. It's just that, in his case, the chosen one was dark-haired … What did the GIs bring in their kits when they went to fight on the battlefields? Of course, if I'd had the misfortune of enlisting I'd have brought Clark Gable or Errol Flynn. But they brought photos of blondes with full lips, in negligees or bathing suits, Betty Grable and others in calendars. Blondes are the great American dream."

"Thank you," says Mimi. She seems a bit annoyed. She is not, nor has she ever been, blonde.

"Blondes are an allegory. But you, you're the ravishing Countess in *Barry Lyndon*, you're Salomé …"

Salomé? She raises her hand in protest.

"No, better still, you're Carmen, Carmen the enchantress … Actually, you know what? I have as much compassion for the carrot as for the donkey. In that game, they both are always being tricked."

She smiles. He takes the last roll. "And I find crooks absolutely fascinating." He breaks it and butters it generously.

She sighs, infuriated. Not that she's criticizing him for eating — these days, there are so many anorexics — even among men, recently, especially young men, singles anxious to look appealing. But the fact is he, who used to be so slim,

is putting on weight and in the United States obesity has
become public enemy number one, held more in contempt,
if such a thing is possible, than nicotine addiction.

"Are you seeing someone these days?" she asks after a
moment.

"Seeing — that euphemism. Why not 'knowing,' like in
the Bible." He smiles derisively. "And you?"

"Me?"

She adopts an expression of feigned surprise. Then "No. I'm
not seeing anyone now. Aside from your father, of course."
Shrewd smiles on both sides of the table. Then Andy frowns
or pretends to. "Don't lie!" he cries. He bursts out laughing.
"Do you remember Izzy when I was six or seven? At the table,
at dinner, when I'd talk about my day. *Don't lie!* I was terrorized. I was always afraid he'd throw the butter dish in my face."

"Admittedly you had a lot of imagination. Too much."

"Too much?"

"For your father's taste."

"Imagination is the only truth."

BRUNO APPEARS AND REMOVES THE plate and the shells, fills
Myriam's glass — she's finally on her second and they haven't
even started in on the Pomerol. "This is promising," he thinks,
amused. The bottle of Riesling is now empty and the critic
looks a bit misty-eyed.

"Did the chef go to Australia to hunt the ostrich?" he asks,
sarcastic.

Bruno smiles without answering.

"Because the wait is particularly long."

"Everything is prepared to order," Bruno explains. "You won't regret the wait. Would you like to taste the Pomerol now?"

Looking sullen, Andy indicates yes. In a few moments Bruno brings the bottle, holds it out so Andy can read the label, uncorks it and pours a small amount in the bottom of the glass. Andy swirls it around a bit, sniffs, tastes, approves.

"As you see, my mother has finished her blinis. I'll be eating my main course alone, which is no fun."

Bruno turns toward Myriam. "Would you perhaps like a salad, Madame — to keep your son company?" Andy answers for her. "Good idea. A salad. My mother is absolutely loves low-calorie vitamins."

"Green," Myriam specifies. "Just plain. And, please bring me the dressing on the side. There's always too much of it."

"I ASSURE YOU, THESE CROOKS are fascinating," Andy repeats. "The lords of finance, the forgers. I've been gathering information for weeks about that whole bunch. Stavisky — that one sets my heart beating and not only my heart: the Russian name, I suppose. Clifford Irving and the fake memoirs of Howard Hughes. The imagination of these people is simply endless. At times I'm overcome with admiration ... And I'm not talking to you about the famous forger, Elmyr de Hory, the brilliant Hungarian painter who boasted he could sketch a Modigliani in ten minutes."

"Apparently Modigliani also painted quickly."

"Even he mustn't have painted a Modigliani in ten minutes ... In any case, Orson Welles brought Irving and Hory together in a film, his last, if I'm not mistaken. With Picasso. Perhaps not his best but unquestionably his most spiritual. Irresistibly, scathingly ironic."

"I remember," Mimi nods.

"And it gave me an idea. I want to propose a television series, caustic as well, about all those people. Bootleggers, arms dealers, counterfeiters, traffickers of all types ...

"Because you find arms dealers fascinating now?"

"In a way."

"Now it's you who must be joking."

"Fascinating for the needs of the television series."

A few moments pass. Andy thinks he wants to smoke, but it's no longer deemed acceptable, and even though he likes to provoke, that provocation is simply impossible. So the moralists have decreed. As Nietzsche wrote — him again — morality says no to life. Yet going outside to satisfy his vice in the rain, his feet in a pond of icy water, is out of the question. Fortunately, Bruno returns with the dishes, first placing the salad and small dish of dressing in front of Myriam. "Extra virgin olive oil, organic lemon juice." Then "Careful, it's very hot," he says turning toward Andy. The escalope of ostrich is topped with a purplish sauce, accompanied with two golden salsifies, and a burgundy-coloured timbale (the beet soufflé), a greenish rosette (the puréed celery-rave), on which a sprig of marjoram is skewered. "Bon appétit," he wishes them, once again. He notices the empty basket. "Would you like some bread?" Andy indicates yes. Myriam shrugs her shoulders.

"AT THAT RATE, WHY NOT serial killers, pedophiles and all the rest?" she asks. Her tone is a tad acidic.

"People already talk about them far too much," replies Andy, cutting a first mouthful of the escalope.

He holds out his fork to her, but she shakes her head.

"Thank you. It doesn't appeal to me."

"You're wrong . . . There's nothing the least thrilling about those sadistic butchers" he continues, "even if the public seems mad about them. No, I'd like to talk about elegant, intelligent criminals, high-end crooks who play with billions, tycoons who control empires without ever having blood on their hands."

"It's their henchmen whose hands are stained."

"I don't intend to talk about henchmen. I'll devote a program to Adam Worth, of course. The neglected artist. All in all, brains are more interesting than muscles ... That is, in certain cases," he specifies a little unnecessarily. "But to get back to the question you asked me earlier, no, I'm not seeing anyone in particular."

"What do you mean, no one in particular?" She seems alarmed all of a sudden. "You pick up anyone who comes along? Do you take precautions, at least?"

"Mamouchka!"

He calls her Mamouchka when she is particularly maternal, or else in slightly absurd moments of nostalgia — while their ancestors may have been born in the fields of Ukraine, neither he nor she has ever set foot there.

"Of course I take my precautions, what do you think? Ramses is my king, I submit, as it were, to his law … I'm not seeing anyone in particular, but I swear to you that there's someone I would see without hesitation."

"Ah … And the lucky guy is called?"

"Iouri. He teaches Russian conversation at the Institute of Living Languages, where I'm studying French. Iouri Chernenko, like the first secretary of the Communist Party during a few months in the 1980s, after Brezhnev. An old guy, behind the times, do you remember?"

She shakes her head. "Not really."

"I wonder if they're related. An athlete's body, the angelic face of an intellectual, small glasses with metal frames, like revolutionaries wore at the beginning of the last century. I can't resist him. An angel, yes, even an archangel. As handsome as Lucifer must have been. The overtures have been made. I'm preparing for battle, as they say …" He gives another aborted chuckle. "But I still haven't managed to determine on which team the blond of my erotic dreams plays. A significant problem. As a result, I'm proceeding with caution. I don't want to frighten the bird away … Thank you," he says to Bruno who has just brought some bread.

They eat in silence for a few moments. Then: "So we can expect an all-out savage attack? You found favour with nothing?" asks Myriam, coming back to the duchess.

"Nothing. Or rather yes, one thing. Georgiana's hat."

He stuffs down the last mouthful of his filet of ostrich.

"I intend to congratulate the costume designer."

"I recently read Arthur. Miller's autobiography," says Myriam. "According to him, critics are far from infallible."

"Arthur Miller …" He pouts disdainfully. "You have time on your hands, it would appear."

"He did win the Pulitzer Prize for *Death of a Salesman*."

"That was in 1949. Other times, other mores. You want my opinion?"

She smiles — the question is purely rhetorical.

"Playwrights and their critics rarely get along well."

"He describes them as little dictators who arbitrarily promulgate the laws and govern good taste."

"So?"

"Snobs, really!"

"I'm a snob and don't deny it."

"He did write *After the Fall*, a play that moved me a great deal. Back then."

"Hmm … Perhaps the least deadly, and even then … Social message plays are so dull. If just one playwright from that time period should survive, it's Tennessee Williams, and for just one play, the unforgettable *Streetcar*, and perhaps especially thanks to Elia Kazan's film … Because Miller … When he's not unbearably demagogic, he's desperately Freudian, everything I hate. With him, there's no end. Committed art, my foot. That's a craze, a myth. Art will be free or it won't."

"You can be committed to freedom."

"Come on. The two words are contradictory. Were Shakespeare, Homer, and Chekhov committed?"

"In their way, perhaps."

"They were not. And can you tell me what you find inspiring, or even vaguely titillating in an expression like 'proletarian dictatorship'?"

"That's not the question."

"Quite the reverse. A proletarian dictatorship doesn't turn anyone on. And I want to be …" Now he's beginning to get fired up again.

"Calm down, my dear … People are looking at us."

"I am calm … And I like to be looked at … I want to be moved, taken to new heights, carried away."

"I know."

"Art is like religion: it has to be separate from politics. It also has to be separate from religion. I am against any kind of impediment — I'm in favour of freedom."

"You are rather pitiless. I actually suspect you rejoice when you find fault with a play. Then you lace into the author or the actors."

"Which doesn't displease me."

"Perhaps you're not being completely honest."

"Demanding, intransigent, subjective, subversive, yes.

Unpredictable occasionally. I contradict myself at times, I'm the first to admit. But dishonest, never. Anyway, why should a critic be objective, I ask you? It's absurd. I demand the right to be subjective. And while people in so-called enlightened circles may take me for a reactionary, deep down the true revolutionary is me."

How to answer that? She sighs. With Andy it's impossible to have the last word. Even when he was little he was like that, an arguer, his father said, an attitude that irritated him intensely. The irritation, alas, did not go away with time. There's nothing Izzy likes about Andy's recently declared homosexuality. He won't have descendants, while his brothers and sisters already have flocks of grandchildren. At family reunions, Bar Mitzvahs, and other celebrations, he feels ignored, like an orphan, looked at pityingly by the rest of the family. The sterile branch. And in Izzy's eyes, his only son is a dilettante, a dandy who wastes his time on trifles, which doesn't help things. Because highly regarded though it may be in the theatrical milieu, *The Big Apple Scene* has only a ... limited, shall we say, circulation. The other offspring of the tribe have already made a name for themselves as lawyers, tax consultants, or cosmetic surgeons. If Andy at least wrote for *The Times* or the *Wall Street Journal* ... Izzy would like to see him earn his living more honourably. Myriam shakes her head. Perhaps Doctor Proust, she thinks, didn't see things differently.

"Come on, finish your vegetables, my dear. You've scarcely

touched the beets. They're healthy. Beets are packed with antioxidants."

Docile — it does happen — he cleans his plate with a few quick stabs of his fork, takes a piece of bread to mop up the rest of the sauce. Myriam has finished her glass of Riesling. "A bit of red?" he offers, gesturing to the bottle. But Bruno beats him to it and fills both their glasses before leaving with the plates. He knows this type of woman well: they always begin by saying no. In crude language, people call them "teases." But when the goal is finally reached, it's like the Trans-Siberian ostrich: it was worth the wait.

He reappears a few moments later: "Cheese?" he suggests, smirking. Andy wouldn't say no to a runny, raw milk, aromatic cheese, if only to complement the rest of the Pomerol. He knows that the restaurant has a farmhouse reblochon it imports on the sly and reserves for a few discreet, hand-picked customers. But Mimi would shriek in protest, so he refrains. Bruno hands them the dessert menu. Andy knows it by heart. He only looks at it for the pleasure of reading the words in French. Queens, kings' favourites, and famous courtesans are much in evidence. *Catherine de Russie — croustillant praline farci de baies sauvages et sa crème fleurette —* praline crunch stuffed with wild berries and crème fleurette; *Hélène de Troie — tatin aux trios poires et parfum de fleur d'oranger accompagné de son sabayon —* three-pear upside-down cake flavoured with orange blossom served with a sabayon; *Reine de Saba — gâteau mousse au chocolat et noisettes grillées —* chocolate mousse cake with toasted hazelnuts; *Lola Montès* — *chocolat noir en millefeuille et son coulis de reines-claudes* — dark chocolate millefeuille with greengage coulis. He already knows he'll choose *Marquise de Pompadour*, the chartreuse soufflé. "Divinely airy," Bruno agrees. "After the escalope of ostrich, an excellent choice." Myriam hesitates between two rival empresses: *Josephine* — *figues rôties la vanilla des îles* — figs roasted in Tahitian vanilla — and *Marie-Louise, un duo thé vert-liqueur d'abricot en sorbet* — a duet featuring two kinds of sherbet: green tea and apricot liqueur. She chooses the *Marie-Louise*. For its lightness, even if, according to all accounts, *Josephine* was the lighter of the two.

"And two strong coffees ... Or would you perhaps prefer herb tea, Mimi?"

She would. "Linden," she specifies.

"THE PLAY WAS TOTALLY OVER-THE-TOP, I told you," Andy continues. "Anyone who has read Conan Doyle, even slightly, who knows the horrible Professor Moriarty, knows it. Not that I'm against the absurd. I adore Arrabal and Ionesco, as you know, I can even appreciate Gombrowicz — when he's not overdoing it. But this was ... they have good expression for that in French ... *cucul la praline*. Corny. Forgive my accent," — he pronounced it *coucou* — "And, moreover, it was poorly acted. That I can't forgive."

"The two male leads weren't very significant, I'll grant you that. But that little Marjorie Dubois is a rising star, and very pretty, which doesn't hurt, wasn't bad at all as the duchess."

"Rising? Shooting star, you mean. If it were up to me, that is. And my article won't help her."

"I read she's going to act in a remake of *Broken Wings*."

He makes a gesture of denial. "Following in the footsteps of Marjorie Martinez? Don't make me laugh."

THE DESSERTS ARE POLISHED OFF. "If I listened to myself," says Andy, setting down his napkin, "I'd treat myself to a slice of that *Reine de Saba*." Myriam casts him a look of horror. "Don't worry, I'll be sensible," he continues. "It's just that I wonder ... Queen of Sheba. In that corny old movie Gina Lollobrigida emerged from a rolled-up carpet, appearing before a flabbergasted Solomon. Very scantily dressed. The ancestor of those pin-ups who spring out of gigantic cakes at businessmen's banquets ... Gluttony is a sin, I know. In my opinion, it's the least serious, even if Dante, a true sadist, sent the greedy to burn or, worse yet, to some circle of his hell. But I won't give in to temptation. Just this once I'll make an exception. I give in so often."

She takes a sip of linden tea.

"We have a lot in common with the Proust family," he says suddenly.

"Are you going to write an immortal work for me?"

He reflects. "*In Search of Lost Paradise*."

"Nice, but people will accuse you of writing a pastiche."

"It *will be a pastiche*. What do you think? That's my ambition — to do a pastiche of Marcel Proust. Besides, he wrote pastiches too. I'll write pages and pages about your latkes, or better yet, about your chocolate chip muffins that I'd gorge on coming home from school and that later I used to dunk in ... in my martinis."

"Your martinis ..." She seems unconvinced.

"Yes, my martinis, and your muffins will become immortal, they'll be quoted for centuries in polite conversations. Filled with admiration, my biographers will repeat the unforgettable words I will utter with my last breath on my deathbed. *I loved her. I only loved her*. And of course, it will be you, Mamouchka." Suddenly he utters a stifled cry. "Good God!"

"What's going on?"

"I must be dreaming," he murmurs. "The tall handsome blond, over there, near the exit. It's Iouri. I was telling you about him earlier. The object of all my fantasies, the guy who makes me make an ass of myself. And he's the carrot! I'm just waiting for him to become the stick *up my ass*."

"Andy!" This time it is she who has raised her voice. "I will not tolerate ..."

"I know ... I know very well what you will not tolerate. It just escaped. Excuse me."

She shrugs her shoulders. He must have drunk too much. Then she glances at the blond in question. Her eyes, approving, return to Andy. "Not bad," she says, her voice softer.

"Isn't he? Can he have been there all the time and I didn't see him? And now he's taking off!"

"Well, don't let him fly away, my dear. Go over quickly and greet him."

"I'll be right back, Mummy."

He said "Mummy." He must really be flustered.

HE COMES BACK SOON WITH the athletic Russian in tow. "Allow me to introduce my mother." She extends her hand. "It's a great pleasure, Madame," whispers Iouri. "An unexpected pleasure." He grasps her hand in both of his, bows elegantly, turns it over, lightly touches the inside of the wrist with his lips. "Gardenia?" — that voluptuous way of rolling his r's. She nods her head. "And lily of the valley."

"The heart of the perfume."

"Do you have time to have coffee with us?" interrupts Andy. "Sit down? Or perhaps you'd prefer a liqueur?"

"Thanks, but no, I really don't have time," replies Iouri, nevertheless sitting down beside Myriam. "I was just leaving. You know the Tzigani in the Village? This evening absolutely phenomenal gypsy musicians will be playing there all night … Interested?"

"What a great idea! Really a great idea," repeats Andy.

He's overexcited, is becoming a bit silly, he realizes. Unless the last glass of Pomerol has dulled his mind. It's as if he's at a loss for words, he who ordinarily is so voluble. Forgetting his French, as it were. Forgetting his English too. But tonight will be his lucky night, he feels it, would stake his life on it. He just has to borrow — surreptitiously — a little money from Myriam. Drinks in those gypsy bars cost a fortune.

His vision is a bit blurred. Yet no, it isn't, he clearly sees Iouri cast his glacial blue eyes — he didn't put on his Trot-skyist glasses with the metallic frames — into Mimi's China night eyes. And she, what does she do? She bats her lashes. Andy can't believe his eyes.

"I think Mummy would prefer to go home," he hastens to declare. "I'll take her back and join you in under a half an hour. Okay?"

"No, no, not at all," protests Myriam. "You're the one who has to go home, my son. You have a paper to turn out ... But I gladly accept Iouri's invitation. I adore Gypsy music."

"I thought that ..."

A kick beneath the table — right in the shin, and it hurts — shuts him up. He's been warned.

"Could you ask for the cheque, dear?" she chirps. Because now she's chirping. Chirping and batting her lashes like a bird fluttering its wings. On the verge of flying away, definitely. Of getting it on, of experiencing seventh heaven. He wants to say: "Stop it, I'm ashamed of you. Stop acting. You're making a fool of yourself. He's too young for you."

"The cheque," she repeats. "Your head's in the clouds, son." This time her voice is a bit sharp. As if in a dream, he complies. He even produces his credit card quickly — hoping there's enough room on it to cover the bill that he presumes is astronomical. Usually he doesn't concern himself with such details. But this evening, in front of Iouri, he'd be mortified to let his mother pay.

"SHE OUTFOXED ME," HE SAYS to himself over and over, still stunned by the realization. "Outfoxed me. My own mother. Mimi." He has often reiterated to her his admiration for women who jump the fence. Good for him, really.

Once outside, he lights a cigarette. Iouri hails a cab. "Can we drop you?" asks Myriam. No, no, he'll walk a bit. She looks up, kisses him on the cheek. The floral scent is more intense. She's put on more perfume. "Have fun, Mummy." And she: "Don't smoke too much, my dear." He opens his umbrella and walks away in the opposite direction.

He can't help but be impressed. They'd often spoken of it together, joking, but he had never seen his mother at work — flirting. She just batted her eyelashes three times and had the guy eating out of her hand. Whereas he, Andy, has been struggling away for months without the slightest result. What must have gone on in Italy While Izzy was taking his siesta? She's a charmer. "There is no justice," he grumbles inwardly. Madame Proust would never have behaved like that. Never. But perhaps Proust would have been inspired by the affair.

On the way, a few ideas form in his mind, the beginning of a play or novel. He hesitates. It would be a story more perverse than *Lolita* or *Dangerous Liaisons* — an incestuous *ménage à trios*, the threesome from hell. Or a kind of *No Exit* more unrelenting than Sartre's. Although he doesn't like him any more than Arthur Miller, he recognizes that, for once, Sartre had been right; hell is indeed other people. Or a tragedy about betrayal, when an abyss opens beneath our feet. Even more poignant than Oedipus. Never seen before, never written. In any case, Mamouchka would be in the middle. And the title is the one he found earlier "*In Search of Lost Paradise*."

4

IN THE AIRPLANE
BETWEEN SOFIA AND PISA

*When you think about it for too long you
regret being born, because then you have
to die and end up in one of those places.*

Lasciate ogne speranza, voi ch'intrate.

Gluttony is a sin.

"I WANT TO SEE MY Tuscany again," Ernesto Liri wailed,
groaned, whined, stamped his foot. At his age, just imagine.
"My Tuscany." An obsession, absolutely. Nothing else interested
him anymore. Sitting in his wheelchair in front of the Black
Sea, gaze intent. Or empty? To think that before, the sight
of the sea and its tumult enchanted him. He no longer interrupted Stefan when the man read to him, no longer lost his

temper upon hearing what he called the "webs of lies" shame-
lessly related in biographies. He, such a gourmand, now picked
at his food with the teeth he still had — dishes that had been
prepared so carefully by Maria. Even the white jam. Even
the *banitsa*. With a weary gesture, he would wave away the
small glass of *rakia* that Stefan raised to his lips at the end of
the meal — what an actor, really! Or, more often, he would
knock it back in one gulp rather than savouring it in little
ecstatic sips, as he used to do, a blissfully calm expression on
his face. He hardly even begged for his cigarette, which he
used to call the "condemned man's last cigarette," with that
little disillusioned grin he put on when he wanted to make
someone feel sorry for him. Maria was desperate. "Oh!
The poor man, look at him, he's wasting away. He's letting
himself die." Perhaps she was telling the truth. "He has one
last dream, my God, let him fulfill it. Let him leave with his
soul in peace."

"I want to see Tuscany again." So it was the last dream,
the last desire. And being the last meant it was no less
intense; quite the opposite. It had come upon him suddenly,
in early March, just after the departure of Nini (Jennifer),
his granddaughter, the youngest, who'd come to spend ten
days in February — her university spring break. "See Tuscany
again," a refrain sung day and night — he sleeps so little —
in every possible way, in his raven's voice — more precisely
a crow's voice, thinks Stefan, with a smile. In his high-pitched
voice.

At the start, Doctor Markov had vetoed it. The long trip, the change in diet, the excitement — none of that was recommended. Too much effort on the old heart. Too many emotions. But Liri refused to back down. "Understand me, Markov. I was born in Tuscany. It's a return to my roots. It's a pilgrimage. I absolutely must make it." Markov shook his head, knitting his thick brows. Liri insisted. "It's my *Santiago de Compostela* pilgrimage. I'll earn my place in heaven there, and I really need it. You're not very well going to pretend otherwise?"

"When it comes to questions about God, I'm no specialist. Contact the Pope," retorted the doctor, a confirmed agnostic.

"My soul is suffering."

"I don't treat souls. Bodies keep me busy enough."

"But I have one, and it's suffering —" repeated the other one.

"My dear Liri, you're really getting on my nerves," interrupted Markov, scribbling a few illegible words on a scrap of paper. Here, I'm prescribing a tranquilizer for you. Two tablets a day, one when you get up, the other when you go to bed. You'll feel better." Then he put away his instruments in his satchel.

The next day, Liri tried again. "If I don't do it now, when will I? My days are numbered." On this point, the doctor certainly could not say he was wrong. Liri continued his whining. His reserve of metaphors seemed inexhaustible. He spoke of salmon that, to spawn, swam upstream to the place where they themselves were spawned. Monarch butterflies that flew down from Canada, going through the United States and a part of Mexico to land, always at the same date, at a very specific place north of Michoacán. Magnificent. They look like orange clouds when they land. He had seen them with his own eyes.

What nonsense. What eggs had he spawned? As for his wings, let's not even talk about them. They haven't worked for a long time now — the poor soul is confined to a wheel-chair most of the time. But finally, doctor or not, Markov shrugged his shoulders, as usual, defeated by this profusion of arguments. Or tired of arguing. "Well, he has to be careful," was all that he said. Careful? *Of what, exactly, are you supposed to be careful when you're almost a century old*, Stefan wondered. *Tell me, doctor. Should I forbid him to spend his nights boozing it up? Make sure he doesn't dance tango and salsa until the wee hours of morning? That he doesn't whoop it up at raves and other wild parties? That he doesn't smoke three packs of cigarettes a day? I won't let him abuse cocaine and ecstasy? I'll make sure he doesn't fornicate his brains out with all the damsels passing through?* Stefan nearly shrugged his shoulders in turn. Come, doctor. Be serious.

Then, upon learning the news, everyone made a terrible fuss, the family in Italy — most had moved to the north and now lived near Milan, assuming various functions, or not, holding various important positions, or not — and the others lived in Switzerland, Canada, and the United States. In recent weeks, the phone had not stopped ringing. Everyone in turn tried to dissuade the stubborn grandfather. They simpered, chided, scolded, begged. *What is this new whim of yours? Aren't you comfortable in your villa in Nessebar? You find the view of the Black Sea so inspiring. You could start composing again. And your beloved roses, you're not very well going to give them up. Don't Stefan, Yuri, Maria, and all the others take good care of you? Come, Dad, you're in clover there* — as if there were anything so wonderful about clover. *And the trip is too long, it'll exhaust you. Stay in Bulgaria. We'll come see you there this summer. Stay, Grandpa. Stay.* Knowing his personality and his idiosyncrasies, they — that is the Milan clan — must have shuddered at the idea of seeing him turn up in their territory, perhaps even settle down in the area. Because while he might talk of a simple pilgrimage, how could one really know what he was thinking? He'd always been a lunatic. With him, you could expect anything, even, and especially, the worst. Old age had changed nothing; it had come without wisdom. We have our jobs, they insisted. Everyone works, everyone is swamped. No one has any free time now. *Who'll look after you if you get sick?* He retorted: "I'm never sick." "Come on, never sick! And your Parkinson's, your emphysema, your sciatica?" He remained unshakeable. "In any case, whatever happens, I'll have Stefan with me. He's used to my aches and pains." And he, Stefan, confidant, companion, private secretary for years, really wanted to go there, to Italy. If only to see with his own eyes the old man's place of birth, near Pisa. It would be useful if not indispensable for his book, Ernesto Liri's biography, that he secretly — for him, only "unauthorized" biographies are valid — is writing. Ernesto Liri, adulated composer, living legend. Practically mummified, perhaps, but still very much alive. Besides, Stefan understood. It wasn't a whim at all. The images of butterflies, of fish returning to their place of birth were accurate — even though Liri was certainly not going there to spawn. No, this wasn't the whim of an old man lapsing into childhood. Or perhaps it was, in a way. Childhood catching up with old age, like the beginning, the conclusion. Come full circle.

A SEVEN-HOUR DRIVE FROM Nessebar to the capital. Stefan drove. It would of course have been simpler to go to the Sarafovo Airport in Burgas, very close by, and from there take a plane to Sofia. But Liri insisted on making the trip by road. Two consecutive flights would be too much for him. So he said no, and Markov agreed with him. And Stefan took the wheel — which suited him fine: driving relaxes him.

It was still dark when they left. A grey light spread little by little over the landscape. The weather overcast, the sky low, as they say. A funny expression, when you think about it: the sky, even if there were a concrete entity to which we can give that name — isn't it actually the void in which we have floated and turned since the dawn of time — the sky neither rises nor descends. It remains immobile in its place in the far reaches of the universe. At least until we find evidence to the contrary.

Hélène Rioux

When they arrived in Sofia, Liri was amazingly high-spirited, contrary to all expectations. It must be said that, comfortably ensconced in the back seat, wrapped in his mohair blanket, he had dozed for a large part of the journey, emerging from his lethargy only to ask, "Where are we now? Where are we?" at more or less regular intervals. As if that really mattered. He didn't even know the names of the small villages and towns they were passing through ... Or he'd announce at the top of his lungs that he wanted to go to the bathroom. The years accumulate: prostate, bladder, intestines, all these organs are less and less reliable. *Tempus fugit.* It flies leaving its scars. All sorts of insults lie in its wake. The digestive system is particularly affected, but it's not the only one. There are also loose or missing teeth, dry and thinning hair revealing a dusty pink scalp, defective hearing, memory loss, shaking. Aging requires a good deal of humility ... So Yuri would accompany him to the bathroom while Stefan quickly drank a cup of coffee. Maria had prepared a basket; they ate in the car. There was even a plum and nut cake, Liri's favourite. Today was his birthday — his ninety-seventh — and Maria hadn't forgotten. He likes boasting that he was born with the spring, which makes him a kind of bird of good omen. A swallow. When he says that, Stefan thinks more of crows: in cold countries at least, crows also return with the good weather.

And now, in the airplane bringing them to Pisa, it's as if he can't stop chattering. In his high-pitched raven's or crow's voice.

"Is there something funny, Stefan?" he caws.

"Nothing."

"I saw you smile."

"Yes, that's true, I smiled."

They are seated side-by-side in first class. Yuri — twenty-three years old, responsible for massages and other special care — is also on the journey. The old man said that travel broadens the mind. The truth is he can't do without him. Four seats face one another, they occupy three: a window for Stefan, the aisle for the two others. The fourth is vacant. The old man paid for all four, not wanting to run the risk of seeing a stranger disturb their privacy. At present, Yuri is leafing through the in-flight magazine — photos of islands and palm trees, enticing suggestions of dream destinations where the airline flies. So all three are travelling in first: in clover. Ernesto Liri may be criticized for many things, but stinginess is not one of them.

"You're right to smile. We're going to have a wonderful trip."

Stefan glances out the window. They've just taken off; Sofia recedes. Then the airplane breaks through the cloud cover; nothing more to see. But sunshine is forecast in Pisa, twenty-four degrees. "I'm convinced of it," he replies.

The flight attendant, pretty, about thirty, with porcelain skin, copper-coloured hair tied at the nape of her neck, and irreproachably even, white teeth, is now miming the safety directions. No one could care less. What can you do, really, when your airplane falls into the sea? When it crashes against a skyscraper and everything begins blazing in an apocalyptic roar. You scarcely have time to repent for your old sins. And as for slipping on a life jacket … In the panic, no one would be able to find it beneath the seat, or know what cord to pull on to inflate it.

"It's the first time we've travelled together," continues Liri. "Other than in Bulgaria, I mean … I haven't left Bulgaria in …"

"A dozen years."

"Since I arrived. And even in Bulgaria I haven't seen much, come to think of it. What have I seen, Stefan?"

He shrugs. "Nessebar. Sofia."

"Sofia. And two or three towns with overly complicated names, with monasteries and castles, old battlefields. I was already an old man when I arrived. In Nessebar. I'd lost my interest in tourism. Lost the curiosity."

"The sight of the Black Sea was always enough for you."

"It was enough. Rightly so … It's been a long time … Far too long, Stefan … Yet I was used to traveling. The United States from north to south, Mexico, Spain, Portugal, France, Canada. You could say I've seen many countries. North Africa, the Emirates, Baghdad in its years of glory. Beirut as well. Now who wants to go there?"

"War photographers, I suppose," replies Stefan.

Liri gives a contemptuous pout. "War photographers. No better than the paparazzi. The new scavengers."

"Witnesses," corrects Stefan.

"Call them that if you like. Personally I call them scavengers, vultures who prowl around mass graves. Thirsting for blood and tears."

"Blood and tears?"

Liri sometimes has a pompous way of expressing himself.

"How does it help us knowing who killed whom and how and how many victims there were? Does it change anything?"

Stefan sighs. "No, it changes nothing. But at least the rest of the world is informed. Other massacres are perhaps avoided. We live in a global village. No one wants to remain ignorant."

"What's the point of being informed? It doesn't bring the dead back to life and doesn't improve the living ..."

"No doubt."

"Definitely. I've lived enough to know. And to lose my illusions. Because I had them in my youth ... I even went to China way back when. Did you know that?"

Stefan indicates yes.

A magnificent city, Shanghai. And the wall ... the Great Wall ... It was impressive, the Great Wall of China. The only man-made object visible from the moon ... They called their emperor Son of Heaven, did you know? In the past, when the Chinese had an emperor. They weren't even allowed to look at him, apparently. Those who dared look up as the idol passed were punished with death ... A cruel ... and slow death. They don't talk about about Chinese torture for nothing ...

Even Mao, their Great Leader — I'm not sure they were allowed to look at him."

He giggles. Stefan shrugs his shoulders. Indifferent. Yuri continues to turn the pages of his magazine.

"They didn't look at him, but they bowed down before his portrait chanting passages from the *Little Red Book*."

"The cult of personality."

"There you go ... In Canton, they eat snakes. But I, of course, didn't eat any ... Would you eat snake, you two?"

"It would all depend on the sauce," replies Yuri, deadpan.

Stefan says no. Or maybe, if there was nothing else.

"Fortunately there was something else ... My music took me all over the world. I was invited with great pomp. Crossings in transatlantic liners called *Empress of* I don't know what anymore. *Russia*. Suites in top hotels, an interpreter, almost always young and cute, at my disposal, meetings with big shots in industry, cocktails in the late afternoon, an abundance of caviar ... I'm not crazy about it, but just the same, there was lots of it. By the bowlful. And can you imagine what it cost?"

"An arm and a leg."

"Indeed ... The festivals, Berlin, Cannes, Venice, the red carpet, the most beautiful women ... Denise ... was it Denise? Or Catherine?"

"Deneuve perhaps?"

"In any case, it was a very elegant blonde. Her name escapes me ... I had an exciting life, I don't deny."

He falls silent for a moment. In his mind, he is travelling

in his memories — both genuine and invented — they often get confused. Stefan must sort through them for the book he's writing. But, well, imagination is a form of truth, he is well aware. Perhaps the most revealing.

"There was a price to pay, of course. The critics, for example. I was criticized for going to Spain during Franco's rule. I was accused of being for the dictatorship, against freedom. What nonsense. What the hell did I care about Franco? It wasn't the Generalissimo who invited me. It was Pepe Gomez León, the choreographer. I went for the inauguration of a flamenco ballet set to my music. Later, I was attacked for directing a concert in the former Soviet Union. Stalin was dead, though. But even if he had been alive ... I made that trip in 1967. The first secretary ..."

"Leonid Brezhnev."

"Yes, in the middle of the Cold War, can you believe it ... In any case, no matter where I went, voices were raised left and right in criticism ... I was an artist, a musician, I didn't get involved with politics."

"You weren't a politically committed artist."

"Not on one side or the other. Always in the middle, like virtue ... I lived in the United States during the witch hunt."

Stefan pricks up his ears: Liri has never addressed McCarthyism with him.

"My name wasn't on the lists. So, of course, afterwards I was criticized for that as well. Yet I had friends who were on the famous lists. I never betrayed anyone."

"Were you questioned?" Stefan asks.

"They questioned everyone. At least everyone who had a name, and I had one, especially after *Broken Wings*. I had a reputation. And then, I was a foreigner, which obviously made me suspicious. Arthur Miller speaks about it at great length in his autobiography, without ever mentioning my existence. A serious oversight. But people talk about what they want in an autobiography. Most of the time, to make themselves look good. Or to justify themselves … Of course, no one mentioned Elkis's role either."

"His role?"

"I know what I mean."

He likes to let some nefarious mystery hang in the air when Bob Elkis's name comes up for discussion. A kind of posthumous vengeance: Elkis died immediately after completing the film that made him immortal. Liri is hanging on forever while his name is increasingly forgotten. Hard to swallow.

"*Bird in the rain, just see me falling, broken wings,*" he hums in his broken voice.

Overcome with giggling, Yuri turns his head away, begins to cough.

"Have you caught a cold, Yuri?"

The young man rises suddenly, rapidly heads for the washroom.

"What's with him?"

Stefan prefers not to answer. *Broken Wings* is the song that made Liri famous. A delicate topic.

"Perhaps he's air sick."

"Perhaps," agrees Stefan.

"Or it's the recycled air. Hard to breathe, crawling with bacteria ... I should have written my memoirs. Before someone gets it into his head to do it for me."

He looks at Stefan strangely, as if he suspects something. But perhaps that's exactly why he is describing his memories. To have a witness before the vultures throw themselves on his carcass.

"It's never too late," says Stefan.

"No, it's not too late. I'll think about it when we return from Italy. You could help me."

Another intent look.

"Nothing would give me more pleasure."

WEARING HEADPHONES, YURI HAS TILTED his seat back, wanting to relax and listen to music. But the old man sees things differently. The crow holds out a claw, grips the knee of the man opposite him. "What's gotten into you? You want to ditch us?" Yuri removes his headphones without answering. The tension is almost palpable for a moment, then, as usual, it fades. Old age has its eccentricities and its weaknesses. And, in the case of Ernesto Liri, its rights. But there exists a kind of tacit understanding between the three men. Each knows more or less how far he can go, when to surrender. Besides, Yuri sees the old musician as somewhat of a grandfather — he did not know his own; they both died before his was born.

A discreet whiff of perfume: the flight attendant leans over toward them, all smiles. She offers them the menu. Liri's eyes light up. "What are we going to eat?"

Stefan opens the menu, begins to read the menu aloud. For Liri, hearing the dishes named is a pleasure that now almost surpasses eating them.

"Smoked Scottish salmon ..."

Appearing knowledgeable, Liri approves. "The best."

"*Châteaubriand Bouquetière*, dauphine potatoes, or panache of shrimp, with wild mushroom risotto. Chocolate marquise," Stefan finishes up.

That what it's like in first class. Even in the middle of the afternoon, you're entitled to a three-course meal, while the rest of the passengers, shoved in behind the curtain like sardines in a can, make do with a rubbery sandwich and a Coca-Cola.

"Good, good ... I'll take the panache. I like mushrooms, especially wild ones ... And as for marquises ... Well, they still set me dreaming. Do you dream of marquises, Stefan? And you, Yuri?"

Yuri makes a face. He says he doesn't give a rat's ass but adores chocolate. Stefan smiles without giving an opinion.

Liri waves a claw-like finger. "Come, Yuri, *a rat's ass*. You lack respect. What way is that to speak about the noble ladies of yesteryear? No, you must treat them with a minimum of consideration. Even when you are for class equality. History, especially the history of France, is punctuated with it —

marquises in crinoline petticoats, a *mosca* at the corner of their lips."

"*Mosca?*"

"A small patch of black taffeta women of the nobility stuck to their faces. A fly, literally!"

Yuri makes an exclamation of disgust.

"A code," Stefan specifies. "The meaning changed depending on where the patch was applied. In that way, the beauty could make a romantic rendez-vous or break off with her lover."

"That's totally disgusting."

"It at least had the advantage of not being permanent," interrupts Liri. "Today girls pierce their lips, eyebrows, and God knows what else."

Yuri nods his head. His latest conquest has a ring in her left nostril, a pearl in her belly button. And a butterfly tattooed on the small of her back.

"We ... Or rather the French, had their Pompadour," continues Liri, "Du Barry, Maintenon ..."

"A countess, it seems to me, Du Barry," interrupts Stefan. "They guillotined her in the Revolution. She asked the executioner to wait."

"A countess, perhaps ... You must be right, as always ... And she wasn't the only one to be guillotined ... Madame de Pompadour protected Voltaire. I'm not wrong, this time?"

Stefan replies no. In the end, what does he know? He just doesn't feel like talking about it. It's been a long day, and it

isn't over. As for the history of France, he only knows —
and vaguely at that — the Revolution and a few Napoleonic
episodes, the Russian Campaign, Waterloo, the Isle of Elba.
And St. Helena, of course. The decline of the Empire, in
fact. It's not like Liri, who had to gather a lot of information
to compose music for all those spectacular swashbucklers ...
As for poor Madame Du Barry's prayer on the scaffold, Stefan
knows it because it inspired a popular song a while back.
A Bulgarian song, but the entreaty was repeated in French.
Encore un instant, monsieur le bourreau — *One moment more,
Mr. Executioner.*

"In the sixties, people were fond of costume pictures,"
Liri sings to himself. "Powdered wigs, feather hats, hoop
dresses, stampedes, golden horse-drawn carriages, and sword
fights. The nobility still fascinate commoners. Strange, when
you think about it, eh?"

"It doesn't fascinate me in the least," concludes Yuri.

"People say that ... If it isn't the nobility, it comes to the
same thing. All your movies and games are filled with castles,
knights, and all that. Even on the stars you put princesses
and kings. Just because I'm an old man doesn't mean I don't
keep up to date ... But what were we talking about?"

"You were talking about swashbucklers," replies Stefan.

"Yes ... CinemaScope, Technicolor, the whole shebang.
No special effects back then. And the stunts were carried out
for real, at the actor's own risk. That is, the stuntman's, more
often than not, and more than one got banged up. Crowds

rushed to the movie theatres. Guaranteed success at the box office. Afterwards, they were shown during prime time on television. Then in the lesser time slots, in the afternoon, to let housewives dream before their brats returned, or at the end of the evening, to put insomniacs to sleep. Now they never show them anymore. I'd be surprised if any copies even remain ... Dane Hubbard, Errol Flynn, Chiara Galiano ... Do you recognize their names, at least?"

Stefan thinks, then replies that Errol Flynn vaguely rings a bell. Yuri shakes his head. The conversation is getting on his nerves; he has trouble following. They're speaking too quickly, both of them, and he doesn't know those movies and actors. He doesn't speak English as well as Stefan. He doesn't need it usually; his tasks are mostly manual and Liri remains silent during the massages. Besides, the old man doesn't know a word of Bulgarian, despite the twelve years he's spent in Bulgaria. He has learned nothing, not the language or the history. Says he doesn't have the patience or the memory for it.

"I think they're all dead now," Liri continues. "Quite young, even, in the case of Flynn. About forty years old. I know that for you, Yuri, forty years old is tantamount to an old fart ... He portrayed a rather convincing Robin Hood ... You at least know who Robin Hood is?"

Yuri shrugs his shoulders. Yes, he knows Robin Hood.

"One of the marquises was mixed up in an obscure affair involving poison. Galiano played the title role. Dazzling. I was the one who composed the music for that one. *Scandal at Court*, or something like that. Was that it, Stefan?"

"I think so. *Scandal* or *Cabal*."

"Nothing unforgettable, it's true. I took my inspiration from Lully, naturally ... They then forced a Marquise of the Angels upon us. A rather insipid blonde, to my mind. But they didn't consult me for the casting. Angélique. A whole series based on that tacky marquise's adventures ... You're too young, Yuri, you didn't know her. And you didn't miss anything, believe you me. The music was banal and syrupy — not by me. They couldn't very well ask me to compose them all."

The captain's voice is then heard. Passengers are asked to return to their seats, fasten their seatbelts. "We will be experiencing some turbulence."

"We're going to see the Holy Week procession," continues Liri — nothing, no turbulence, will prevent him from holding forth; he is like a broken music box, its tutu-clad ballerina turning around without stopping. "And the San Ranieri Regata, in June ... Well, if I'm still in this world."

Stefan remains silent. He no longer reacts to that kind of remark.

"You think that I will be?"

He sighs. "Why not?"

"Why not, you're right ... In this world or in the other ... Pisa," he continues, "Are you happy, Stefan? A beautiful city, a superb city, you will see. You too, Yuri. Superb. Where did you reserve? Downtown, I hope."

Stefan represses a gesture of impatience. Since morning, he has answered the same question at least twenty times. "At the Excelsior. As you requested."

"You did well. Old hotels are reliable. The service is always good. Don't talk to me about those chains where all the rooms are identical anywhere on the planet. You'll see, when they colonize Mars or the moon, the first thing they'll build will be a Hilton, with the same insipid decor, the same watercolours on the walls ... The Excelsior still exists. So much the better. When I went to Italy I, of course, stayed with family, but I did stay at the Excelsior once, for a whole week, and have not forgotten it. A superb city, on the Arno, our beautiful Tuscan river; superb. And not only the tower. Even though the Allies bombed our beautiful city of Pisa mercilessly in 1944. Pounded it, that's the word they use, I believe ... 'pounded.' Not very pretty, if you ask me."

"A word that really says what it means."

"Yes. Pounded. They also use it for sexual relations ..."

"Violent ones."

"Brutal, violent. Loveless. If we didn't have the word, would we have the thing? I'm talking about the bombings. What comes first, do you think?"

Stefan replies that it's like with the chicken and the egg: he doesn't know. The two came simultaneously, perhaps. He has never asked himself the question.

"You should, though. It's an excellent question. I often ask it of myself, and haven't found the answer ... You feel as if there are hammers, gigantic masses beating down … Mortar fire or, I don't know what. They have those expressions. Mortar is to build houses, not destroy them. Or to make pesto."

"It's also a type of canon."

"They suggested I compose the music of a film about World War Two. I refused, of course. No way would I mix my name with that carnage. They respected nothing. Not our monuments or our churches. The soldiers couldn't care less about world heritage. But I was no longer there when they pounded Pisa. I was with the Allies. In the United States. I perfected my music. And that duality didn't make life easy. You no longer knew whom you were betraying. You tried to make yourself invisible, to remain neutral. But how could I have predicted that they'd declare war against one another? When I left Italy, no one was talking about it."

"Wars are unpredictable. While being always predictable. We just don't know when and between what countries."

"We pretend to ignore them, you mean. In the end, it's all part of the same plan, and everyone knows it. So they pounded Pisa. Destroyed monuments, killed people. The most part, civilians — innocents. And bombed the countryside as well. Of course. It's always the poor who pay. Members of my family were in the Resistance. And others, I must admit, others were." He closes his eyes for an instant.

"… were fascists," completes Stefan to himself. Mortifying to admit it today.

The pretty redhead — smiling mechanically, her voice

crystal-clear — now comes to offer them drinks. Liri wants champagne. Veuve Clicquot — the idea of the effervescent widow has always delighted him. "You too, Stefan? And Yuri? We'll toast our trip to Italy."

In a manner of speaking. Liri trembles so much that in the time it would take him to make a toast, he'd spill the contents of his glass over his pants. For a long time now, it has been Stefan — sometimes Yuri or even Maria — who helps him drink and eat. So Stefan holds the glass to the lips of the old child.

"To your birthday," says Stefan.

But Liri would rather drink to the journey. He says that when a person, like him, is a hundred years old, or nearly, celebrating a birthday is grotesque if not indecent.

"It was because of the times," he continues apropos of fascism, bombings, betrayals. "Very troubled times. And Mussolini had a lot of charisma. He hoodwinked them all. Perhaps it began with good intentions; who knows?"

"Hitler had charisma too," says Stefan.

"He had. He had it for too long. Then he stopped having it. As for his feelings, who knows?" he repeats. "The human soul is an unfathomable mystery."

Stefan raises an eyebrow.

"Hitler, a soul?" exclaims Yuri. "That would amaze me."

"Everyone has one, good or evil. But I grant that for Hitler, you wonder."

"A soul that was damned," says Stefan.

"Damned without a doubt. In any case, our city was used to suffering. It was inured. Had survived many ordeals. Conquered and re-conquered over the centuries, annexed to one kingdom then to another. Genoa, then Florence, notably. The famous conflict between Guelphs and Ghibellines."

"It also had its hour of glory," interrupts Stefan, who has made enquiries. "It was also a conqueror."

"Of course. It conquered Sardinia, then Corsica. Then they plundered it. Italy did not yet exist. Each city was a kingdom. And each swallowed the other in turn. That's the way things happened then."

"Nothing has really changed."

"No, nothing changes. We still annex and surrender just as cheerfully. The names of the countries change at the speed of ..."

He seems sad, all of a sudden, he who was so fired up. For some time now, he has been going, without transition, from the most exuberant joy to inexplicable despondency. He has always been more or less like that — bipolar, they call it nowadays — but lately his mood swings have intensified.

"Would you like something? Water, perhaps. I'll call the flight attendant."

"No, no, Stefan. No water, not right away. Give me a sip of the Veuve Clicquot — to make my heart light. I am thinking about my city, about Pisa. In the fourteenth century, we experienced the plague, you know, the black plague, the wicked death with its skeleton mask and its scythe, its black cloak. But of course, we weren't the only ones. All the cities of Europe, at the time. You'll say you have to die of something."

"People no longer die of the plague, I think," says Stefan. "Or they die from it less often."

"In Europe, you mean," interrupts Yuri. "There are still epidemics in Africa."

"Nothing compared to what went on in the Middle Ages, when it decimated a quarter of the western population. Today, the disease is almost eradicated. Fortunately."

"Fortunately? I don't know," says Liri. "With that kind of illness, there was the advantage of going quickly. Of being expeditious. A quarter of the population, do you realize? Now, people die anyway. Only it takes longer ... Look at me, I'm dragging on forever."

"That's because life expectancy is longer."

"Expectancy? You joke. What do you think I expect at my age?"

Stefan sighs. "To see Tuscany again."

"You're right, Stefan, to see Tuscany again. But I'm boring you, I feel it. I'm boring both of you. I'll stop telling you these black thoughts."

"You're not boring me."

Yuri has closed his eyes, he no longer even pretends to listen.

"Come now, no fawning. It is not like you. We're going to see the Piazza del Duomo, they call it Campo dei Miracoli, the Field of Miracles, or is it the Court? The Court of Miracles? What do you think?"

"One or the other, as you wish."

"So the Square of Miracles, it's more romantic. I can't remember why they call it that. And then that sublime fresco, *The Triumph of Death*. I was very impressed, as a child. Imagine, three open coffins, the corpses lying inside, merciless death striking them, the destitute with their hands out, begging, one moment more, like the marquise on the block, and then the angels and the devils. Have you read Dante, Stefan? Dante Alighieri?"

"I read him in Bulgarian translation, a long time ago. A few excerpts. It's a bit hazy in my memory."

"He's been translated into every language. You read the part on hell, I suppose. People always begin with the part on hell, then stop there. *Lasciate ogne speranza, voi ch'intrate.* 'Abandon all hope.'"

"Ye who enter here."

"That's it. 'Ye who enter here.' Was it in verse in the translation?"

Stefan thinks for a moment. "In prose."

"Some translators choose the easy way and we lose the music. When the music is all that matters. Yes, all that matters. Myself, for example, without the music — I don't know what I'd have become. Perhaps I would have been worse than I am."

"Blessed be music," murmurs Yuri without opening his eyes.

"Yes, blessed be it," approves Liri, who does not seem to have grasped the irony. "We didn't have books at home. Well, we had a few, the Bible, of course, but not that one, not *The Divine Comedy*. We weren't rich, you know. I come from an environment that was very ..."

"Modest."

"My father farmed the land, my mother sewed. From dawn till dusk, good weather, bad weather, every day of the week. Farmed, sewed. And cooked. Nothing was handed to us. You must wonder how I learned music."

"You were an altar boy; the organist, an old maid, or was it a nun?"

"A nun. Mother Cecilia, a prophetic name."

"She detected your interest, your gift, and taught you the rudiments. Then your uncle ..."

"The eldest in the family, the one who had inherited the olive grove and the mill ..."

"Paid for your piano lessons. At age sixteen, you entered the Conservatory of Pisa, then obtained a scholarship to continue your studies abroad."

"And that's how I ended up in the United States at age twenty." Liri squeaks out a small laugh without too much joy. "I see. I've told you all that already, many times. Seems as if I'm rambling."

He falls silent. Stefan gives him a sip of champagne.

"So we had no *Divine Comedy* at home and I went to the school library. And if I've already told you, what's the difference, I'm repeating myself. I was leafing through an illustrated copy. In black and white. Terrible, the visions of hell. Terrible. I was hot, trembling in every limb as I turned the pages. Yet I kept on turning them. Children like being afraid."

"Not only children."

"Fear tickles; that's what children like. It's almost erotic. As I grew older, I began to like it less. The harpies in the Wood of Suicides, violence under a rain of fire, snakes attacking thieves. You see, I haven't forgotten the images. Memory holds up. I lose everything else, but memory, long-term memory, I mean. Because short-term memory ..."

"... is less sharp. That's natural."

"In the long term, it resists. And many have lost even that, once they've reached my age. Mr. Alzheimer gave his name to the amputees of memory, and it is, after all, more dignified than 'doddering' or 'gaga.' A generous gesture from him. The doddering are no longer doddering; they are ill, have a proper illness recorded in the medical dictionaries, with symptoms, development, treatment. It's more reassuring, you must admit. Because when there's no name, you don't exist ... I see the images again. All the damned were naked. In purgatory and paradise, the souls wore long robes. White, of course. Bizarre, don't you find?"

Stefan smiles. "Not so much."

"What's our Yuri doing? Is he sleeping?"

"The journey must have tired him."

"Tired him? At twenty you're never tired. I wasn't. Unless it's the champagne. He's not used to it. But anyway, whether he's asleep or pretending. You and I are wide awake, right? Except that I forget what we were saying."

"Souls in white robes."

"Yes, the souls were wearing robes, in the end, that's what's bizarre."

Stefan thinks for a moment, then: "The illustrator must resort to subterfuges to draw the souls."

"Of course. The unfortunate gluttons, our moralistic poet put them in the third circle. Condemned to spend eternity beneath an icy rain. 'To pay for the baneful crime of gluttony.' In my opinion, he exaggerates. Because gluttons ..."

"Don't deserve that. I agree with you: Dante is at times too austere."

"Gluttony is a venial sin. Those people frighten me, Stefan. They've always frightened me. Even as a child, I was terrorized."

He breaks off seeing the flight attendant appear. She serves them the smoked salmon appetizer and offers Chablis. Yuri awakens — if indeed he was asleep. Stefan takes out the silver-gilt pill box from his jacket pocket, selects a blue tablet, gives half to Liri with a bit of water, then cuts his salmon into small pieces and feeds him.

"I can't help but ... I can't help thinking of them. Perhaps because I'm approaching them. The circles. And I don't know which one is my destiny."

"None, perhaps. Why do you absolutely want to end up in hell?"

"Don't want to, in fact."

"I imagine you very close to paradise, playing music with the angels."

Liri makes a face. "You imagine me on a cloud, with a lute?"

"Or a lyre. You would play *Broken Wings*."

"He's making fun of me," he says, turning toward Yuri.

"He's right. I also imagine you. There's a very pretty guardian angel, beside you on the cloud. Her wings are quivering, her nipples hard beneath her white dress."

All three begin to laugh.

"Meanwhile, in Pisa, we'll eat *ribollita*. My mother always prepared a big pot of *ribollita* for the week. A good childhood memory. Memories of food ..."

"Are a consolation."

"We need something to console us at the end. Console us in going away and leaving everything behind. I remember *ribollita*. It's a thick soup, with *fagioli*, red cabbage, olive oil, the oil of Tuscany, so fruity an oil that's almost green, with just a touch of bitterness; the very essence of the olive." His teary eyes sparkle. "Herbs from the bush, tomatoes," he lists, counting the various ingredients on his fingers. He pushes his fork away. "Thank you, Stefan, I've had enough."

There is now eagerness in his expression; once again he is the child hovering around his mother in the kitchen, intoxicated by the fragrances.

"*Ribollita*, it means 'reboiled,' because it's better when you reheat it. My wife, God rest her soul, prepared it as well.

But it wasn't the same; something was missing. To begin with, she wasn't from Tuscany. She was born in the United States. So, you see, there's no comparison. I met her in New York; we married there before the war. The second, I mean. There aren't many like me left who knew both world wars. Do you know what year I was born, Yuri?"

"You are from prehistoric times." He bursts out laughing. Liri's thin lips stretch out in the shadow of a smile.

"A fossil, you're right. I was born in 1911, and married Bianca in '36. Sicilian parents, great music lovers. They're not all in the mafia. Besides, the Mafiosi appreciate music too. A very pretty girl at the time, Bianca, and an excellent cook. An impeccable tomato sauce. Just enough garlic, a touch of basil, a half lump of sugar to offset the acidity. Her veal roast was always very tender, it would almost melt in your mouth. She prepared it with rosemary. Her secret was to brush it with a mixture of mustard and honey. She made the *cornetti* herself. Our guests feasted. But her *ribollita* was not up to par, alas. To accompany it, you rub thick slices of bread with garlic; good country bread, our country, without salt. A good, well-aged, aromatic pecorino, and very thin slices of *finocchionna*, the best sausage in the world, with fennel seeds, a hundred times tastier than that of Genoa or Bologna, the reputation of which is overrated, believe me. You know what? Gluttony ..."

He is going to say: "Gluttony is the last sin." He's been repeating the same sentence for years. And every time, it's as if he had just invented it.

"… is the last sin," he finishes, as the two others expected. "The first and last. The first because, have you ever seen an infant feed at its mother's breast? Babies are little gluttons. Even Jesus must have been with the Virgin Mary, his mother." This image seems to make him joyful; he emits a little chuckle. "Am I blaspheming, do you think, Stefan?"

Stefan shrugs his shoulders. He says he doesn't know, doesn't know much about blasphemy.

"Of course, you're too young; you weren't raised with the same precepts as I was. The same rigid commandments. *You will not swear* was the second. There were ten; you had to learn them by heart, and seven deadly sins. Seven, like the planets in heaven, like for the creation of the world."

Yuri raises an eyebrow.

"God created the world in seven days," explains Stefan.

"Six, in reality," corrects Liri. "On the seventh day, He rested."

"According to the Bible," continues Stefan. "That was before Darwin proposed his theory. In any case, some people still believe it."

"We can't say they're wrong. Does it please you, the idea of having a chimpanzee and its female as ancestors? Not me. I would rather Adam and Eve, a hundred times over. Even if I don't believe it."

Stefan cracks a little smile, winks at Yuri.

"Seven sins, then," continues Liri. "One for every day of the week, you could say. Even on Sunday; sinners don't rest

... Pride was the first. But I've had reasons to be proud. Do you agree?"

Good, Stefan thinks. Now he'll go over all the sins he was able to commit in his long life. With a bit of luck, I'll glean some new details — the biographer in him is always on the lookout. "You had your reasons," he asserts. "Everyone has."

"You're wrong, Stefan, everyone does not. For most people, humility is the sole option, but they don't know it. Or don't want to know it. I was a good musician and was aware of that. Perhaps too much so. They won't hold it against me in the beyond. Because, it was justified pride, right? False modesty is nothing but hypocrisy. As for miserliness, no, no one can criticize me for being miserly. On the contrary. I was not extravagant though, far from it. I earned a lot of money, it's true, and knew how to make it grow; there is no harm in that. Even Christ advises it in one of his parables. Do you know what I'm talking about?"

Stefan shakes his head.

"Of course not. But well, no matter. I made a lot of money with *Broken Wings*. I didn't squander it. Think of Lola Montès, of Sagan: rich women who ended up practically penniless. Cleaned out, ruined, fleeced. Once I read the story of an English duchess, don't ask me her name, I forget it, who ended up losing her entire fortune gambling."

"Men ruin themselves at the casino too."

"Men too. The women at least seem less attached to the money than the men. Or perhaps they're not as clever? In any case, this one was English. They had planned to make a film about her life. I was approached for the music. In the end the project didn't materialize. I forget her name. Gainsborough did her portrait. You don't remember?"

Stefan shakes his head.

"She had quite a few lovers, the Duchess. Quite a few lovers."

The arrival of the main course provides a diversion. Both have selected the panache. Yuri has opted for the chateaubriand. New wines are offered. Stefan holds out a mouthful of risotto to Liri, then a half a shrimp covered in a creamy sauce, then a mushroom, a scallop. Liri waves a trembling hand. "Thank you. Give the rest to our young friend. I know you want some, Yuri. At your age, you're hungry enough for two. Personally, I want to save room for the marquise. The beautiful marquise."

His head nods gently, he raises his right hand, as if wanting to beat time. Musicians in his memory are tuning their instruments: the ball may begin.

"The third sin is lust. Ah! Dante did not spare them, the libertines and the lustful. What was the punishment in store for them?"

Stefan says he doesn't remember. Or perhaps he has not read that passage.

"I read it. That type of thing titillates you when you're ten years old. But I got nothing for my trouble; there is no ... explicit description, as they say, in *The Divine Comedy*. It's coming back to me. The ones who yield to the sin of the flesh are condemned to violent storms for eternity. There are more cruel punishments, of course, and Dante, a discreet man, did not punish them where they sinned. Even so, they will never have any rest and it must be difficult to spend eternity being tossed about by the wind. Exhausting. Give me a bit of water, Stefan. My mouth feels like sandpaper."

"It must be the recycled air. Too dry."

"It's because you're talking too much," says Yuri. "You're talking too much about Dante. Personally, the only one I know is Dante Sullivan, a police inspector in a TV show."

"My days are numbered, that's why I'm talking. And the Dante I speak of is not a police officer, though he's not far from it. No, he's an Italian poet, of the fourteenth century. Lust, then. There was this couple of lovers — do you know the story?"

Stefan indicates no; Yuri shrugs his shoulders.

"A girl, Francesca, I think, one day was married — against her will — to a twisted guy, a real toad of a man, who had a brother that was, as they say, not hard to look at and very courteous to his relative. In short, the inevitable happened. Can you blame them?"

"Certainly not!" exclaims Yuri, his voice resonant.

"Yet Dante punished them. Such intransigence staggers me. Yes, it staggers me. I don't like Dante, I think. Despite the beauty of the language and all that."

"It was another era," says Stefan.

"Another era, perhaps. But that is not enough to excuse him. I too am from another era, am I not, Yuri?"

"Prehistoric times, I told you."

"I wonder why people continue to read him," murmurs Liri. "Dante."

"People listen to your music."

"Thank you."

"I doubt people read Dante much these days," interrupts Stefan. "It's like Homer and many other immortals. We only know them by name."

"But we revere them."

Stefan gives him some more water.

"I succumbed, obviously. What man worthy of the name does not succumb? Do you know any? They have a song in French," he continues, not waiting for an answer. "'*Il faut bien que la chair exulte*' — 'You have to indulge the flesh.' A man does not experience that indulgence with his legitimate wife. My late wife, may she rest where she is — certainly not with the lustful — my late wife, well, she was a good wife, Stefan. A very good wife, an excellent mother, I have nothing to criticize her for. But what can you do? A man needs to …"

"Indulge."

"Have fun. I already told you all that, Stefan, I won't go over it again. I'll burn in hell for all my fun. Or in purgatory. After all, God is a man. He must be able to understand."

"The Devil, too, is a man."

"The Devil too, you are right. An angel of the male sex.

Even if they claim angels have no sex, Lucifer is indeed a man, has all the attributes … But I wasn't lustful, not like that two-faced Bob Elkis — a whited sepulchre. Not lustful, no. I succumbed out of love for Marjorie. Marjorie Martinez."

Stefan knows. He has already recorded the entire episode in his biography.

"Ah, our marquises are here."

The marquises are shaped in the form of stars. Three raspberries, a star fruit and slice of kiwi accompany them. Swirls of red coulis decorate the plate. All three abandon themselves remorselessly to the sensual pleasure. Liri, however, is less avid than usual before the joys of chocolate. Each time Marjorie is brought up, he's like that, wavering between euphoria and nostalgia. Each of us carries a thorn in our side. Marjorie is his. Has been for a long time.

"You were speaking of Marjorie," says Stefan.

"I had a weakness for blondes. My wife may well have been called Bianca, but her hair was black, and she was rather hairy, which excited me at first, then … It's like everything else. You've seen the photos, Stefan. So you know what I'm talking about. You'll tell me that Marjorie was not really blond. It's true, she was brown-haired — caramel, let's say, caramel everywhere. As sweet as candy. Is there any champagne left?"

"I'll call the flight attendant."

"Don't call her. Give me a bit of Bordeaux; I want to drink to Marjorie. To her memory."

Stefan gives him a sip of white wine, wipes his chin with the napkin, then he and Yuri clink glasses.

"She was a nice little girl, in the end. Too sensitive, perhaps, for the milieu. Hollywood in the forties, fifties. I don't know if you realize; it was merciless."

"Still is today," says Stefan.

"You're quickly replaced in Hollywood. The go-getters arrive with their gangs of friends, and then — no mercy. Quickly adulated, driven away, kicked out the next day. The Academy sometimes awards you an honorary Oscar to set its conscience at ease. To appear generous. A meagre offering. You should see those old farts arrive, trembling all over, tears in their eyes. And the audience rising to give them an ovation, as if nothing had happened. A great moment of emotion. I have to laugh ..." But he does not.

"They didn't give me one."

"You received the Oscar for best original score for *Broken Wings*."

"Yes, I received that, but no honorary Oscar. When you think they gave one to Bob Elkis posthumously. Posthumously! What are they waiting for? For me to kick the bucket? And then put my photo with those people who have passed away during the year. I got out of that nest of vipers on time. But not her, Not Marjorie."

He sighs deeply, staring into space.

"I can't believe you only succumbed once," jokes Stefan to chase away the melancholy.

He doesn't succeed; Liri still looks morose.

"I had other temptations and I admit it, I didn't always resist. What I also admit, and am not proud of, is that I've forgotten the names."

"You should have kept a diary."

"My wife would have found it, and then ... Nothing escaped her. I remember the circumstances most of all. And even then. An extra in a blockbuster, a script girl in another. Stewardesses, interpreters, secretaries, babysitters, nurses. A violinist. A flamenco dancer."

"Babysitters?" Stefan is surprised.

"Well, next to you, Don Juan was an altar boy," scoffs Yuri.

"Well, then, you were listening?"

"I always listen. You were boasting of having good long-term memory, I think."

"That's because those things didn't happen that long ago. Fifty or sixty years is not really that much, you know, when you consider a man's whole life. A man my age. You have to go back a lot further in time. It's when you reach childhood that things become clear. I was not a faithful man. Or else I was weak."

"It's the flesh that is weak," says Stefan.

"The flesh, yes. And my wife — it's like I told you. You couldn't really have fun with her. And after fifteen years of marriage, we had run through our resources; there wasn't much left to discover. to discover. Nevertheless, I loved her in my way, respected her. I always took care of her and the children. Provided for all their needs without making much fuss. Never contemplated leaving her."

"Never?"

"Or rather, yes, I thought about it, just once. During my affair with Marjorie. The poor girl was pregnant. But divorce was unthinkable. Bianca would have bled me dry. I already told you all that, didn't I?"

Stefan nods his head.

"So now it's your turn to tell. It's true; I know nothing of your love affairs. You don't very well live like a monk."

"Perhaps."

"I don't believe you. A few times I've caught a glimpse of Yuri's girlfriends. Speaking of which, the latest one is very cute, have I mentioned?"

"Which one?" asks Yuri.

"What do you mean, which one? The latest, the one who was there at Christmas, Martha or Natalia. Anyway, you know the one I'm talking about. The one who wears glasses."

"That's the one before last. Now I'm going out with Julia."

"Do I know her?"

"No."

"Well, anyway. At least they're visible. Where do you hide yours, Stefan?"

"In my room, under the bed."

"That's not true," interrupts Yuri. "He hides them in the attic. He's Bluebeard, don't you know? He has seven shut up there, in all colours. Redheads, brunettes, blondes, black. Seven different nationalities. He sets one free each night, and at dawn, he returns her to her dungeon. Last night was a Chinese woman."

"You've uncovered my secret, Yuri, I admit everything. And my Chinese woman is called Raspberry Scent."

The old man smiles lewdly. "Delectable."

"And how!" Yuri bursts out laughing. "I know; I saw her."

AFTER THE FLIGHT ATTENDANT SERVES them coffee, Ernest Liri continues to enumerate his sins. Envy — no, he says, he had nothing to envy anyone, except for the great Johann Sebastian Bach, but what musician doesn't envy him? Gluttony — that, yes, and many times, but that's not a real sin, it's more a way to glorify the Almighty, show him we appreciate his blessings. It's true that alcoholism is a part of that; in the world of movies, you can easily become an alcoholic, the opportunities for celebrating — or for drowning your sorrow — are practically unlimited. He did not become one. Anger — he often lost his temper, he admits, he was far from gentle with his musicians, but a man seeking perfection cannot let himself be indulgent. Christ himself denounced the lukewarm. He never hit anyone, except his children, a clout occasionally, when they deserved it. That doesn't count. As for laziness, no.

He says no, but what has he been doing all these years? What have been his memorable achievements since *Broken Wings?*

His voice calls to mind a kind of rasping purr, the worn-out music box with its ballerina in her pink tutu who keeps turning. Yuri has just put his headphones back on — he's very lucky, because, for three weeks now — between Liri's whining, the untimely telephone calls from the family, and the preparations for the journey — Stefan hasn't had much time to hear himself think. He may well be used to it, but his head is spinning a bit. He just hopes the old man will calm down once he's in Tuscany.

"If I were you, I wouldn't worry," he says. "Your sins are forgivable. You're not going to roast in hell. Besides, that isn't our destination. We're going to Tuscany, as you well know, to paradise, to see processions, attend regattas, and eat *ribollita*."

"Yes, *ribollita*. The first and last sin. Not bad, eh? We end as we began. And too bad for the doctor and his never-ending recommendations. I'll eat *ribollita* and lard from Colonnata on warm bread fresh out of the oven, slices of *finocchionna* with a glass of Chianti, Brunello or even Vino Santo. Do you want me to tell you, Stefan?" He is no longer croaking. Now his is the whining, annoying tone of a child yearning for attention.

"Tell me," Stefan replies patiently.

"When I leafed through the book, as a child, *The Divine Comedy* with its black and white illustrations, I told myself that eternity didn't look any more delightful in paradise. I kept that to myself, of course — if not, there would have been a scandal! I would have been casting shame on my family. And the slaps I would have received for my candour. But all those souls on their clouds who formed figures, rose patterns, or I don't know what, who floated in a kind of unreal light, they all seemed so ... so ..."

"Severe?"

"Forbidding. Their company didn't look very appealing, that's for sure. Forbidding, and in the end not really happy. It's funny, they always talk about seventh heaven. Dante imagined ten circles. I remember a drawing of Lucifer, enormous, brows knit, head in his hands, his enormous wings spread. Well, I found him, but didn't mention it to anyone. I found him more interesting than God the Father, a venerable bearded man sitting on his throne, all the way at the top, at the tenth circle. The problem is I have no more hope."

This time Stefan has no answer.

"It's not so much death I fear," says Liri again. "It's afterwards."

"Who's talking about dying?"

"I am. I'm talking about it. Sometimes I regret being born since, after my death, I'll have to find myself in one of those places."

"Heaven and hell are only suggestions. Perhaps something entirely different awaits."

"Reincarnation? I wouldn't like that any better. Beginning all that again, childhood, trying, disappointments, old age and death once again. No, I don't want to be reincarnated.

All in all, I'd prefer oblivion. If the plane crashed now, we'd arrive in the beyond at the same time. I'd be less afraid, I think. I'd be less afraid if we arrived there together."

Stefan places his hand for a moment on the trembling hand.

"And afterwards. Do we still exist afterwards, do you think?"

"This is my last journey, Stefan."

Stefan could protest for the sake of form, but what would be the point? He too knows it is the last journey. And he also knows he'll miss the cantankerous old musician. His old crow. Suddenly his heart is heavy. He feels as if he is attending a funeral, a bizarre feeling. As if this airplane were a hearse, and they were headed to bury Ernesto Liri in the family cemetery.

He can indeed eat all the sausages he wants, he thinks, *all the bean soup, drink all the Vino Santo. Satisfy all his desire, his whims. Dance, if he likes, smoke like a chimney, mentally undress all the girls in flower strolling along the banks of the Arno.*

At present the old man seems to be dozing. He has closed his eyes, leaned his head on the back of his seat. But he is not dozing, Stefan knows. Stefan looks out the window. The clouds have disappeared. They are flying over the Ionian or Adriatic sea. Everything is blue.

5

EIGHT O'CLOCK IN THE EVENING IN SEVENTH HEAVEN

It's a faraway land people long for
without knowing it.

Julie thinks she recognizes Daphné.— a
Chinese girl with blond hair ...

And my Chinese woman is called Raspberry
Scent.

THE PROGRAM IS LIVE. IT begins at eight o'clock. They've been through make-up and now here they are, as fresh as daisies. In a manner of speaking. Beneath the layer of foundation, they all are hot. That's because tonight, the stakes are considerable. Nervous or not, they've been waiting for twenty minutes. Around them, a beehive of activity. Technicians are buzzing about, calling out to one another, hook up this, unplug that, connect two or three wires; assistants flit here and there with clipboards, check off points on grid paper.

The decor can be summed up in one word, and it's easy to guess which. The background is sky blue — of course. They've been placed in a semicircle in uncomfortable cloud-shaped chairs. Boy, girl, boy. A Black guy as sleek as ebony, a bleached-blonde girl with almond eyes, a rather good-looking Latino guy. One holds his guitar on his knees as if cradling a child. Another has set a chef's hat on her curly hair.

To determine the order of the performances, candidates' names were drawn at random a week previously. Daphné will be eighth, which augurs well; eight is a lucky number in China, an omen of prosperity. She believes in signs — all Chinese do. Indeed, life constantly talks to us, advises us to do something or not, always with infinite wisdom, you just have to be receptive to its voice, a continual whispering. The signs are there, you just have to recognize them. Hold out your hand and touch them, open your eyes and see them, prick up your ears and hear them, smell the wind. Stay on the lookout, receptive like the earth. Hone your sensitivity. Who taught her that? No one. Heredity. Wisdom thousands of years old etched in her genes. A date, a number, a butterfly landing, on what does it land? A bird taking flight — is it blue, is it black? Daphné knows that nothing is insignificant, the future is determined in the colour — auspicious blue, unlucky black — the flower, branch, or number. She's been gathering information for a long time on the customs of China, its knowledge as old as the world. Transformations, yin and yang, equilibrium of forces of nature: it's all there, within our reach.

Today, Daphné is in auspicious blue.

Strangely, she has stage fright. Strangely, because for the last two years she's been dancing buck-naked five nights a week, if not six, and has never been nervous. But this time it's different. Even though she's dressed from head to toe, wearing a turtleneck, a miniskirt that falls like an inverted corolla on her perfect thighs, sheer pantyhose, and ballet shoes — only clothes that have never been worn — it's as if she's never been so naked. She's afraid of perspiring beneath the spotlights.

She wants to win.

Miguel, the Latino — a lost cause of a seducer, she thinks cynically, condescendingly — flashes her a smile. What kind of smile? Of complicity? She doesn't want it. They're not partners, they're rivals. *Leave me alone*, she grumbles inwardly. Antoine, the sleek black guy, seems as wrapped up in his thoughts as she. He too wants to win. They all do; that's why they're here.

They are sitting on horribly synthetic white foam rubber cushions that make her itch. These are placed on a transparent plastic frame, so that contestants look as if they're floating. At least that's the impression the show has tried to create. You sink into them. Later they'll have to extract themselves from them with a minimum of elegance. To add to … what? To the discomfort? The feeling of helplessness? To top it off, Daphné has her period. The second day. In her case, the worst. It started without notice, her cycle completely off kilter. Yesterday she could have screamed, discovering her misfortune. The body, always ready to let you down. Betraying you when it's needed most. The idea of leaving a red spot on the cloud when she gets up terrorizes her. A pimple mars her face. The body is a traitor, the spirit — or the soul — is at its mercy. She feels as if her head is in a bank of mist. Is it the beginning of sinus trouble? An allergy symptom? Something — the synthetic wall-to-wall carpeting, the air conditioning — is attacking her respiratory system. It can't. This evening, more than ever, she needs her concentration.

But she is eighth, and that augurs well.

She fleetingly touches the fragile jade bird hanging from her neck on a black silk cord, the only jewellery she lets herself wear. She bought it yesterday in a store in Chinatown. It was essential that it never had been used before this evening. *Fly with me*, she prays, not moving her lips. Miguel sees the gesture, leans over toward her. "A good-luck charm?" he asks.

She nods her head without answering. *Mind your own business, buddy.*

"Me too," he continues, not letting himself be thrown.

He is wearing a gold chain with a little cross around his neck.

"It was my grandmother's."

Well, good for you.

"She left it to me. On her death bed."

How does one answer that? Is he doing it on purpose to throw her? Daphné makes a small gesture open to interpretation.

Finally they call for silence.

Now the music of the credits can be heard: a few notes reminiscent of the sound of a lute, but created by computer, surely; no one plays the lute anymore. A curtain, a kind of gossamer veil — everything is trying to be light here — opens stage right and the blond host, Angélica Dumas — a real blonde? Is that her real name? — undulates to the microphone on stiletto heels, turns graciously around to show off the little white-feathered wings applied to the back of her golden dress. Applause, laughter, shouts of approval.

The show is live in front of an audience.

Angélica — in the end, perhaps they chose her precisely for her name — now explains the rules and the sequence of events of the game. *Seventh Heaven* is the name of the program. Sixteen competitors selected from thousands — many came, but alas, so few were chosen, she pretends to lament — seven weeks, a variety of challenges concocted expressly for them by a team of researchers, two eliminated each time, except for the final week when three will be eliminated. However, rest assured: no one will leave empty-handed. She lists the prizes offered to the losers by the sponsors, including a week-long stay in a five-star hotel on Paradise Island. Not bad for a consolation prize. *It makes you almost want to lose, don't you think?* The last one, male or female, to reach seventh heaven will take home the bundle, a hundred thousand dollars, tax free — like in the lottery.

Daphné thinks only of that; she has never coveted anything so much. To win and leave for China. Goodbye, green Canada. Flying first class — with all that money, no way will she be squished into coach — crossing the continent from east to west, gliding over the forests, the interminable open country, proud mountains, then flying over the Pacific Ocean, the China Sea, to finally land at the extreme east — the round-ness of the Earth always fills her with wonder as does the absurd idea of going from east to west to arrive again at the east, but at the other end of the world. As a little girl, when she thought of the Chinese at the other end of the Earth, she saw them upside down. All kinds of far-fetched — and insoluble — questions arose: how do the pointy hats stay on their heads? How do they manage to eat without spilling everything? And the furniture in the houses, was it glued to the ground? Did people sleep fastened to their beds? China was a great mystery.

She hasn't asked herself these questions in a long time now. She has others, and will find the answers. Her plane will land on Chinese soil, in Shanghai, perhaps, or in Canton, in Peking. The plan obsesses her. Once there, she will perfect her Mandarin, two or three years full-time. She has been taking courses since last fall.

It is not the desire to find her parents — biological, as they say, one sperm and one ovum among billions of millions — that motivates her. She couldn't care less about them. They abandoned her: too bad for them. What she wants is to gaze with her own eyes at her native country, a land of history and legend. History that goes back to the Palaeolithic. *You did not exist yet*, she thinks, *the world hadn't even imagined you when they were already making ceramic objects and tools from stone and bones*. She dreams of the landscapes, has memorized hundreds of names. Their sounds enchant her: the rivers, Huang He, Yangtze; the peninsulas, Liaodong, the high plateaus, Yunnan-Guizhou; the plains, rice fields, mountain ranges, islands, Hainan. The provinces: Yunnan, Fujian, Hebei, Shandong, Sichuan. And the big cities, Nankin, Haikou, Canton, Xian, Peking, Shanghai. The Great Wall — on which construction began seven centuries before she existed — that can be seen from the moon. In a notebook she copied down the names of the dynasties, Han, Mongols, Ming; of warlords; of tyrannical or enlightened emperors, all Sons of Heaven; of empresses held in contempt; adulated concubines; of philosophers and poets. Life there is like the powerful current of a river, implacable, crossing through centuries, a multitude of images dancing upon it, peasants in the rice fields, wearing cone hats — yes they remain on the heads — courtesans with painted cheeks in brothels in the pleasure district, mah-jong players, opium smokers, the silk road, junks, monsoons, tea ceremony served according to unchanging ritual, palanquins, china, cherry trees in blossom, operas, dragons, kites, wind chimes. She even tried to read *The Little Red Book*. An arid, arduous read — she did not persevere.

And now tonight she is on the set of a reality TV show, more determined than ever.

"The first program is the simplest," coos the hostess, while Daphné empties her mind. "Each candidate — they have never seen one another before tonight — will have three minutes, duly timed, the time it takes to sing a song," she specifies, grinning ear to ear, "to sell his or her … product." She turns to the contestants. "That is, to introduce yourself and, above all, sell yourself." They have had only one week to prepare their performance. Spontaneity, above all, was encouraged. "This part will last an hour in all, counting the time for commercial breaks. Next comes the moment of truth, the highlight of the program: a second very intense hour during which there will be a crossfire of questions and answers between the competitors. They will not get off lightly," she promises, frowning in a way meant to be threatening — without quite succeeding. "They will be merciless. Wolves, lions, that will tear one another to pieces before our eyes. Unchained beasts in the arena. *Grrr* …" She pretends to shiver, rolling wild eyes. "All blows, including blows below the belt, are allowed. Two psychologists will act as referees, orienting or modifying the debate as needed. And finally, two contestants, a girl and a boy, will be sent away, and the fourteen survivors will enter the first circle of Paradise. There.

they will submit to various challenges until the following week. These challenges will of course be broadcast live over the Internet, twenty-four hours a day, throughout the week."

"The decision will be made by the public — both the TV viewers (via the Internet or by phone; the email address and phone number will appear in due time on the bottom of the screen) and by people in the audience, who will fill in the voting card handed to them when they entered. They will select the chosen and," she concludes, theatrically indicating a door at the back of the stage, "the damned." This door carries the word *Hell* in letters of fire. The audience noisily expresses its joy. In decadent Rome, a similar crowd stamped their feet while watching gladiators fight, their blood saturating the sand. The crowd revels in her power to save or condemn. *Who talks about evolution? Who says that humanity changes*, Daphné wonders.

"The basic idea," Angélica continues unperturbed, "is that candidates must be of diverse origins, have lived in Quebec for at least five years and of course, have their citizenship — which does not exclude the 'pure laines,' obviously. A question of multi-ethnicity and reasonable accommodation. The concept has been in vogue for some time. The new face of Quebec in transformation. We will help this Quebec emerge from its cocoon."

Inwardly, Daphné shrugs her shoulders. *Whatever*. In addition to the two boys flanking her, she spots in the group a Latin-American beauty with very strong features, probably

Brazilian with three drops of African blood in her veins, two candidates of Arab origin, a black girl, and two other Asians besides herself, a girl and a boy. As for the other competitors glimpsed in the make-up room, she's not too sure. Pure laines, probably. Besides, from where she's sitting in the centre, on the eighth cloud, she does not see them all clearly.

She's not used to speaking in public — in her profession it's body language that counts. She mentally rehearses her text. *My name is Daphné Laframboise. I have almond-shaped eyes because I'm Chinese.*

"This inaugural program is therefore the simplest," declares Angélica. "The ones that follow, with their challenges, will be a surprise. Only one thing is certain: all tastes will be satisfied. Our competitors have no idea what's in store, but will have the opportunity to display their courage, sense of humour, artistic gifts, resistance and more. Seventh heaven — and the beautiful hundred thousand dollars that go with it — well, they have to be earned, right?" Again the ambiguous smile promising novel sensations. "One last point: as opposed to programs of this type on other channels, this isn't about forming couples — although of course if that happens, so much the better. No one will complain. But there will be just one winner. Male or female."

Female, thinks Daphné. *Me*.

"Let the game begin!" the angelic one decrees, clapping her hands. She turns around, her wings quivering. A concert of applause.

A boy stands up, introduces himself. Bulgarian on his mother's side, Italian on his father's. His name is Gino. He dreams of becoming an actor. Physically speaking, not bad — green eyes and black eyebrows. But now he's launching into a monologue from Molière's *Don Juan*. "There is, besides, an inexpressible charm in the first stirrings of a new passion, and the whole pleasure of love lies in change. Nothing can withstand the impetuousness of my desires: I feel my heart capable of loving all the earth; and, like Alexander, I wish that there were still more worlds in which to wage my amorous campaigns." An odd idea, in the end. Why do they all consider themselves seducers? This one is certainly nether old nor cynical enough. The audience, made up mainly of women, does not seem convinced or won over. The reception is lukewarm. Daphné gives an imperceptible sigh of relief. If they're all this hopeless, she doesn't have to worry.

Sophie, the second one, now approaches the microphone. Daphné can't concentrate, too much stress, but she hears a high-pitched voice — too high-pitched — then laughter. The audience is jubilant. Anxiety, that unlucky black bird, a crow, suddenly touches her with its wing. She latches onto her own text, which is not funny in the least.

My name is Daphné Laframboise. That's not my real name. I'm not a true blonde either. I'm Chinese; beneath the dye my hair is as black as night. I'm twenty years old; I was born very far from here, in China. Abandoned by my parents at birth. Who will laugh? Who will cry? They'll think: consider yourself lucky. You were adopted, while others … Others are thrown into the river — what is it called again? Huang or Chang something, a funny name.

Bringing up her uninteresting childhood is out of the question. A few images, some dull photographs, are put away in the drawers of her memory — they can stay there. A little girl with slanty eyes, a slightly chubby face framed by pigtails, playing all alone in the yard of a bungalow. An average-looking brown-haired woman, her adoptive mother, a sad look in her eyes. Her monotonous voice in the background. *Daphné, supper. Have you done your homework, Daphné?* Books with covers all the same — couples embracing in the moonlight, beneath a palm tree — lying on the living room coffee table. Or else open on the armrests of the beige sofa. Enough to turn you off love forever, that is, at least if that's what love is. The TV's on and the woman is snivelling in silence watching the movie, a Kleenex box beside her. A man in a jacket and tie enters at the end of the day, carrying a briefcase. Childhood in a Montreal suburb. Idyllic? My foot! Memorable? Anything but. You just want to forget it. Muffins on Saturdays, the rubbery cheese sandwiches, the shepherd's pie they call *pâté chinois*. Nothing Chinese about it! Her pink bedroom. Not even a tragedy to tell. She'll only say a few words, has chosen them carefully. *Above all, don't show bitterness.* That would look bad.

SOPHIE MOVES AWAY FROM THE microphone to the sound of prolonged applause from the audience. Steve takes over. He's brought his guitar and harmonica; he speaks French with a slight English accent. His appearance calls to mind a sharp image of the end of the mythical sixties — long caramel-coloured wavy hair, faded jeans, embroidered shirt, shell necklace. Looking either crazy or candid, depending. A peace and love sign is drawn on his guitar. The songs of Bob Dylan were a part of his childhood, he explains. The idiot tells how he was born in Seattle, but grew like a plant — marijuana with its bitter-sweet smell — in the Quebec countryside. His marvellous parents, *I love you Mom and Dad* — were hippies as invincible as Astérix's Gauls. Delighted chuckling in the audience. His song couldn't have been more predictable: he has set his own ecological lyrics to the tune of *Knockin' on Heaven's Door* and sings it nasally with almost touching fervour.

Daphné touches the jade bird. She's too warm; she'd like to pull herself off her cloud. It's the lights. Too strong, violent. Too warm. She blinks. The Latino brushes up against her arm. "It'll be okay." She does not respond.

My name is Daphné Laframboise. My Chinese parents — certainly not marvellous — did not want me. Probably because I'm a girl. There, girls are poisoned gifts of nature. Even if nature encompasses the yin and the yang with the same impartiality. It's the same in western civilization. If you don't believe me, reread your history. My adoptive father ended up taking off; I won't criticize him for that. He remarried, has three children; I'm not his priority. My adoptive mother became even more tearful than she was already. Personally I didn't cry. "You're hard Daphné," she told me time and again.

Well, what are you supposed to be? Soft? I left, at eighteen years old, to live my life.

The words chosen are perhaps too hard. She'll change "told me time and again" to "repeated." No, she'd be better off dropping the entire passage, stopping at "priority." Even adoptive, mothers remain a taboo topic. And "take off" is perhaps too offhand. "My adoptive father fell in love with someone else. It's always about love."

Then she'd tell things the way they are, call them by their name. Assert herself. She has never had therapy — no problem with her ego, but she knows all that, she knows the vocabulary by heart. To assert oneself, to come to terms. There is no other secret.

I dance nude. I dance nude in bars, Olé Olé, Geisha, Sexy Sadie. Yet I'm not a prostitute. I never sleep with the clients.

You want to know how it began, this dancing business? How do you become a nude dancer? By answering a classified ad, as simple as that. "Pretty dancers required. With or without experience. $$$." Full columns in the newspapers. Never any unemployment in that field. There you go. A cowboy hat, lasso, high-heeled boots. Nipple tassels. At the Pussy Cat, my number was all the rage. In Montreal East, at the American border, in the depths of Abitibi, on Côte-Nord all the way to Labrador, and into Ontario; success was guaranteed everywhere I went. Cities and villages with French names, English names, Native, cities and villages of which I know nothing other than the gloomy bars found on the side of the highway, between a MacDonald's and a Réno-Dépôt hardware store. Interchangeable. Like the dancers.

I never sleep with clients. I'm twenty years old and am a virgin, believe it or not. Sex doesn't interest me.

Will she really tell them that?

~~∽~~

TWO OTHER COMPETITORS HAVE HAD their turn. The Brazilian, Alicia, performed an exuberant samba. Daphné remained unmoved. No danger, though; people won't vote for her: she's too beautiful. Beauty is power, but when it reaches that level of perfection, it becomes a handicap. It intimidates, discourages, frightens. It has been statistically proven that in this kind of situation people just want to recognize themselves. They'll vote for someone ordinary. A juggler followed her: the audience was lukewarm. A small cloud-shaped ball with wings escaped. He made a sheepish gesture. A real comic. Daphne felt no pity.

At present, a slender redhead, a chef's hat on her head, is standing in front of a microphone, cooing her story in the form of a recipe, a tempting dessert she has christened *Empyrean*. "The most elevated of the celestial spheres. The dwelling place of the divinities," she takes the trouble to explain for the spectators — the majority if not all — who have not understood. "Reduce to cream, beat with a whip, but not cruelly" — such wit — "to create an airy mousse. Melt chocolate on low heat, add the zest of this, three drops of that. Incorporate, fold, soak, flambé."

A microsecond of ecstatic silence follows the description

of the Empyrean. Then, a round of frenetic applause. In fact, things are going exactly as Daphné had predicted. All the competitors would want to compete for originality, she knew. No one, except her, will think of simplicity. Well, let them compete. Compete and make fools of themselves. She will be original in her simplicity, will be the only one to dare use it.

She is eighth and that augurs well. In China, eight is pronounced "Ba" and attracts luck. That's all they talked about at the Olympics, inaugurated on the eighth of the eighth month, at eight o'clock in the evening, in 2008. In the bars where she dances, she's the most popular dancer; they shout with joy — *heehaw!* — when she clicks the heels of her boots, twirls her lasso. Queen of the night. But tonight, she has another number, one she has not broken in. Her assurance — blue bird, black bird — her assurance wavers all of a sudden.

Commercial break. Extras in white gowns cross the stage, moving their fake paper wings, fake lutes in their hands, while others, in black leotards and red masks, with fake long tails glued to the small of their backs, brandish fake pitchforks and pretend to jab the candidates.

Daphné had planned to tell only the truth — after all, this is a reality TV show. But while people may claim the contrary, fiction surpasses reality. Truth, especially her own, is banal. Imagination is what counts and wins. They want something juicy. Or something sticky — blood, sperm. Something that flows — tears. Something touching. Or hilarious. They want to get their money's worth. And she offers her tale. Is it true? They don't give a damn. True stories are only interesting when they are colourful. Or when they make people laugh loudly. Otherwise, be on your way. They want heroes, victims, survivors. Not anonymity. They're at a show. They want to laugh or cry. They want amazing feats. Physical abuse. Or miracles.

Antoine, the seventh — in the West, seven is a lucky number — stands up slowly, an unfurling vine, and approaches the microphone. "I come from Africa," his low voice quivers like a tom-tom in the savannah. Civil war, corpses with stomachs ripped open, fleeing on desolate roads, refugee camps, child warriors, the litany goes on and on. "You've saved me. Thank you." Even Angélica seems moved; her eyes are moist. What's he talking about now? With money, he wants to relieve misery, save lives in turn. Daphné feels like plugging her ears; she plugs them mentally, doesn't want to hear those words, going immediately after him, saying she is called Daphné Laframboise, a salmon returning to its place of birth — fish that swim against the current in rivers are somehow touching. She'd decided to conclude with this metaphor.

In her head, the images now follow at a frenzied rhythm. Is that how you die? When your entire life, it seems, passes before your eyes? Perhaps she's dying and doesn't know it. Bits and pieces whirl about, collide, the castle in China crumbles. The door to hell will soon open for her. In she'll fall.

To the bottom of the hole, the Geisha Bar or even worse. Back to the beginning. My God, help me!

What God?

She sees herself leaving at the end of the program, head down, with the clumsy juggler. Or perhaps they'll take pity on his clumsiness, perhaps they'll spare him. She'll leave with the nasal-voiced ecological singer, or another who's even more hopeless. The unconvincing Don Juan. In her hands, the sorriest consolation prize: seven tanning sessions at the Paradiso tanning salon.

Quickly, find something, invent another scenario. There's no time left; her name is called. Like a zombie she walks to the front of the stage. The time has come to improvise. In high school, in her improv group — an extracurricular activity — they all said she was the best.

She touches the jade bird lightly, lets her arms fall to her sides. She closes her eyes, as if to collect herself. *Remember, uprightness, simplicity. You are this image. You assert yourself.* The words emerge from her like a wave she had not predicted. A voice is speaking through her own. "My name is Raspberry Scent. That's my Chinese name. I have almond-shaped eyes because I am Chinese. I was born in Shanghai, the largest port in China." They want to shiver, remember, they want miracles. "They found me in a garbage can, among the peelings. The sun was setting; I was completely naked, the pink light poured over me. I wasn't crying. It was so unusual that people took note. I was the baby who didn't cry. At first they thought I was dead. My heart was still beating. I was tiny, a small fruit fallen in the pink light. They called me 'Raspberry Scent.' It was the first day of spring, the day of the equinox. I am twenty today. For twenty years, I have been suffering."

It doesn't matter whether it is true or not. Someone said imagination is the only truth. Now she opens her eyes and stares at the audience. She knows what she must embody. Wounded innocence. Assassinated purity. She wants a tear to roll down her cheek. It does. "I was five when my adoptive father began to abuse me. My adoptive mother knew about it. She never protected me. He remarried; he has another daughter who ran away three months ago. Not difficult to figure out why. Her name is Fanny; she disappeared in Florida. Perhaps you heard about it."

Indignant murmurs ripple through the audience. She has them — it's like when she whirls her lasso. She is going to win.

6

MAR AZUL, THREE O'CLOCK
IN THE AFTERNOON

This reminds me of another little girl,
last winter, in Cabarete, who claimed
she was a tour guide.

... miniskirt falling like an inverted
corolla on her perfect thigh ...

THE SUN IS AT ITS highest in the sky, at least that's how it
seems; in any case, it's certainly at its hottest. The brightness
hurts the eyes. Not a breath of wind, not a cloud today and
the cancerous UV rays roast the skin mercilessly. The sea is so
calm it seems to be dozing. It, too, must be exhausted by the
sun beating down on it. And so must the fish swimming in it.
Fewer and fewer of them, the fishermen bemoan. Exhausted.

Perhaps the harmful rays penetrating the water give them skin cancer too. Or else, disgusted by procreating only to end their days in a fisherman's net, in a frying pan, on a plate surrounded by lemon wedges, or worse yet, in the form of insipid fish sticks at the frozen food counter — often in a country where neither they nor their parents have ever ventured a fin — they've stopped reproducing. Anyway, the sessions of egg-laying and fertilization, all things considered, aren't really pleasurable: just think of the salmon. The great circle of life? A sinister farce, in their case. Everyone marvels at the phenomenon — atavism, they say. Everyone, but them. So the instinct to perpetuate has left them. They are on strike. *Adios. Go see if you can find us somewhere else. Go eat plankton or jellyfish if you like, but not me and mine, you're done eating us.* You can hardly blame them.

The sun is at its most torrid — it's three o'clock in the afternoon. On the beach in Cabarete, in the Dominican Republic, a crowd of resort vacationers gleaming with sunscreen are nonetheless sprawled on the burning sand beneath umbrellas, and the little bar with the thatched roof — Mar Azul — is almost deserted. There is of course Concha, faithful to her post, leaning on the counter before her eternal Coca-Cola. There are also a couple of vacationers, in their early twenties whom she's never seen before, smooching in a corner, his right hand fiddling with and feeling the weight of her left breast — is he trying to fiddle with and feel the weight of her heart, her lung? — beneath her candy pink T-shirt.

"Some people have no shame," grumbles Concha.

The barmaid, Maria Flor — Florita shrugs her shoulders. "What's gotten into you? They're not bothering anyone. I find them kind of cute."

Good-natured, Maria Flor. For her, everything is cute. "Besides, it adds a bit of ambiance," she adds.

"What are hotel rooms for, then?" spits out the other one.

Not that Concha is a prude. She isn't. She is, so to speak, paid not to be one. But today she seems to have gotten up on the wrong side of the bed. Or else burned her tongue with the first sip of coffee. To be handled with the utmost care, three pairs of white gloves at least.

The song that was playing — "*Broken Wings*," the salsa version by the Dominican group Olé Olé — has just ended. Maria Flor glances at the pile of CDs, and finds the one she's seeking. Now we hear the first notes of "*Bésame mucho*," a retro tango version this time, sung — or sobbed, or begged — by Paolina Sanchez in her tragic quavering voice. Maria Flor winks at Concha who gives an exasperated sigh.

"Don't look so glum. You're going to scare away the customers."

"The customers? I sure would like to know what customers you're referring to? Personally, I don't see any."

"I'm talking about the ones who are going to arrive. If they see you there like a policeman, for sure they won't want to come in. And I'm talking about that guy who's already here."

Maria Flor subtly points her chin at the loner, a man whose pale face is accentuated by a well-trimmed grey beard, reading a book at the back of the room. Now it's Concha's turn to shrug her shoulders. She's not in the mood for banter, as she's made clear. Nor for flirting. She's melancholy today. The little one, Paquito, is sick. A kind of gastroenteritis. He vomited all night, Paquito, her son, even though she seems rather young — she's eighteen, but doesn't look it — to have a child. Her mother, who usually takes care of him, has caught the same bug, and her sisters, at least two among them, have gotten up in a bad way this morning, with greenish skin, glassy eyes, one unable to go to school, the other to go to work as a chambermaid in the Paradiso Sol Hotel. What did they eat, what did they drink, *madre de Dios?* Rotten food? Polluted water? So she, of course, spent the night going back and forth between the bedroom and the bathroom, baby in her arms. She didn't close her eyes for even a minute. Result: she is washed out, her nerves on edge, a splitting migraine, as if a team of determined carpenters out to get her were hammering six-inch nails into her cranium. Maybe she'll get sick too. What's more, it's three o'clock, and she hasn't yet swallowed a bite. Hasn't been hungry all day. And not being hungry, in her case, is rare. A date to mark on the calendar.

For the moment, her sister Merce — the virus hasn't affected her — has taken over, and is seeing to the household. As for Concha, she went out for a change of scenery. To breathe.

Maria Flor sets down a small glass of rum next to the flat coke. "To fortify you." Concha needs fortification in times like these. Usually she doesn't drink alcohol, but now … Everything's going badly and she doesn't see how things can improve. Tourists have less money to spend. Or they pretend to. Or they find her less appealing. Or they're all going to Cuba now; they say it's quite a bit cheaper there. Whatever the reason, she usually goes home empty-handed. Like her cousin Manolo when he returns from fishing, one morning out of two. No, at the end of her tunnel, there's an electrical outage; no light turns on. "It's because you don't smile enough," claims Maria Flor. "Before, you used to smile all the time. And it worked." She's right. But who feels like smiling now? Concha would like to see Maria Flor in her shoes. Maria Flor says that people come to Cabarete to forget their troubles and that's why she has to smile, or they won't come back. And with the increase in the price of fuel and airline tickets they need a lot of persuading, that's all they talk about on TV. All the commentators look devastated. Hotels are half full. Or half empty, according to the optimistic or pessimistic point of view one has of the situation. There are more and more hurricanes, increasingly ferocious. Igor ravaged the Yucatan coast last month, Jenny is close to Haiti, and Karl, since yesterday, is spiritedly approaching via the Atlantic: none of this helps matters. Here, in Cabarete, they've been spared, but for how long? And, Maria Flor points out, there's not exactly a shortage of tropical islands on the planet. "Do you know how many there are, just here in the West Indies, aside from us? At least fifty. Cuba, the Barbados, Jamaica, Puerto Rico, and ..."

"It's OK. You don't have to name them all for me. I know."

"The tourists could easily decide to go tan on other beaches. And what would become of us in Cabarete without them?"

Concha shrugs her shoulders. To hear Maria Flor, you'd think smiling at vacationers was almost a patriotic gesture. "Tourism is the country's largest industry." The only one, as it were. She says that, for most of these foreigners, a chaise longue on the beach, or a glass of rum beneath a palm tree, is paradise on earth for one week a year. And they're entitled to that. It's so cold where they live. "Minus twenty-five some-times. With what they call the wind-chill factor, they say it goes down to minus forty. Can you imagine?" Perhaps, but where will she, Concha, go to forget her worries? For she has plenty. Where is her earthy paradise?

To add to her troubles, a real string of them for some months now, Concha has just gotten out of the slammer. Christmas vacation had gone badly for her: families with their swarms of brats; honeymooning couples gazing into each others' eyes; most in all-inclusives, with their own bars, shops, excursions, orchestras, group leaders. And their social direc-tors, of course, always women. As rum consumed on the premises is part of the package, they spend all their evenings there. Not a peso more to burn in Cabarete. No one needed her. In fact, it was as if she had become transparent. She could put on her shortest skirt — the one she's wearing today, yellow flowers on a white background — her tightest jeans, no one saw her. After that, business was only so-so for two weeks. So, at the end of January, in desperate straits, she stole a wallet from a vacationer's beach bag. A woman! What got into her, *madre de Dios?* With a man, she'd have been able to settle the affair amiably, with no one being any wiser. She would have known how to bring a man around. *Disculpame. Perdón. Lo siento.* For you, it's free, *cariño*, I'll do anything you want, I only ask that you wear a condom. *Ven conmigo.* She'd have exhibited her skills for an hour or two, and in the end, would have been absolved of her sin, like at confession. Perhaps even richer, with a green bill slid into her bra. Go in peace, sin no more.

But that's how it is. She gave in to an impulse; she herself wouldn't even be able to explain why. She was looking for her brother Raúl when she fell upon it. The straw bag with purple and yellow stripes, like an Easter egg that had materialized there just for her. It practically jumped out at her. A kind of miracle. The immaculate, shiny, still-crackling straw. Not at all misshapen. New, undeniably — its owner must have bought it in some fashionable, expensive store just before she left. A high-quality bag, nothing like the ones they sell here in the *Made in China* souvenir stalls. And it was there, alone, open, without a zipper, lying on its side on the deserted beach towel, with the wallet visible amid the usual odds and ends: a small bottle of sunscreen; paperback romance novel with a glossy cover featuring a couple embracing beneath a palm tree, a hair brush, a mirror, lipstick, dark glasses. If that's not provocation what is? Around her, everyone seemed to be sleeping. She thought she heard the wallet murmur, "Take me." It's true, she swears, a murmur amid the lapping of the waves, nonchalant. She did not resist the call. She bent down next to the towel as if to pick up a shell. Her hand inched its way in, keen and furtive like a little lizard. She didn't see anything coming. All of a sudden, that loud exclamation — was it a shout or a yelp? In any case, one thing is certain: it awakened all those who were dozing.

That was her first attempt. She had never stolen anything; she swore it to the judge, hand resting on the Gospel, tears flowing like a stream, a cascade, a torrent down her cheeks. Mascara mixed with her tears. "Besides, who's talking about stealing, Your Honour? They didn't understand; they falsely accused me; I'm as innocent as a newborn. I just wanted to look at it, it had fallen on the sand, I just wanted to know who it belonged to, just put it back in the bag, so that it would not be stolen, in fact." A lame, weak appeal that convinced no one.

So she had to get caught in the act by the swimmer's friend, a hysterical redhead, as thin as a rail in a fluorescent green bikini who arrived from God knows where just as she was going to slide the object of the crime in the pocket beneath her skirt. A dozen scandalized tourists approached. *Santa Maria*, what were they going to do to her? Cut off her hand? Lynch her? Hang her from the first coconut tree? She needed to run, of course, but how do you run when your legs refuse to obey you, when they're just two sticks of wood stuck in the sand? It was impossible even to take a step forward. She was transformed into a statue.

The judge was tough, inured; he had seen plenty of tears before. "Thieves are a shame upon the country," he had raged. She kept her eyes lowered. "And that pocket beneath your skirt, what do you use it for?"

"To put shells in, your greatness. Afterwards, my sisters and I use them to make necklaces."

"You sell them? You have a permit for that?"

She wanted to sink into the earth. A permit? First she ever heard tell of that. Here, permit or not, everyone offers what they have; it drives the local economy, and in the end everyone comes out a winner. It's well-known that tourists love handicrafts. They go back home with a suitcase full of authentic souvenirs to give their family without having spent a fortune. "We've put in the request, Your Honour," she had stammered, despite everything. "We're waiting for it." He hadn't believed a word. "Well, in the meantime, a month in prison at Santiago will teach you." The gavel banged down, sounding like a thunderclap.

"Don't complain," Ernesto said by way of consolation. "In the olden days, thieves were hanged or sent to the galleys. Even today, in China, the punishment meted out to pickpockets is re-education training in the depths of the countryside. For second offenders, a bullet in the back of the neck. As expeditious as that. No room in prison for small fry, and certainly no desire to spend money to feed them. Public execution, to set an example, or edify the people, after a trial that lasts a five minutes at most. In Singapore you would have received the cane, I can't remember how many strokes. Publicly, once again. It hurts. It leaves scars. People who have tasted the medicine don't soon forget it. They don't have a sense of humour in those countries." Ernesto knows whereof he speaks; he spends his time reading. He has just finished a Chinese detective novel. "Don't complain ... Easy for you to say," she had retorted. Nevertheless, she shuddered: a bullet in the back of the neck for an insignificant stolen wallet — without knowing what it contained — seemed to her disproportionate, even in countries where laughter doesn't exist. And even in detective novels. But perhaps detective novels are like romance novels: they say just about anything.

Ernesto is her cousin. Not an angel, either, far from it — not when you account for all those aging female tourists, completely enamoured, whom he swindled. But well, no one ever lodged a complaint against him; he's very lucky. He came to see her three times in jail. He brought her food to eat: fruit: mangoes and papayas, and chocolate. And cigarettes, fortunately. Otherwise she wonders how she would have survived. Incredible how long it is, a month there. At the thought of cigarettes, she begins rummaging in her bag, finds the Marlborough Lights, lights one, inhales sensually. *Gracias*,

Ernesto. He continues to give her a package from time to time, menthols sometimes, Concha's favourite. He has contacts in all milieus, does all kinds of favours, and receives all kinds of gifts in return. And as he has a generous nature, doesn't forget his less fortunate or less resourceful cousins. In prison, he also brought her news of the family. "Manolo caught a thirty-pound marlin. Paquito is teething."

She only had to hear Paquito's name and the tears began to flow again down her cheeks; she moaned *!Ay Mi bébé! !Mi pobre niño!* Ernesto waited for the shower to pass; gave her other news. "The Paradiso Sol is half empty. They kept Loli, but they threw out Merce. Temporarily, they said." Merce is Mercedes, and Loli is Dolores, Concha's sisters. There is also Soledad, Sole, who still goes to school. All five daughters received, at their christenings, an old-fashioned first name representing an attribute of the Virgin. Conception, mercy, distress, solitude. Not very cheerful. Strange to mark your daughters like that from the day they're born. But their mother worships the *madre de Dios* almost fanatically. Religious images and statuettes clutter the entire house. She places flowers in front, lights candles. The youngest one, who's eight, is called Rocío, in honour of a sanctuary in faraway Sevilla, where *Mama* dreams of going one day on a pilgrimage, in May — while knowing this dream is impossible. We all long for an unattainable star.

Concha imagined the confusion in the house, with her sister out of work and herself in prison."

"Your mother is beginning a novena."

Another one.

"And is Raúl selling any paintings?"

"Times are hard for him, as for others. The recession —
right now, people are dancing on the edge of the crater."

"The crater?"

She opened her eyes wide.

"The apocalypse is not far off," he concluded.

She quickly made the sign of the cross. He continued in a
lighter tone: "Enrique now has a fiancée from Quebec."

"Quique?"

"Yes, Enrique, himself, our little cousin Quique, and guess
where he met this real treasure?"

She shrugged her shoulders.

"At Mar Azul. He's contemplating going to live there.
In Canada. That is, if his lady friend comes back to marry
him. Then he'll have his citizenship. If you want to know, I
wouldn't be surprised if she does come back. She seems to
me rather smitten."

"You saw her?"

"Older than him — I'd give her at least thirty-five. Works
at the Department of Immigration in Ottawa. Sure that will
facilitate matters. Her name is Dorothée."

"Good for him."

It certainly wouldn't be her, Concha, who'd have luck like
that. A smitten fiancé, a public servant at Immigration Canada
to bring her out of the doldrums.

No sooner had she returned to Cabarete then one of the soldiers who patrolled the streets, machine gun slung across his shoulder, shouted at her roughly. "Watch out," he warned her. "We're watching you." *Why me?* she'd almost protested. *There are crimes far worse that are committed here.* But she refrained. You don't argue with an armed man. "We're watching you." She considered herself warned. She'd paid dearly for that wallet — if someone forgot one stuffed with bills in front of her, she wouldn't touch it, even with her fingertips.

Now the girl with the pink T-shirt has slid her hand beneath the table. Not difficult to figure out what she's doing. The sound of her companion grunting can be heard across the room. Concha sends her a dark look.

"GO ON, HE'S BORED ALL alone, the poor guy," continues Maria Flor. "Go keep him company. He'd be only too pleased."

"Too old."

It's true, she's tired of old men.

"Generosity comes with age."

"You must be joking!"

A few memories come back to her and they're not great. She thinks of the taxi driver she met right here a few months ago. A Québécois with a Russian name. Fédor Savine. In his own way, he wasn't that bad. She'd imagined him thirty years before, trim and tanned, standing on a surf board riding the crest of the waves, as proud as a peacock. His hair blond, rather than grey, and curling a bit at the nape of the neck. That's what she often does with clients who are her grandfather's age. She closes her eyes. It helps her swallow the pill. But in the end, on the beach, he had bargained. She'd asked for fifty American and he had offered her forty Canadian. So she had refused. Usually, she doesn't refuse. Especially as he, looking rather uncouth, hadn't displeased her that much, despite his bull neck and heavy blotchy cheeks. Things usually go well with that type of client; their demands are more or less predictable, and they're easy to satisfy. They behave tenderly, sometimes, happy to have a young thing in their arms. And after all, with forty dollars, even Canadian dollars — it was before their dollar had begun to climb, which of course didn't last — she wouldn't have had to count on Ernesto for the cigarettes. And the whole family would have eaten their fill for a good ten days. *Mama* has the most economical recipes imaginable — soups made with bones boiled a long time, chilies, a lot of rice with fish when Raúl fishes at night with Manolo — and her accommodating friends give her good prices in all the local stores. It wasn't the fact that he'd bargained. She's used to that. They all want to get more for their money, the vultures. But he'd said that he'd paid for her meal, and that had insulted her. The meal had nothing to do with it, did not enter into the transaction. After all, he too had eaten, and eaten well. At her uncle Rafa's restaurant — the best grilled meat in all Cabarete. In fact, it was her cousin Quique who'd served them, and you couldn't ask for a friendlier waiter. Fédor Savine had insinuated that she received a commission. But if he was satisfied with his meal, what did it matter to him if she received something or not? In a self-respecting family, you stick together; it's natural. Just because there's sunshine and palm trees doesn't mean life is easy. A vale of tears; *Mama* says so and she knows what she's talking about. You earn your place in heaven, impossible otherwise; it's all Adam and Eve's fault. Eve's mostly, the glutton. The guys land here and what do they think? That people like her can afford to eat in restaurants? They eat in restaurants when they're invited. And as Ernesto says, family has to show solidarity to survive. Especially when her father and his boat were swallowed up by the sea. It happened five years ago, the night of an unexpected storm. Their mother tells them that that's the sea's way of taking vengeance on all the evil done to it. The poor and innocent pay the bill; it's been that way since the world began. Don't expect justice down here. Where then? When you ask her that question, *Mama* rolls her eyes toward the blue sky. Justice is in the hereafter. We'll be glad when we get there. In any case, without her, Fédor Savine would have eaten a mediocre meal, no doubt, and far more expensive, alone like an orphan. A widow, rather. She had kindly kept him company. And when you are a surly old taxi driver looking like — what do they say again? There's an expression that makes people laugh a lot — *la chienne à Jacques*, that's it. *La perra de Santiago*, no matter what you mean by that. She sees him again in his awful old synthetic pants, his brown polo shirt (or was it olive green?), his big shoes, his socks full of holes. Yes, when you're that badly dressed, don't expect company to be free. She had insisted: despite what people may think, even girls like her have their pride. It was fifty American, not a peso less. She didn't budge an inch, he neither, and in the end she'd gone home empty-handed. A bad memory, yes, but there are worse. No matter, Fédor Savine remains like a bone caught in her throat.

"This one is different," insists Maria Flor. "To begin with, he ordered whisky. Chivas; no one ever asks for that here. The bottle must have been sitting here for almost ten years, from when Mar Azul opened its doors. He said *Por favor, señorita*, and *Gracias, señorita*. Very polite. Not to mention the tip he left me. He has class, I assure you. A *caballero* like they don't make anymore."

"He looks like Santa Claus with his beard."

"Come now. Santa Claus has a white beard. His is grey. Besides, it's not really a beard. Just along the line of the jaw. If you want my opinion, it makes him look distinguished. And his book, his glasses. I assure you that if I were you ..."

"What would you do if you were me?"

"I wouldn't hesitate."

"LA CUENTA." THE COUPLE TAKES off. Florita tells them the amount in Spanish. Of course, they don't understand. They only know those two words that they utter at the top of their lungs, *la cuenta*. Concha translates. They count their pesos, convert to dollars, try to calculate the tip. A very laborious process. But finally they leave. Her hair is a mess, her T-shirt crumpled, and he's as red as a boiled lobster, and not from sunburn. They're going to finish it off in their hotel room. About time, too.

"If he interests you so much, that guy ..." Concha begins.

"What do you mean, if he interests me?"

"Nothing."

She'd better keep quiet. She was going to say: "If he interests you, don't worry about me, you can have him. I don't intend to compete with you." She caught herself in time. Because while she was vegetating in prison, Raúl — her own brother, the painter who sells his canvases to tourists on the beach — began to go out with Florita. And it's serious. Now she's wearing a ring on her finger. Not a diamond, but it shines, and Florita displays it proudly. They're even talking about getting married before the summer, having children, all that. *Mama* is crazy with joy. Imagine the scene if he learned she was trying to encourage his fiancée to cheat on him. He already has a grudge against her since the episode of the almost-stolen wallet. He claims that rumours have spread and it's hurting his business. He'd never forgive her. Raúl is so jealous. A monster. *Of course, here everyone has something*, thinks Concha spitefully. *A jealous lover, good contacts for cigarettes, a real gem willing to do anything at Immigration Canada.* Everyone except her.

"He's looking at you," whispers Maria Flor.

"He's reading his book."

"No, he's pretending. I'll bet he's going to offer you a drink. I give him five minutes. Come on, smile. You're going to have a nice evening."

~~

AND SO IT IS THAT *jealousy is interminable ... One doesn't have to be with someone, it suffices to be alone in one's room, thinking, to experience new betrayals by one's mistress, even if she were dead. As well, we mustn't fear in love, as we do in everyday life, merely the future, but even the past, which often only emerges for us after the future.*

John Paradis looks up. That Proust, really. No one has ever known how to talk about love and its manifestations like him. About love and its torment. Passion, desire, jealousy. The fear of losing the loved one, of not being loved in return. Of not receiving the exclusive, perfect love that we ourselves think we give. Of not being loved enough. And all that without practically ever leaving his bed. It compels admiration. Long sentences in which the narrator wonders interminably about the meaning of a look, a sigh, a smile, or lack of such. John Paradis is very happy to be rereading *In Search of Lost Time*.

His first attempt goes back about forty years. He was still a student. First year of a Master's degree in English literature. Proust was not on the syllabus, of course, but everyone was talking about him. Everyone was spouting quotations, putting forth his or her interpretation of the madeleines and the linden tea. Were the young girls in flower in reality boys? Who was hidden behind Albertine's mask? Wanting to judge for himself what was going on, he borrowed the complete collection from the university library and read it in one go, over one summer. Now he understands that perhaps he was a bit too young, perhaps he read a bit too quickly. He remembers reading the work without appreciating it much, complaining about the length — which today delights him — of the sentences, with their old-fashioned turns of phrase, the extreme use of relative pronouns, asides, and the imperfect of the subjunctive, and of the artificial and entangled atmosphere of the salons where anachronistic duchesses held forth. Because, at the time, John Paradis swore only, of course, by the dictatorship of the proletariat. The universe of Dickens — the capitalist rapaciousness and hypocrisy, exploitation of the working class, and particularly of children by the odious wealthy — seemed to him incontestably more real, more genuine and even more moving than petit bourgeois Combray described in infinite and fastidious detail by Marcel Proust, genius or not. David Copperfield and the pitiful Nell in *The Old Curiosity Shop* — more touching than Swann, Verdurin, Charlus and, above all, the hypersensitive and sickly narrator of *In Search of Lost Time*. Of course, everyone speaks of what he knows; everyone exorcises his childhood as he can. At age twelve, Dickens slaved away in a factory like his characters, while his family rotted in prison for his father's debts. At the same age Proust let himself be cosseted by a mother and a grandmother who were pathetically indulgent.

Today, John Paradis believes that the world described by Proust has the artificiality of the world it reflects. And that this very artificiality is genuine. For the world is just as real in private mansions as in the slums, and suffering is not felt less intensively by wealthy people than by the oppressed. Well, he admits he is not completely certain of that. Suffering is not the same, of course, and some have compensations to console them that others cannot even imagine. A syringe of morphine in hand, compassionate nurses lean over some, then tuck them into their satin beds. Others, alone, spit blood and phlegm as they wallow on their pallets. How can you compare them? Yet the rich suffer as well, they just have another kind of hunger. Everyone suffers. And everyone dies at the end of their story. There's a kind of immanent justice. John Paradis has at least reached the age — sixty-one — where he knows that.

Nor does he want to deny the ideals of his youth. Marx and Engels, Trotsky, the Nietzschean theories, *Gott is tot*. Che Guevara, *Libertad o muerte*. And even Nechayev's *The Catechism of a Revolutionary*. He immersed himself in them, fired up, as the early albums of the Stones and the Beatles, Bob Dylan and Léo Ferré played on his cutting-edge stereo system, the hashish smoke hanging heavy his room and his blood boiling in his veins. Sweet sixties. No denying that. He lived his youth like it should be lived. He had the privilege, he is well aware, of living it in those years when everything was changing.

When he was born, the war was over, the economic crisis almost forgotten. The Age of Aquarius was beginning to break through, an age full of promise. The horizon was opening up; prospects looked bright, a thrilling time. And people thought that love was finally freed from its straitjacket. But sometimes he feels it is his ideals — his gods — that have abandoned him. It's absurd to think that way, he knows. Ideals do not abandon. They remain the same, perpetually. They are handed down from one generation to the next. It is in adolescence that God dies. After that, his existence is given the benefit of the doubt. To put things mundanely, are we trying to have our cake and eat it too? John Paradis does not see himself as an opportunist. His position is closer to philosophical doubt. Thinkers, and not the lesser ones, have been sceptical long before him. No, ideals do not change. It's just that one day you stop fighting to impose them. You're tired. He thinks again of all the slogans that he chanted frenetically. *It is only a beginning, let's keep going.* Faraway shouting and hopes. You move away from that; the shouting and hoping now only an echo. As teenagers we ardently and creditably believe that we can change the world. Years go by, and we see it will always remain the way it is, for better or — too often — for worse.

HE GLANCES AROUND THE ROOM. The atmosphere leaves something to be desired, to say the least, despite the bartender Florita — small flower, she told him her name earlier —

who does her utmost to put on lively music. No matter what CD she selects — or perhaps because of the choice — customers are conspicuous by their absence. They're all on the beach. Presently, a group is singing at the top of their lungs in Spanish to a hybrid rhythm, a kind of cha-cha-cha revisited with maracas and congas for accompaniment. Not very convincing, if you ask his opinion, especially in the middle of the afternoon. In the evening, it's one thing, when a crowd bent on partying sways their hips like — he was going to judge harshly, before remembering that, at twenty years old, he too swayed his hips and his wriggling was hardly more elegant. Earlier, a young couple had been fondling each other with a lot of conviction — even absorbed in his reading, he made out their explicit panting and smiled into his beard. They've left; good luck to them. The only one left, with the exception of Florita, is a girl — a bit scrawny, but otherwise rather cute — who's brooding, leaning on the counter, palm against her cheek.

HE PICKS UP HIS BOOK again, goes back two pages. He quite likes doing that, especially with Proust, rereading the tortuous sentences, mulling them over in his head, never sure of having exactly understood what the author intended. *We end up, by way of suspicions, absorbing daily, in huge doses, this same idea that we are being betrayed, a very small quantity of which would be fatal, infected by the jab of a cutting word.*

Exactly. He's experienced that as well, many times. Two

marriages and as many divorces, not counting the liaisons, short-lived or long-lasting. That's because back then freedom and infidelity too often went hand in hand. It's not easy to experience love in such conditions. People think those years were one constant party. Not so. Besides, all parties come to an end. He remembers wake-ups that were decidedly not triumphant. His two marriages, his affairs as well, short-lived or not, ended bitterly. Cries of rage, tempers flaring, doors slammed. And the bickering, my God! Who's keeping the set of Japanese dishes? Who's taking the cat?

There is an age at which to read a book — a work, in the case of *In Search of Lost Time*. That's what he always tells his students. What he told them, actually. He retired last year. An ideal moment for each book, or else it's too late, or too early. He told them that approaching a book is like approaching a person. A genuine meeting, osmosis, is only possible at a precise, given moment in our history. He had them read Emily Brontë, Thomas Hardy, Percy, and Mary Shelley. For John Milton — *Paradise Lost* — he advised them to wait. Yes, an age to read a book, an age to love it. *Besides, love is an incurable ill, like these constitutional predispositions, in which rheumatism provides some respite only to give way to epileptiform migraines.*

LOVE — IN THE END, IT is always about love. The love we seek, find, lose, destroy, and begin seeking again. He sighs deeply, glances at his watch. Three fifteen. He wonders if he wouldn't be better off going elsewhere, but just the thought of walking under this leaden sun exhausts him. He'll finish his glass, read a few more pages, and see.

LAST SEPTEMBER, AT A USED bookstore, Outre-mots — sagging couches, rickety tables offering old gilt-edged Nelson editions, original editions of the old série noire collection, art books, sometimes even numbered and dedicated copies — he came across an old edition of *In Search of Lost Time* published in Montreal during the war. Sixteen volumes, in quite good condition — despite the yellowed paper. But that defect, if it is one, instantly seemed to him to add something nostalgic to it all. No, it was not a defect; in this case it was a quality, in perfect harmony with the theme of the work. He smiles faintly. *Bonsoir Nostalgie*, a program broadcast on the radio on weeknights. He is a loyal listener. If his students knew — had known that, they would have found it tacky. It is. We can't help but treasure certain memories, and songs from our teenage years are a part of them.

In short, he didn't resist buying the sixteen yellowed volumes, and doesn't regret it. They all featured a name of the flyleaf, Marie-Ange Sullivan. In a way, that name had convinced him, go figure. No doubt for the nostalgia, once again. The bookseller, a young woman, impeccably cultured, always ready to recommend books, gave him a very good price. He didn't need the discount — his pension keeps him more than comfortable. But she's like that. With all customers? Or only with him? *Too bad*, he sometimes thinks, *that the fairies who*

handed out charm and beauty weren't there the day she was born.
He thinks that each time he enters the bookstore and she
greets him with teeth the colour of old ivory. On his last
visit, however, she appeared less jovial. While she was preparing his bill, he glanced at the book she was reading, propped
up close to the cash register, a bookmark — an angel on
fuchsia velvet paper — emerging from about two thirds of
the way through the volume. The biography of Ruddy Wallace,
who'd nicknamed himself Thoth, after the ancient Egyptian
god of evil and night — really, these guys with their over-sized
egos — pedophile, sexual predator and noted serial killer,
who's been waiting for about ten years to go to the electric
chair on death row in Florida. With that type of reading, no
wonder the bookseller looked so gloomy. Why read that, he'd
almost asked, when there are so many admirable works in
which to immerse yourself? He said nothing. He already knows
the answers. To become immune. To overcome. Because we
are all voyeurs. Because death, cruel death, fascinates us.
The Roman emperors were well aware of it when they sent
Christians and beasts to face one another in the arena. Who
speaks of evolution? Who says humanity is improving? In any
case, the novels he gives — gave — his students to read
were not, for the most part, any more cheerful. Tess of the
d'Urbervilles dies on the scaffold; Mary Shelley created a
monster. Books are our mirrors. What is reflected there is
not always beautiful to see. He took back his credit card, placed
his purchase — a monograph on Gainsborough, a painter

he likes — in his backpack, murmured "Goodbye, Béatrice."

For her name is Béatrice, a name that doesn't suit her at all. If she'd been prettier, just a little, like Florita or her friend, for instance, he would have perhaps made advances. He is angry at himself for reacting like that feeling — repulsion? — but, well, that's the way of the world; we won't change it, at least not in his lifetime. Men are attracted to beauty. Call it atavism. He is no worse or better than others. Women, well, women are different; intelligence is worth more in their eyes. If not, how can one explain their infatuation for a short-sighted runt like Woody Allen, or Serge Gainsbourg at his worst. They're right, no doubt about it. Beauty fades, as is said. Nevertheless, if Béatrice had just been a bit more good-looking, if those acne scars had just been a little less obvious the poor thing must have suffered a lot during her teenage years — he would have made advances to her. She'd be only too pleased, he was sure. A man feels those things. She was very much alone, surely, once outside the bookstore, in her living room, surrounded by books, a glass at arm's reach, within reach of the other, a ton of goodies — sweet, salty, perhaps — dreaming of him having come that same after-noon, wondering about the meaning of a look, a smile. Or of their absence.

He's already read the first ten volumes. In his edition, *The Prisoner* has two volumes. He is well into the first; here in Cabarete, he'll have time to read the second. When he has completed *In Search of Lost Time*, he intends to tackle Dante's works, a plan that has been continually put off. Then Homer's, *Iliad* and *Odyssey*, and, to finish off with a flourish, Ovid's *The Art of Love*.

The morose girl standing at the bar lights another cigarette. She smokes a lot; she seems tense. He quit smoking five years ago after one bout of bronchitis too many, but the taste, the desire, the craving, never go away. It almost hurts, sometimes. He wonders if they allow people to smoke on death row, in Florida for example, where a pseudo-god of the night rots, if they offer them the traditional final cigarette — final pleasure, final sin — before leading them down the corridor, or if there, like elsewhere, their health is protected up to the final second. He looks at the smoker from afar. She is inhaling sensually, head back, eyes closed, like he used to do. Small triangular face, beautiful silky black hair, lanky body, flexible and smooth, he thinks, like a vine. Former colleagues, men his age, describe having young "friends" in Cuba. They go see them once a year and receive all kinds of favours in exchange for small gifts. He chases away these thoughts, shaking his head. His book is still open in front of him.

PEOPLE WONDER: HOW DOES A man like him, a retired English literature professor, land in a place like Mar Azul, in Cabarete? He doesn't really, how to say, look the part; he doesn't look like a water sports enthusiast or a salsa dancer. Has he gotten lost? Taken the wrong airplane? He smiles to himself, imagining the faces of his ex-students or colleagues if they could see him here. True, he could be more easily imagined strolling elegantly around a city filled with history, coming out of a museum and entering the house where such and such a famous composer or poet was born, in Prague, for example, which is supposed to be marvellous, or Vienna, London, Mexico City, or Paris. He too, in a way, could more easily imagine himself there. If he were in Paris, he would now be tasting the same Chivas at the Procope or at the Café Voltaire. He had also planned a trip to Corsica this spring; he's never been there. Calvi appealed to him. A kind of return to beginnings — Christopher Columbus was, they say, born in Calvi back when the city belonged to Genoa.

What he's doing there is actually the result of a rather far-fetched story. He retired last year. He sold his house that was too big for him in Notre-Dame-de-Grâce, and moved with his books, LPs and CDs — classical music, cult bands from his youth, old singer-songwriters — and his memories into the house he had inherited on the river in Sainte-Marguerite-du-Lac-Masson. Told himself he'd spend his remaining days there — twenty years, perhaps, if he followed in his father's footsteps — reading, thinking, and writing, aphorisms at first. He has a weakness for aphorisms. *Imagination is our only truth; A woman remains a woman; whatever her outward appearance and however unrefined, there is still a female heart beating inside its cage; You only wake up once from a dream.* He was quite proud of that one, until he recognized it on a television show he was watching absent-mindedly. One of those programs that are in fashion, its plot unfolding more or less in a scientific police laboratory. The show was in English, but the idea was the same. *You only wake up once from a dream.* In the mouth of a particularly perverse serial killer — who hacked up his victims with a jigsaw — no doubt inspired by Wallace, a victim of God knows what childhood trauma. Must have suffered from enuresis; it's always the same story more or less. The child who wets his bed is cruelly punished and spends the rest of his life abusing innocents as he himself has been abused. In a microsecond, John Paradis experienced a shock, the feeling he had been despoiled, plagiarized. After all those years teaching literature, he should have known that everything has already been imagined. We never invent anything. The sentence was perhaps borrowed from some philosopher or poet. If you believe the thrillers, all murderers are men of letters, each of them quotes Nietzsche, Plato, Edgar Allan Poe, of course, and Dante, and even the Bible with a vengeance. The ex-professor must have realized: as an author of maxims, he would not go down in history. Better to give it up than make a fool of himself, even in his own eyes.

What he did next was also unlike him. A classified ad in *Le Devoir* on a Saturday. "Retired but passionate literature professor seeks F for love and more." Had he really written that? On some melancholy evening? During a night of insomnia? It was the end of November, winter already set in, a good foot of snow in front of his window and the tall pine trees covered in white on his property. Had he begun to miss love and its torments? Hadn't he anticipated the boredom? Was he yielding to the saying "man wasn't made to live alone," as someone, in his great wisdom, had declared one day? He preferred to think of it as an experiment worth trying, a kind of harmless game to fill gloomy evenings of a winter that was shaping up to be particularly tough that year. He could have tried the Internet; social networking sites were apparently all the rage. One of his colleagues who went in for that "sport" claims he had met a few more-than-acceptable candidates. But John Paradis was anxious that the chosen one be a reader, and that she read *Le Devoir*. He didn't want a woman glued to her computer screen night and day, sending and receiving messages — lies? — written in truncated metalanguage.

So there it was. a classified ad like a bottle cast into the river, a seed sown in the earth, and then waiting for the outcome. To be frank, he didn't put too much stock in it. And yet, sometimes he let himself imagine idyllic scenes. A sunny kitchen; a woman, mature in her beauty, wearing a soft dressing gown, newspaper open in front of her; a bowl of café au lait covered with foam on a cloud-shaped placemat; a blue earthenware bowl; a homemade jar of jam — apricot — decorated with its old-fashioned tartan cover; a loose bun from which a few wisps of hair escape; perhaps a cat brushing against her legs. The power of the imagination, and so forth. He believed he could almost smell the sickly sweet aroma of coffee, the classifieds page. The reader couldn't help but smile before this profusion of prince consorts and other suitors for queen of the hearth. She'd fall upon his intriguing proposition and decide to give the suitor a chance. Or a redhead, in a classic raincoat, kid boots, reading the newspaper on the subway, suddenly dreamy at the prospect of meeting this passionate academic. Another one who would read in bed, listening to music, Chopin waltzes, Erik Satie, falling asleep thinking of him. Or else, and here he recoiled, Béatrice or someone like her. She was the type to read *Le Devoir* on Saturdays, and also, he swore, the type to fantasize about taking her pen, dipping it in her tears. Would she recognize him? "Dear Professor, seek no more. You have found me."

He looks up. Feels the eyes of the two girls at the counter upon him, mocking, in the case of Florita, almost kindly. The other's are indifferent, even disdainful. Must be weighing him up, evaluating his abilities, on a dance floor — probably no great shakes — or in bed — hardly any better. She's wondering, perhaps, if he has a date with someone. In a way, he too is asking himself that.

THE WAIT HAD BEEN A short one and a flower soon grew in the snow; that is, an avalanche of letters followed. To tell the truth, he had not expected so many forlorn women. A student claiming boys her own age disappointed her, a few married women languishing in their suburbs between the creative cooking courses and their gymnastics, yoga, aerobics; divorcees, happy widows, tearful widows seeking a friendly shoulder to lean on, single mothers overwhelmed by children at an awkward age. Civil servants, teachers, nurses, a translator, two psychologists, four massage therapists, several retirees — like himself. A budding novelist, who revealed neither her age nor her marital status, seeking a mentor — her letter written on the computer, two verb tense errors, an Anglicism. Some claimed, candidly he thought, to have read the interminable historical novels — full of anachronisms — by Juliette Evanelli, or the complete works of Hope Spencer, as if such admissions were likely to win him over. A few photos accompanied the mailings. None resembled the muse hoped for, yet he let himself dream a little before the variety of faces offered, he thought, with the same touching naiveté. "Whatever her outward appearance," and so forth.

He conscientiously replied to all letters. The selection was made naturally, without distress. In February, he had only three correspondents left: Suzanne, Coralie, Marie-Ange, like the unknown woman — surely almost a hundred years old, in an old-age home losing her autonomy, perhaps even dead and buried — whose yellow books he owns today. March came, and he hadn't met anyone. Among other things, his second wife still criticized him for his tendency to waver. In the end, he really didn't know what he was seeking. To make a name for himself as a letter writer if he had to give up becoming an author of aphorisms?

He had Suzanne's photo — a face with regular features, glasses. Coralie described herself as an athletic brunette, a bit plump — the bit, for him, was ominous. Marie-Ange was more discreet; she preferred to converse with him about his reading. He liked her fine, careful calligraphy, her style worthy of — well, of a minor author no doubt, but all the same, she wrote well, on watermarked stationery. It was she who had mentioned Cabarete. The interminable winter had sapped her strength, her sprits, she declared. She needed a week in the sun before facing the spring, in Montreal the most depressing season of all, when the snow is filthy and boots are ruined in the slush. Was she throwing him a line? Without thinking too long, he reserved a plane ticket, a room for a week at the four-star Paradiso Sol Hotel at a more-than-reasonable price, not saying anything to her. A way of continuing the game and even spicing it up a bit. It would be fun to meet this Marie-Ange in a place he had never imagined vacationing. Images from old movies floated in his memory. Running in slow motion on an endless beach. He planned on following her without her knowing for one or two days. Then he would decide. If he didn't like her, nothing obliged him to reveal his true identity. Ève, his second wife, also had criticized him for being manipulative and it infuriated him. He replied that you have to look out for yourself. A few days of warmth wouldn't hurt him. He had nothing to lose. There would still be time once he returned to go visit Calvi.

Marie-Ange had spoken of the spring equinox — today. He'd arrived yesterday. He didn't want to risk travelling on the same plane as she. He wanted to explore the place, see where he was likely to find her. If she had taken the same airline, she must have been there since eleven o'clock this morning. In the late morning, after swimming in the pool for an hour, he went into a few bars, shops, and restaurants. No woman alone on the horizon. The beach? Packed. Impossible to expect to find anyone — and certainly not a stranger — in that jumble of stretched out bodies.

But suddenly he thinks of something: she never told him she'd be alone. Perhaps there was some old mother, brother, sister, childhood friend, colleague, cousin, child — he himself has two, from the first marriage, or, as the French say, "du premier lit," from the first bed, with a candour that makes him smile, implying that children are always conceived in a bed. He has two grandchildren as well, Arthur, in honour of Rimbaud, and Albert, for Einstein. Strange, the old-fashioned names that are coming back. Sometimes he's sorry that the second one wasn't a girl. Then perhaps he could have had an Albertine in his lineage.

Perhaps she is not alone. And he has no photo of her. It's off to a bad start. The risky, even incongruous aspect of the undertaking now clearly appears to him. The whim of a teenager. Ridiculous. He's annoyed at himself. He's read too much Marcel Proust. Or read it too late. In any case, he knows full well that life is not a novel.

Perhaps it's not such a bad start as all that, however. Tomorrow he'll start searching for Marie-Ange. For the moment, perhaps there are better things to do. A girl sulks, leaning

against the counter. Or else she is waiting for something. Someone. Him? Her flowered skirt looks like an inverted corolla
on her slender thighs. One can't help but think of the young
girls in flower in *In Search of Lost Time*. A scratch on her right
knee. She must have fallen running, like a kid. He imagines
the tip of the sandal getting caught in a crack in the sidewalk
— admittedly the sidewalks here, when there are any, are in
terrible condition. All in all, it makes her even more touching.
Now she's looking at him with undisguised insistence, almost
impolite. A little earlier, she was evaluating his merits. A spark
of interest lit up in her eyes. He must have passed the test.

~

HIS GLASS IS EMPTY. HE closes the book on his bookmark —
the toothless smile of the face of his grandson Arthur — puts
his reading glasses away in their case, stands, approaches the
counter. "*Lo mismo, por favor.*" Then, indicating Concha: "Y
¿para la señorita?" Concha hesitates a fraction of a second.
She shrugs her shoulders imperceptibly. "*Coca-cola con hielo.*"
Her singsong voice is not unpleasant.

Maria Flor drops five ice cubes in a glass, one at a time.
Five minutes. She had predicted correctly.

Now John Paradis has sat down on the stool next to
Concha. She half turns toward him. Not bad at all, in the
end. Old enough to be her grandfather, perhaps, but a well-
preserved grandfather. His grey beard is carefully trimmed,
not a hair out of place. Florita says he looks distinguished.

It's true. Certainly he's not the type to bargain. At least he's well-dressed: beige cotton pants, well-ironed, pinstriped shirt, sleeves rolled up, and wearing a good watch.

"From Quebec?" she asks.

"John Paradis," he introduces himself, holding out his hand.

"Paradis?" Like *Paraiso?*"

She smiles. The smile reveals even, white teeth. Better and better. "I'm Concepcíon," she says. "Concha."

7

EIGHT O'CLOCK IN THE EVENING IN OUTREMONT

Since the "events" ...

And it was her first attempt. She had never stolen anything, she swore it ...

THE EVENTS — IN FLORENCE'S HEAD, it is still the "events" — she cannot resign herself to refer to what happened in St. Petersburg three months ago any other way. The "events," that is the runaway, the disappearance of their eldest child, Fanny, almost thirteen years old. She who always says you have to call things by their name — naming is the first step, that's what she repeats to her patients — cannot manage to do so.

Since the events, she's been less vigilant with the two boys.

One child is missing, but two others are there, two others call out, their silences resonate as loudly as their shouting. What should be done, what is the secret, how do you live? She doesn't know. She who had always a solution to propose. *Watch over the ones who remain.* Before, that was what she would have answered if she'd been asked the question. She doesn't manage to answer, or does so badly. Now, tonight for example, it's after eight and at their age, six and seven years old, Balthazar and Jonathan should be in bed; they have school tomorrow. Yet hearing their voices in the living room she does not intervene. They're watching television. Their grandmother Claude — Florence's mother — is with them. Florence doesn't want to mix in. The rules have changed, sleep comes less easily, they need to be told stories. She has no more left; she has only one and doesn't want to tell it. For them, too, it's hard. Balthazar has begun wetting his bed again at night. Jonathan has nightmares and wakes up screaming. Their grades at school are dropping quickly — in class they can't concentrate, hardly surprising. They're too young for such an ordeal; they don't understand. She doesn't either.

Robert hasn't come home — another meeting with his support group, the Association of Parents of Missing Children. Some people have been waiting more than twenty years for a child who perhaps they wouldn't even recognize if he or she resurfaced. Some have horrible stories. Some break down and cry; it's the same thing each time. Florence doesn't go. Horrible stories: she's heard too many of them, seen too many tears.

She is less vigilant and it's contradictory. She is — how to say? — distracted. Her mind is elsewhere, a winged insect, dragonfly or butterfly flitting around, not landing. Everything seems enveloped in a mist. Because this vigilance at every moment, this severity — more Robert's, in fact — what purpose has it served in the end? Fanny disappeared all the same.

All the years of studying psychology, all the years spent listening to others confide their problems, their disorders, their disasters, the years spent trying to understand them, help them reconstruct the shattered image, mend the tattered ego, in the end, why, Florence wonders. She didn't even understand her daughter, apparently. And yet understanding is her profession. Something escaped her, the fragility, the taut rope ready to snap. The shoemaker's children go barefoot. We've been told that for a long time in every way possible. Old popular wisdom has expressed itself, once again. And popular wisdom is rarely optimistic. If you play with fire expect to get burned. If youth but knew. Once the first step is taken, there's no turning back.

The disappearance, the running away, took place in St. Petersburg, Florida three months ago, over Christmas vacation. That is, what should have been two weeks of vacation together as a family, sunbathing and swimming in the ocean, golf for Robert, a half dozen books for her. It happened the first day, scarcely a few hours after they arrived. The afternoon was coming to a close. Florence keeps seeing the moment, the last moment she saw Fanny lying on her stomach at the edge of the pool. Her two-piece yellow and blue striped bathing suit, her slender body offering itself up. A touching sight. Small henna butterfly tattooed on her shoulder. She seemed asleep, a book close to her face, the headphones of her Discman on her ears. Florence had bought her an iPod for Christmas; she'd been asking for one for months, said that Discmans were passé, completely passé, no one had them anymore at her school; she looked ridiculous. Like a dinosaur. "It's hell," she concluded. Hell, that's the only word they have in their mouths to describe anything. To hear them, nothing is liveable; they're always pitiful. And they don't even know what the word means. They haven't been raised with religion. Nor was she, in fact. Hell is supposed to be the worst of punishments. It's supposed to last for eternity. Well, no. Hell is now. They used to be in paradise and didn't know it.

But she'd bought Fanny an iPod, telling herself perhaps she'd stop looking so put upon. Perhaps she would concede a smile, even fleetingly. Her beach bag was beside her. The two others, Jonathan and Balthazar, were jumping in unison in the pool, their floaters around their arms. No danger of them drowning. Besides, they swam like fish. It was she, their mother, who forced them to wear floaters, saying you can never be too careful. The concert of protests still resonates in her head. She remained immovable. Never too careful. Later, she remembers, they played cards; she saw them from her perch. A few children were bickering — *don't push! Asshole! Coño!* — the two boys as well. From the balcony she intervened. Present, vigilant; that was how she was. Calm returned. The sun on her skin, a caress, while in Montreal a snowstorm was raging. She was almost purring, prize idiot. Blissful, yes, blissfully ignorant, she planned Christmas Eve dinner — roast capon, fine peas, potatoes au gratin, fruit salad, coffee ice cream — thought of the dress she would wear for the occasion, the blue one with the daisies. She remembers all the details; they've been playing constantly in her head. She's searching for what went wrong. The moment she was too vigilant, or not enough. She was reading about historical events in Tsarist Russia, a grand duke who'd stolen his mother's icons, and Nicolas Savine, his soul dammed. *In debauchery he attained heights that distinguished him*. That distinguished him! Such style. She laughed to herself. The balcony was on the second floor, she wasn't far off; she read with one eye and kept the other on the children. It's very clear in her memory. She has nothing to reproach herself for. She could not have acted otherwise, short of putting a ball and chain around their feet. She doesn't believe in such methods. The ball and chain are not a solution. She only has to think of the confidences told to her in the secrecy of her office. Tie up children and they'll only want one thing: to escape you. She is a good mother. She always prepares balanced meals, supervises homework, looks after cuts, tells stories, cuddles and consoles, gets up at night when they're sick. She breastfed all three of them until they were nine months old. She is an exemplary mother. At least, she was. She prepared, supervised, looked after, told, cuddled, consoled. Consoled Fanny. Everything has changed.

She'd had them drink a large glass of orange juice — oranges she'd just squeezed — right before letting them go down to the pool; in the evening they'd eat out, fried chicken, which the boys love. Nothing. Nothing to reproach herself for. The sun had been about to set; Robert came home and they'd had a drink together; whisky for him, Diet Coke for her, a bowl of salted nuts. She'd daydreamed out loud, spoke of vacationing in St. Petersburg, Russia, next summer, just the two of them. Robert wasn't against it, their talk was carefree; she told him that the kleptomaniac great-duke had been mad about a dancer named Fanny. She quoted a few lines of a poem she loved. *The moon glows, russet-coloured in the white night. Its shadow wanders like a ghost and is reflected in the Neva.* He asked who wrote it and she replied "Alexandre Blok." It's all very clear, for three months she's been thinking about, seeing it over again in her head. He'd said: "Florence, you dazzle me." It was carefree, full of promise. "You dazzle me." She felt the light shine from her, a dazzling woman. She dreamed of white nights and mist, balalaikas; she remembers these images, the red moon on the black water. And then suddenly Fanny wasn't there anymore. As if the earth had opened up in a micro-second and swallowed her up. Do such things really happen? Happen other than in books, happen in real life?

They searched everywhere, not finding Fanny. A photo in his hands, looking demented — she had never seen that look in his eyes — Robert had gone knocking on all the doors.

She, retreating into denial, kept repeating to herself that Fanny would come back. "I know her, she forgot the time; she always does. I was like that at her age. She's walking on the beach, went too far, is trying on T-shirts in a store." Like a mantra. She'd come back. Come back.

They ended up calling the police. Two officers, a white man and a black woman, came. Sitting in the living room they took notes, asked questions. *Did Fanny have money?* A few dollars in her pocket. *A drug problem?* No. *Anorexia, bulimia?* No, no. *Was she rebellious? Like all teenagers, no more. Had she been depressed lately, or a victim of bullying at school?* No. *Had she been disappointed in love, or had a fight with her parents?* At thirteen years old, the slightest disagreement begins to look like the end of the world. Robert had shaken his head, but Florence replied that yes, there had been a conflict: Fanny hadn't wanted to come to Florida this year; there was no point in pretending the contrary. They nodded their heads. Her friends, in Montreal, had planned an end-of-the-year party, she specified. Fanny was ... She sought the right word. Fanny was mortified. Was that the right word in English? A runaway, the police officers said, then; some young people run away when they're upset. It is their way of defying authority, most of the time they're found. Or they come back on their own, contrite, after a few days. How many days? They shrugged their shoulders.

Then a night of waiting — the worst night of her life, the longest. It was that night she started smoking again. Robert got drunk.

The next day he noticed that two-hundred and eighty American dollars was missing from his wallet. The conclusion was obvious: Fanny hadn't drowned in the ocean, hadn't committed suicide, hadn't been kidnapped. She'd taken the money, two one-hundred dollar bills, four twenties, and had left deliberately. She'd planned it all; the clothes were in her beach bag with the stolen dollars. She'd even thought of her Medicare card. At the time, Florence had felt almost impressed. Comforted, at least. *Resourceful, my daughter*. But that hadn't lasted. Because how far do you go with two-hundred-eighty American dollars when you're thirteen, and don't know anyone, and speak barely three words of English? Not far. She remembered how guilty, yes guilty, Fanny looked coming out of the bathroom. Then suddenly she understood what happened. Fanny had stolen, Florence was sure it was the first time, and was afraid to face the consequences. Florence had seen that too often, girls incapable of accepting themselves, who gradually end up finding themselves behind bars. Drugs, fraud, prostitution. Violence. Grief and despair. She did not want any of those scenarios. She wanted to rewind the film of events, see the bathroom door opening, her daughter's guilty face, cheeks aflame, looking evasive. Freeze-frame. She would have said. "Ok, Fanny, enough, let's talk face to face. You can tell me everything; I'm used to it, I've already heard everything. Nothing is irreparable." Fanny would have ended up confessing, the money would have been returned from whence it came, and Florence would have promised to remain

silent. Nothing is irreparable. The film would have played out
with another ending. That is, it would have started up again
with the ending planned: sun bathing and swimming in the
ocean, Christmas Eve on the terrace, opening the presents.
A Walt Disney day — another surprise she'd had in store for
them.

She repeated to herself, is still repeating, that that's not
a reason to leave. You don't leave on account of missing a
New Year's party. Because of a few miserable dollars stolen
from your father's wallet. You don't ruin your life because
of that. And yet, yes, you do leave on account of that, she
knows it. You leave for far less than that. You ruin your life.
When you want to leave, she knows, any reason is good. When
you want to die. Die, yes, the word sometimes crosses her
mind and she hastens to chase it away.

After the event, there was no more question of vacation,
obviously. Her parents had cut short their trip in Tunisia and
rushed to join them to take care of the boys. She remained
close to the phone smoking cigarettes; Robert went all over
the surrounding area. A girl matching Fanny's description —
shoulder-length brown hair, braces on her teeth, jeans, turquoise T-shirt — had been spotted at a McDonald's on the
highway, at the exit of the city. The employee who'd served
her, a fair-haired boy, none too bright, had noticed her foreign
accent. She was alone, had ordered a chocolate milkshake,
of that he was sure. It was about seven o'clock; he knew
because he'd started at six and she hadn't been the first

customer. Afterwards, quite few people had come in and no, he hadn't noticed anything unusual. Other employees thought they remembered a man in black who looked suspicious. The trail stopped there. Impossible to know if someone — the man in black — had approached her, or how long she had stayed. Florence rewinds the film once more, reconstructs the story. They report the disappearance more quickly; police officers in a car stop at that McDonalds to get an apple pie, coffee — they all do — and recognize the distraught girl in the turquoise T-shirt and bring her back. Repentant? Rebellious? What's the difference, they bring her back that evening. Robert gives up golf, Florence her reading, they spend the remaining days not letting the children out of their sight, not even for a fraction of an instant.

At the end of two weeks, they'd returned to Montreal. What else could they do? Sick at heart, paler and more tired than when they left. The news had preceded them; journalists hungry for catastrophes, vultures, awaited them at the airport with their cameras, and microphones. Live, the "tearful parents of the young runaway" share their impressions. She hadn't wanted to say anything. Robert did the talking.

Her father remained in St. Petersburg; he telephones daily; the investigation is stagnating, he says, discouraged, the investigation is stagnating. He's thinking of hiring a detective there, locally, to resume the search. Her mother, here, is taking care of the house. Florence is on sick leave — she works at the women's prison. She no longer has consultations with prisoners. She has nothing left to offer them; she's empty. For three months, she hasn't slept more than three hours straight. Fanny, her absence, takes the place of sleep, especially at night. Now when she does sleep, it's in the afternoon, curled up on the living room sofa, or sitting in front of the computer in her office. Sitting, yes. As if sleep, a bird with large black wings spread open, were swooping down on her, flooring her. She doesn't know how many pounds she has lost. About twenty. She's a shadow of her former self. Her clothes float on her; her hair is dull; she has bags under her eyes.

She tries to occupy her mind. That's what she would recommend to her patients. She advises them to read, study, knit, keep a journal, anything. Occupy the mind, above all; do not remain idle. The paper, for example, that she has to give at the University of Washington in Seattle in September. The Department of Women's Studies is holding a conference; she was so happy to be invited. Every day, every night, she goes into her office, turns on the computer, opens a book, tries to think about it. She's even written a few pages. Nothing worthwhile. It's as if there is no more room in her head for ideas. But she tries. She forces herself to keep a few threads of her life. Otherwise the earth could open up and swallow her up as well.

The boys have had their baths, put on their pyjamas; they're with their grandmother in the living room. Florence hears the murmur of the television. She doesn't interfere. She only insists they not watch detective series. Because, those series, even if the police win — and they don't always — invariably begin with a murder. She doesn't want them to think that a murder … that a murder has taken place. Sometimes you see girls lying on an autopsy table, very young girls. You see their swollen faces, hear words like "sexually assaulted," "mutilated." Fanny was crazy about those series, especially the one with a hero called Dante Sullivan. She wanted to become an expert in forensic medicine, like him. Florence freezes. She has just thought of her daughter in the past; she forbids herself to do so. Her eyes fill with water.

A sweet smell — muffins, cookies — floats through the house.

Robert has created a website, loads of people send emails, think they have recognized Fanny here or there, in the most improbable places. Mediums offer their services. Gullible fool, he follows the trails. They all lead to dead ends; at the end the walls are cold and grey and hope vanishes. He's started to work again, but his heart is no longer in it. He too has bags under his eyes, a leaden complexion. Florence knows he goes to pedophile sites; perhaps he'll see Fanny in a clip, a photo. He says that thousands of children are involved in those goings-on. Tens of thousands. You have no idea. She does. She doesn't want to see him doing that. Those sites are the cesspool of the world. She says: "You're corrupting your soul. You won't forget those images." He nods his head, replies he must save his daughter, will go get her wherever she is. At the bottom of the cesspool, if necessary.

The entire family is shattered.

For now, Florence is in her office, blankly staring at the computer screen. "Known and Ignored: Women in History," is the theme of the conference in which she's agreed to participate. Before the events. She clings to it, the conference is her lifeline. She's received a draft of the program. It's there, on the screen, the panels, papers, sessions. She knows they'll talk about two exemplary figures of the female rebellion, Flora Tristan and Sofia Perovskaïïa. Perovskaïa in St. Petersburg. Florence had in fact just been reading about her that day, the day of the disappearance. An anarchist hanged for her role in the assassination of Czar Alexander II. She wonders if anyone thought of Charlotte Corday; her name doesn't appear on the list. Heroine or visionary? The line between the two is not always clearly drawn. She'd like them to talk about Charlotte Corday, guillotined at age twenty-five — André Chenier had written a poem for her. There's a paper on the Marquise du Châtelet, who was treacherously nicknamed "Madame Voltaire," or else — more treacherously — "Madame Newton Pompon du Châtelet," one of those learned women people make fun of, as if, for a woman, to be learned was the height of ridiculousness. Mistress of Voltaire, translator of Newton. And another on Christine de Pisan, of course. She has read books on all those women. A portrait of the beautiful and wise Christine, with her writing case, adorns the wall of her office in the prison. The prisoners said she was beautiful. The first woman known to have earned a living from her pen, Florence explained to them, to raise her three children. They nodded, admiring. *La Cité des dames.* That's the title of Daphné's latest CD — Fanny swears, swore only by her. Scholars classify Christine de Pisan next to Dante among the major writers of the Middle Ages, Previously, only scholars knew her. Now, prisoners hum her ballads *"Seulette suis et seulette veux être"* — All alone I am, and all alone I want to be — they find that beautiful. The CD has just come out Does Fanny hear the song where she is? Feminist even before the word existed, and at a time being a woman, well. You only have to think of the despair of the unfortunate women when they had the misfortune to give birth to a daughter. Repudiated, scorned. Called all sorts of names: mediocre, incapable, incompetent. A daughter! Anne Boleyn had paid for that misfortune with her head. Florence likes — liked — history. Had she not become a psychologist, she would have been a historian. She wonders sometimes if she hasn't missed her calling. New films play out in her head. Her life in a past or future that does not exist. She'd teach in a CEGEP, a private college, a university; she'd have another husband, Philippe or Pierre, a history professor like herself, or a literature professor, or else they'd be researchers, both immersed in unintelligible writings. They'd have another type of discussion, another way of making love, more tender or more passionate or more perverse, other children, a daughter whom they'd perhaps name Fanny, or Flora, or Natacha, a daughter who wouldn't have run away, because her father, more understanding, less authoritarian, would have allowed her to spend her vacation in Montreal with her friends. This evening, Florence's heart would be light as she prepared her presentation for the conference. If she'd had boys, they'd be in bed; her daughter would be listening to music in her room, she'd send messages to her innumerable friends on Facebook. Would chat online. Pierre or Philippe would be at home, he too, another house. He would enter her office, place the frothy bowl of café au lait near her, and ask: "Everything going the way you want?" A kiss on her neck, one near the temple. If he had a moustache, she would say, laughing: "You're tickling me." His lemony cologne would linger for an instant after he'd left the room. How life would be if it were another life. Her female clients do that all the time. She stops them. No, she says, no. It's pointless, leads nowhere. Look at reality, call things by name. What life would be. Pedophile websites, vanished children would be news on TV. They, watching the news, would shake their heads thinking of the suffering of parents who have lost a child.

She wants a glass of wine, but refrains. She would have to see her mother, be subject to her critical gaze. Or worse, sympathetic. She already drank half a bottle at dinner. She lights a cigarette instead. She only smokes in her office, never in front of the children.

One hand on the mouse, she scrolls through the program, reads the names. A translator will speak about La Malinche, Cortés' interpreter — Florence doesn't know who that is. So many unknowns, ignored, swallowed by up history. Voices almost inaudible, shadows shifting at the bottom of dungeons. So Hernando Cortés had an interpreter. Forgotten. And his own name, venerated or held in contempt, is no longer unknown to anyone. A musicologist will draw a parallel between Clara Schumann and Cosima Wagner, both known, but for the wrong reasons — both gone down in history under their husband's name. *If people remember me, it will be under my own name, Jordan — that of my father, in fact. The children have both names, Jordan-Laframboise. Fanny hated that. She wanted to sign Fanny L. Jordan. I was flattered. Robert of course made a scene.*

A few books on the work table, within reach. The life of Renée-Pélagie, Marquise de Sade, an essay on daily life in pre-revolutionary France, and her own work, *The Missionary Instinct in Women: The Wish for Self-Destruction*. Published by Éditions Pensée nouvelle just a year ago. An eternity. Fanny's exuberant pride when she held the book in her hands. The name of Florence Jordan in red letters on the cover, the small black and white photo on the back cover. "Mom, you're famous!" A heartfelt cry. They were still close a year ago. Florence had planned on writing a sequel, drawing on history to establish a parallel between the same instinct in men and women. She had the title: *Missionary Instinct: Domination or Abnegation?* She thought of the men in cassocks, Jesuits and others, who had travelled the world, to unknown pagan lands, brandishing their crucifixes, lighting stakes. The ones who had gone with Cortés to Mexico, had gone to the heart of Africa,

China, Indonesia, Canada. She thought of the Crusades. Of the revolutionaries, anarchists — Perovskaïa and Charlotte Corday were exceptions. Ready to give their lives, no doubt, but why? In their case, the idea of power seems more or less inherent. Whereas other women ... "Through wanting to save, they lose themselves."

There is a passage that she could use for her paper, or for the sequel, if she ever starts writing again. She nervously flips through the book. It's there, almost at the end, on page 253.

The missionary has a heightened maternal instinct. For her, the offender — even the murderer — always represents the misunderstood child, the one in need of love. She believes she alone is capable of giving the child this love. The missionary becomes attached to alcoholics, drug addicts, and violent men. To justify them, she invents scenarios of abusive mothers, brutal fathers, and childish shame and terrors. Her heart fills with compassion; she wants to repair past injustices. These scenarios sometimes correspond to reality, understandably, and more than one murderer has had a pathetic childhood. But when it comes to serial killers, for example, does whether or not the scenario is true make their murders less odious?

Cora-Lee, Florence's American translator — they correspond regularly; the book is supposed to be published in English at the end of the summer — recently told her the story of a woman she knows, a divorced mother of two, who is moving heaven and earth to receive permission to marry, a recognized criminal on death row guilty of particularly cruel murders. This is not an isolated case. These women are more numerous than people think, writing to prisoners, going to visit them in prison. As if they all want to play the role of Sister of Mercy in *Dead Man Walking*. They call them pen pals, and that seems almost innocuous.

Do you realize, the translator had written, *that guy, Ruddy Wallace, perhaps you've heard of him, has killed — I'll spare you the gory details — teenagers who were more or less the same age as her daughter? This woman has two children, a girl and a boy, twins. Do you realize? People can say what they like; personally I find that indecent.*

Other scenes arise suddenly in Florence's head. Fanny leaving a McDonald's in Florida, a man in black following her. Fanny walking along a secondary road. Night has fallen. Does she want to go home? A car stops. The driver suggests she get in. She runs away, her feet bloody. Or else she gets in and is carried away by the night. But why did she leave there? In that McDonald's, she must have felt safe. Why didn't she phone? And they, why didn't they think of that, a McDonald's not even three kilometres from the condo? Why didn't they look there? The horror film must stop. Florence refuses to watch it. To see the ending. Monsters kill girls like Fanny, and women want to marry them. In February, a body was found in a forest in Virginia. A naked body, a teenage girl's. They thought of Fanny, and Florence's heart stopped beating. For how long? She doesn't know, but it stopped. The DNA didn't match. She is like a condemned woman whose execution has constantly been postponed. A naked body in a forest in

Virginia, a head in a garbage bag in Arizona, a mass grave near Victoria, on Vancouver Island, a child fished out of the Saint Laurence River. Sometimes she thinks: "Bring me a head in a garbage bag, a hand, a heart, a liver. Anything of hers. So I can bury her finally. So I can bury her. So I have a grave to place flowers on."

She doesn't want to listen to the news anymore, never wants to open a newspaper again.

The missionary is an abyss tormented by an unquenchable thirst for love. Inexplicably, she doesn't seem to need to be loved in return. Giving is enough to appease this need. She is, to quote an old Tuareg proverb, the "mother who prefers the baby before he's grown, the sick child before he's healed, and the one who travels before he returns." Her indulgence is limitless. If she herself has children, she tends to prefer her sons. With her daughters she displays a severity that is often obsessive.

But not her. She was never extremely severe with Fanny. The rules, the famous rules, Robert alone has decreed. He had — has — the impression he failed with his adopted daughter, Daphné. The baby that with his first wife — sterile — he went to fetch in China. She left school at age seventeen, now she dances. Ballerina, Robert thinks. Ballerina! Is he really that gullible? Florence can recognize a nude dancer when she sees one. Dozens have gone through her office. Each one with her story. And their stories buzz about now in Florence's memory. Some were scarcely nubile when they began. She imagines Fanny undressing in a cheap whorehouse, or in one of the select, posh clubs, on the Costa del Sol, on the islands, or on one of those giant liners that sail international waters, evading all laws. She's heard tell of them. Everything is permitted on those boats. She imagines — and doesn't want to — the obscene contortions. But no, Fanny's body is not obscene. It is slender, the body of a teenager with prominent shoulder blades, a touching sight to see. What is obscene are the eyes and hands placed upon her.

How to stop thinking of it? She closes her eyes that burn; Fanny is behind her eyelids. She opens them, looks at the screen, reads the names.

Cosima, Clara, Alma Mahler, all three great lovers — they do exist. Devoted, body and soul, to the glory of their men. In *Human, All Too Human*, Nietzsche criticizes the "wives of those artists who offer themselves as sacrifices." "My life consists of raising my children and copying out his scores in ink," Cosima wrote in her diary. "After the meal, we are happy to play a duet." Florence remembers that sentence; she used it in her essay. "Was it a life?" she asks. "Does love explain all? In wanting at any price to save a person, some women lose themselves. Others seem to forget that they exist." She, it must be acknowledged, is not a part of this select group of great lovers. Does she regret it? Nostalgic for a feeling she has never experienced: a great love? Perhaps more simply, she has never met the man she would devote herself to body and soul. Geniuses don't roam the streets. The wives of these artists were exemplary figures, of course;

they didn't experience degradation. Personally, Florence has rubbed shoulders with cases that are less, how to say — less exemplary: bikers' girls, prostitutes devoted to their pimps, and so on. Nothing but a miserable life.

Misfortunes — she has heard so many of them in consultation. Rape, incest, people beaten up, abuse of all kinds. She thinks of her daughter, imagines the worst. Dancing naked in a dive, exposed, soiled, bound hand and foot, wounded. She refuses to imagine it. Can't manage. Sometimes thinks she'd rather see her dead. She refuses to think of it.

～

A SOFT KNOCK ON THE door of her office. Jon, her brother, comes to see her every other evening, the way you visit a sick person. He enters, carrying a tray. It's like at the hospital, really. An orderly. All that's missing is the white coat. She feels bad-tempered and is angry at herself.

"Were you working?"

She nods. She no longer works. She pretends. And others pretend to believe that she's working. Everyone's playing a game.

He pushes away the ashtray filled with cigarette butts, places the tray on the table, glances at the books.

"Renée-Pélagie de Sade," she says. A woman ignored by history. People prefer to remember her husband."

"Sade. You're speaking of the divine Marquis?"

"The diabolical."

A small teapot and two blue china cups, a souvenir of a

trip to the Netherlands with Robert just before their wedding, when the future was still bright with promise — two muffins on a plate. In Amsterdam they conceived Fanny. They were coming out of the museum, the Rijksmuseum — she remembers the cats drawn by Gainsborough — they'd drunk a beer in a café, and the sudden desire, incredibly strong, risen up from so faraway, from the soul, it seemed. They'd almost run to the hotel.

"Mom tells me you didn't eat anything at supper."

She makes a gesture of impatience — to think that before, she was a model of patience.

"When I eat, I throw up."

He pours the herbal tea into the cups. "Camomile mint, you won't throw up. What did she make today?"

"Overcooked pasta, sauce out of a can. Jell-O."

He sighs. Their mother is not, and never has been, much of a cook.

"The muffins are right out of the oven. Carrot and date, orange-flavoured honey, whole wheat flour," he recites. "I made them from scratch. A recipe by Victor Karr. You know, the cookbook I was translating in December."

As if that changed anything. She's forgotten the sensation of hunger. And the other one, satisfaction. She's forgotten the satisfaction of desire. Because she doesn't have any more. She has only one. He's going to say she must keep up her strength; they've all been saying the same thing over and over for three months.

"I made other muffins for the children. With chocolate chips."

She says nothing. Not so long ago, she made muffins with Fanny, on Sunday mornings. Fanny played her CDs. "Oh! Listen to this one, Mom. It's my favourite."

"The conference organizers want the topic of my presentation. I've made my choice."

"I thought you'd said Lola Montès."

"I did, but I changed my mind. There was nothing missionary-like about her. And as you know, missionaries are my specialty."

"Mathilde — you know who I'm talking about? My friend Mathilde ..."

"The translator."

"She's going to the same conference as you. She's writing a paper on La Malinche, the Aztec interpreter of Cortés."

"The problematic of betrayal in translation or something like that. I saw her name on the program. I didn't make the connection with your Mathilde."

"She was in Mexico City in December. She was doing research on La Malinche, in fact. I talked to you about her."

"I forgot."

She forgets everything.

"A controversial character," he continues. "Fallen out of sight. An Aztec slave sold to the Mayas then sold again to Cortés's Spaniards. She took the side of her last master. In love with him, no doubt. How do you explain it, otherwise?"

"Not everything can be explained. Nor can love explain everything."

"Mathilde thinks she shaped the destiny of Mexico."

"As for Lola Montès, she was the mistress of the grandfather of Louis de Bavière, Maximilien. He was crazy about her, absolutely crazy. He'd given her a chateau. And then she ended up penniless, an old dancer in second-rate night clubs, in the southern U.S. In love up until the end with horrible men who exploited her. I find that type of fate touching. Cruel life. And La Malinche, how did she end up?"

"We don't know. Disappeared … Sorry."

This is a word that everyone's been avoided uttering for three months.

"Fanny had begun to read *Lolita*."

He averts his gaze. Talking about Fanny, especially with Florence, is too much for him. He no longer knows what words, what tense to use. The present or the past. The future? Even more absurd. Whatever the tense, the words always sound false.

"She was reading it in Florida. Robert was furious when he discovered the book. She left it on her towel. At the pool. Or else forgot it. She wanted, she wants to become a profiler, or work in a forensic science laboratory."

"Profiler, that's rather like following in your footsteps."

"More like those of her heroes. That famous Jaguar, you know. On TV. Métis, long hair, dark glasses, muscular. The kind that makes thirteen-year-old girls fantasize. Dante Sullivan.

He spends his time declaiming excerpts from *The Divine Comedy*."

He says nothing. He too has dreamed. His fantasy was called Stanislas, the type who sets naïve seventeen-year-old guys dreaming. Stan dressed in black, smoked gauloises, declared himself an anarchist, a direct descendent of Nechayev. He recited *The Catechism of a Revolutionary*. A mythomaniac. And he, Jon, repeated after him. *The revolutionary is a man condemned in advance; between society and him, there is war without mercy.*

You dream, then you awaken suddenly. The marks are still visible on his wrists.

"When she was little, she wanted to become a veterinarian," continues Florence.

He starts.

"She adored, she adores animals."

"Yes," he says. "Partial to goats."

"Passionate about them. She wanted to become a specialist in goats, do you remember? Always asked me for *Monsieur Seguin's Goat* before going to sleep. I must have told her the story at least a thousand times. At the end she would cry, "Run away, goat." Before the wolf arrived.

"She imagined the goat could win against the wolf."

"And when I told her the story of *Little Red Riding Hood*, she rooted for the wolf."

She stops, on the verge of tears. Narrows her eyes, breathes in deeply. Then: "It's going to be Renée-Pélagie," she says.

"What?"

"The Marquise de Sade. For the conference."

"Oh, yes. The Marquise, good idea ..."

Fanny's ghost is there, almost palpable; he feels it move about the room. *Later, I'll be a goat specialist. I'll have a flock, a hundred thousand goats. And a grey wolf as well, tamed. I'll give each one a name, Pâquerette, Frisette, Blondinette. The wolf will be called Loulou.* He'd answered "*Of course, Biquette.*" She was seven years old. Fanny is dead; he knows it, is certain. Her ghost is there; he feels its breath on the back of his neck. Florence knows it as well, impossible for her not to. The ghost is breathing on her cheek, her eyes are closed. "I just want her not to suffer," she whispers. "Not to have suffered."

He nods his head. "Eat something."

He's said it imploringly. Florence takes a muffin — still warm — brings it to her mouth. The sweet smell makes her nauseous. She puts it back on the plate.

"An innocent young thing at the beginning of her marriage. Renée-Pélagie, I mean."

What an effort she is making. What an effort to survive. Jon breathes — the ghost has moved away. For how long?

"I can imagine her surprise seeing the strange bird she'd married."

"The innocent young thing quickly transformed into a tigress. Rushed up each time her husband got into some new mischief, ready to defend him, showing her claws, each time he called for her support."

"You have to believe that she lóved him."

Florence shrugs her shoulders.

"Loved him? Perhaps. Apparently, yes, she loved him. Like your Malinche loved the conquistador. To her great misfortune. Or happiness. How do we know? I'm not in a good position to judge. I don't even know what love is."

"Come on."

"I assure you."

"In the end, who does?"

"It's a word."

"They're all words."

"If there were no word, would the thing exist? Would love exist? Would death exist?"

An awkward pause. Then: "Is your mind still made up?" he asks. "You haven't changed your mind?"

She shakes her head.

Because the unthinkable — she's forty-one years old, for her it is unthinkable — has happened. She's pregnant. Jon is the only one to know. A stupid accident. They haven't made love often in the last three months. One time. Her IUD had come out.

The appointment was made at the women's clinic. The procedure is to take place the following morning; Jon will go with her. She doesn't even want to discuss it with Robert. A pregnancy now, in her condition? In the condition he's in? Unthinkable.

"I'd feel as if I were trying to replace her," she says.

Jon has nothing to reply: they are like-minded. She lights a cigarette.

"I should have gone to Florida with you," he says finally. "You'd suggested it. I could have brought my work. You don't know how angry I am at myself."

He is a translator. In December he was translating a cookbook, *Recipes from the Ends of the Earth* by Victor Karr. It was a rush, as usual. It's always a rush. Now those details seem unimportant. Florence wanted him to spend Christmas vacation with them. He'd refused. He could have watched over Fanny.

"It wouldn't have changed anything. What do you think? That I didn't know how to take care of her?"

He had hurt her.

"I mean that ..."

"You could have. I could have. Everyone could have done differently; everyone has something to reproach him or herself for. I could have been at the pool with the children rather than reading on the balcony. Robert didn't have to race to the green the minute we landed. He could have allowed her to remain in Montreal; she wanted to so badly. I could have insisted, demanded. The boys could have stayed close to her. And she — she could not have stolen from her father, she could have admitted it to me, could not have run away. You know what? I hate her for having done that. She destroyed us all. You see what I've become?"

He nods his head. He sees.

"If she wanted to destroy us, she's succeeded. Thank you, Fanny."

THE OFFICE DOOR IS SUDDENLY flung open. Both boys in pyjamas — a hockey player for Jonathan, Harry Potter for Balthazar, Christmas gifts from the grandparents — are in the doorway, overexcited. They both speak at the same time.

"Mom, you smoke?"

"Mom! Come see, Mom!"

"Grandma wants you to come. Daphné is on TV."

"She's sitting on a funny chair. She's all in blue."

"She's going to win a hundred thousand dollars!"

8

PROVIDENCE, RHODE ISLAND, IN THE MIDDLE OF THE NIGHT

*And all those islands in shimmering
seas, tropical paradises ...*

*As if they all wanted to play
the role of Sister of Mercy in
Dead Man Walking.*

IT'S A QUIET NEIGHBOURHOOD IN Providence, near the university. The street is called Angell, a name that augurs well. Of course, Lovecraft lived on that street; that's where he created his monsters. But now he's dead, and his monsters with him. At least we hope so. Dentists, psychiatrists, craft shops, florists, delicatessens, cafés: you can find everything you want. It's a pleasant neighbourhood in which to live, where, on fine days, it's pleasant to linger — certainly not today — where it's nice to raise children. There's the giant skating rink nearby; people like to see the skaters glide in rhythm to the music broadcast over invisible loudspeakers, waltzes by Strauss and other very well-known tunes, there's the pretty park with a stream and white ducks, where you can picnic in the summer. Tree-lined streets: elms, maples, pines. The irresistible charm of New England. Visitors are unanimous: the East Coast has tremendous charm. They are right. The river is within walking distance. A well-to-do neighbourhood, no doubt, but unpretentious. It is in the smallest of the United States, Rhode Island. Its flower is the violet, its motto is *Hope*, and its past is closely linked to the American Revolution. Stately residences dating to the beginning of the last century, built of wood or brick, with gables, have been transformed into duplexes with modern kitchens and bathrooms. It's three o'clock in the morning, everything is asleep, everything is plunged into silence — a silence haunted tonight by the howling of the wind

Yet no, everything is not asleep. We can make out light on the second floor of one of those large houses. An insomniac?

Eva, Eva Williams — no relation to Roger of the same last name, preacher and Puritan, who founded the city in the 1630s when he and his flock fled persecution. She's forty-three years old, works in the university library where she began as a clerk and now is in the acquisitions department. She lives in this apartment with her children, Judith and Jeremy, twins. That is, one week out of two. Shared custody for the last five years. This week they're with their father, Steven, a few streets away. The son looks like Steven, athletic — he participates in national diving competitions — and blond; Judith takes after her mother, black hair, brown eyes. She too has the vulnerable look of short-sighted people. At age twelve she insisted on wearing contact lenses; it was that or nothing, "And if you refuse, too bad. I'll get run over crossing the street." Eva has given her own up. She suffers from chronic conjunctivitis. Her glasses have black, rectangular frames and her shoulder-length straight hair is parted in the middle. She is reminiscent of a singer popular in Europe in the seventies.

An almost normal existence. She shares custody of the twins with Steven; that's how it is now, times, customs have changed. Evolved, according to some. Is it better or worse? We don't know. The wheel keeps turning, you can't stop it. We follow the movement. We move forward with the hands of the clock of time. Life is not like it was in centuries past, when large residences housed families with their swarms of children, servants wore black dresses and white aprons, women received their friends for afternoon tea, and the piano would sit imposingly in the living room; today, it's the television. Of course, all the city's memories are certainly not idyllic. Episodes that are nothing to be proud of — slave trade, organized crime — taint its memory. We are not, have never been, in a valley of roses. Paradise is a nostalgic hope;

we believe we remember it without ever having known it; paradise is an illusion. The history of cities is like the history of the world, of humanity. No history is moral, we're all built upon ruins, flowering on mass graves. The cries, they say, remain imprisoned for a long time in the stones; when we pay attention, apparently we can hear them. We're built upon these stones, upon these cries. Our houses moan and so do our bones, especially at night.

It's three o'clock in the morning; Eva feels as if she hears them — what a racket. She's still dressed, in black: wool pants and a wide-ribbed sweater. At her neck is a small chain on which she has strung silver ring of Ruddy's that is too large for her. It came in the envelope with his last letter. Ruddy Wallace, a prisoner on death row in Florida. They've been corresponding for three years.

Outside, the rain has stopped, but the wind still howls just as forcefully; it pounds against the bare-branched maple, as if determined to throw it to the ground. The poor thing resists as best it can. Its branches crack eerily; you'd think you were at Wuthering Heights. Perhaps the cries of people who have met their end cruelly take shelter in the wood of the trees? The moon is conspicuous by its absence, hidden behind the clouds at the back of the black sky.

There have been many unexpected visits this evening. Two, in fact. But that was still two too many. Reverend McBain showed up after supper, and later, Steven. A procession, really, these men who appeared out of the storm, downcast, severe, shivering, mouths full of reproaches and admonitions. She didn't need that.

She had made a walnut cake; she likes to cook when she comes home from work, especially on cold evenings. Then she concentrates on the recipe, doesn't think of anything. The sweet smell still lingers in the house. She'd just taken it out of the oven when McBain rang the door. What did he want? He'd heard a rumour, wanted her version of the facts. She served coffee. When she finished speaking, he shook his head, looking concerned. "I'm afraid you're overestimating your strength, Eva." She's not overestimating.

"But Christ pardoned all offences. On the cross, he promised heaven to the thief who would share his suffering," she'd replied — words she hadn't anticipated.

"Christ?" He raised his eyebrows "I'm not sure I understand. What are you seeking? To be crucified? To save the world?"

"We all can be saved. It is written."

He had looked at her, severe, almost scandalized. "Pride is the first sin." He saw her as too proud. Perhaps she is.

"Think," he repeated to her as he left. His tone had softened. He placed a hand on Eva's shoulder. "God does not ask so much of us. He does not demand the impossible from us."

"What would you know?" she'd almost asked. "What would you know about what He's asking me?" She'd refrained. "Our motto is hope," she'd murmured. He'd nodded his head without answering. He wrapped his scarf around his neck, buttoned his coat and raised his collar, donned his hat. Outside it was a miserable, just below freezing, well below with the wind-chill factor, almost a record for the spring equinox. It was the tail end of a hurricane that had raged a bit earlier in the week in the Caribbean. Or was it somewhere else? For a few years, hurricanes have been following one another at a disturbing rhythm. Some visionaries see in this acceleration early warning signs of the end of the world. Others claim that our mistreated planet is taking its revenge.

Eva handed him his gloves. "I will think it over," she promised. But she has no more time to think. When she opened the door, the wind swept into the house. Bent over — the poor man is not in the first flush of youth — one hand holding his hat, Reverend McBain headed toward his car, parked in front. When the headlights came on, Eva thought for an instant she was seeing the empty eyes of a ghost open onto the night.

SHE HAS A HEADACHE, a sharp pain behind her eyes. It went very badly with Steven. He stayed two hours, slamming the door as he left. The vibration is still echoing in Eva's bones, mixed with the moaning of the wind.

That's why she's not sleeping.

The television is on. War zones, buildings in flames, injured people on stretchers or lying in the dust, always the same succession of horror and misery. Eva muted the sound; the images themselves are sufficient; commentary would be superfluous. In the end, what do the names of the cities and countries, the number of victims matter? It's all interchangeable and while the names of the cities and countries change, in all languages cries and moaning resemble one another. Suffering is the same everywhere — an abscess festering on the face of the world.

She cut the sound, put on a CD — Erik Satie. In order to calm the night, the blow dealt to the table, the glasses that trembled, the door slammed.

Her decision is made, her word given: she'll marry Ruddy Wallace. They can say what they like, lecture her, admonish her, beseech her, threaten her. She must. It was not an easy decision. She'd thought a long time before making it. Ruddy is on death row in the Florida State Prison. He's given himself the name of Thoth, god of the shadows in ancient Egypt. All recourse has been exhausted; all the appeals, rejected; only clemency from the governor remains. He won't get it, of course; his crimes are too horrible. He tortured and killed children. In Florida, the condemned can choose between lethal injection and electrocution. He informed her in a letter he would choose the chair — *Old Sparky*, they nicknamed it, almost affectionately, because it makes sparks. "I'll end up frying like Ted Bundy," he specified. Cynical until the end. Eva wants to marry him before the sentence is executed.

It was supposed to be a secret. But everyone knows, apparently. She had only talked about it to her sister Rose. And to the children; she had no choice.

Her close relations are desperate. Last week, that Cora-Lee whom she scarcely knows — Rose's friend's cousin, that's how rumours get around — sent her excerpts from a book she is translating. *The missionary has a heightened maternal instinct. The offender — even the murderer — always represents for her the misunderstood child, the one in need of love. She believes she alone is capable of giving the child this love.* Her sister brought up the troubles of pre-menopause. Hormonal changes, she believes, makes certain women lose their sense of moderation. They get carried away, act on impulse, and sometimes ruin their lives — and those of their close relations. But it isn't that. She's in her right mind. And she has her periods regularly — no pre-menopause on the horizon.

"You're an intelligent woman. Balanced," her minister said to her. "Think of your children." She's been thinking of them since they were born. "Don't saddle them with a burden they won't be able to carry." Last week Judy cried, "If you do that I'll die of shame." Die. Jeremy doesn't seem to understand either. But the burden she carries alone.

AS A CHILD, EVA SPENT every summer in Nantucket with her family. That's where she conceived a project to visit every island on the planet. She began cutting out photos from magazines — a solitary coconut tree, the red sun upon the sea. She memorized names. She read and reread *Robinson Crusoe*. A book for boys, people said, but she wasn't too fond of shepherdesses and their princes, or of blondes who slept for centuries in castles. Her idea of happiness was completely different: to be shipwrecked on a stormy night, wash up in the morning like a piece of driftwood on a shore, discover an island and — wonder of wonders — discover the island was uninhabited. Beginning the world again. Building her house little by little, one day the walls, one day the roof, up to the seventh. Like God, in the beginning.

Before her marriage, she'd travelled in Europe alone three summers in a row; jeans and a backpack, hair streaming down her shoulders. Three summers, three islands: Crete, Sicily, Ibiza. A Marcello, an Alex, sleepless nights on the beach with a bottle of cheap ouzo, her head heavy in the morning, good-byes on the side of the highway, then climbing into the packed bus. She was afraid of nothing. The word "freedom" had the meaning she gave it. Today, it has another. The words remain the same; it's only the meaning that changes.

The fourth year she went to Iceland and met Steven at summer solstice. Three months later they were married. Other journeys followed; they made them together: Margarita, Guadeloupe, Paradise Island, St. Lucia, Newfoundland. They went to the Marquesas Islands; Eva wanted to see Gauguin's tomb and his "House of Pleasure" on the Island of Hiva Oa. Then it was Hydra, in the footsteps of Leonard Cohen and his *Beautiful Losers*. They planned Nordic odysseys, Ellesmere, Elsinore, declaiming speeches from *Hamlet*. Bundled up in parkas, snowshoes on their feet, exploring virgin areas, where they say the last infinite spaces can be found. But the twins were born. They remained in New England.

They divorced when the children were seven. That year she visited the Leeward Islands. Her heart wasn't in it. The following year, she was a little less sad. She spent a month on the Isle of Man.

The last journey was to Corsica, three years ago.

After that, she understood that she too was an island; it was time to explore herself. There are things and causes that are greater than we.

She decided to correspond with a condemned man. She chose the worst, the most cruel, Ruddy Wallace, and that's why she chose him. A question of an ordeal, of redemption. In her head it is very clear. Only she can't find the words to explain it.

The plane ticket has been bought, the date set at Florida State Prison. In three weeks, she will marry Ruddy Wallace. She wonders if he'll be in his orange uniform. The one he was wearing when she visited him, once, two years ago.

But the marriage is just symbolic. What do they think? She's not going to screw the monster in his cell. It's a gesture. A gesture of compassion. Amid the shouts and cries of rage. Weapons of mass destruction, ultimatums. A gesture of compassion. While war brews, while, on TV, you see bodies fall in slow motion. Going to the limit.

STEVEN HAD BURST OUT OF there, a gust of wind, thunder. The noise of the door slamming continues; it's slamming inside her. No, it's the blood coursing through her veins, raging; it's her heart pounding.

Live out your neurosis. Live out your neurosis; "I'll ask for custody of the children. And get it. You'll never see them again." Steven said that to her, teeth clenched, before slamming the door. *In another century, I'd have been a saint. Today I'm overly proud, unbalanced, pre-menopausal. A neurotic.*

The world is sad. War thunders, troops are massed at the borders, missiles are ready to be launched. The predator watches his prey. *I'm descending to the bottom of the cesspool, torch in hand.*

Death on the move. I see the corridor where you move toward your destiny. Yes, death is on the move. And love?

Perhaps it's like paradise, an illusion. It's a mirage, like the horizon that recedes. We believe we remember. We keep on seeking it.

The road is long.

～

LET US LEAVE ANGELL STREET and Eva William to her morose cogitations. She has made a decision and will not budge; no one can do anything about it. Everyone lives out their destiny. We will not judge her. That's how she wants to explore her island. Well, let her do it, at her own risk and peril. Missionaries have been travelling throughout the world since the dawn of time, with their good news and their crosses.

Outside, the wind is raging furiously; let's hurry. Two other insomniacs await us a little further on, on Benefit Street, this time. And the atmosphere is scarcely any more serene in that house. But what's going on tonight? The monsters of Love-craft, Cthulhu, Azathoth and others, slimy, sprawling, evil, have they risen up from their abysses to torment the living?

We are at the home of Steven, Eva's ex-husband, the father of the twins. He's just come in. He has exhausted his reserve of patience; he's had enough. He awoke Bea, his companion — Salvadorian, fifteen years his junior. Now they're in the kitchen, he's drinking beer, she, tea. The door is closed; they don't want the children to hear.

"She's completely nuts," he fumes. "She spoke of Christ on the cross, a Sister of Mercy in that movie, you remember the movie, and of a guy in Spain, one Mañara, who, after a youth of debauchery, devoted the rest of his life to the poor. According to her, he took them down from the gallows, to go bury them. It happened in the 1600s, can you imagine? She's obsessed with his story, wants to be like him. You think you know someone and then bang. Nothing, *nada*, *nichts*. It's like talking to a stranger."

Bea nods her head. She'll certainly admit that Eva is unhinged — in fact, has always known it — but demanding custody of the twins is another story; she's not sure she agrees. That is, she is sure of the contrary. As it was, when she'd met Steven, he'd undergone a vasectomy and she, who would have liked to have children, had to resign herself. In the name of love, what won't people do? She's not even thirty; is that a life? These two are fourteen, a difficult age. With Jeremy, things are okay, but the girl! Constant confrontation. This evening for example. They almost had a fight over nothing: the impossible girl had left her damp towel on the bathroom floor, the bottle of shampoo and tube of toothpaste open. She takes her for a slave, no more, no less. As for the meal of chicken, rice, salad, and peas, she barely touched it. You should have seen her picking at her food, with that disdainful expression. And Steven is basically never there. He's always working, renovating houses; the entire city is fighting to get him. So who'll be stuck with all the chores? She shudders in advance.

"*Cariño*," she begins.

Then she falls silent. But did she say or only think it? *Cariño*. Darling. How to explain to him without him flying off the handle? Besides, he's not listening. He's continuing to rant and rave. He's roaring like the wind.

"Apparently Madame is looking for meaning in her life! Meaning in her life, when she has two children."

"Exactly, while we're talking about the children ..."

"They like you. Fortunately. The transition will be less difficult for them."

So. Less difficult for them. Her opinion will not be asked. From now on, chores, humiliations every day of the year. She could say no and go away, but where? Not that she's staying with Steven for the house. Mind you — it counts, a house. Useless to pretend otherwise. She had imagined another life, for sure. Children, that is, her own children, travel. He had done all that with the other one.

"Meaning in her life, I ask you! If she needs to devote herself so much, let her work in a hospital or do something else. There's no shortage of good causes. But no. She'd rather marry a monster. Thoth. Really. You'd think you were in a novel by Lovecraft. You haven't read him and nor have I, but I know he created hideous characters with names like that. Slimy, with tentacles, hidden at the bottom of the water. She's out of her mind, obviously. You know what she told me? She wants to explore her island. What nonsense."

"Her island?"

"That's how she talks now. She's an island. She must see things through. Better to be deaf than listen to that. Yet I tried to understand."

"Perhaps she's entered a sect."

"One more reason to take the children away from her. Apparently there are three forms of love and she has just reached the third. Selfless love. What rubbish I've had to listen to tonight!"

He finishes his beer. Bea rises to fetch him another. "As far as I see, maternal love no longer enters into her priorities."

"Nor mine," murmurs Bea, her back turned, head in the refrigerator. *Nor mine; I don't want your children either.*

"What did you say?"

She uncaps the bottle, returns toward him.

"Nothing," she says. "I didn't say anything."

This is how the night will continue on Benefit Street, in Providence. One fumes; the other nods her head.

~⌒

THE LAST INSOMNIAC IS JUDY, in her room. She has told her father although she'd promised to keep the secret. And now, tragedy. She heard him when he came in. He woke Bea up; they went into the kitchen. She heard his voice. On tiptoe, she went halfway down the staircase, pricked up her ears. Words floated up to her. "Completely nuts." "Entered a sect." "Take the children away from her." Around her, the world collapsed. She returned to her room. Now she's trying to read a book. The story takes place in Russia, when there still were tsars, princes, and princesses. These are called Igor and Natasha; they're drinking tea in a palace. Perhaps it was better back then.

As for Jeremy, her brother, he's asleep. Good for him. At least there is one person asleep in this family. And if he is dreaming, we know not about what.

9

IN A COTTAGE IN
DEVONSHIRE, AT TEA TIME

It is love. And here are little girls immersed in storybooks,
girls in front of the mirror. Musicians tuning their instruments:
the dance may begin.

... It's motto is Hope.

IT IS A SACROSANCT MOMENT, tea time. A ritual from which
they have never departed. Scones, shortbread cookies, sandwiches — cucumber or watercress, cheese, tuna with minced
celery and mayonnaise, very fresh white bread — buttered
crumpets, lemon curd, three cakes, one light, one with fruit,
one dark, in thin slices on an oval service plate, strawberries
— fresh in season, or, like today, frozen — with a bowl of
Devon cream. The tea is Earl Grey — leaves, never bags;

Mummy would turn over in her grave — left to brew for exactly five minutes in the silver teapot. The Royal Doulton china service — their parents received it as a wedding gift, not a single piece is missing — has a tiny rose pattern. The tablecloth is percale, the napkins embroidered with their initials, their rings are ivory — yellowed, but genuine, like everything else in this house. A grandfather was high-ranked in the army, an avid big game hunter, who had had a career in Africa back when elephants weren't an endangered species. Trays are prettily set out on the coffee table in the living room. Teapot, small plates, cups and saucers, napkins and spoons wait on the sideboard. Everything is exactly the way Mummy used to do it, according to immutable rules that seem to have been decreed by Queen Victoria herself. Yes, the way Mummy used to do it. Or almost. When Sir Roderick — Dad — was present, they preferred to take their high tea in the dining room, and more serious, more substantial, savoury food was served: York ham, cold roast beef, thinly sliced tongue — Hope Mary thoroughly detested the idea of eating tongue. Along with three varieties of mustards, a dish of chutney, stilton, and old cheddar also had their place on the table, as well as the two cut glass decanters, containing port and sherry. But he wasn't there often. He had an important position in the county magistrate. He was a coroner, which kept him busy. Crooks, forgers, pimps, murderers and other transgressors weren't any more out of work in England than in less civilized countries, and not more in those days than today.

Kitty, an obese seventeen-year-old spaniel, is snoring on the flowered sofa. The years and the pounds weigh so heavily on him — he is indeed a boy despite his name — that the poor thing can hardly walk nowadays.

It is raining. It's been raining since this morning and doesn't seem to want to stop. Spring equinox. The garden, their pride — they grow subtropical species there, magnolias and camellias — is for the moment but a promise. In summer, when it explodes with colours and smells, it looks the way we picture Eden before Adam and Eve lost it. And for only an apple.

Hope Mary moves away from the window. Today the landscape is sad. She tightens her cashmere shawl about her.

Philip is late. What is he doing out in the rain? He must be walking along the seashore. We are in Torquay, which they rightly call — the climate is milder here than elsewhere in the country — the English Riviera. Yet with this rain — more of a drizzle than a shower, it's even more treacherous — he could get a cold. And in his case, colds most often degenerate into bronchitis. Despite his doctor's repeated advice, he refuses to quit smoking — a pipe rather than cigarettes, fortunately, yet it still can't be claimed to be good for the health. At least he doesn't smoke in the house. The smell of smoke makes her nauseous, as he knows. She put up with her father's cigars long enough.

But now he's late. He has surely lost track of time; he's so absent-minded. He knows full well she likes them to greet guests together; she's told him so at least a hundred and fifty times. Today they're expecting two: the Tuesday ones. Rose, the cook, has prepared everything; now she's gone. Hope Mary gave her the evening off.

She sits down next to the spaniel who scarcely moves a muscle, and takes a little cucumber sandwich — her favourite. Philip is her brother; they've been living in this house since they were born here. She, at least, has never left it. Philip married an Irishwoman about twenty years ago. Margaret, skinny — Philip described her as slender and exuberant, while Hope Mary called her talkative, over-excited, was an archivist at the BBC. He had just begun there as a news writer. A bizarre and particularly powerful virus had killed the unfortunate woman, returning from a journey — the honeymoon they'd taken in India. Life too often has a cruel sense of irony. On the outskirts of Madras, Margaret suddenly came down with nausea and vomiting. By the time they returned to the city, she was delirious with fever. At the hospital, they injected her with a massive dose of an antibiotic or something else, Philip doesn't know what, but he's sometimes thinks that was what killed her. Perhaps she was allergic. Or they used a poorly sterilized needle — how can anyone know? The convulsions had begun in the plane bringing them back to England. A long journey, especially when a person is in great pain, as Margaret was. Her beautiful lips had flecked with foam, her beautiful green eyes rolled upwards. She succumbed two days later, at the summer solstice, not regaining consciousness. No memorable word was uttered at the moment of her last breath. All her hair, her red hair — Philip said Venetian blonde — had fallen out, her rosy complexion had become sallow. That's what remains of our beauty; we are finally so little: death takes perverse pleasure in reminding us. Everything is but vanity. Doctors shook their heads, completely at a loss. The autopsy revealed nothing. In desperation, they concluded she was bitten by an unknown insect; there was a suspicious mark on her left ankle. Such incidents occur more often than people think.

Twenty-seven years old is unquestionably too young to die. Phil was inconsolable. Still today Hope Mary remembers his red, swollen eyes; she would never have thought a man could cry so much. Their father had never shed a tear in front of them, and yet God knows in his profession he had seen tragedy. Incapable of returning to work where he had met Maggie, Philip let himself waste away; he nearly followed his beloved to the grave. Hope Mary convinced him to return to live in their childhood home, at least for a time. Now he no longer cries. Not that he is consoled. But life has reasserted itself, as well it must. He has had adventures, liaisons, some short-lived, others less so. Hope Mary has had hers, romances in her case: to each his own secret garden. It never disturbed their harmony — they each occupy their own floor of the house; she the second, he the third. They share the main floor for common activities, tea at five o'clock among them.

They both write, but only under her name, Hope Spencer

— she dropped the Mary. Philip refuses to be associated openly with the undertaking. Romance novels are not a man's business, he says. When people ask him how he earns his living, he replies that he invested his money wisely; he has a private income. Which is true in a way — their royalties may be seen as a goldmine.

It was she who first had the idea. A kind of catharsis, colon therapy: he was too sad. He spoke of the deceased constantly; it was becoming an obsession. Hope Mary was afraid he would lose his mind. To tell the truth, he was making her crazy; she couldn't take it anymore. So she suggested rewriting Maggie's story — making it into a novel. Philip had only one condition: that they keep their first names. They kept them. Of course they changed the ending. No fatal virus this time, no hideous insect, unsightly convulsions, or bald head, but a love story that ended in a blaze of glory.

It took them four months. Little by little Philip experienced a new sense of purpose; he even took an amazing amount of pleasure in the exercise. It was she again who suggested trying to have their manuscript published. Success. The satisfied publisher asked for more. Since then, they write two, sometimes three a year. The formula is always the same, but at least it is tried and true. They meet, fall in love, face opposition, then love triumphs. Besides, in fairy tales too the formula is always the same. Shepherdess and prince, toad and princess, just a kiss and love triumphs over adversity. Children have been asking to be told these stories for centuries. Seen in this light, men — women, let's say — are eternal children. They want to dream. Can we blame them? Life, real life, is already hard enough. Terrorist attacks, famines, natural catastrophes, epidemics, not to mention crimes of all kinds; you just have to open a newspaper, watch the news on TV. None of that is in their books. Women — men too, it's just that they express it differently, read the same books, but deny it — need hope and wonder, the novelist sees things that way. Humanity needs comforting. It's not for nothing that Hope Mary was so named at birth. Her destiny was cast. Life is sad, yes, she says, but in our novels, injustice is repaired. And if our stay down here too closely resembles hell — purgatory, really — it behoves us to recreate paradise. Philip thinks like her. For them, writing is almost a mission.

Translated into all sorts of languages they don't know, Mandarin, Finnish, Georgian and others, their books sell well, on average, tens of thousands of copies. They earn their living more than honourably, but nevertheless live frugally. They could afford a half dozen servants, but make do with a cook, cleaning lady, and a gardener during the summer months. The rest of their earnings are generating interest in the bank: something for a rainy day.

Most of the time, it is she who conceives the scenario. Philip finds the places, conducts the research, and writes the descriptions of the scenery. Geography was his favourite subject in school. First names and last names, gastronomy, local customs: all that is his domain. Hope Mary describes the dances, dresses, faces, houses, etc. They write the dialogue together.

Sometimes he suggests the place and she creates a story around it. Or it's the other way around; she has the embryo of a story, he describes the decor.

He chooses idyllic sites, Mykonos, the Marquesas, Corsica — he has a weakness for islands. Green Ireland, of course, Cornwall, the Isle of Man. Provence, many times — but never the same city — great mythical Russia — that of the czars, they cherish it, imagining it as both sumptuous and terrible — the Golden Horn, China with its mysteries. India, never. Philip doesn't even want to remember the country exists. In *Sayonara Peach Flower*, the story of an Osaka geisha with whom the heir to one of Japan's greatest fortunes falls madly in love, he described a tea ceremony in minute detail. Tea is his thing, his fantasy. He did it again in *The Desert Fiancée* — this time the story was set in the Sahara; the lovers are called Ahmed and Aicha, the tea was mint, served with honey and cornes de gazelle and other confections made with honey. Then again in *Serenade at the Winter Palace* — St. Petersburg, Igor, Natasha, Morello cherry jam, smoked black tea from a samovar.

At least it was like that before. But for two years now they've had assistants. Not that the well has run dry, far from it. That type of well does not run dry. But time has passed; they tire more quickly, write with less enthusiasm. Besides, Hope Mary is not comfortable with the computer, and publishers now have all sorts of requirements; she doesn't want to be bothered with fonts, counting characters and all that. And no one lives forever, so they have to make sure someone takes over, train those who will carry on. Because these novels, whatever people may think, are not that easy to write. They hired two people to help them, as many authors do without anyone being the wiser. Ghost writers. The French call them *nègres* — negroes. Hope Mary finds that name racist. It would never occur to her to describe her assistants in that way. Besides, one of the ghost writers — she prefers that — is a person of colour, a young Ugandan, Lucie. She writes and pronounces her name, awkwardly perhaps, in the French style; Lucie's family managed to flee the odious dictatorship of Idi Amin Dada, a tyrant who, among other things, gave himself the title of King of Scotland, go figure. Another furious madman who tortured his country. He's dead now, good riddance. Eternity will not be long enough for him to suffer for his sins. Providing something like eternity exists.

Lucie was born in England; she studies languages at Exeter. The other ghost is William, a florist by trade, in his thirties, very refined. Philip suspects he is gay. Hope Mary merely finds him romantic.

FIVE MINUTES TO FIVE, THE door opens; voices resonate in the vestibule. A burst of laughter: Lucie, who spends her life laughing. It's almost annoying in the end, this joviality, this levity at any and every occasion, most of the time without rhyme or reason. Not everything is funny in life, after all.

Philip claims she's laughing because she's nervous, intimidated. Perhaps. Hope Mary has another concept of timidity.

The three enter the living room at the same time. "Coming home, I ran into our friends," explains Philip, eyes bright. "We were coming from opposite sides." Lucie — wearing black and white striped panty hose, a red turtleneck, a short denim skirt, and a dozen jingling bracelets, appearing a bit anachronistic in this old-fashioned setting, exclaims delightedly at the abundance of food. "I'm dying of hunger," she says immediately at the top of her lungs. "And crumpets! I love them! Wonderful Rose. Do kiss her for me." Kiss her! Hope Mary shakes her head. As if she would kiss Rose! Philip smiles indulgently. The appetite of youth — he too was insatiable way back when. William is more discreet. Hope Mary pours tea into the cups. Lucie places a buttered scone and a slice of cake on a small plate with a crumpet she has spread with a thick layer of lemon curd. She takes her tea with milk; Philip takes his with sugar. The two others prefer theirs plain. Philip pours himself a glass of Sherry. Everyone sits.

It's their weekly work meeting — brainstorming as they say.

Two more or less historical novels are underway. They're the ones that sell best. William is inspired by Georgiana, the Duchess of Devonshire, a character that for some time has become fashionable again. A movie about her has just been released, and a play is opening this very evening on Broadway. As for Lucie, she is devoting herself to the tormented idyll of a young Aztec orphan and a Spanish officer at the time of the Conquest of Mexico. She proposed the subject, and has just started.

Here's how they proceed: each Friday, William and Lucie send by email — one has to move with the times — the pages they've written. Philip prints them. Armed with a red pen, Hope Mary spends the next three days reading, commenting, correcting, and crossing out. Philip verifies the historical, and geographical details and gives his opinion. The following Tuesday, they meet to work. Always at teatime: may as well combine business with pleasure. The comments go down better with sandwiches and scones. And today, Hope Mary has added a decanter of sherry and glasses to the table. She has prepared some more or less caustic remarks and these small compensations or consolations will not be unwelcome.

In the case of the Duchess, Hope Mary has imagined the starting point: a kind of homage to the aristocrat who carried the name of their county. In 1803, Georgiana was forty-six years old, and had a punctured eye she camouflaged as best she could beneath a lock of hair. Her innumerable gambling debts — she had always been a compulsive player — have ruined her. A young painter rings her doorbell; he wants to paint her portrait. At first she refuses, but he insists; he sees her beauty beyond the wrinkles. It is this beauty of the soul he wants to immortalize. Gradually a tender rela-tionship develops between the fallen aristocrat and the future genius. She tells him of her tumultuous life, her love with the duke, a haughty man she married at age seventeen, and her friendship with Marie-Antoinette, the unfortunate queen of the French. The unsuitable episodes, notably the ménage à trois, and various other adulterous liaisons, Hope Mary prefers to conceal.

She takes a bundle of papers, gives a faint smile meant to be encouraging.

"My dear William, your last forty pages were almost perfect. Weren't they, Philip?"

Philip approves with a nod, then "I found some improbabilities," he says. "Minor," he specifies, in a good-natured tone. William nibbles nervously at a tuna sandwich. Despite the smile, the "almost" and the "minor" worry him. They always begin, she especially, by the positive. The bombshell — she again — does not take long to fall and often he must redo everything. He expects the worst. It's true that he lacks self-confidence. This is only his third collaboration.

"Certain sentences are too long," continues Hope Mary. "This one, for example. And it is one among many."

Hope Mary leafs through the manuscript, chooses one filled with scrawled comments and crossings out. William represses a groan: all that red, as if the page, lacerated with a knife, had bled. Hope Mary clears her voice, takes a sip of tea, then begins reading.

"*Outside, the autumn wind howled its long monotonous cry and Douglas felt a wave of compassion and tenderness was over him as he observed the Duchess, dressed in her water-silk dress the colour of* rain, *half lying on the cushions of the purple velvet ottoman, bathing in the warm light of the fire that hummed in the hearth, her chin resting in her palm, eyes lowered, in a pose both languorous and infinitely melancholic.*' I counted seventy-four words. That's too many."

"The Emperor Frederic made the same type of reproach to Mozart," remarks Lucie, vaguely ironic. "'Too many notes.' In the movie, do you remember?"

Her outspokenness sometimes verges on impertinence. Hope Mary looks daggers at her.

"Well perhaps the Emperor wasn't wrong. In any case, our readers are not accustomed to such flights. Our mission is to entertain people."

"Not put them to sleep," adds Philip.

"A dress the colour of rain is a stroke of inspiration," Lucie says. "But shouldn't we add something about the famous lock of hair that covers her punctured eye?"

Hope Mary takes a long breath. She must remain calm.

"We are trying to keep things simple," she continues. Between seven and fifteen words per sentence, twenty at the most, is our rule. We insist on that. This is not about adding, but about cutting."

"We are not the sort to show off," adds Philip. "We are neither postmodern nor ..."

"Short sentences reassure people; they follow the story without becoming confused. We can easily make four sentences with yours, William. *The autumn wind* — we know it's outside, the wind doesn't blow in the house after all — *howled its cry*. Period. Obviously it is long and monotonous. And even *howled its cry*, I'm not convinced. *The autumn wind howled*. Period. *Douglas felt* ... etcetera. I made a few cuts, tightened up where necessary. You'll see. Details, trifles, I assure you. Fortunately there was nothing irreparable. The place I don't follow you, though, is when you describe the duchess's ball gown. Canary yellow, really! Would a woman like her have worn yellow? And canary? With her rosy complexion, her hair verging on red ..."

"Venetian blonde," amends Philip.

"But in the portraits, the one by Gainsborough, especially, the most ... well, the most famous, the Duchess is wearing a pale yel ... yellow," William tries to justify a bit awkwardly: he stammers when he's anxious. "I took my inspiration from it for the ... the ... ceremonial dress."

"Perhaps, but in my opinion it's a mistake, an error in taste; anyone can make them, even a duchess. Besides, as you yourself say, it's pale yellow in the painting. In any case, green emphasizes her beauty more, you'll agree. Emerald green."

"That was Maggie's favourite colour."

Philip's eyes mist over for a moment. An awkward silence.

"There's something more serious," continues Hope Mary, unruffled.

"I'd take a drop of sherry," stammers William, desperate. What is she going to criticize him for this time?

"Of course, my friend. But why only a drop?" Philip fills a glass to the rim. "Directly from Jerez, private import. I'm sure you'll like it. Lucie?"

She smiles knowingly. "A drop for me as well."

She grabs a watercress sandwich, polishes it off in two bites, takes a second, cheese this time. The girl eats like a horse and hasn't an ounce of fat," Hope Mary thinks enviously.

"I'll have a dash, Philip."

They all raise their glasses.

"Oh, that makes me think of a joke," says Lucie. "You know what a sad woman replies when she's offered a drink?"

"Please, Lucie" interrupts Hope Mary. "We really don't have time for jokes. To return to our little problem, William, your way of describing the relationship between Georgiana and Marie-Antoinette brought me up. You seem to imply that … I know today we are both open-minded and I myself usually close my eyes to … We can forgive anything in the name of love, I agree, but, well, I'm afraid people will take the heroine for a lesbian. On no account do I want …"

"Didn't she have a ménage à trois with her husband and his mistress?" interrupts Lucie. "The mistress of both of them, if I am to believe what I've read."

"We are writing novels, not historical treatises."

"Besides, it hasn't been proven," says Philip.

Lucie insists: there are letters from the two women in which the allusions are more than clear. But Hope Mary settles the matter: Philip is right, none of that has been proven.

"At the time, people sometimes had an ambiguous way of pouring out their feelings in letters," she explains. "Let's be careful not to reach misplaced conclusions."

"Besides, dear Lucie, are the letters you describe even genuine? If you knew the number of fake documents in circulation," says Philip. "People really have no respect. Do you remember the forger arrested last year who imitated the writing of the greatest authors: Byron, Mary Shelley ..."

"And even if it's true, some things are better left unsaid," interrupts Hope Mary, who does not like to see him veer off topic. "In any case, here the plot concerns the growing love between Georgiana and the painter. Let's not confuse the issue. Speaking of which, I changed his name; Douglas sounds too harsh. Now he is called Shawn, which is gentler, more tender. Do you agree?"

Lips pursed, William nods his head imperceptibly. The question is purely rhetorical. Whether he agrees or not won't make a difference.

"I'd like you to go over the entire passage again, William. Emphasizing the intellectual affinities between the two friends, Georgiana's sorrow when she learns of the queen's dishonourable death. Led to the gallows in a cart, beheaded like a vulgar criminal. But don't dwell too much on the torture. We want our readers to be moved to tears, not horrified. You understand me, right?"

"Y ... yes."

"Do you have an idea for the ending?"

"I thought that she could ... die in his arms. In Douglas's ... Stephen's ..."

"Shawn's."

"Yes, Shawn. The arms of the painter. I already have a ... very moving scene in mind."

"Wonderful!" exclaims Lucie, her mouth full.

Her mouth full! This girl's manners are sometimes beyond belief. Hope Mary looks at her reprovingly. Lucie swallows, and then keeps going. "And after Georgiana's death, the portrait makes the painter famous. Evaluated at millions of pounds, exhibited at the National Gallery. We could even imagine a daring robbery afterwards. Masked thieves enter the museum one night and make off with the masterpiece."

"Believe it or not, it happened in real life," says Philip. "A man named Worth, or was it Ward? I don't remember, an American, in any case, had stolen a Gainsborough painting, in fact. Dad told the anecdote in his notebooks."

Their father, an insomniac, spent part of the night in his office writing about crimes and criminals, famous or not. He left about twenty bound notebooks, a veritable gold mine of information on the defects of humanity.

"Apparently the guy, a notable swindler, fell in love with the portrait; he kept it for about twenty years. He ended up getting caught by an ordinary bounty hunter. Well, maybe not ordinary, because it was Pinkerton, founder of the detective agency of the same name."

"Better and better," cries Lucie, enthusiastic. "Reality

surpassing fiction, I love the concept. So Georgiana continued to be loved madly across the centuries. We could write
a sequel. The thief's passion for the deceased Duchess. I can
already imagine the speeches. Like Heathcliff talking to Cathy's
ghost at Wuthering Heights."

William raises a hand. That was not how he'd seen things.
After all, he's the one who wrote the book; even if he doesn't
sign his name to it, he should have the right to take an active
role in it. But Hope Mary gets there ahead of him.

"Writing a series is out of the question," she decrees. "Our
readers won't follow it. They often buy our books in train
stations or airports and read them during their trip. All the
stories must be contained between two covers."

"It was just a suggestion," murmurs Lucie, resentful.

Then she falls silent. *One day, I'll write under my own name*,
she thinks. *And I too will be rich.* She now helps herself to
some strawberries and a heaping spoonful of Devon cream.
A hundred and fifty calories, at least. The glasses are empty;
Philip fills them. Hope Mary takes a cucumber sandwich.
William takes advantage of the lull to put in a word.

"This story of the ... theft of the painting has already been
to ... told," he says. "The ... the play, the play ... that is opening on ... on Broadway today. They talked about it in ...
in the *Ti* ... *Times Literary Supplement* last week. There is an
interview with ... with the author. Madame ..."

"Evanelli," completes Philip. "I read the article as well. In
the play, the thief is the infamous Moriarty. In reality he was

called Worth, Adam Worth; the name comes back to me now. I remember that Dad had recorded the fact in a notebook. He concluded with this sentence: '*Even the most hardened of hearts may be touched by grace.*' Our father was a great moralist."

"And that concludes the subject, I believe," says Hope Mary.

"As for having Georgiana die in the arms of the painter, I'm not sure," Philip intervenes. "Of course, we're playing with historic truth; we allow ourselves some liberties. I am afraid that in this case were a going a bit too far. That is not how the duchess died."

"How did she die, by the way?" asks Hope Mary.

"I don't know, but certainly not in the arms of a painter."

"Why not?" protests Lucie who has not regained her smile.

"First, because the painter did not exist," scolds Hope Mary, exasperated. "That must be sufficient reason."

"She must have died from an illness," says Philip. "Tuberculosis, perhaps. At the time, one person out of two had TB. I'll do some research. I'll have the answer next Tuesday, same time."

But Lucie digs in her heels.

"If we follow your reasoning, the young painter named Shawn never existed and Georgiana didn't meet him at the end of her life. The story is invented from start to finish. If we absolutely insist upon historical truth, I don't see the point in continuing."

"I've al … already written a hundred and twenty-three pages!" croaks William, dismayed.

The poor man seems on the verge of tears.

"Come, calm down, my friend," says Hope Mary. "No one is talking about abandoning the novel; after all the work it would be ridiculous. We just want to improve it. But Philip is right: we mustn't distort the facts too much. Embellish, yes, but within the bounds of plausibility. Here's what I suggest: let's change the heroine's first name; we'll call her, I don't know, Elizabeth or Julia. I prefer Julia. Let's make her a marquise rather than a duchess. Julia, an Italian marquise. Venetian, even, to make Philip happy. You'll find her a surname. And why does she have to die at the end? It's already distressing enough to have to pass away in real life. No, I think she could marry the painter instead. Let's make her ten years younger. Then she'll be thirty-six. Thirty-five, let's say, the prime of life for a woman. Her beauty is in full bloom. And let's age our bashful lover a bit. Thirty-one seems suitable to me. The age difference will not be too shocking. And the punctured eye, really. You know what I think? I find it rather uncalled for, if not to say sordid. If she was simply short-sighted? Very short-sighted? The gaze of very short-sighted people is touching, especially when they have brown eyes, as do most Italians. What do you think? You're good with the computer, William. These little changes won't take more than an hour or two of work."

Incapable of answering, he chews his sandwich, looking

glum. Too much mayonnaise; he should have taken water-cress. It's even worse than he'd feared. A few hours of work, she must be joking. She's never written if she believes that. What she's asking amounts to a complete overhaul, that will take him days — that is nights; in the daytime he works in his shop. Nights, then, even weeks. Brown eyes now, after all those passages in which he described the liquid sky-blue eyes of the heroine. And the final scene — the apotheosis, the epiphany — that he had imagined has just been scratched. The woman treats him like a slave, no more, no less. And neither of the other two have the guts to defend him. Alone in the arena like an ancient Christian facing the lions. No thumb lifted to save him. If he listened to himself he'd leave immediately. With the manuscript. But they have a copy.

"Bi ... anca," he stammers finally.

"Excuse me?"

"I prefer Bi ... anca. For the du ... the marquise. Bianca over ... Julia."

Hope Mary turns toward her brother. "Bianca ... Is that plausible? I mean was it a name people had at that time? It seems a bit too modern to me."

Philip shrugs his shoulder. "I believe I remember a few Italian noblewomen named Bianca. A Bianca de Medici, if I'm not mistaken."

"It is also a ... a character in ... *Othello*," adds William. "She loves Ca ..."

"Cassio," completes Philip, on the verge of losing patience.

"In that case, go for Bianca. Thirty-five years old, Italian, very short-sighted. And a marquise. For everything else I give you carte blanche."

At least there's that. They breathe. For William, the ordeal is over; now he can relax. He allows himself a scone with hint of cream — Rose makes some with raisins, others with figs. Usually he avoids sugars and lipids. His diet may not be very festive: whole grains, green vegetables, steamed fish, and skim milk, but it does have the advantage of being well-balanced. However, every once in a while — these scones are a sin. Plump and golden, crispy outside, moist inside. Exactly the way he likes them.

"SHALL WE LOOK AT OUR young Aztec?" Hope Mary now proposes. "Xannath, is that right?"

"It's pronounced 'Chanat.' It means 'vanilla flower' in Nahuatl," explains Lucie. "I found it on the Internet."

"Charming," approves Philip. "'Vanilla flower.' It's cool and sweet-smelling. Very evocative. I like it a lot."

"I hesitated. There was also Zanya, which means 'eternal.' Or Nayeli. That's 'I love you,' but in Mayan."

"We already had a Peach Flower, remember, Philip?" In the novel set in Japan. Wouldn't it be redundant? Besides, I wonder: does the heroine have to have an Aztec name? In the end, Aztec or Mayan, would anyone know the difference? Nayeli sounds better, I think."

Philip looks at her, exasperated. "Seems as if changing first names is becoming an obsession with you."

The criticism leaves her disconcerted for a moment. She regains her composure.

"Fine, I won't insist, Xannath, Chanat, whatever you like. I just ask you to make the meaning clear from the start, vanilla flower. Knowing it will make the name more appealing to our readers."

Lucie agrees, nodding.

"That's not the problem," continues Hope Mary.

She pauses, which does not augur well. Everyone holds their breath. You could hear a pin drop. Lucie reaches toward the plate of cakes, then thinks better of it. William drinks his last drop of sherry, sets his glass down on the table. Hope Mary pours herself tea.

"Would you like some?"

They all shake their heads. The tea must be lukewarm now, despite the wool cozy covering the teapot. Which is to say undrinkable.

"I'll speak frankly with you, Lucie."

"Don't bother, I get the picture," the girl interrupts. "You don't like it."

Philip intervenes.

"That's not what she said."

"I haven't said anything yet."

"But it amounts to the same thing. Your tone of voice …"

"Not at all," Philip intervenes. "Don't think that, Lucie. We like your project. Setting the story in Mexico at the time of the conquest is very original. A time and a place we'd not yet contemplated. And the research is well done. What you write is entirely credible. The description of the temple in Tenochtitlan, the flowers, plants, many-coloured feathers, and costumes. We feel as if we're there. My hat is off to you."

"Will you let me speak!?" Hope Mary explodes.

Disturbed from his dream, the spaniel starts, gives a small moan, then falls back asleep.

"The original idea was worthwhile, I grant you. But what you do with it ... First of all, can you explain to me how Xannath can fall in love with Don Fernando, the conqueror, after he massacred her entire family? I find that inconceivable."

"The Stockholm Syndrome," asserts Lucie. "It's been seen quite often. I'm not inventing anything."

"The Rape of the Sa ... bine Women," says William, coming to her rescue. "In Ancient R ... Rome. They fell in love with their ki ... ki ..."

"With their kids?"

"With their kid ... nappers."

"I know what the Stockholm Syndrome is, but Fernando is an oaf! Even physically there's nothing appealing about him. Come on, Lucie, would you succumb to his charms, personally? And when I say charms ..."

"My God, perhaps," she replies dreamily.

"Perhaps? Listen to how you describe him. *Black body hair. Hairy. His bull neck.*"

"Lucie probably wanted to give an impression of virility," says Philip.

"A caricature. And the massacre! She takes sadistic pleasure, I don't know what other words to use, in depicting tongues being pulled out, hands being cut off, feet being slowly burned, bodies hanged from branches of exotic trees, and more. We don't need all that!"

William trembles, almost chokes on a mouthful of scone.

"It's not even properly written," finishes Hope Mary, dealing the final blow.

A microsecond of stunned silence follows. It's the first time she's been so categorical; usually, she proceeds more tactfully. Philip hastens to intervene. "Come now, Hope Mary. Lucie's writing is no doubt colourful ... lively, I mean. Inventive. It's just that certain passages are a bit crude. The collection we publish in ..."

"They're barbaric. You yourself acknowledged that yesterday."

"The times were barbaric," Lucie justifies. "The conquest of America, of Mexico in particular, amounts to genocide; everyone admits that. I didn't invent it," she repeats.

"You didn't have to go into detail."

"Deep down I know what you think," Lucie murmurs. "Barbarity is in my genes."

"Not at all. Dear, dear Lucie, no, that's not true. You mustn't think that way. I forbid it. Neither my sister nor I are racists, you know perfectly well."

Now he is begging, whimpering. Hope Mary can't believe her ears. What's gotten into him? *Dear, dear Lucie.* Poor Philip, to hear him you could think he was in love with the damsel. He's almost pathetic.

For the moment the damsel in question seems frozen — unusual in her case, to say the least. She has lost her arrogance. And her appetite. She isn't eating anymore. She feels dizzy. Biting retorts buzz in her head. "You're the ones who don't know how to write. Your rules are completely outdated. All your sentences resemble one another. Between seven and twenty words; subject, verb, object. All your novels are carbon copies. What am I saying, novels? A bunch of inane little stories." She champs at the bit. She needs money to pay for her education and there's the rub. She has friends who work as servers in pubs, at night. She herself used to work as a cleaning lady, and then as a nurse's aide in a hospital. The work of ghostwriter is more rewarding, despite the injured feelings.

"A bit more sherry, Lucie?" suggests Philip. She shakes her head. "A little sandwich? A slice of cake?" Neither. But William extends his glass. Hope Mary sighs. If they continue drinking at that rate, soon they'll be rolling under the table, especially Philip. Since Maggie died, she's never seen him like this. Where is his composure? She feels as if her eyes are suddenly opening. She observes him carefully. He's smitten; no doubt about it, completely under her spell. Bewitched. She'd never noticed. *How long has this lunacy been going on*, she wonders? Perhaps the girl practices voodoo or casts other evil spells. Indecent, regrettable. She could be his daughter. But … Precisely. But what if Hope Mary is mistaken about her brother's feelings? Perhaps he's simply pining for the child, the daughter he never had. Many men, especially when they're over forty, dream of having one. The prospect of dying without progeny drives them to despair. He's forty-four years old, she, forty-six, the age they had given the duchess. She too thinks sometimes about the children she doesn't have. Life has gone by too quickly, youth has vanished. Writing took everything. All of a sudden she is weary.

"Do you have an opinion, William?"

He rolls his eyes, caught unawares. "I … I haven't … haven't even … read it," he stammers.

"You, Philip?"

"I think we should adjourn. We're all a bit tired today. The winter is dragging on and setting our nerves on edge … Lucie will rework her text. Right, Lucie?"

She doesn't reply.

"Lucie?"

"Yes. I'll rework it," she agrees, reluctantly.

She rises. The two men do the same. "I feel like walking a bit," announces Philip. Well, well. William takes his pages. Hope Mary hands hers to Lucie. "I don't need them," says Lucie. "I'll start from scratch … And thank you for tea."

"It was de … delicious," adds William.

They leave the living room together. Voices murmuring in the vestibule. Door opens and closes.

Hope Mary approaches the window to watch them move away. The rain or drizzle has finally ended.

10

NIGHT BEGINS AT HEAVEN'S DOOR MISSION

> *Their paradise — their quest for the absolute —*
> *is truly lost. And yet, it was so beautiful*
> *when they dreamed.*
>
> *... Sir Roderick — Dad*

THE FOUNDER OF THE MISSION is a former hippie, a Bob Dylan fan. Actually, "fan" is too mild. Ardent admirer would be more exact. A genuine one. That partly explains why he named the shelter *Heaven's Door*. He hasn't believed in heaven, hell, nirvana, or the beyond in a long time. The hereafter? If you ask him, one life is more than enough, and he's convinced he has atoned for more sins in this one than he's been able to commit. So starting over, even in the next world, no thank you.

But he believes in Dylan.

He was thus inspired by the emblematic song in naming the shelter. Found on *Pat Garrett and Billy the Kid* — the movie soundtrack — a record released in July 1973. Side B, between *Turkey Chase* and *Final Theme*. Re-recorded several times subsequently, notably by Eric Clapton, Bob Marley, and Guns N' Roses. All cult singers. Even Daphné, a French singer that teenagers adulate — the new shooting star in the firmament — has had a go at it, without much success in his opinion. While the accent is pretty, he finds her voice really too shrill. The song deserves another treatment. The latest known version is the one by Netchaev, a group from Seattle. Mitch — his father called him Michael, his mother, Mickey, although he hated the nickname of the stupid mouse, his brother called him Mike, his teenage friends Mick, like Mick Jagger; now he's Mitch to everyone — owns the entire collection of records, which he listens to rarely, so as not to further damage them. Some are already quite scratched. He also owns the CDs, which he listens to all the time — all bought, never pirated. Not that he's against pirating. Principles and fine words are often smoke screens; he's lived long enough to know that. He lives in society, but only because he can't do otherwise. All the same, he's wary of set rules. Morality, legality, that kind of notion leaves him cold. Except for stories of pedophilia, of course. And organ trafficking, torture, and antipersonnel bombs that tear to pieces innocent people. Everything that hurts and maims humanity. In comparison, pirating CDs seems a rather minor crime. Even a million CDs don't carry much weight in comparison. But for Dylan it's different. He insisted on giving them to himself as a gift, and a gift is not a real gift when you haven't paid for it. Perhaps this conception is a bit twisted, but that's how he feels. He acquired the records one by one, first through the classifieds, then, for a few years now, through the Internet; everyone has something to sell. It wasn't easy, but he managed. It was important to him.

He doesn't have a favourite song. For him, it's as if the same song plays endlessly, the same nasal, rough voice, the same chords, or almost, guitar and harmonica, violin and background vocals sometimes, the same visionary lyrics. He knows them all by heart. Yet, one particularly moves him: *Knockin' on Heaven's Door*. Because, in the old days, he often, too often, felt like that; like someone knocking, knocking on a door. Heaven's door, or hell's. Begging to be let in. In the darkest days and nights of his life, when he needed drugs, when he was worm-eaten, down and out, chilled to the bone, disorientated, a complete knockout, that's the song he sang, guitar case open at his feet, a few coins inside to encourage the generosity of passers-by. He has not forgotten.

When he opened the mission, about twenty years ago, after finally coming out of his despair, he swore to himself that no human being would ever knock in vain on this door. He set up a sheltered area beneath the balcony, too, for the lost cats of the neighbourhood. A good dozen: mangy toms and emaciated female cats and their kittens have chosen it as their home. He always keeps leftovers for them.

SPRING EQUINOX. OUTSIDE THE WIND is howling like a hungry wolf, or one that has lost its female, or that has just fallen on her body, shot with a rifle bullet, on her blood in the snow.

In the kitchen, Mitch prepares tea. Alcohol, pot and powder: those days are long gone. The only drug he has not given up is tobacco. They can utter every possible warning about cigarettes, frighten him with the most hideous spectres, mouth cancer and all that, he has no intention of quitting. He rolls his own, which fits his personality. And it does him good. Going without them is out of the question.

He places three cups on the tray: his own, featuring a red lobster on a black background, a gift from Corinna; one that's solid yellow; and another that's blue with stars. He adds the sliced whole-wheat bread, a jar of peanut butter, an apple, a banana, and a few homemade oatmeal raisin cookies, courtesy of Molly, on a chipped plate. The boy must be hungry. When you know hunger, or have known it, you know how to recognize it in others. You feel it, you read it in their eyes. Some signs are unmistakeable.

For Mitch, hunger was a long-faithful companion.

AT THE END OF THE sixties everyone was hitch-hiking to Vancouver, then going down the coast to California. A real frenzy. Long hair, wooden jewellery, embroidered shirts, bare feet in sandals. One guy in two lugged along his guitar. At night, bonfires were lit on the shore; they sang Dylan and Leonard Cohen while a joint was passed from hand to hand. People screwed in the grass, out of the way, changed partners joyfully or not, fell asleep as dawn rose. Flower Power, Peace and Love. In Vietnam, the war was dragging on; in Canada there were the deserters the conscientious objectors and pacifists who had stepped across the border. There were words on everyone's lips. What words? Mitch shrugs his shoulders. Words. But at the time, he believed them.

He'd made the journey in the opposite direction. From the Pacific to the Atlantic. From Vancouver to St. John's, Terra Nova: a Portuguese explorer, João Vaz de Corte-Real, gave it that name twenty years before Christopher Columbus docked a little further down with his three ships. And people claim he was the one who discovered America.

Terra Nova, then. Once there, he stopped moving. As if run aground. It was impossible to go any further without diving into the icy ocean, and end up mingling with the fishes — there still were some back then.

A BIT EARLIER THAT EVENING, he had driven to Cape Spear. His dog Lady — an exuberant six-year-old Labrador he took in when she was still a baby — needed exercise; she likes to run there. And he needed tranquility; a half an hour after supper, while there were still volunteers in the place. He likes the old lighthouse standing like a sentinel, projecting its light into the night. He especially likes that the lighthouses exist to guide lost boats. If people could choose to be incarnated as something, he would choose to be a lighthouse. In a way, that's what he is. He read that in times past, before people planted flags there and it was officially recognized in the name of such and such a king, Cape Spear was called Cauo de la Spera, a word that means 'waiting' or 'hope.' The Portuguese had named it thus. The cod fishermen gathered there, awaited favourable winds. Later, with the same idea, the French named it Cap d'espoir. The English changed the name to Spear. Only the sound — distorted — was preserved. The meaning disappeared. A pity. It's as if hope is no longer there.

They say the place attracts people who are suicidal. Last year, on the same date, there was one who did it. A guy in his thirties threw himself into the ocean at the end of the point, at the eastern extreme of the continent, into the grey, icy water amid the rocks. You have to be at the end of your rope to decide to dive in there. At the end of hope. At certain times, continuing to live requires too much courage; you don't have it. Mitch too, sometimes, in the past, looked into the grey water at the same place. What was he thinking then? *I'll merge into the movement, a wave washed away. I'll caress the fish, sunken ships, galleons, galleys, schooners, rusted submarines, buried treasure, and the drowned, beautiful women in ball gowns, the old cod fishermen, the soldiers, my memory will merge into the memory of the world, my despair into its hope.* Things like that, stupid things he chanted in his head, a song he could have composed. A quick

---

301

way to end it, for sure. The attraction was almost irresistible. What stopped him? He no longer knows.

This evening, it was a boy of about eighteen. Lady noticed him first. A sociable dog, she rushed toward him, began to leap about, barking joyfully. He didn't react. He was standing, immobile, staring at the waves. It was like a mirror; Mitch saw himself there, at the same age. He recognized the outline, skin and bones, the jeans hanging down, his stance, the weight of the world on his shoulders. Even without seeing it, he could have described the expression on his face, the emptiness in his eyes. He approached noiselessly. He knows what must be done in cases like this. Fingers numb from the wind, he rolled a first cigarette, held it out to the boy, then a second for himself. That is called brotherhood. Or compassion. No matter, he knows what must be done; it had been done for him. They worked hard to light it in the gusting wind. When they finished smoking, Mitch slid his arm under that of the boy, led him toward the car. "It's too darn cold, you can't stay there. By the way, I'm Mitch." No reply. No resistance, either. He could have just as easily been a serial killer. And now the youth is in the office. He still hasn't said a word; they don't even know if he understands English. Stan is keeping him company.

Mitch pours boiling water over the teabags.

Newfoundland. Terre-Neuve. Terra Nova. When Mitch arrived in St. John's, it was as if he had just reached the end of the world. There was the feeling he had travelled from one extremity of the world to the other. At seventeen he had taken the ferry from Vancouver Island — his father, a major in the army, was in charge of some service, discipline, undoubtedly, at Nanaimo military base. With his guitar, and a book, just one, *Thus Spake Zarathustra*, why that one, he doesn't know, probably because he could open it at any page, read a passage at random, he had crossed the country from west to east, ending up in St. John's and has not budged since. Like the people he shelters today, he had wandered in the port, shivered beneath the rain, hand out, at the mercy of vicious winds blowing in from the North Atlantic. Like them, he had experienced jail, detox, shelters, had even belonged to a cult. Yes, for a time, he believed or wanted to believe, that Jesus loved him. Not that it made him more serene. Fortunately, he came through that as well. Twenty years of wandering, running away and returning, so many setbacks, how can he forget that hell? Needle marks on his forearms, bloodshot eyes, emaciated face. Who said that times were good? Who said they were easy back then?

Did they look for him when he left? If so, they didn't find him. In a way, it's just as well. But he'd be surprised if they made investigations. Good riddance, his father the Major must have thought. Roderick Morgan; you always wanted to call him sir, Sir Roderick, like the usual army officer in India in an old British detective novel. Perhaps his mother shed a few tears in silence. She never made much noise. He imagines her in the kitchen, wiping her eyes with her apron, murmuring that the onions were making her cry.

And now Mitch is approaching sixty; he's fifty-seven, yet he hasn't changed his look at all. It's too late to change it. Long hair fastened at the back of the neck with a leather string, greying beard taking up half his face. He looks like an old hippy and knows it. Anyway, that's exactly what he is, a scrawny old hippy. A kind of boy scout. What is it they say, again? "Once a scout, always a scout." Awful childhood memories. He had even succeeded in getting expelled from the pack, to the great shame of Sir Roderick. For what reason that time? Insubordination, no doubt. There was never any other.

The old man was often ashamed. The height of humiliation came when Mitch was caught in the act of stealing a record in a store. "You deserve the gallows," the major had hissed, on the verge of apoplexy. Is that the kind of thing a father says to his son? Mitch doesn't have children; at least he doesn't think so. If a casual affair resulted in a child, he knew nothing of it. But if he'd had one, he'd never speak to him or her like that. Worse still was the time he had been discovered in the basement with his friend Chris, smoking a joint. A joint! That was the final blow — added to the others that had rained down on the Major. "You're not worth the rope it'll take to hang you." Always the image of punishment awaiting him, the black sheep. Sir Roderick was so proud of his eldest son, Rod, enlisted in the army. A carbon copy — brush cut, square-shouldered, steely-eyed. But when you're saddled with the same first name as your father, what else to do but follow in his footsteps? Mitch had inherited his mother's name. That is, the male version; she was called Michelle. And that was about all he'd inherited from her. She never said so, but he often thought she would have preferred a girl, that she felt a bit alone in the male household. He has not been in touch with them, nor has he ever heard from them. But she appears sometimes in his dream like a ghost, somewhat sad, looking at him unsmilingly. She didn't smile often.

An old hippy, then. In any case, his guests — he calls them his "guests" — couldn't care less about his look. Their trajectories too have stopped somewhere in time. Alcoholics, drug addicts, overmedicated people, unrecognized geniuses — so they like to think — failures, overly fragile, staggerers. One evening at supper, they talked about Ryan Larkin, the great animation filmmaker who had just died. It was in February 2007. He had lived on the streets in Montreal, reduced to begging, having had his hour of glory: an Oscar nomination. Then he'd ended up at the Old Brewery Mission. "Ironic, really, the name, Old Brewery, for an alcoholic," someone said. And someone else replied that "Heaven's Door" was also ironic. Premonitory, added a third. Some didn't understand the word. But it made Mitch's flesh crawl. Premonitory. He hadn't seen things that way.

His guests: wandering souls at the gates of paradise. Some come only to eat and take a shower. Others need the computer: Mitch never says no. So much the better if they want to communicate with friends and relatives, if they maintained ties. He just makes sure they don't go to obscene or racist sites: there have to be some limits, or chaos would quickly ensue. Others have practically made a nest there, especially in winter. Unlike the birds, they leave when the good weather returns.

A QUARTER TO ELEVEN. IN the rooms upstairs, the concert has begun. Most snore, a few moan or even cry out at times in their sleep, prisoners of dreams Mitch would rather not imagine. There have been no cases of sleepwalking in some time. He touches wood. Sleepwalking is not easy to manage. Mitch sleeps with one eye open; a sleepwalker can hurt himself tumbling down the stairs. But tonight everything seems calm aboard ship. Neither seasickness nor mutiny on the horizon.

He takes the tray, heads toward the office.

The boy — they don't know his name, and Mitch is not the type to ask his guests for ID — is slumped in the armchair, his long thin legs stretched out in front of him, Lady lying at his side on the floor. Black hair, high cheekbones, a scrawny beard, bronzed complexion. But very blue eyes. A Métis? Black hair, blue eyes. Corinna was like him and claimed to be Métis. In the early years she was always there at the shelter. Silent, as well. She drew. He has a drawing by her, a garden — the vision of earthy paradise of a girl like her — hung on the office wall. Trees, giant flowers, unicorns, and birds entangled, done in black pen on white paper. She had worked on it diligently an entire evening. He set limits for himself;

he never touches the girls who come to the shelter. He says sometimes he lives like a monk. Even monks succumb, and with Corinna, it happened once. Just once. Afterwards, he explained to her they couldn't continue; he had a code of ethics and all that. He could kick himself for it now. For succumbing, as well as for trying to explain why. Because the next day she didn't show up. Nor the day after. Nor any other day. He was eaten up with guilt, he searched for her throughout the city, imagined her at the end of the point, staring at the grey water, carried away by the waves. Her absence left a kind of hole. She must be about forty now, perhaps older. Mitch thinks of her when it's cold, when it snows, when it rains. He can't help but have a heavy heart. Even though he knows he mustn't become attached.

Stan is tapping away at the computer keyboard. He stops by the mission a few evenings a week, helps out with the paperwork, fills out grant applications. He has given himself the title of assistant. There are others, kind souls, Frances, Molly, Martha, Chris, Jason, and a French speaker named Justine, who come at suppertime and leave once the dishes are done. Today Molly has made cookies: the aroma still lingers in the house. The guests had a feast. Without his assistants, Mitch doesn't know how he'd manage. For breakfast, he can get by alone. The first meal isn't really complicated: orange juice — the guests need vitamin C — toast, peanut butter — fibre — strawberry jam, bananas, sliced cheese, coffee. Three out of four food groups isn't bad. Hard-boiled eggs every

other day, for the protein. Thus filled, they're ready to face
the day. There are twenty-four beds distributed in six rooms.
The kitchen, dining room, office, and living room with a TV
are on the main floor. The mission closes at eleven o'clock and
re-opens at five in the afternoon. They always have a full house.
The afternoon is devoted to shopping, laundry, repairs, and
cleaning. When Mitch gets a chance, he takes a nap; he certainly needs it. And then everything begins again. Seven days
a week, all year long. No vacation for the destitute. Nor for
those who take care of them.

Mitch doesn't know much about Stan: he rents a room
somewhere in the city, earns a frugal living giving French
courses. Forty years old, more or less. He too seems to have
had something go wrong in his life, he too seems to have fled.
When he speaks, most of the time, it's about the revolution,
a kind of obsession with him. He tells how his ancestor was
an anarchist, or nihilist, one Nechaev, like the group from
Seattle — they spell it differently, but Stan says it's the same,
a well-known philosopher. Mythomaniac, more or less; Mitch
has met more than one like him in the shelter. Sometimes
he spews out terse phrases, eyes feverish. *The annihilation of
the old is the creation of the future*, that type of thing. *The nihilist
is a man who bows before no authority*. Mitch lets him speak,
approves with a nod. He doesn't know if he can define himself
as a nihilist, he sees himself more as a humanist, but has never
bowed to authority either.

Otherwise, they put on music, or a movie; Mitch has a few.

Often they watch the same one *Pat Garrett and Billy the Kid* by Sam Peckinpah, for the unforgettable scene in which the old sheriff is dying in front of his wife and children while Dylan sings the famous song. Not that the film is a masterpiece. But it's that or the news, which Mitch doesn't really feel like watching anymore, or an old episode of Columbo, or a James Bond movie with sharks, submarines, girls in bikinis, and casinos where men win or lose fortunes, and always the planet about to explode, about to be rescued by the same casual hero. You don't believe it and that's what's relaxing. Most of the time he falls asleep long before the end. When he wakes up, Stan is gone.

HE SETS DOWN THE TRAY on the desk. "Dig in, guys."

Stan takes a cup of tea, the blue one with the stars, and dunks a cookie in it. Mitch rolls himself a cigarette. He smokes only in the office and even then, not much. Never in front of the guests. Tobacco has now been banned in the shelter because of the grants he receives from various government organizations. If an inspector were to show up and detect the hated odour, the grants would go up in smoke, unquestionably.

"I've finished," announces Stan. "All you have to do is print the three pages, sign the last one, and mail them. Wait for the cheque."

"Thank you."

"No problem. I do what I have to do."

"Thanks all the same."

"I do what I have to do," repeats Stan. "Between society and the revolutionary, it's war without mercy."

"Uh-huh."

"*The Catechism of a Revolutionary*," specifies Stan.

"Nechayev."

Both of them start, stunned. From the deep in his armchair, the youth has spoken.

"You ... you know Nechayev? You've read him?"

Stan's eyes light up. Now the litany will begin again. The story of the ancestor, the rhetoric and all that. Mitch already feels exhausted.

The boy arises, approaches the desk. Lady follows him. He makes himself a sandwich — peanut butter and sliced banana. Then a second, identical, and gives the dog a cookie, takes a cup — Mitch's, with the lobster — and returns to the armchair. He probably won't say another thing all evening long.

That's fine. No problem. Sometimes you have nothing to say, so may as well be quiet. Or you have too many things you want to keep for yourself. Mitch understands that. Everyone is entitled to his secrets. He takes up his guitar. He hasn't played in a long time. Before, when Corinna came, he played for her while she drew. Sitting in the armchair, she too not speaking. A sudden question arises. It's as if a hand is inching its way beneath his ribs, crushing his heart. What if ... blue eyes, black hair, high cheekbones. *Your mother's name wasn't Corinna?* He bends his head over his guitar.

He begins with his favourite song.

The boy closes his eyes. Outside, the wind continues to howl.

"Riel," he says.

Riel?

"That's my name. Riel."

He has a name, that's already something. A nice name, even. What will he say when he makes up his mind to speak? That he's a descendent of a hero in Canada's history? Louis Riel had no descendents, Mitch knows. But what's the difference? In a movie, there was a guy who took himself for Don Juan. So why not Riel? He himself, not a minute ago, was imagining a son heaven-sent. Everyone is entitled to his dreams.

11

LATE AFTERNOON
IN LOST PARADISE

A letter from his friend François, the so-called
poet, the one living the good life in Spain
at taxpayers' expense.

The only drug he has not
given up is tobacco.

Lost Paradise, Calvi
March 21

MY DEAR TÉPHA, YOU DIDN'T reply to my last — actually
my first — missive, written at the winter solstice. Perhaps I
was too insistent that you drop everything and join me in
Spain, which I painted in glowing colours: thousands of castles,
flamenco dancers, and other exquisite delights. Calm down,

I'll stop insisting. Even if I don't understand. That is, if worse comes to worse I can understand your not coming — you don't have the plane fare; you're painting a masterpiece and can't stop. But to not answer me? We had a pact, remember: send each other a handwritten letter at each change of season. I've respected my side of the bargain. What are you waiting for? Is it because what I told you about Julie? Are angry at me? Sulking? I'm becoming lost in conjecture. Between friends, between brothers, I thought we had nothing to hide.

But what did I say, really? That I'd seen Julie dance naked and I'd not been impressed. So what? You could have simply replied telling me to mind my own business. I would have. You don't actually think I did it on purpose, followed my cousin to that Geisha Bar or somewhere else to see her wiggle her hips. For starters, how could I have known she was dancing there? Even you never knew where she worked. It was just a guys' night out, to celebrate my receiving the grant. I'm only sorry you missed it. I was as surprised as she, I swear. Did you show her my letter? If so, I can easily imagine her anger, can imagine her giving you an ultimatum: herself or me. Or — anything is possible — she opened it without your knowing it and my confidences ended up in the first available garbage can. I repeat I am becoming lost in conjecture — if not in sinister premonitions. (If indeed that is what you did, what you are doing again this very moment, Julie, well, please accept my apologies. But you disappoint me.)

No matter, armed with my pen, I'm reoffending, and faithful to my promise, am writing to you on the equinox.

Once again, I won't describe in detail all my adventures; besides, they're less varied than the last time. I already spoke to you of Seville and of my Sevillana, Manuela. She continues to bewitch, delight, and inspire me. So, if you read the name of the place from which I'm writing you, you must be wondering what the happy man I am is doing in Corsica, in Calvi.

The happy man is on the trail of Don Juan, at least the one I described to you in my last letter. Remember? Miguel de Mañara. In December, I was in Montejaque, in his *palacete*, with my beauty; I wrote you from there. For two weeks, I've been wandering like a lost soul in Calvi, seeking his ghost. An obsession, you say? Perhaps. I want to get to the bottom of things, drive the guy back against the wall, make him spill everything he knows, everything he has in his guts, all that he is.

And I'm writing, writing. I'd told you I was beginning a series of poems on the character. For the Calvi episode, I had writer's block; in Seville, I was getting nowhere. I needed to be here in person. Manuela understood and let me leave.

I've rented a studio with a kitchenette. The place, however basic, is costing me an arm and a leg, but I have no choice. The poet must bow to the demands of his muse. I live frugally. I've given up almost everything. The only drug on which I still depend is tobacco. And I cherish my dependency.

OKAY, FORGET EVERYTHING YOU'VE JUST read. I can do anything but lie to you. Or lie to myself. The truth is that the happy man is not happy, and the lover is less and less in love. As for the poet, he's not writing. When he tries, it's absolutely worthless. The work, alas, is not progressing. I've come to a standstill. I'm wandering around Calvi. What am I missing, Tépha? A chromosome, a gene? I left Montreal my head full of plans; I travelled as I wished. In Seville I found the woman I loved. And now, nothing. The muse I mention, and whom I call upon, has slipped away from me. I tear up pages as I write them.

The woman I loved. I wrote that in the past, and not only to respect the sequence of tenses. I'm no longer sure of anything. It has nothing to do with her. The problem lies with me. In December, I couldn't find words enthusiastic enough to describe my bliss. The situation is the same; it's I who have changed. We're going to have a child at the end of the summer — am I cut out for fatherhood? I've read too much about Don Juan, apparently. Here I'm drooling over the women on vacation. I lust when I see them half-naked on the beach. And for the moment I'm preparing for battle. I feel myself on the verge of giving into one of the available temptations. As Molière's Don Juan said, "the true pleasure of love consists in its variety." But what will happen if I give into one and then another?

I've thus been wandering on Calvi, the island of beauty, as it is called, for three weeks. What to tell you about the city?

I could describe the citadel, visible from the balcony of my studio. At dawn, beneath the pink sky, and at night, as if emerging from the black water beneath the stars. Omnipresent. The first and final image of the city. An impression of solidity, permanence — the complete opposite of me. Resistance to time, resistance period, stubborn, almost obtuse. Something in the mass of arrogant, immobile stone, standing in the face of time that passes, erodes, ravages, in the face of elements that rage furiously, annihilating monuments that men persist in erecting, proudly, this mass of stone standing, still standing despite wars begun again. Something in its harsh beauty calls to me — a magnetic force, mineral force, inertia. Something, too, distresses me. Sometimes I need all my strength to resist the impulse to throw myself into the waves.

No, the last sentence is also false. I'm making literature. I'm revelling in romanticism — the tormented poet and all that. I keep lying. Be reassured, I'm not suicidal. Just lost.

It's you I miss, Tépha.

Since I'm not writing, what am I doing with my days, my nights? I'm reading about the history of Calvi, and it's fascinating. Here's a small sample, at random. The city is Corsican, as you already know. In 1356, however, it took an oath in Genoa. *Semper fidelis*, forever faithful. The two words are inscribed above the gateway at the entrance to the citadel. As wars were fought and treaties signed, other oaths were taken — funny how an oath means a solemn declaration or commitment as well as a curse. Languages are full of truisms — each one has its peculiarities. Many unusual associations. And contradictions. But this oath, carved in stone at the entrance to the citadel resists time. Even if it doesn't mean much anymore.

You must be wondering what the connection is between the Corsican or Genoan city and my Don Juan: Miguel de Mañara, the proud Sevillian. His parents were born here: that's the connection. But too many misfortunes — the plague, fires, barbarian invasions and all that — rained down on Calvi back then, and they preferred to make their home in Seville, where their offspring was born in 1627.

I spoke to you of his admiration for the character of Don Juan — he and I have that in common — of his plan to seduce a thousand and two women, not one less — I am somewhat less ambitious. Seems he devoted all his energy to that for some time. And then one fine day the unrepentant seducer decided to take stock of his conquests. One imagines, in illegible scrawl, first names, dates, personal information and suggestive little crosses. Only incest, the ultimate taboo, was missing from his list of conquests. No problem. He had a half sister he didn't know, in Corsica. He sailed for Calvi and introduced himself as a friend of the Seville branch of the family. You can imagine the rest.

The damsel was called Vanina; she was soon conquered — she had only known rugged, laconic Corsicans. But however vile Don Juan was, he still had a code of ethics. He insisted the beauty giving into him have full knowledge of the facts. So he revealed they were related. Horrified, the innocent young thing called upon her entire contingent for help. Our seducer, unmasked, was forced to confront his host in a duel. After slaying him with a thrust of the sword, he escaped via a secret staircase. Sounds like a dream, right? Well then, let's dream. Dreams are our reality. The following day, he snuck onto a ship at anchor in the port of Calvi. I don't know any more, but the story is enough to feed my imagination. And I haven't lost hope of discovering the staircase. The story obsesses me. He wanted to incarnate Don Juan; I want to incarnate him. In my own skin, I'm suffocating.

During the day, when I'm not at the citadel, I walk along the seashore, filling my lungs with salty air. The water is cold, but not too bad. I swim sometimes, when I'm brave. At the marina, I dream before the names of the moored boats. *Quiet Man, Queen of the Sea, La mouette*. Many women's names — there is even a *Vanina*. I stop for a beer. My first day here I adopted a small café called Lost Paradise, which has become my home base. I am writing you today from there.

Let's be honest: the only *paradise* here is the name. In fact, it isn't much to look at, just a place to stop off. But it's across from the sea, the Mediterranean, and as they say, that's something.

An orange-coloured banner supported by stakes driven into the sand is unfurled in front of the establishment, displaying on the first line the words "LOST PARADISE" on the next "BAR – SNACK – ICE CREAM" in black capital letters. "Live Jazz at ten o'clock every evening; Julius Milton on saxophone" is announced in sky-blue italics on the third line. Strange, this coincidence: Milton in Lost Paradise. John Milton, the seventeenth century British poet — blind — wrote the poem *Paradise Lost*.

Three daily specials are written in chalk on the board. Today we are offered *Arlequinade* of peppers, a bacon omelette, or grilled sardines. Yesterday was almost the same, except it was a mushroom omelette. Nothing out of the ordinary, really, except for the *Arlequinade*. I ate one earlier. It's actually a simple fried dish — red and green peppers, as you can imagine — along with onions, that they renamed to make more appealing. A salad — garden salad, of course, they're not going to write it's from the supermarket — is served with the three dishes. Rickety faded wood tables on the terrace, painted olive green inside. A cooler filled with Nestlé products. On the walls, posters of Julius Milton, a three-day beard, shadows under his eyes — imagine a worse version Gainsbourg, if that's possible — dating from when he and his saxophone performed in various jazz clubs, various festivals — never in Montreal and that, he admitted to me, is one of his greatest regrets — with various short-lived groups. A few nostalgic movie posters, *Broken Wings* — the unforgettable Marjorie Martinez playing Lola before her mirror, the final image of the film you and I both worship — and *Casablanca*. All in black and white. Marlon Brando in a leather jacket, Brigitte Bardot, hair tousled, straddling a motorcycle. One is of Marilyn Monroe, the most famous, her skirt in the air, a flash of white panties. The usual row of bottles behind the bar. Wine glasses hanging from their stems, espresso machine, ashtrays on the counter.

Jazz, then — very average — at night, at Lost Paradise, but during the day, the loudspeakers broadcast sentimental old songs as far as the beach — Serge Lama, Stevie Wonder, Joe Dassin. Right now it's Henri Salvador — he would like to see Syracuse. Listening to him, I tell myself that I would too.

Paradise is not very busy. A few regulars, including myself, birds of passage — right now, three beaming Vikings who've just ordered beer in English, and a little Asian couple in their mid-twenties, very quiet, sharing an ice cream construction on the terrace not far from me. Is this a foretaste of what awaits us in the beyond? Eternity is likely to be rather dismal if you want my opinion. Or, if it's a reflection of the famous Eden, we can't blame Adam and Eve for wanting to jump over the gate. I feel a bit like them.

Another couple came in a bit earlier this afternoon, from Quebec; I recognized — with a kind of perversely nostalgic pleasure, I admit — the accent. As I understood, they had just landed. They were emphatically describing the freezing rain battering Montreal when they left. I imagined myself braving the elements and was almost jealous. Actually, I've had enough of good weather.

When I'm not writing about the history of Calvi, I'm burying myself in Byron's *Don Juan* in English, his last work, unfinished. Recently I devoured his biography — ordered from Seville on the Internet, delivered to my door three days later.

I'll briefly paint a portrait of the devil. His ancestors were called Lord Evil, Jack Storm, and Crazy Jack. Admit, it's a good start, especially when you're from a romantic century. I, being from a rationalist century, with ancestors whose names are merely Joséphat, Armand, and Eusèbe, am green with envy. No problem; one day, I'll invent a biography for myself. But let's return to our Byron. He had a club-foot; he limped. He was afraid the handicap would make girls despise him. As a teenager, he was pudgy. Plump. Afterwards he went on a very strict diet. He had a tamed bear. He liked dogs. He was perpetually in debt. He treated women badly, except for his half-sister Augusta, with whom he had a very intimate relationship. He kept prostitutes he called nymphs. He increased his conquests. He arranged orgies in his abbey in Newstead during which, disguised as a monk, he drank wine out of a human skull transformed into a goblet. His admiration of Napoleon knew no bounds. He had homosexual affairs and an incestuous — tumultuous? — relationship with Augusta, his half-sister. A girl was born from the union, Fedora, like one of his characters. I can't remember if he named his daughter after the character or the character after his daughter. He sought a cause greater than him. For some, the simple cause of life is not enough. They need words greater than themselves, the words to fill the emptiness. He was disillusioned. He took up cause of the Greeks against Turkish oppression, raised a small army. He died in Missolonghi of pernicious fever without having fought a single battle. A very ordinary death. He was an ironic man. Perhaps he appreciated this final irony. I'm not sure, but I hope so for his sake. He was thirty-seven. "If thou regret thy youth, why live? ... Look around and choose thy ground, and take thy rest." These are the last words written in his journal. Or something like that; I'm quoting from memory.

Disenchanted, he also wrote that love is utter nonsense, merely a blend of compliments, romance, and deceit. He was an incarnation of Don Juan, one among many others, but perhaps the most convincing. Or touching. After Miguel de Mañara, of course. Women threw themselves at him. One of them, whom he had left — he left them all — wanted to kill herself. Another — or was it the same? — sent him a lock of her pubic hair in memory of their lovemaking. A melancholy poet, adventurer — pirate? — he set them dreaming. Perhaps a remarkable lover, he who didn't love. For these who love too much make love badly, as someone wrote, Cocteau, I think. In a way — admittedly twisted — I feel nostalgic, reading about his life. I would like to be him, to have been him.

To tell you the truth, I would like to translate his *Don Juan* in my spare time, to alleviate boredom. It's often translated in prose, and the music is lost. I know; I read excerpts from both versions. It's worthless in French. There's no music. I'm not a translator, but I have a theory: translating is rendering the untranslatable, the soul. Everything is connected, intermingled. Strands of colours compose image. Thought is given form by rhythm and sound; it edges its way into the complexities. In wanting to be faithful to the meaning at any cost, people end up distorting thought, betraying it. I want to enter Byron's thoughts — and Don Juan's. Translate him subjectively. I am seeking possible music. I think I'll use the alexandrine. I have even turned out a few. The magnitude of the task exhausts me in advance.

This is how I spend my days and nights.

Other than that, I'm thinking of you. Conjecture and premonitions, sinister at times, as I mentioned above; I imagine the worst scenarios to explain your silence. While painting, you splattered yourself with turpentine; you got it in your eyes, you're blind, can no longer read my letters or write to me. You fell on the ice, broke your right arm, can no longer paint — or write to me. You're dead. What did you think of at the moment of ... At the end, when they say time contracts and your entire life flashes before your eyes? Of the frescoes you wanted to paint? Of Julie? Of all the others? Of your friend, your brother, of me? And what will I remember? What will flash before me? Horrible images, as if in a nightmare, memories we thought were forever banished from memory? The frogs we tortured in our childhood, the girls we made cry? Does the murderer see his victims flash before him? Do we see the errors we committed along the way? The shameful, the contemptible? Because I have to confess something: that evening at the Geisha Bar, while I was watching Julie wiggle her hips, well, my thoughts were rather base, in the gutter, to be blunt. And I was ashamed. I don't want to exhale my last breath with the memory of that shame. Where are the images of happiness that flash by, all the times we said I love you and it was true? *Forever faithful* ...

I'M STOPPING THIS MOROSE LETTER here. You don't need this. Evening is falling, everything is becoming red. I'll go back into my lair.

Before closing, I'll briefly sum up the rest of my plans. I intend to return to Seville in May, for the procession of the Virgin of Rocío. Manuela assures me it's a spectacular celebration: missing it is out of the question.

In June I'm invited to a literary festival in Moravia. No idea what I'll read. But they say the beer there is wonderful. I'll give you all the details in three months.

Then I'll return to Seville in time for the child's birth. If it's a girl we'll call her Nadia. You know perhaps — no, you don't — that in Russian it means (more or less) hope.

Afterwards ... well, afterwards, I don't know.

As I told you, the only drug I've not given up is cigarettes. I'm actually lighting one now, a Gitane filter, and I'm smoking to your health.

Well, so long, old chap, as another guy would say, Byron
perhaps. *Hasta luego,* as Don Juan would say.

> Your friend,
> François
> (who despite your silence, just hopes
> you have not forgotten him).

12

NIRVANA, AT SOME POINT
IN ETERNITY

It's called heaven, or nirvana;
It's where the righteous go after they die.

John Milton, the seventeenth century British poet
— blind — wrote the poem Paradise Lost.

IS DAY BREAKING? NO, HERE it does not break. Here nothing breaks and nothing falls, neither day nor night. If not for the dazzling whiteness, if not for the pleasantly temperate surroundings, you could almost believe you were in oblivion. But if you are, it's because you tumbled down there. Here you float, and glide; you fly. Oblivion is damp and grey. "The colour of ice," as someone once described it. Oblivion — the word says it, they are all forgotten. Here they remember.

In oblivion, they are all forgotten. Here they endure forever in the memory of humanity.

All the images of cherubs playing the lute on a cloud are, indeed, images. The white robes in which Gustave Doré modestly adorned the souls do not exist here either. The chosen, as that is usually what they are called, are here, and remain forever as they were when they arrived: in togas, doublets, suit and tie, crinolines, tutus, blue jeans, or pyjamas — this last outfit, not very flattering, is the one we find them in most often. Only the rare few who show up nude receive, as dictated by decency, the famous tunic. And if they are in nirvana it is because they have been decreed, rightly or wrongly, to be immortal. A kind of learned society, as it were.

The dictionary describes it as a state of eternal bliss where all desire is suppressed, which would make the stay a bit monotonous, admittedly. Others believe on the contrary, that all frustrated desires on earth are fulfilled in nirvana. They are also mistaken. Those who are frustrated when they land — so to speak — in heaven remain so for eternity. For this reason their blessed status is rather ironic.

A melancholic trio is meditating in a corner — the great Dante, his guide Virgil and Beatrice, the beloved. If Dante is melancholy, it's because he hasn't found the circles he toiled for years to describe. Everything is on the same level, and he's reduced to rubbing shoulders with the unpunished wicked, as he did on earth. What, for example, is the Marquis de Sade of sinister memory doing here? Dante obviously didn't know

him in his lifetime, else he would have thrashed him, as he
deserved, in the last circle of his hell. He would have boiled
him in a cauldron with his kind: Nero, Caligula, Heliogabalus
and other Idi Amin Dadas — whom the poet did not know
either. No, here the only idea is not to be forgotten by those
living on the other side. For better or for worse. Enlightenment
or horror. For some find a kind of sensual pleasure in horror,
much good may it do them. The depraved old man that some
blasphemously nickname 'the divine Marquis' struts about, as
conceited as a peacock, flabby cheeks, slovenly, potbellied,
crumpled shirttail hanging out, an appalling sight — and
while strutting about he endlessly declaims or spews passages
from his degrading works — if they can be considered
works. *The Misfortunes of Virtue*, what a disgrace! A mad-man.
He actually ended his career — career! — in an asylum at
Charenton. You would not have expected to be subjected to
his company in nirvana. To add insult to injury, the vile man
says that he only laments the absence of his "chicks," the
unfortunate young servants, scarcely nubile, that he had
corrupted in his Bluebeard's castle, and who have long been
sunk into oblivion. For the chicks in question enter the great
category that is also designated, with blood-chilling realism,
as "cannon fodder," "unknown soldier," "silent majority" — as
if the anonymous did not cry when they were hurt —
or, more simply and contemptuously, as "the multitude"
"the masses," or "the riff-raff." All those who, in the end, will
never have access to nirvana.

But there you go, people still read Sade on Earth; they even study, quote, and dissect. He is translated, commented on, analyzed, and pastiches are written about him. A free spirit according to some, precursor of nihilism, existentialism, and psychoanalysis according to others, the last word on Catholicism — that definition from Flaubert. He spent thirty years in prison for what he wrote, and for some people that proves something, go figure what. It wouldn't take much for him to be raised to martyrdom. There have even been feminists — which, you'll agree, takes the cake — who have studied his case and found merit in him. Yes, merit. Moral pornographer, concluded one of them, not turning a hair. As if pornography could be moral. The infatuation that persists nevertheless opened the door to nirvana for him. And don't think he regrets anything. That breed doesn't know what it is to repent.

Those who spoke of a land of the just were cruelly mistaken. It is no more just here than it was over there. Or, if there is justice here, its mystery remains unfathomable. Proust, for example, who suffered from asthma on earth, still suffers from it just as much, and you hear night and day — so to speak — his wheezing breath, which is not restful for him or for those subjected to hear him. But is it just? And Milton, the great John Milton — whose masterpiece *Paradise Lost* almost compares with *The Divine Comedy* — who spent the last twenty-two years of his life blind, has not regained his sight here. Is it just?

This injustice plunges Dante into gloom, despite the presence of Beatrice at his side, who tries in vain to comfort him.

"Don't worry about those people," she says in a soothing voice, referring to the tyrants whose existence here, rather than in hell — the only place suitable for them — is a thorn in Dante's heart. "Who knows if, sooner or later, they'll not be thrown into Gehenna? Perhaps God is biding His time."

God ... Dante shakes his head. He has come to doubt His existence. If He does exist, He made fun of him.

Beatrice is therefore at his side, and, in a way, that is another thorn that makes the poet's heart bleed. He can never possess her. She is married, and when you are, it is for eternity, alas. "*Whom God has brought together*," and so on. Impossible to contest this dictum. When you think about it, Simone de Bardi was married for two short years to the beautiful immortal, the *gentillissima* — it was no doubt the fellow's earthly paradise — then he tumbled to the bottom of oblivion like a nobody. For what do we know of him? *Niente*. Even Beatrice in nirvana never mentions his name. It's as if he had never existed. But he does exist. The centuries may have passed and water flowed under the Ponte Vecchio, yet it is this man who prevents Dante from knowing the delights he had secretly imagined. Sweeping his fingers through the sweet-smelling, silky hair of the beloved, kissing her ivory forehead, pressing her white hand between his, he abstains. On earth too, even such innocent ecstasies had been denied him. Prey to the pangs of desire, Dante must be forever content to stroll close to her, confide in her platonically, listen to her speak. We are far from the dreamed-of harmony. Is it just? Ah! Even the punishment that he, in his fifth canto, conceived for Francesca and Paolo Malatesta, the guilty lovers — delivered for eternity to the violence of the winds — even that torture seems preferable to his existence here. At least they can continue to say they love each other, even if they're crying. Whereas he scarcely dares to allow himself the slightest allusion to his feelings.

"You tricked me," he grumbles, now blaming Virgil, his former guide in the maze of the beyond. "You led me on a journey that inflicted unutterable suffering on me — places that didn't exist."

"But I did it for the cause of poetry," Virgil justifies. "Why do you reproach me? Thanks to my care, you created a major work people still read today."

"So? Whether people still read me or not proves nothing. They read others. That villain of a Marquis, for example."

"My gentle friend!" cries Beatrice, her cheeks flushed. "I beg of you. Do not compare yourself to that dreadful man!"

"They certainly don't read him for the same reasons," Virgil adds. "And I predict one day they will cease reading him."

"I no longer want to believe your predictions." Dante plunges back into his mediation. The two others remain in silence.

Let us leave our trio to brood, the vain to strut, the sardonic to snigger. Others among the chosen merit our attention.

DANTE IS UPSET AS IF nirvana were, a few exceptions aside, inhabited by loathsome creatures. He is wrong. It's far from true. If it were, where would the good people be? Philosophers, sages, artists, inventors, and benefactors of humanity hold a place of choice here. Nirvana is totally democratic. Bribes, paybacks, and other underhanded practices are strictly prohibited. No angel or guardian would ever let himself be corrupted. The few controversial personalities you bump into actually give the place its charm.

Because, let's be honest, without a nutcase like the Marquis de Sade, say, eternity would be a tad boring. He spices it up a little and many do not complain.

Robert Elkis, for example. Upon his arrival — he reached nirvana as soon as he exhaled his last breath — the filmmaker tried to strike up a friendship with Dante Alighieri of course. After all, the man was elevated to the rank of myth and even though Elkis had never read him — so many works to read, life rushes past, we never have time — he, like everybody else, still knew him by name. In a way he venerated him. How could one do otherwise? His name is synonymous with poetry, with perfection. Places and streets carry it proudly; monuments in his honour adorn practically the entire planet. Dressed in a flowing robe, his forehead encircled with laurels, frowning, sometimes an arm outstretched, like Christ on the mount enlightening the flock.

Elkis, however, quickly tired of it. His company was really too austere, no levity. The poet had no humour, was a paragon of virtue. Raised to such a height, virtue repels and even in nirvana a bit of humanity would be welcome, imperfect as it may be. His discourse, without a doubt poetic, is limited to admonishments, recriminations, and other imprecations, occasionally punctuated by heart-rending sobs. Five minutes of such a diet and you're guaranteed a migraine, take Robert Elkis's word. And one day, with no hidden motive, when he wanted to tell a little to joke to Beatrice, a charming young woman, incidentally — the other maniac practically leapt at his throat.

In the shade of an apple tree — artificial, nothing grows here, of course, nothing withers, nothing dies — they were drinking their nectar. What he wouldn't give for a good whisky on the rocks from time to time, Elkis sighed to himself. Especially when you've lived through the shackles of prohibition — the dreadful Volstead Act passed in January 1920 by a handful Puritans with an excess of virtue: that again. He was still young at the time, but remembers it as if it were yesterday. All those evenings washed down with Coca-Cola or fruit juice. It was deadly dull. As he's always said, without a drop of rum to console it, Coca-Cola is a mighty sad beverage. Of course, you could find rum and other consolations, but at your own risk. Eliot Ness and his team of untouchables were never far. The torture lasted thirteen long years. But well, you can't expect to experience the slightest intoxication in nirvana — they don't even offer communion wine — he learned that from the outset.

Nectar then. Dante, as usual, had been soliloquizing and, as usual, his words were hardly cheering. The poet, we have seen, is not exactly the life and soul of the party. On that day — or night — in nirvana, the sun doesn't set; there is no sun, for that matter — he was beside himself with anger because he had just learned his name had been given to the hero of some television series. "A fop!" he shouted. "Conceited, he quotes me without rhyme or reason — and wrongly! The price of fame, they say. But what a price! To begin with, what did I do to pay this price, what crime did I commit, can you tell me?" No one could.

Seeing Beatrice's goblet empty, Elkis had quickly moved the carafe nearer. "Do you know, beautiful lady," he whispered, to lighten the atmosphere a bit, "what the jealous woman replies when offered a drink?" The beauty shakes her head. "A trace. The unhappy woman asks for a tear, and the voluptuous woman asks for a touch." Admit, that's nothing to make a fuss about. That little joke had been told to him by one of his writer friends, a witty woman from Quebec, and he had repeated it many times — in French it was even more suggestive — always with great success. The *gentillissime* stared wide-eye: she hadn't understood. But Dante saw red. "How dare you!" he roared. And so on. No sense of humour. No levity.

Without Virgil's intervention, Elkis would have lost an eye.

From now on he avoids the trio, whom he merely greets from afar when passing.

TO AMUSE HIMSELF, HE SOMETIMES glances at what's hap-
pening on earth. Various film societies have scheduled *Broken
Wings*; a retrospective of his work is planned at the Film Library
in Florence, an impassioned young filmmaker — rather
talented, as it were — plans to film a remake of his swan song.
A few doctoral theses have been added to the bouquet of
laurels. This is all rather good news. Even though, he thinks
a bit melancholically, at that rate he won't be leaving nirvana
very soon. He shrugs his shoulders. All in all, better to be
here than in oblivion, even without whisky. An angel passes
with his tray. It's time for refreshments. Elkis beckons to him.

There is a less comforting piece of news, and it is called
Ernesto Liri. He is still maligning him. Right now, in the
airplane carrying him to Pisa — a pilgrimage — Liri is calling
him lustful, two-faced, a whited sepulchre. Whited sepulchre,
honestly! And the lucky dog is entitled to champagne. He's
not denying himself. He's toasting his confederates with
Veuve Clicquot, no less, while gossiping about him behind his
back. To think that some say you find justice in the beyond!
They are quite naïve. In nirvana, as on Earth, justice is in
illusion.

At present, Liri is intimating — he was always the type to
insinuate — that Elkis gave names, betrayed people during
the witch-hunt. A shameless lie! Bob Elkis always stayed far
away from politics, was not even questioned. And the other,
the so-called secretary, is swallowing it like the Gospel, taking
notes in his head. Elkis wouldn't be surprised if he repeated

the slander in his book — he's cooking up an unauthorized biography of … of the tyrant, to tell it like it is.

Why does Liri have such a grudge against him? God alone — if He even exists — knows. After all, *Broken Wings* won him the Oscar for best original score. Without *Broken Wings*, he would have remained the unknown that he was. He could show a minimum of gratitude. It would be too much to ask, apparently. Has old age made him lose his sense of reality? Is his memory failing? Is he off his rocker? These things do happen. Some old people have obsessions and nothing can make them listen to reason; they start finding an innocent man guilty of all their evils. But old age cannot explain everything: Liri has been ranting and raving for sixty years. Since Marjorie, in fact. The eternal triangle, once again. *Cherchez la femme.* The musician moped for the actress who pined for the filmmaker. Such is the world; we won't change it. And at least it makes for successful movies. In the end, what is *Broken Wings* if not a tragic love triangle — Bromsky, Stephen, Lola? Okay, the poor thing didn't survive very long. She is in nirvana, too, the immortal Lola, as they call her down there. And she still loves him. He sighs. She loves him. That's their karma.

The worst is that the senile old man will soon make his entrance — he must be on the verge of kicking the bucket; he's almost a hundred years old. With the music of *Broken Wings*, a major work, as they say, his *pièce de resistance* — the only worthwhile one — he's not likely to tumble into oblivion.

Elkis dreads this arrival. Because with Liri on the scene, nirvana won't be very nice.

NOW HE'S WALKING IN FRONT of the small round window. He approaches, then changes his mind. He's sick of contemplating oblivion. Before, the sight amused him: he felt he was at the movies, a blockbuster, an epic set it antiquity, with its thousands of extras. Not anymore. There's that guy, what's his name again? La … something. Laflaque? A ridiculous name to remember, in any case. Let him wallow in oblivion, everyone has forgotten him. He's the author of the mediocre detective novel that inspired Elkis to create his masterpiece. Lafargue, that's it. Francis Lafargue. Another who swears eternal hatred to him. Why? Frustration, spite, it's always the same story more or less. There wasn't much in his novel; Elkis took the names, the embryo of the plot and the city, Southampton. Everything else — the scene with the broken heel, the final words written in lipstick on the mirror — he invented. *Broken Wings* is unquestionably his work, no matter what the insipid hack claims. But, like all failures, he spills his venom, claims to all and sundry he has been despoiled. Didn't he declare the other day that Elkis had distorted his novel? Distorted? That little nothing was rubbish, just a pack of platitudes, his characters nothing more than caricatures. As for the dialogue, forget it. Elkis gave a soul to what had had none. Lafargue should be grateful. But it's the same with Liri: such people don't know the word "gratitude." What's

more, the horrid Lafargue got it into his head to devote
eternity to tormenting his benefactor — virtually, of course.
He invents tortures. One day, he burns his feet with a blow-
torch, the next he binds him hand and foot, covers him with
honey, on ant ants' nest. Good for him if it keeps him busy.
Because oblivion is remarkably lacking in entertainment. A
bit like nirvana, all in all.

In the beginning, the sight amused Elkis. In company
with the Marquis de Sade, with whom he had struck up a
friendship, he had some very good times, eyes glued to the
small round window, both of them roaring with laughter. "By
gosh!" cried the aristocrat, splitting his sides. "And I thought
I'd imagined everything! I tell you: this guy is even more
sadistic than I."

No doubt, but imagination or not, this type of performance quickly becomes repetitive. And even though they are
imaginary, the mistreatments inflicted on him by Lafargue
send shivers down his spine. One had almost poked his eye
out, another called him every name imaginable, and a third
singed the soles of his feet: none of it is very cheerful.

Today, Elkis is melancholy. He looks around for the Marquis.
The divine one's conversation has a knack for cheering him
up, which he really needs. In fact, now he's waddling around
in his greyish night shirt, a goblet in his hand. "Donatien!"
Elkis calls. "Donatien Alphonse! Over here!" The man in
question arrives with his rolling gait. "My dear fellow!" A
wide smile reveals drooling gums and stumpy teeth. Not

very appetizing, to tell the truth. And yet, as decrepit as he may have been — thirty years in the dungeon didn't help — the fellow appealed to women. Even at the end of his life a damsel, aged thirteen, the daughter of one of his jailers, became attached to him. That commands admiration. If Elkis were a jealous man ... he is not.

"Where are you headed?" he asks.

"Where do you expect me to go?" Sade replies, bursting out laughing. "I'm headed nowhere."

"In that case, I'll go with you."

"And you, what were you doing?"

"Nothing. What can I do?"

"That suits me perfectly."

Arm in arm, our two comrades walk off to an improbable elsewhere.

"You know," begins Elkis, "for a long time I contemplated making a movie of your Justine. At the time, alas, censorship made it impossible."

"Damned censorship! If anyone has suffered from that, it is I," grumbles the Marquis. "Thirty years in jail, thirteen in the nuthouse."

A copse appears at a bend in the road, an unoccupied glider swing. They sit down, let themselves be rocked. A slight breeze carries its sweet scent to them. They begin to feel drowsy. Elkis nods his head.

"Would you tell me about your chicks?" Elkis suggests.

13

MIDNIGHT AT THE END OF THE WORLD ... EATING IN THE NIGHT

... regular or Italian-style poutine with extra cheese,
or a version with chicken and peas.

... without a drop of rum to console it,
Coca-Cola is a mighty sad beverage.

VICTORIA EXITS THE ELEVATOR, WALKS down the hall of the hotel — high quality carpet with an oriental motif, subdued lighting, hushed atmosphere — and heads purposefully toward the revolving doors. A glance at her wristwatch: twenty-five minutes to midnight. She buttons her raincoat, raises the collar, slips on her gloves and goes out into the storm. Appearing as if from nowhere, a porter in a uniform trimmed with braid materializes. "Taxi, madam?" She nods her head.

He immediately opens his umbrella — Victoria's, very small and basically more decorative than practical, is in her purse — escorts her to the first car parked in front of the entrance and opens the door. "Thank you," she says slipping a dollar coin into his palm — they call it a loony; she finds that charming, more poetic in any case than "quarter" or "dime." Or worse still, "buck," harsh-sounding, evoking nothing as bucolic as the Nordic loon.

What weather! Freezing rain is coming down   has been all day, accompanied by gusts of wind. Yesterday as well. She arrived yesterday from Paris in the early evening. It was raining there too, but not as hard. She had planned on taking advantage of the afternoon to stroll around the city. After glancing out the window this morning, she deemed it wiser to abandon the idea. So she spent the day in her room, consulting her notes, transcribing them on her computer. She had her breakfast of grapefruit juice, a bran muffin, plain yogurt with zero fat, and coffee in the dining room. Toward eight p.m. she had a tray sent up — smoked salmon, rye toast bread, mesclun, and Earl Grey tea — which she accompanied with a half bottle of Ontario Chardonnay found in the little refrigerator. Why not? Trying local wines is part of her job. She ate while watching a detective series on TV. They're always the same, no matter where you are on the planet; it's funny when you see the same episode three times in a row and each time Dante Sullivan speaks in a different voice and in a different language. Then she took a scalding hot shower, put make-up on carefully, and is now ready to face the night and its surprises.

So this is what they call spring in Montreal. She didn't hear the weather forecast, but in New York it must be more or less the same — enough to discourage anyone from venturing onto the sidewalks, but not her. Besides, she has no choice; she must return to New York tomorrow — by train, which at least is more relaxing. She has that novel on the civil war — a hefty six-hundred pages full of twists and turns by Juliette Evanelli. Excellent travel reading; she read almost half of it yesterday on the plane. She'll continue tomorrow on the train.

So tonight her odyssey here in Montreal comes to an end. She tells the driver her destination: Saint-Zotique between Saint-Denis and Saint-Vallier — saints everywhere, my God! She has no idea what these two could have done — were they martyrs, popes, or crusaders? — to earn their place in paradise.

She's been travelling for six months. For her new book, *Eating Late at Night*, she's been trailing around, from one city to the next, on five continents. She's beginning to grow tired. And the experience has been rather hard on her stomach, which explains the frugality of her meals today. She has one left, and based on what she's heard, she shouldn't expect anything light.

After the success of *Gourmet & Gourmand* — it's unquestionably more appealing in French, more erotic, the repeating of the "our" sounds; repeated; you think you hear a large contented cat purring by the fire — and *Recipes from the End of the World,* her latest creation, about forty thousand copies — she's lost count — sold in the U.S. alone. She wanted to treat herself to this trip around the word discovering unusual, too often disparaged, delicacies.

By now, it has become clear: she is Victor Karr. The ruthless critic, the columnist with the vitriolic pen, tirelessly smoking out exotic flavours. She. In her profession, anonymity is desirable. Perhaps even preferable; without wishing to be alarmist, some not very reassuring anecdotes get around. She can't forget the food columnist who received death threats; another had the phalanxes of his right hand broken by mafia henchmen after daring to criticize the *vitello al tonno* of one of its protégés. Godfathers, we know, mean business. How do you write then, especially when you're right-handed? Even eating becomes a complicated undertaking. No, being a critic, be it of books, theatre, music, or food, is far from easy work. So Victoria keeps her nose clean beneath her mask and signs her writing Victor.

Few people are aware of this. There is of course her publisher — always the same; she is exemplary in her loyalty — her ex-husband, and her three daughters. All four as silent as the grave. Did they need a photo for the back cover? She didn't hesitate. Here is His Majesty Victor Karr the first, she announced to her publisher, holding out a snapshot of her father — round-faced, jovial, bearded, pot-bellied, exactly how people expect a gourmand to be. She was not fifteen when the poor man succumbed to food poisoning. A cruelly ironic end for such a *bon vivant*. The autopsy detected the presence of E. coli bacteria in his intestines. Not surprising, in the end. Although people repeatedly told him to be careful, he insisted on eating his meat rare. Almost raw!

Could gourmandise be a family defect? But Victoria is not really a gourmand. She considers herself curious. Fortunately, she has what she calls a cast-iron stomach. She tastes everything — that is, almost — and most of the time is no worse for it. The secret is she does not eat to excess. She has been less reasonable in the last six months, which explains the sensation of heaviness, of upset stomach. The waistband of her skirts cutting into her. She swears to go on a strict diet once she's home.

Her father, Victor, was not a food columnist, but liked to eat. And cook. More gourmand than gourmet, actually, an epicurean. She sees him again in the yard of their house, in summer, armed with a spatula and a large fork, grilling steaks bigger than plates, the word "Chef" emblazoned on his apron, a chef's hat perched lopsidedly on his mane of hair, a glass of bourbon on the table, within arm's reach. Or else rum and Coke. Without a drop of rum to console it, he claimed, Coca-Cola would be far too sad a beverage. He followed that up with a slightly bawdy joke. "What do the weeping woman, the jealous one, and the voluptuous one answer when offered a drink?"

He must have told it a thousand times. Regardless, no one could help but laugh. It was he who sliced the bread contemplatively, saying: "Man does not live by bread alone, but without bread, he doesn't live." Couldn't stand bread being wasted, even a crust. It was he who tossed the salad. Always a lot of garlic in his dressing. Or he would say: "Garlic is the universal panacea. Do you know that in Marseille during the plague it protected a gang of corpse robbers from the epidemic?" Alas, all the cloves he ate did not protect him from E. coli. It was he who uncorked the bottles of red wine. "Even Christ enjoyed it." A great lover of aphorisms. He plunged lobsters into a pot of boiling water, after rocking them to sleep, so that they would suffer less, he said, his voice almost tender. All his desserts — he was partial to pecan pie — were accompanied by whipped cream or ice cream without exception. After the meal, he enlivened his coffee with a drop or two of brandy. They'd find him in the middle of the night in the kitchen, in pyjamas. "I'm famished," he'd explain, acting contrite, showing his sandwich of raw onion overflowing with mayonnaise, and his pickles.

His profession was unrelated to cooking: he taught history. Although it is perhaps less contradictory than one would think. He said that of course world history was that of wars and conquests. But what was at the origin of the wars and conquests? Hunger. Hunger rules the world. Makes it go round. He always had anecdotes to tell, proverbs and poems to quote. Did he see Victoria spreading honey on her bread at breakfast? He spoke to her of Democritus, who, in the evening of his life, gave up eating and kept only a jar of honey, feeding himself on its fragrance. He asked: "What did the Egyptians in Antiquity say when they ate honey?" She replied: "Truth is sweet." "Bravo, honey." If they were drinking tea, he'd say: "The Arabs brew tea three times, to symbolize love of life, love of love, and love of death." Victoria was impressed. In choosing her profession, she felt as if she were taking up the torch from her father.

SO WHAT DO PEOPLE EAT in the middle of the night? A quarter, perhaps a third of humanity — hard for her to be precise — lives at night. Ambulance drivers, fishermen, doctors on call, nurses, taxi drivers, bartenders, disc jockeys, nude dancers. Writers and journalists, police officers, private detectives. Burglars and drug dealers. And all the insomniacs — most of them wandering souls. What do they eat when they're famished — as her father was — at hours deemed ungodly?

To answer this essential question, Victoria has been travelling around the planet for six months. She has eaten French fries both tender and crispy in a Brussels tavern one night when it was raining buckets. On the beach in Calvi, in Corsica, at Lost Paradise — a small jazz bar, not the best, but she hadn't gone for the music — an *Arlequinade* of peppers had been offered — entirely acceptable. A plateful of goulash, red cabbage and dumplings in a brassiere in Prague, all washed down with wheat bear brewed on the premises. In Tuscany, at a family trattoria on the outskirts of Pisa, she was served a bowl of *ribollita*, the unforgettable cabbage and white bean soup drizzled with olive oil: enough to restore any reveller from his or her nocturnal excesses. Oh! Recipes of farmers, poor people, of those who since the dawn of time have dealt with hunger, recipes handed down from one generation to the next — each mother has her own, each family venerates its mother's recipes ... A hearty and reviving French onion soup in a small café near a market in Lille. In Mexico City she tasted fried pork rind — *chicharones preparados* — garnished with firm slices of avocado that melted in the mouth, tomatoes, crème fraîche, and spicy sauce. Mexicans, like their former conquistadors, are incredibly devoted — culinarily — to the pig, and both groups on either side of the Atlantic prepare it with all kinds of sauces, at no matter what hour. Thus in Barcelona, in Madrid — where *movida* is an institution so to speak — she was treated to *callos*, tripe in sauce; she's still smacking her lips. The good-natured chef agreed to give her his recipe: cow stomach, calves feet, pig's snout, onions, tomatoes, peppers. And in Seville, my God, in Seville, in a *taberna* called *Gamba alegre* — irresistible happy shrimp — she tasted a plateful of *jamón Serrano* — pigs haunches covered with mould hanging from a beam above the bar, placed on the *jamonera* and cut up into very thin slices by the *camarero*, undeniably a rather attractive man — manchego cheese aged just right and black olives, while sipping a glass of chilled jerez, during an authentic flamenco show. An unforgettable memory. Recalling it, she can't help but suppress a chortle of pleasure. The driver glances at her, perplexed, in the mirror. "Are you alright, Madam?"

"I'm fine. Perfectly fine. It's just that I'm dying of hunger."

"Be patient, it won't be long now. Ten fifteen minutes and we'll be there. You see the weather. We can't go any faster."

Not always easy to eat at night. Just last week in Normandy, more precisely in Le Tréport, she set her heart on a restaurant in the port that in fact was called À la fortune du pot — pot luck — how could she resist? But it was on the verge of closing; the cook had already put on his oilskin, and the kitchen, tidied up and shining, looked like a new penny. She had used all her charm and begged them to give her something to eat, anything, saying she hadn't eaten a thing since noon, had lost her way in the rain — it was raining there too — on the poorly marked and poorly lit roads. It was almost true: that very afternoon, she had taken the wrong secondary road and driven about fifty kilometres for absolutely nothing. But it wasn't true that she'd eaten nothing: she'd stopped in a bistro for a warm chèvre salad and a coffee. All ended well: the chef, won over, removed his coat and prepared her a delightfully runny mushroom omelette accompanied with a basket of still-fresh bread, a wedge of runny brie, and a glass of Muscadet. She had managed well that time. Others who are starving are not so lucky. She has also been to florescent-lit hospital cafeterias and other similarly depressing places, where she had to make do with rubbery sandwiches, shrivelled up slices of pizza, bars of pseudo-chocolate peering out from behind vending machine windows, watery coffee in cardboard or Styrofoam cups. Not even worth talking about. Yet she remembers, and can't help but smile, a surrealistic card game in a hospital cafeteria — it was just before her departure from New York, where she had begun her research — with a group of sick and disabled people in bathrobes, alongside their ivs. On the menu: microwave popcorn and cherry coke. A night worthy of an anthology.

SHE NEVERTHELESS MADE THE MOST of the trip to take notes for her next book, *The History of Gourmandise* — and there anecdotes are legion. A fascinating history, if not edifying. A history that is, in two words, profoundly immoral. Some, like her father, claimed the history of the world is the history of its hunger, and above all, satisfying that hunger. Victoria thinks that it's the history of its gourmandise. Take cinnamon; who remembers the wars raged in the sixteenth century for control — it's always about control — of a spice that, when all is said and done, is quite innocuous? Victor said it was only used to flavour apple pies. He was wrong, of course: one has only to taste Indian curries, and North African tagine or pastilla to be convinced. Or even a Bolognese *ragú* — an old recipe Victoria came across in her research. In any case, cinnamon has nothing to do with hunger. It is gourmandise, period. But coming back to its history, for cinnamon, the Portuguese imposed a reign of terror from Oman to Goa,

sank merchant ships on sight that approached the coasts of
Ceylon, hanged Venetian or Genoese agents who wanted to
sell it. The Dutch and their East India Company soon joined
in, and things worsened. Then England got involved. Victoria
devotes an entire chapter of her work to this dreadful episode.
And what to say about those drinkers of coffee, a beverage
that formerly was strictly and arbitrarily forbidden, who
were thrown in the Bosphorus, enclosed in leather bags,
without any form of trial? About the slaves torn from their
Africa, imported by the boatload and put to work on sugar
plantations in the New World? What to say about the salt
mines? About tea? No, we find no moral in all that. But it's
still history, and Victor would be proud of her, she knows;
she's made the connection between his two passions. From
where he is — in heaven, he cannot be elsewhere — she sees
him nod, hears him urging her: "Don't give up, Victoria." It
will be her major work, her swan song, always the most beautiful. She has been working on it in her spare time for years.

But that was the dark, technical side of her work. The other,
the recreational side, was to eat in the company of night
owls. She has not denied herself.

IT IS IN MONTREAL THAT she has chosen to end her spree. At
the End of the World, a haunt of taxi drivers and famished
night owls. According to her informer — she has them in
every country — they serve the best poutine, Italian-style or
regular, in the city.

She wonders if her driver also goes to the place.

He bursts out laughing. "The End of the World. Of course I know it. Saint-Zotique near Saint-Denis, that's where you're going?"

"That's right. I was told about their poutine."

"I recommend the version with chicken and peas, called *galvaude*. You'll tell me what you think."

"*Galvaude?*"

"Potatoes, sauce, cheese curds, pieces of chicken, coleslaw and peas," he recites. "More nourishing than a regular one."

She digests the information.

"So a kind of hot chicken sandwich?"

"If you like. Hot chicken without the bread, but with cheese. All in the same bowl. Trust me: once you've tasted theirs, you'll never want any other. If you insist on bread, just ask for a basket. On the house. That way, you have all the four groups of Canada's Food Guide."

"I think for this evening three groups will be enough. And for dessert? I mean, if I'm still hungry."

"Try the *pouding chômeur* — poor man's pudding. Marjolaine makes it. There is no better. Are you a foreigner?"

"A neighbour, let's say. From New York."

"So you can't know *pouding chômeur* — it's typically Québécois. A kind of white cake, but heavier, with caramel sauce. You can add table cream if you like. It's to die for, especially served hot. Did you come on business? Or as a tourist?"

"To sample the specialities."

"I recommend beaver tails; it's a kind of donut, but without a hole. If you like the sound of it, you need to go to Chez Victoire."

Victoire!

"I'm thinking ... I could come back and fetch you, if you like. I always eat one in the middle of the night with a good cup of coffee."

It's more than she could hope for. Now she has a guide.

"Fantastic," she says.

They ride for a few moments in silence. Rain hammers the windshield; the wipers squeak melancholically. "Damned spring," grumbles the driver. Then, "Sorry."

"No, no. I'm with you. The month of March is atrocious in New York too."

"Say hi to them from me," continues the driver. "At the End of the World, I mean. Good evening from Raoul, Raoul Potvin ... No, don't say anything. I'll surprise them. I can't wait to see their faces when they see me walk in. I haven't set foot in there in quite a while. I used to go there all the time."

He seems to be yearning to confide.

"You don't go there anymore?"

"It's been a while. A couple of months. We used to play cards every Wednesday. There were six of us: Diderot, Boris, Laure, Denise. And Doris."

"And you."

"And me."

He sighs deeply.

"So you played cards," Victoria encourages him.

"The last time, a Wednesday in late December, in fact, something happened. Doris passed away in the bathroom, and no one noticed ... Too caught up in playing. It's true we were losing the game, my partner and I."

"Bad loser?"

"Do you know any good losers? Everyone plays to win. All the same, I have regrets."

"And you never went back."

"Once or twice, at the beginning. But my heart wasn't in it anymore. And now, you're going to think I'm crazy, I regret not going anymore. I feel as if I've let my friends down."

ONE MINUTE TO MIDNIGHT. THE taxi pulls up in front of the End of the World. Victoria pays the fare. "Don't forget to say hi to them from me."

"Raoul Potvin."

"That's right. But don't tell them I'm taking you to Chez Victoire. It would hurt Marjolaine."

THE STROKE OF MIDNIGHT. VICTORIA, a modern-day Cinderella, opens the restaurant door, rushes in with the wind. A few damp locks escape from her jet black bun. She shakes her umbrella. Everyone — two well-built guys that look like Slavs, a little runt with black skin, two middle-aged women, a pale, thin guy with a pen in his hand — stare at her, as if she were an apparition come from another world, appearing out of the night. A bittersweet sounding song is playing on the radio. Victoria recognizes the word "Syracuse." One day she enjoyed an exquisite *caponata* there. An order pad is lying on the floor in the middle of the room. A pretty girl in a pink T-shirt is crying her heart out; one of the two women is trying to console her. *Have I walked into a drama?* Victoria wonders.

"Messieurs dames," she greets them politely.

With the exception of the girl in the pink T-shirt who is still crying, they exchange dumbfounded looks. Yes, a drama has surely just taken place.

"I've come for the poutine," she announces, after hanging her raincoat on a hook.

Marjolaine regains her composure. "Yes," she stammers. "Poutine, of course. Please have a seat. I'll bring you the menu."